AFTER THE END TRILOGY

This is a work of speculative fiction. All of the events and dialogue depicted within are a product of the author's overactive imagination. None of this stuff happened. Except maybe in a parallel universe.

First Printing: July 2019

Cover by Vincent Sammy

JOIN THE READER LIST

Do you love Post-Apocalyptic, Dystopian and Horror fiction?

Mark's a busy author and he releases regularly in these genres so if you enjoy what you read here and want to be notified whenever there's a new book out, join the reader list. Just click the link below. It'll only take a minute.

www.markgillespieauthor.com

(The sign up box is on the Home Page)

You can also follow Mark on Bookbub.

THE CURSE (AFTER THE END 1)

For the real 'Eda'...

1

The endless barrage of rain crashed down to Earth. It poured out of a dark sky smothered in thick, bloated clouds that hung low over the once-thriving metropolis.

The man who rode on horseback down 42nd Street didn't seem to mind the rain. Not judging by the contented, almost serene glow in his eyes. There was a smile on his face too. The soft clip-clop of the horse's hooves on the wet road was the sound of a leisurely stroll in progress; it was a gentle, even soothing noise, and in stark contrast to the angry weather.

There were over a hundred women lined up on either side of the street, waiting for the man to pass by. They watched him – all of them, a silent and tentative welcoming committee with their heads buried under a sea of brightly colored umbrellas.

Every now and then, an anxious face would peer out from the rim of an umbrella, eager for a glimpse of the latest visitor to their community.

A man.

There was a man in town.

Eda Becker stood in line too, but unlike the majority of the other women, she didn't bother to shield herself from the deluge with an umbrella. Eda had always liked the feel of the rain – even the icy cold variety – on her head. The books had a word for that – they said she was a *pluviophile* – a lover of rain and it was a good thing too, considering the nature of the weather these days. The older women in the Complex liked to say that Mother Nature was overworked, that she was still trying to clean the last traces of blood off the streets from the war. Eda couldn't see any blood on the streets, no matter how hard she looked. The others would be quick to remind her that just because she couldn't see the blood, that didn't mean it wasn't still there.

Eda wasn't sure what they meant by that.

The rainfall grew more intense. By now it sounded like there were a hundred horses on the road, their heavy hooves stamping off the hard surface, all of them galloping at full speed.

At last, Eda was forced to pop up the hood on her maroon rain cloak.

She watched the man on horseback pass her by and decided to follow him as discreetly as she could. Quietly, the sound of her footsteps lost in the downpour, Eda took a step backwards, removing herself from the long and rigid line of women that had gathered outside to greet the grinning man.

She walked behind the line, keeping her head down. Her eyes stayed alert however, tracking the man's path as he made his way towards the entrance to Grand Central.

Eda wasn't doing anything wrong or expressly forbidden. But nobody else had stepped out of line to get a better view. Their loss – it wasn't every day a man showed up in New York. As she walked parallel to the visitor, she could hear the horse's hooves still clicking on the ground. It was a strangely satisfying sound, completely new to her. Eda glanced over and saw the permanent grin on the man's leathery and red grizzled face – it was a gargoyle smile that stretched far and wide. His gray trenchcoat dripped endless streams of water. So did the cowboy hat, tilted back on his skull at a slight angle to allow a better view of the surroundings.

The women broke into a sudden round of applause. It was a

muted but joyful gesture of appreciation. They clapped one hand against the knuckles of the other – the one that still gripped the handle of their umbrellas. Although the end result was somewhat muffled, it was at least enthusiastic.

The grinning man waved to the women standing on both sides of the street. There was something regal about the gesture. At that moment, he was like a beloved hero coming home after a long, painful absence. As he smiled, the deep lines and grooves on his old face got deeper.

At last, the horse was brought to a stop close to the entrance of Grand Central. The man dropped the reins, dismounted and as he stretched his stiff limbs, he took a long look around at his surroundings.

The women's applause began to fade and soon there was only the sound of the rain again.

Eda crept forward, still intent on getting as close to the action as possible. Fortunately nobody was paying much attention to what she was doing. As she approached the end of the line, not far from the station entrance, she watched the grinning man as his eyes scoured the bruised and battered surroundings of Manhattan.

His grin slowly faded and Eda wondered if he was remembering the past.

The area he was looking at had been a major crosstown street in the borough of Manhattan and housed some of the city's most recognizable buildings. Some of them were still intact but many were gone now. The New York Public Library was a pile of rubble, as was the former Headquarters of the United Nations. Times Square looked more or less like a crater, but Grand Central Terminal had remained untouched – a minor miracle considering its importance during the war when it had performed a crucial role in supply transportation.

A tall woman with an umbrella stepped out of the station entrance. She walked onto the street and approached the man at a steady pace. Like Eda, this woman appeared to be undisturbed by the intense rainfall that had besieged the city. She wore a bright red rain cloak – the sort of garment that was worn by all the women in the

Complex. These were essentially old raincoats with large hoods and long cloak-like tails that trailed down the back, stretching almost to the heels. These had been stitched together from a variety of different items scavenged across the city. The rain cloaks weren't pretty by any means, but they were warm and bulky, so much so that it looked like the wearer had a tent wrapped around them.

Long strands of greyish-brown hair poked out of the edges of the woman's hood.

Upon seeing the woman in the red cloak, Eda stepped back into the end of the line. Mission accomplished – she was now only a short distance away from the grinning man and his horse. She lowered her hood and tried to act like she'd been standing there all along. Despite this, Eda could feel some of the women in the opposite line staring at her, or maybe she was just imagining it. It didn't matter. With any luck she'd be able to listen in on the upcoming conversation with ease.

"Welcome to New York," the woman said.

She raised her umbrella, positioning it over the grinning man's soaking head.

"Welcome to the Complex," she said, offering an outstretched hand. "My name is Shay and I'm very pleased to meet you."

The man didn't say anything at first.

He patted his horse on the side and a long time seemed to pass before he accepted the offer of a handshake.

Shay turned around and gestured to someone standing behind her. Almost immediately, a middle-aged woman in a brown rain cloak came up behind them. The woman pointed to the horse, then said something to the man that Eda couldn't hear. The man nodded and a moment later, the woman took the lead rope in hand and led the horse away from the station.

"This is the Complex?" the grinning man said.

"Yes it is," Shay said with a nod. "Have you traveled far?"

The man nodded. For a second, he looked old and exhausted in the face. His body sagged a little too. Eda guessed he was probably in his early sixties but it was hard to tell with people of that generation –

the war had put so many years on them that most were older than their appearance would suggest. No matter how much they smiled, the past would show up sooner or later in their eyes, that little trace of leftover heartache that always wore them down gradually.

He was a big man. He literally towered over Shay, which was quite a feat considering that Shay herself was at least six feet tall without her boots on. As she stood beside him, she had to work to keep the umbrella over his head.

"Well I met your ambassador," the grinning man said, wiping the damp hair off his face. "She was quite a gal."

"Which ambassador?" Shay asked. There was a curious glint in her eyes.

The man shrugged like he didn't really care. Eda saw him glance towards the tip of the Chrysler Building, its distinctive presence still towering above the city skyline. The grinning man's eyes lingered there for a few seconds before he turned his attention back to Shay.

"Oh I'm not sure," he said. "Deborah? Deirdre? Any of those ring a bell? It was definitely a 'D' name – of that much I'm sure. She was about fifty years old, maybe a little older. Real skinny bag of bones type. She looked hungry as hell but a real determined gal you know? It looked like she'd crawled through Hell and swum across the Lake of Fire before she found me."

"Denise," Shay said. "So you came up from the south?"

"Yeah," the grinning man said. "Been in Pennsylvania for a while but I wandered up from Virginia originally."

"Virginia?" Shay said. "What's it like down there?"

"Dead," the man said, shaking his head.

"You saw no one?" Shay asked.

"Virginia's a ghost state," the man said. "There's no one there anymore. I bumped into a couple of old-timers living out of a bus in Pennsylvania but that was it. I'm telling you, America's gone – it's really gone. You gotta see it to really appreciate that fact. This here's the biggest crowd I've seen in a very long time. What have you got here anyway? One hundred, two hundred people? And all ladies too – guess that makes me kind of special, right?"

Shay's lips curled into a half-smile.

"And what did Denise tell you?" she asked.

"She told me what I needed to know," the grinning man said. "Told me you little ladies got a special project going on right here in New York. What a story that was – fascinating."

He raised his eyebrows. The grin on his face was devilish.

"Project with a capital 'P'," he said. "Isn't that right?"

"Yes," Shay said.

The man looked over his shoulder at the women who'd welcomed him to the city. They were still standing in two neat lines on either side of the street.

"I know what you need," he said, turning back to Shay. "So where is she? Is she standing over there with the rest of them? Where's the girl with the face that launched a thousand ships?"

"You don't waste any time do you?" Shay said, with a soft laugh. "I thought you'd be exhausted after such a long..."

"Helen of Troy," the man said, butting in abruptly. "I've had a long journey and it was all to meet her. To do what we have to do. So where is she?"

"She's not here," Shay said.

The grinning man frowned.

"I hope she's somewhere close," he said.

Shay nodded. "Of course she is," she said. "Didn't Denise tell you? Helen is kept separate from the rest of the women in the Complex for many reasons. She resides in the Waldorf Astoria on Park Avenue and right now she's getting ready to greet you."

The man laughed loudly, a spluttering noise that sounded like something was clogged up in his throat.

At the same time, Eda caught Shay looking over at her. There was a strange look on the older woman's face – something that Eda couldn't quite pin down.

Pity? Amusement?

"Eda," Shay said. "You weren't standing there earlier."

Eda felt like all the eyes in New York had turned towards her. Her skin was burning. She opened her mouth to say something to Shay but the words were stuck on the tip of her tongue.

Shay smiled.

"If you're going to take such an interest in our conversation," she said, "why don't you come over and offer to carry this gentleman's bag while I show him around? Make yourself useful, yes?"

Now it was the grinning man's turn to have a look at Eda. As he glanced over his shoulder, his eyes narrowed. It was as if he was looking at a rare and peculiar species of animal – some form of life that he didn't quite understand.

He licked the rainwater off his lips.

"Cute," he said.

Eda's body stiffened.

"Eda?" Shay said, beckoning the young woman over with a curled finger. "Get the gentleman's bag please."

Eda nodded and crept forward. Despite the discomfort she felt at being singled out, she would at least get to follow Shay and the stranger around for a while longer and listen in further on their conversation.

"You don't need to show me around," the grinning man said, looking at Shay. "Truly ma'am. I'd prefer to get right down to work if you don't mind. Or isn't she fertile right now?"

"As a matter of fact she is," Shay said. "Usually men show up at the wrong time and so we'll put them in a hotel until Helen's body is ready to receive. As far as I can recall, you're the only one who's ever arrived at the perfect time. It's almost like it's a sign, wouldn't you say?"

The man nodded. "Lucky me."

"Yes indeed," Shay said. "Nonetheless, Helen isn't quite ready for you yet. She won't be long and in the meantime, why don't you let me show you around? I can tell you a little about what's happening here in the Complex. After that, you can go straight to work. I promise."

The man looked too tired to argue with Shay.

"Sure thing," he said.

"Eda!" Shay said. "Come on. Get the gentleman's bag please."

Eda nodded and hurried over to where Shay and the grinning man were waiting. She heard some of the women sniggering at her back but she didn't care. Let them stand there in the rain and get soaked.

"Can I take your bag?" Eda asked the man. She kept her distance from the newcomer but couldn't fail to miss the peculiar smell of aged leather that drifted off either his clothes or skin.

There was a withered backpack at the man's boots.

"I can carry my own bag," he said. "There's not much in there."

"Nevertheless," Shay said, stepping forward. "You're our very special guest and if we treat our beloved Helen like a queen then you must let us treat you like a king. It's only fair."

The man smirked and scratched at the jagged stubble sprouting up off his chin. With a nod, he picked up the small bag and thrust it into Eda's hands.

"Whatever makes you ladies happy," he said. "There you go sweetheart. You'll take good care of that for me, won't you?"

"Thank you," Eda said. "I mean, yes I will."

He laughed.

Eda slung the bag over her shoulder and it weighed next to nothing, almost like it was empty. She imagined that the long hunting knife strapped to the grinning man's waist was the most important possession he carried around with him. He must have been quite the skilled hunter to survive out there with just his wits and a sharp blade.

The three of them walked towards the entrance of the station. Eda kept a few paces behind the others, hoping that they'd forget she was there.

"Why this place?" the grinning man asked. "Why Grand Central?"

"It's intact for a start," Shay said. "But we don't live or sleep here – it's more of a gathering point for the women. It's the heart of our community."

"So where do you sleep?" the man asked.

"Nearby," Shay said. "The women help themselves to whatever accommodation they can find. Hotels, abandoned apartments or stores – it's entirely their choice when it comes to where they spend the night."

"And where do you live Shay?" he asked.

"In the Waldorf Astoria, close to Helen."

"The Waldorf Astoria," the man said, chuckling quietly. "How lavish you are. It's still in good condition then?"

"It's in perfect condition," Shay said. "The looters never got anywhere near it, thank God. It's a piece of history as far as I'm concerned."

The man pointed to the station as they approached the door.

"This one's a piece of history too," he said. "Grand Central, I'll be damned. I remember this place from back in the day – it's classic New York."

"For me it's a symbol," Shay said, looking up towards the roof with a proud eye. "This place, it changes with the times – this was actually the third station to occupy the site here. Back in the early twentieth century this building embodied the ascent of New York. It expanded in harmony with the city's growth, a constant symbol of change, going back to when they razed the old building to construct a new station, replacing the steam locomotives with electric trains."

"You know your history," the man said. "Well done."

"I'm a proud New Yorker," Shay said. "Born and bred. And I'm sure this building survived for a reason. It represented regrowth in the past and that's what we're all about now. What *this* is about. The Complex. The Project. That's why we sent out the ambassadors and it's why you're here today. This building will oversee the preservation of the human race. And not a moment too soon – we're running out of time."

"Yeah," the grinning man said.

"Let me show you inside," Shay said.

As they walked towards the door, Shay pointed at a row of long, rectangular flowerbeds outside the building's exterior. Short stretches of awning leaned over the flowerbeds, offering at least some shelter from the strong winds that often accompanied the rain.

"We call them the gardens," she said, lowering the umbrella and closing it before walking inside. "But really it's just a small collection of plant foods that we grow – they're our lifeline. We keep mostly, low-maintenance crops – potatoes, beetroot, carrots, kale, onions – and some others. A quick weed, water and little fuss."

She pointed a finger towards the sky.

"The water comes easy – that's one good thing about all the rain. It's low-input, high-output in terms of the food we grow here, and that's good because we have over a hundred and fifty mouths to feed. We have some wonderful gardeners and chefs here at the Complex. And you help out too sometimes, don't you Eda?"

Eda was still lagging a few paces behind.

"A little gardening sometimes," she said with a shrug. "Nothing much."

"How do you store the water?" the grinning man asked.

"We have large barrels to collect the rainwater," Shay said. "There's plenty of water kept in storage. It's a crude system overall but it works extremely well. It's amazing how much water we can accumulate from just one large rainfall. There's no excuse for dying of thirst anymore."

The man glanced over his shoulder at Eda.

"That your kid?" he asked Shay.

"Eda?" Shay said. "No. Eda never knew her mother, not really. She was orphaned at a very young age during the war."

"What is she?" the man said. "Thirty? Thirty-five? I haven't seen anyone that young in a long time."

Shay nodded. "Considering how things are, I'd wager she's one of the youngest people left in the country. Most of us in the Complex are in our fifties, sixties or older."

"Yeah I noticed," the man said. "And what about Helen?"

"She's roughly around Eda's age," Shay said.

"Thank Christ for that," the grinning man said.

As they walked further into Grand Central, he whistled his appreciation.

"This place is gorgeous," he said.

"Yes it is," Shay said.

The main concourse in Grand Central was almost three hundred feet in length. A massive celestial ceiling, twelve stories high, adorned the concourse, painted with two and a half thousand stars and zodiac constellations. The information booth and the ticket vending machines gave the impression that the station was still operational. Eda's favorite feature however, was the four clock faces located on top of the information booth, all made from opal.

"So this is where you girls hang out?" the grinning man said.

"This is where we gather," Shay said. "This is where we grow, think and plan for the future of our species. The Project – the dream of reconstruction was first born here."

The man made a loud snorting noise.

"You're sure as hell clinging on to the past," he said, shaking his head. "Who says we even deserve a second chance? After everything that happened."

"We're clinging onto life," Shay said. "And it's not the past we're interested in, it's the future." She pointed to a variety of large and small pot plants on the outskirts of the concourse. "Life goes on, inside and outside this building. It will continue to do so with the right amount of love and care. Life surrounds us. It's stubborn and has an inherent will to survive, and yet the one form of life that we seek to prolong most of all eludes us."

"Guess that's why I'm here," the man said. "Right? You need somebody to water that special plant you're keeping in the Waldorf."

There was a grim look on Shay's face. Her skin looked pallid and thin.

"If only it were so simple," she said in a quiet voice.

The grinning man frowned. Eda imagined that he'd been quite a physical specimen many years ago. He was still a force now but age, along with life's wear and tear, had manifested on his giant body in the form of gray hair, wrinkles and a slightly protruding gut.

"It's simple enough," he said to Shay. "I move into the Waldorf and put a baby inside your queen. Look, I might be sixty-something years old but I'm probably the most fertile man you ever saw in your life. I had four young boys before the war and..."

He stopped all of sudden. It was as if he was unable or unwilling to continue down that line of thought.

"Never mind," he said.

"You're very confident," Shay said. "I can see that. But so were all the other men who came through here before you. Just like you, they said all the right things before they went to see Helen. Tell me something if you please. Why don't you fear the curse?"

"Because I don't believe in the curse," the grinning man said. "Because the curse is a bunch of made-up, voodoo bullshit."

Shay smiled. "Really?"

He nodded.

"Well your ambassador – Deirdre or whatever her name was again – sure had a lot to say about it. That just made me all the more curious but whatever this curse is lady, it's got nothing to do with me. I work just fine in the downstairs department I'll have you know."

"They all say that," Shay said. "And yet it's always the same excruciating disappointment at the end. Sometimes I ask myself, why would anyone go through that by choice? Do they ignore the curse because they want to go out in a blaze of glory by sleeping with the most beautiful woman in the world? Others truly believe they're immune. They believe that they're the chosen one, the father of the future. Tell me, is that what you think? Because if so, I hope you're right."

"I can't speak for other men," the grinning man said. "But I'm operating just fine under the bonnet. It's like I told you, I don't believe in any of this natural hoodoo. How does a curse just magically appear out of nowhere?"

"You underestimate the wrath of Mother Nature," Shay said. "I would advise you strongly against doing that. She despises us."

"I think old Mother Hubbard is starting to forgive us," the grinning man said with a laugh. "Listen lady, the panic's over. I'm the special one you've been looking for. All praise goes to the lovely Deirdre or Denise or whatever she's called for finding me. Now, just show me where the most beautiful woman in the world is and I'll go take care of the rest."

Shay smiled and took a backwards step.

"Are you an arrogant man mister?" she asked.

He shook his head. "Just speaking the truth."

"Tell me something then," Shay said. "Truthfully. Did you fight in the war?"

"Sure did," the man said.

"Some people say that it's because of the chemicals in the air," Shay said. "That it's not a natural curse but a manmade one. That wouldn't surprise me either."

The grinning man sighed. He was starting to look bored with the conversation.

"Hey kid," he said, looking at Eda. "Tell me something and I want you to be super honest with me. Is this Helen of Troy as beautiful as your ambassador said she was?"

Eda frowned and shook her head.

"I've never seen her."

The grinning man squinted his eyes. "What?"

It was Shay who answered.

"I mentioned earlier that Helen is kept apart from the others," she said.

"Why?" the grinning man asked.

"We can't risk her contracting an illness of any kind – she's too important around here. She doesn't garden, she doesn't cook, she doesn't do any of the everyday things that the rest of the women do – her sole job is to conceive a child. Her entire existence revolves around that. Helen is too precious – she's protected night and day, fed well and exercised. I'd wrap her up in a giant cotton ball day and night if it meant keeping her from harm."

"I can't wait to meet her," the grinning man said. "Speaking of which, shall we…?"

"Would you like some refreshment first?" Shay asked. "Water? Some food? You've come a long way for this – I feel it's only right that we should take care of you, feed and water you, before you go to Helen."

"I'm not hungry," the man said with a shake of the head. "Not thirsty either. What I am, is ready…"

"You're sure?" Shay asked.

"Right now," he said.

They stopped at the door while Shay opened up the umbrella again. It was still raining heavily outside and the weather showed little signs of letting up anytime soon. Most of the women who'd lined the streets earlier to greet the visitor were now gone or moving back towards shelter.

"I wish you good luck," Shay said, looking up at the grinning man with a tight-lipped smile.

Eda thought she saw a hint of sorrow in the older woman's eyes.

2

Eda clamped her hands over her ears and closed her eyes tight. At the same time, she retreated backwards down the corridor, moving away from the Presidential Suite like it was spewing out a storm of toxic fumes that were chasing after her at high speed.

But it didn't matter how fast her legs pedaled in reverse or how much distance she put between herself and the hotel room.

The screaming didn't go away.

Eda's body felt icy cold from head to toe. She shook her head back and forth, trying to rattle the noise out of her system. But the scream was so intense, so overwhelming, that it was like the floor and all the walls around her were trembling.

She opened her eyes and looked once more at the white double doors that led into the Presidential Suite. It sounded like a large animal was being tortured somewhere behind those doors.

He was still screaming. Wouldn't he just die for Christ's sake?

Eda was standing in the hallway on the thirty-fifth floor of the Waldorf Astoria. She was furious at herself for hanging around that place long after she'd been needed. Why hadn't she just gone home after watching Shay and the grinning man walk into Helen's suite? She'd carried his bag upstairs and that was it – job done. Go home

Eda, that's what Shay had said to her. And as usual, Shay had been right. Eda should have been back in her own hotel now, far away from...*this*.

Instead she'd insisted on lurking around the corridor like a ghost.

There had been no exaggeration, not even in the most dramatic and frightening accounts of the power of the curse. Eda had heard some terrible sounds in her life. She'd lived through the wild years, the violent slow decline that had plagued the country after the war and yet she'd never heard anyone scream like that before.

The scream cut off suddenly.

There was a series of loud thudding noises that sounded like someone banging furniture against the walls. Eda's heart was racing. She was still backing away, still staring at the double doors with terror-filled eyes.

"No," Eda said, shaking her head. "No way."

She turned around and ran as fast as she could. She tore down the empty corridor towards the stairs. Barging shoulder-first through the double doors, Eda rushed into a reckless descent, still running as fast as she could. It was a long way down to the first floor – staircases in luxury hotels had been little more than emergency exits before the war. Back then people took elevators between floors, but the elevators in the Waldorf and everywhere else for that matter had long ceased working. Even if they had worked though, Eda had no interest in being confined in a little compartment and leaving herself at the mercy of a bunch of steel cables.

Her feet thudded off the stairs in a loud tap-tapping noise. She gasped for breath, ignoring the desperate voice in her head that told her to slow down or risk falling headfirst and breaking something.

The adrenaline pumped through Eda's body, fueling her frantic charge downstairs.

She occupied her mind during the descent with one question:

Why the hell did Helen and her people have to live all the way up on the thirty-fifth floor? There were forty-something floors located inside the Waldorf Astoria. What was wrong with the second or third floor for God's sake? But Eda already knew the answer. She wasn't asking the question because she didn't know. For the men who traveled far and wide to visit Helen of Troy, the long walk upstairs was a final ceremony of anticipation. It made them feel like they were walking towards a queen, which only enhanced the excitement of the moment.

And if Helen was a queen, then wasn't it true that all these men were kings? How good must that have felt after a life of nothing in the American wasteland?

Eda had seen the rapture on the grinning man's face as he'd ascended the stairs to the thirty-fifth floor.

The poor bastard.

Eda charged downstairs, her feet barely glancing off each of the many steps. Eventually she reached the lobby and with her lungs grasping for oxygen, she staggered to a clumsy stop.

Her heart was about to explode. Both her legs were completely numb.

She fell into one of the many chairs that were scattered around the lobby. Her still trembling fingers dug deep into the cushioned armrests in an effort to regain control of a world that was spinning wildly around her.

The lobby appeared to be deserted. Usually there were guards posted on the first floor of the hotel. They'd been there earlier when she'd walked in with Shay and the grinning man but for the moment at least, the lobby was empty.

Eda looked around as she caught her breath. The stylish, wood-paneled lobby was huge. There were black marble pillars scattered throughout and she imagined that this was like sitting in a European royal palace of old – the sort of place she'd read about in history books and that although very much real a long time ago, might as well have been something out of a dream.

Directly in front of Eda, there was a nine-foot tall bronze and mahogany clock tower with a gilded Statue of Liberty on top.

"I know," Eda said, looking at Lady Liberty. "It was stupid of me to stick around. Well don't worry, as soon as I catch my breath I'm..."

Footsteps.

Eda leapt back to her feet. She wasn't supposed to be there in the hotel at this time and right now she didn't want anybody to see her, not the way she was feeling. Not the guards and definitely not Shay.

But it was too late. Somebody paced into the main lobby.

Eda heard the sound of someone breathing hard, like they'd just been running at breakneck speed. She took a deep breath, then spun around and looked over towards the staircase.

It was Linda.

Linda McAvoy was Helen's live-in chef. Eda didn't know her that well as the majority of Helen's assistants, Linda included, spent most of their time in the Waldorf, keeping their distance from the rest of the women in the Complex. Linda was approximately in her late sixties and she was dressed in a dark blue rain cloak that trailed almost down to her feet. Her long silver hair was ruffled, the bangs thick with sweat.

Eda guessed that despite her age, Linda had taken the stairs in a hurry too. It was of some strange comfort to Eda that she wasn't the only one who hadn't been able to handle it up there. But there was one big difference – Linda had been inside the room when it happened. She'd seen everything and not for the first time.

Linda stopped and pulled out a pack of cigarettes from within her back pocket. Still breathing hard, she slid the cigarette in between her lips and struck a match. As she brought the lit match to her mouth, Eda noticed that the older woman's hands were shaking badly. It looked like she was ill, rather than scared.

Linda took a long, impatient drag on the cigarette. Then she started to walk forward, like she was on her way to the front door to finish her smoke outside. But as she started walking, she noticed Eda standing by the clock. Linda stopped. There was a puzzled look on her tanned face.

"Eda?" she said. "What are you doing here?"

Eda felt an onslaught of all the wrong words flood her mind. Instead of blurting something stupid out, she left an uncomfortable silence in the air and gathered her thoughts slowly.

Somewhere in the back of her mind, the grinning man was still screaming.

"I carried his bag over from the station earlier," she said, "After that, I came back and sat down for a while. I must have fell asleep or something, I don't know."

Linda tapped gently on her heart.

"Jesus kid," she said. "You really gave me a fright there. Thought I'd seen a ghost or something."

"Sorry," Eda said. "Is everything alright?"

Linda hesitated. Another uncomfortable silence followed.

"I was just going outside for a smoke," she said, glancing towards the door. "Maybe a little fresh air. What's it like outside? Still raining or is that a stupid question?"

"Still raining I think," Eda said. "Just bracing myself for the walk back to the Fitzpatrick. It's not far but sometimes it feels like it is when the weather hits hard."

"Some days are just plain ugly," Linda said. "Best staying indoors and hiding under the covers. See what tomorrow brings, you know what I mean?"

Eda nodded. "Yeah."

Linda closed her eyes and blew a long trail of smoke into the lobby. She no longer seemed interested in going outside.

"Linda?"

"Yeah?"

They looked at each other in silence.

"Is he dead?" Eda said, pointing a finger to the ceiling.

Linda nodded slowly.

"Yeah," she said. "Yeah he is."

Eda fell back into the seat. She shook her head back and forth slowly in a trance-like motion.

"He seemed so sure," she said. "Back over in Grand Central, you should have heard this guy. He was so damn *sure*."

"They're always so damn sure," Linda said. Her face glistened with a fine coat of sweat as she spoke. "It's a form of denial if you ask me. I don't know, can you blame them? I mean it's a pretty fucked up thing to come to terms with – the fact that Mother Nature doesn't want us around anymore. Still, we have to try to persuade her to give us one more chance. Every time we leave Helen and a man in the bedroom, I pray to God, hoping that he still cares enough to give us a second chance. To take the curse away. Then we hear that horrible screaming and I know..."

"Know what?" Eda asked.

"That we're screwed," Linda said. "That maybe it really is all over and we're just pissing in the wind here."

Eda listened to the dull thud of the falling rain outside. It might have been easing off at last.

"Is Helen okay?" she said.

It was a stupid question, but one that Eda felt compelled to ask.

"She's a little shaken up I guess," Linda said, stepping away from a freshly fallen clump of ash on the floor. "This probably sounds terrible but it's nothing she hasn't seen before."

Linda inhaled deeply and the tip of the cigarette glowed bright red.

"Poor girl," she said. "Who am I to say how she feels? Just because she's had more than one of them die on top of her, that doesn't mean it gets any easier."

"I'm sure it doesn't," Eda said.

Linda exhaled and then fanned the smoke away from her face like it was a swarm of biting insects. There was a pallid, yellowy tinge to the older woman's skin. Her face was sunken in around the middle, more so than Eda had ever remembered seeing before.

"Worst thing about it," Linda said. "I think she's starting to get used to it. The craziness is becoming normal and that can't be a good thing, not ever."

"The men's orgasm," Eda said. "Is it really that bad?"

Linda looked at Eda as if she was a child who'd just asked yet another silly question.

"You're asking the wrong person," Linda said. "Although nobody sticks around long enough to tell us for sure. But yeah, it's that bad.

The lucky ones die outright – it's done and dusted but that doesn't happen often. Usually they live through the pain and then..."

She paused.

"What?" Eda asked. "Go on, please."

"I've seen them thrashing and rolling around on the floor like madmen," Linda said. "It's like they've been stung by something so bad that they can't stand being alive anymore. Jesus, the look on their faces. I'm talking about the worst pain you'll ever imagine Eda, one that no matter how hard you try, you can't ever get rid of, not while you're still alive."

Linda kicked the growing pile of ash at her feet away. It scattered, making even more of a mess in the lobby. Linda didn't look like she gave much of a shit. With a short burst of gargled laughter, she pulled both sides of her rain cloak closer together, as if feeling the cold all of a sudden.

"Sometimes I think it's all for the best," she said. "Failure I mean."

"What are you talking about?" Eda said.

"You haven't seen it up there Eda," Linda said. Now it was her turn to point towards the ceiling. "For the men who survive the orgasm, death is the sweetest comfort they'll ever know. In a way, death becomes the orgasm and they'll do anything to get there. They'll run to the kitchen, grab a knife off the rack and stab themselves repeatedly in the throat. I've seen it. They'll pound their heads off the wall until it literally turns to mush. One of them tried to jump out the window but he was so messed up by the pain that he couldn't figure out how to open the damn thing. I guess what I'm saying is, do we really deserve a second chance? Because God, Allah, the Universe, Mother Nature or whoever put the curse on us, they don't seem to think we do."

Eda shivered. She could taste the cigarette smoke in the air and it smelled rancid.

"Is Helen as pretty as they say?" she asked.

Linda smiled. "She's beautiful. Poor thing, Jesus."

Eda nodded. "Did the grinning man do everything right?" she asked. "Did he do the relaxation ritual? And the fertility blessing?"

Linda raised an eyebrow. "How do you know about those things?"

"Shay told me."

"Right," Linda said. "Shay always said you were the curious type. Anyway, he didn't want the relaxation ritual. Thought it was a bunch of mumbo jumbo, sitting down and talking with Zahra, a woman who used to be a hypnotist. Said he didn't need to relax. Said he wasn't nervous because the curse was bullshit. I'm sure he thought the same thing about the fertility blessing but Shay always insists on saying the words. He was so eager to get into the bedroom. What a dickhead. Well now he'd a dead dickhead."

Eda glanced upwards. "I'm glad I'm not up there," she said. "That's the last place I'd want to be right now."

As soon as she said it, Eda held up a hand in apology to Linda.

"Sorry. That wasn't the best thing to say."

"Don't be sorry," Linda said, brushing it off with a sweep of the hand. There was an ugly wheezing noise as she sucked hard on the last of the cigarette. It was a desperate, almost pitiful sound.

"Nobody in their right mind would want to be in the Presidential Suite now," she said. "That son of a bitch ain't grinning anymore. He split his head open off the wall. You should have seen it – it was like he was being burned with hot acid and electrocuted at the same time. I saw the madness in his eyes. He'd gone all the way to Hell before he'd even died."

Linda's body trembled. It was obvious that one cigarette wasn't going to be enough.

"Thank God I'm just the chef," she said. "I wouldn't want to be Lucia for the rest of the day."

"Lucia?" Eda asked.

"That's the cleaner. What a shitty job she's got ahead of her tonight. Picking up all that..."

Linda winced. "Still, she never complains. She's a trooper."

The chef reached for another cigarette, even though they were in scarce supply these days. As she lit up a second smoke, Linda stared towards the front door of the hotel.

Her eyes were distant.

"There are at least fifty ambassadors out there looking for men," she said. "If they're not all dead then they're working. And if they're working that means more men will be showing up in New York and soon. That's a lot of bad news waiting for poor Helen. She's a smart girl too, she knows what's coming."

"I'll bet she feels sick every time someone knock on the door," Eda said.

Linda looked at Eda and nodded. "Yeah," she said. "Wouldn't you?"

3

Eda leapt out of bed and ran towards the window.

She'd heard a scream.

She pressed her face up tight against the filthy cold glass and looked outside. It was dark out there as it always was in the early hours of the morning. These were the witching hours, when the dark forces of the world were at their strongest. Nothing good ever happened at this time of day, that's why most people chose to sleep through it.

The third floor window of the Fitzpatrick Grand Central hotel faced directly onto 44th Street but there was nothing out there, at least nothing that Eda could see.

The rain had stopped at last. It was quiet, a little too quiet.

Had she been dreaming? That wouldn't be a surprise, not after what happened with the grinning man earlier on in the Waldorf. After talking to Linda in the lobby, Eda had walked alone through the rain back to the Fitzpatrick. There were only a few women from the Complex living in the Fitzpatrick, which held over a hundred and fifty rooms in a ten-story building located opposite Grand Central. The hotel was run down, partially by age but the looting and vandalism that had been so rampant after the war hadn't exactly helped to keep it in good condition. Unlike the Waldorf, the owners of the Fitzpatrick hadn't bothered hiring private guards to protect their property. Those who'd tried to protect their investments, like the Waldorf people, had hoped that the trouble would blow over and that somehow, as crazy as it sounded now, things would eventually get back to normal.

It never did.

Eda didn't mind the wear and tear of the Fitzpatrick. The smell of old things, of decrepit furniture and worn carpet, was a strange source of comfort to her. Most of all however, she liked it there because there were less people and that meant more privacy.

She stayed by the window, looking down both sides of the street as far as she could see. The soft hair on the back of Eda's neck stood up and there was a cold feeling inside, like a warning alarm going off in her mind.

She wondered if someone else had turned up outside the station. Could it be another man? Usually months passed between the arrival of different men at Grand Central.

It was possible, but unlikely.

As Eda stood with her hands gripped tight to the window ledge, her mind wandered back to the years after the war. The wild years. They were full of things that couldn't ever be forgotten by those who'd survived to talk about them. There were always screams in the middle of the night back then. The younger Eda wouldn't have blinked at such a disturbance as the one she'd just heard or imagined, but the world during the wild years had been a louder, even more frightening place than it was now.

Eda felt a chill in the air and shivered. Then she turned around and went back to bed.

But it was no good – she couldn't sleep. All she was doing was lying there, staring up at the yellowy-white ceiling.

It was times like this, with her mind working overtime that Eda missed her best friend, Frankie. Eda had shared a room with Frankie, real name Francesca, in the Fitzpatrick for three years before her friend had all of a sudden gone missing. In all likelihood, even though it wasn't easy for Eda to accept, Frankie had run away from the Complex.

Eda had been devastated by the loss.

Afterwards, Shay had encouraged Eda to move out of the Fitzpatrick and into one of the more populated hotels so that she could mix with the other women. But Eda stayed where she was. Most of the women in the Complex were a lot older than she was and besides that, they had little in common with Eda. Frankie on the other hand, had been about Eda's age and they'd shared the same endless curiosity about the world that had existed before the war. It was that curiosity that inspired them to spend long happy days ransacking old bookstores in the city together. Not surprisingly, few bookstores had been looted after the war. Eda and Frankie mostly raided the history, science and biography shelves and dumped everything into an old wheelbarrow they carried around with them. After that, they'd bring the books back to the hotel and disappear inside the Fitzpatrick for days.

Sometimes they'd read for hours at a time, shouting out interesting facts to one another from across the room.

Eda couldn't help but think that it was those same discoveries that had inspired Frankie's wanderlust. She'd been a curious, highly intelligent girl and she would have fitted in well with the world before the End War and all its marvels.

If only she'd asked Eda to go with her...

Eda struck a match and lit a lemon-scented candle on the bedside table. She then pulled out a tattered hardback book lying under her pillow and thumbed lazily through the pages. It was a general history of the twenty-first century, which had been published a few years before the breakout of the war.

She was re-reading a section about the arms race between the USA and China when she heard a booming voice shouting from afar.

The book fell out of her hands.

Eda stared at the window. Her heart was pounding.

It wasn't a scream this time. She could hear the sound of a man yelling from afar and there was something else too – a faint rattling or churning noise that sounded like something heavy clattering off a distant road.

"Another man?" she said. "It can't be. Two in one day?"

Eda jumped off the bed and stood paralyzed in the middle of the room. Her mind was temporarily frozen with fear. A moment later, she heard frantic footsteps charging downstairs. Loud voices filled the hotel. Eda recognized those voices as belonging to two other women from the Complex who also lived in the Fitzpatrick.

"C'mon," Eda said, talking to herself. "Do something."

She hurried over to the coffee table next to the window and picked up her dagger. The dagger was a strange, exotic looking weapon with a distinct medial ridge on the blade. Eda kept the blade sharp at all times, even though there had been little use for it in recent years.

She blew out the candle and ran towards the stairs. As she reached the first floor of the Fitzpatrick, Eda heard more shouting on the streets – it sounded like it was coming from a couple of blocks down. And it was getting louder all the time. It was the same male voice she heard over and over. He sounded angry and damn loud about it.

Eda stepped outside the hotel. The cold air was like a slap in the face.

She started walking towards the disturbance, keeping tight to the buildings and cloaked in darkness. With a light step, Eda moved off 44th Street and onto Lexington Avenue. From there she hurried south, ignoring the warning bell voice in her head that told her she was crazy.

But something was happening and it was like a magnet pulling her in.

As she approached the corner of 42nd and Lexington, Eda saw two women huddled tight together with their backs facing her. They were both peering out from the edge of the building, pointing down East 42nd Street towards the entrance of Grand Central.

Eda caught up with the two women and when they heard her coming, they spun around and nearly jumped out of their rain cloaks in fright. When they saw it was Eda, they looked both relieved and angry at the same time. Eda vaguely recognized them both as gardeners. She didn't know their names but they were in their mid-sixties approximately and both worked inside Grand Central, tending to the crops.

One of the women, short and skinny, with Oriental features and smooth brown skin, raised a hand as if to halt Eda's progress.

"You can't go any further," she whispered.

"Why not?" Eda asked, trying to get past them so she could look around the corner. "What's going on for God's sake? Who's doing all that shouting?"

The other gardener – pale-skinned and with frightened blue eyes – pressed a finger tight to her lips.

"Not too loud," she said.

Eda scrunched up her face in confusion. There was no way anyone on 42nd Street was going to hear them talking. She forced her way past the two women, just enough to poke her head around the corner and see what was going on for herself.

She looked down 42nd Street towards Grand Central.

"Holy shit," she said.

There was a brown horse pulling a small wooden cart with massive spoked wheels. The cart was parading back and forth in front of the station entrance like it was performing in a parade.

Eda crept out further. She slid around the corner, all the while getting closer to the action. She ignored the faint protests of the women behind her.

She had to see this.

A fat, heavily bearded man stood up in the driver's seat of the cart, holding the reins and yelling wildly at the top of his deep voice. He bellowed an ear-splitting command to the horse and it turned left, spinning the cart around yet again. The cart then raced back along the center of 42nd Street over the faded white lines that had once divided traffic. Now that she was closer, Eda saw something at the back of the horse-driven vehicle.

Two dead bodies.

She gasped.

The corpses were attached to the cart by two long stretches of gnarled rope tied around their legs. It was two women and they were lying flat on their backs, their arms outstretched in a cross-like pose. Their bodies shuddered violently on the wet road as they were repeatedly dragged up and down the street.

"What the fuck?" Eda said. "What is this?"

Further back, a large group of about thirty men stood at the side of the road. They were dressed in a variety of torn rags and even from a distance, Eda could see – she could *feel* – the ravenous, inhuman look in their dead eyes. Their long hair and thick beards made them look like a pack of wild animals that had just crawled out of the woods.

Eda looked back at the two gardeners. They were still hovering at the corner of the street. The Asian woman gestured with her hand, urging Eda not to go any further along 42nd Street. Her pale-skinned friend looked like she was about to be sick.

A gentle rain began to fall.

Eda looked up at a black, starless sky and smelled a fresh, earthy odor in the air. Another big downpour was imminent.

The man driving the cart let out a loud, primal roar that would have been heard for miles across the city. He was like a conquering barbarian and he roared with unrestrained laughter as he continued to drag the two corpses behind his rickety chariot like a pair of mangled trophies. The bodies were covered in dirt, bruises and patches of dried blood – it was hard to discern their features and even harder to guess how long they'd been hooked up to the cart and how far they'd traveled like that.

Eda turned back to the gardeners. They were gone.

She looked at all the men gathered in close proximity to the station. She hadn't seen so many men standing in one place, not since she'd been a child. It was a miracle of sorts, albeit an unwanted one. Linda had been right – the ambassadors were out there in the waste-lands telling the world all about the Complex and the Project.

But at what cost?

Further down 42nd Street, the cart finally rolled to a stop close to the station entrance.

"Where is she?" the fat man bellowed. He was still up off his seat with arms stretched out, displaying the sheer enormity of his girth for all the world to see. Like the other men, he was dressed in worn, colorless rags.

"Where's your beautiful queen?" he cried out. "Where's Helen of Troy?"

The man roared yet again and then clumsily stepped off the cart, landing on the damp road. He lifted his head towards the falling rain, opened his mouth and caught a few drops on his tongue. When he'd tasted enough, he smacked his lips together like a contented animal.

"Where is she?" the fat man called out. He took a look at the empty streets and let out a long, exaggerated sigh. "There's no need to hide from me ladies of the Complex. Your friends here told us all about your little community in the heart of NEW YORK, NEW YORK!"

He sang the city's name in a strange warbling melody.

"You have food, women and purpose," the fat man said. "But you're incomplete. You need men. Well, your wish has been granted and it's all thanks to the brave efforts of your dead messengers right here. They found us a long way away from New York. They told us about your Project and the matter of reconstruction. We've traveled a great distance to help you – won't you come out and say hello?"

He laughed and turned to face his wild-looking colleagues further down the street. They were still standing in the rain, watching everything happen with a chilling silence.

"Some things don't change," the fat man said, gesturing to his comrades. "Civilization has crumbled, the human species is teetering on the verge of extinction but a woman will still – STILL – keep a man waiting."

Eda's fingers gripped the wooden handle of the dagger. She crept closer still, keeping in the darkness at all times.

There was a sudden flurry of movement.

Somebody stepped out of the station's main entrance.

Shay, dressed in her bright red rain cloak, walked slowly towards the center of the road. She moved in a ghostly silence. Seconds later, a few other women followed her out of the station and approached the unexpected, late night visitors.

Shay stood facing the fat man who greeted her with a cold, menacing grin. The other women quickly formed a tight semi-circle at their leader's back.

"What took you so long?" the fat man said.

Shay pointed to the two corpses tied to the cart.

"Why did you kill our ambassadors?" she asked. Her voice rang out loud and clear as if she wanted everyone in the vicinity to hear her. "They traveled this land in peace, seeking nothing more than to find volunteers for the Project. There was no need to harm them – no need to kill them."

"Wrong," the fat man snapped. He pointed a finger at Shay's face. "Your ambassadors tried to murder us in our sleep. Before that they tried to steal food and water from us. You know, you should be careful what sort of people you use to represent you. If you send out thieves and murderers, well, it might give the wrong impression."

"Whatever the initial act of wrongdoing was," Shay said, "we both know that it wasn't committed by my people."

The fat man smirked. "Are you calling me a liar?"

There was a pause.

"I'm calling you a cheap bandit," Shay said. "You're all bandits and you've come here to loot and destroy what I've worked so hard to build. To take what isn't yours."

"That hurts my feelings," the fat man said. He looked almost sincere.

"Oh really?" Shay asked. "Well if you haven't come to steal and murder, then why are you here?"

"I want everything your messengers promised and more," the bandit said. "You have food and gardens, am I right? You've got water. You're organized and most importantly, you have women everywhere. Thank you God! Granted, most of them are a bit old and saggy around the edges but beggars can't be choosers, not in the United

States of Armageddon. I hope however, that Helen is a lot more attractive than what I'm seeing out here. Is she? Please say yes."

"You want to breed with Helen?" Shay said.

"*Breed*?" the bandit said, roaring with laughter. "Of course I want to breed. It's going to be glorious. We're going to rebuild the world together, take the human race back to its former glories. And to do that we're going to need people – lots of people and that means a lot of breeding."

"What about the curse?" Shay said.

The bandit shrugged. "What curse?"

Eda heard Shay laughing from afar.

"Do you think I'm impressed?" Shay said. "Do you think anyone here is impressed when you play the fool?"

The man smiled and tapped a finger off his forehead three times.

"I remember now," he said. "Your ambassadors *did* say something about the curse and how Mother Nature was pissed at us. They talked about a lot of things – a low sex drive, painful orgasms and a childless, barren world – blah-blah-blah. To be honest, I had no idea what they were talking about but they said if we came all the way here to New York and successfully bred with Helen that we'd be the heroes of our fledgling species. That we'd be treated like kings for the rest of our lives. *Can you defy the curse?* That's what they said to me."

Eda could see the back of Shay's head nodding slowly.

"Have you had intercourse lately?" she asked.

"Not lately," the bandit said. "Had your messengers over there not insisted on fighting to the death I would have tested your curse out on them. Now I'll be the first to admit that my sex drive isn't what it used to be but that's only because of all the chemical shit floating around in the air. And it's also because I hardly ever see a woman these days. So trust me when I say that right now, looking at you all, I'm horny as hell. I'm going to ask you again – where's Helen?"

"Let me tell you something," Shay said, taking a step towards the bandit. "If you have an orgasm you'll die. And it'll be a terrible, terrible death like nothing you could ever imagine. I've seen it so many times now."

The man roared with laughter. "You know something lady," he said, "you remind me of a Sunday school teacher I had a long time ago. Good to see all that fire and brimstone shit survived the end of the world, you know?"

Shay lifted the hood of the rain cloak over her head.

The bandit's hand moved to the hilt of a short sword hanging off his belt. His fingers tapped the handle in a slow, contemplative rhythm.

"Maybe I'll take you as one of my wives," he said, examining Shay from head to toe. "Yeah, I like you. It could be Helen for sex and you for conversation afterwards. Because I get the feeling you've got a big set of balls swinging under that red coat of yours sweetheart. And I like that."

He looked at the huddle of women standing at Shay's back.

"C'mon," he yelled. "Don't look so worried ladies. Think about the positives here – you'll be a lot safer if we stick around. I speak from experience – there are bad people wandering about out there nowadays. Not many it's true, but the ones that are out there, they're sick in the head. Almost everyone you'll meet has been driven mad by hunger and loneliness. And they're always on the move. It's only a matter of time before they get here and find your little Complex. When they do, you'll be glad you've got us to protect you."

The fat man raised a hand in the air.

At this signal, the other bandits began to walk slowly towards the station. As they got closer to the old building, Eda noticed that they were all carrying the same type of short sword as their leader. At the head of the pack, a giant man swaggered with loose, simian limbs flapping in the breeze. He had to be at least seven foot tall and his extreme height combined with a sturdy build and straggly brown beard, made it look like a grizzly bear was running loose in New York.

Someone else caught Eda's eye.

She saw a younger man hanging slightly apart from the others. He was probably about thirty or a little older. A mop of dark curly hair flopped over his forehead. In contrast to his heavily bearded comrades, there was only a thin coat of boyish stubble growing on the man's face. He looked like a stranger in the crowd, like he didn't belong with the others. As he walked at the back, his eyes darted around with uncertainty. Several times, he glanced over his shoulder like somebody who knew they were being watched.

"You don't want to fight us," the fat man said to Shay. "Look at my boys back there, right? They're battle-hardened and as mean as a pack of rattlesnakes. And we don't want to fight you either. All we want is to be part of one big happy family together. Is that so bad? We can do great things here in the name of reconstruction. Will you let us in nicely? Peacefully? Or do we have to force our way in? It's entirely up to you."

Shay stood in silence for a moment. The horse made a fat snorting noise and tugged on the cart, as if it was eager to move along and start dragging those corpses up and down the street again.

"You're right," Shay said, nodding slowly. She pointed a finger at the advancing bandit pack and her shoulders appeared to drop a little. "It *would* be foolish of us to try and fight you."

"No," Eda whispered from the shadows.

The fat man moved his hand away from the hilt of his sword. "Good girl," he said, patting Shay on the shoulder. "Smart girl too. I'm definitely claiming you as one of mine."

"Take what you want and go," Shay said. "Take the food. Take a woman – but just one if you please. Don't kill us or damage our supplies – don't destroy everything that we've worked so hard to build here."

"*Destroy* it?" the bandit said, looking genuinely surprised. "You have me all wrong sister. I don't want to destroy anything – I want us to build a beautiful world together. *Together*. We're staying, we're not going anywhere."

He stepped forward and slid a chubby finger down Shay's cheek. The finger kept going until it slipped inside the rain cloak and landed on Shay's pale neck. The fat man then pulled at the cloak, opening up a small gap between the fabric and Shay's skin. He leaned forward, staring down at Shay's body, all the while licking his lips.

"I'm going to like it here," he said, his eyes lighting up.

He let go of Shay and turned to his left. It looked like something had caught his attention over by the station.

Whistling loudly, the bandit walked towards a row of flowerbeds lined up neatly outside Grand Central. He leaned closer to inspect the assortment of vegetables growing there and when he was done, the bandit turned around and nodded his approval.

"You've been busy," he called over to Shay. "Well done. I take it you gals know how to cook this stuff as well as you grow it? Oh boy, busy, hardworking women – just like my Angie back in Philly before she went batshit crazy."

Shay walked towards the bandit. It looked like she was gliding over the center of the road.

Eda saw the bandit's hand instinctively reach for the sword at his waist.

"Gentlemen," she said, coming to a sudden stop. "Yes, we've been busy. In fact, you've no idea how busy we've been here in our dear Eldorado. But it would give me great pleasure to show you."

Shay looked up towards the night sky.

"Now," she said.

Eda heard something – a brief, high-pitched whoosh that cut through the sound of the pouring rain. It was followed by a loud, yet muffled shriek.

She saw the fat man staggering backwards away from the flowerbeds. He was bent double, one hand reaching for something on his head.

Then he dropped onto one knee.

There was an arrow lodged in his neck.

4

More arrows rained down with lethal precision.

The bandits were thrown into a sudden, desperate panic. Most of them ran for cover in the abandoned buildings opposite Grand Central. A few however, charged boldly towards their leader who by now had collapsed onto his back in the middle of the road. But it was too late to help him. The fat man's saucer-like eyes stared blankly up at the dark sky, his mouth like that of a dying fish, opening and closing, gasping for breath.

There were people shouting everywhere. Angry, frightened voices filled the night.

Eda tried to stay small. She was still tucked in at the edge of the street, clinging to the old storefronts that were cloaked in darkness. After moving forward a little, she looked up and saw a shadowy line of figures standing on the Park Avenue Viaduct, which extended outwards like a ramp or a bridge above the street level entrance to Grand Central.

The archers.

"Yes," she said, throwing a fist in the air.

Most of the bandits realized that the sudden attack was coming from the viaduct. It was too late for many of them to get out of the way. Eda watched as an older man with a mop of straggly gray hair, stood in stunned silence, staring up at the long row of female assassins. He yelled something to the women, something that sounded spiteful, and then seconds later took an arrow in the heart.

A woman's voice bellowed out the command 'FIRE'. This happened every five seconds and Eda, still looking up towards the viaduct, realized that there were two lines of about ten archers standing on the bridge. These two lines were taking it in turns to shoot at the bandits down on the street. After the front row had fired, they'd immediately duck down and pull another arrow from a quiver that was fastened onto their backs. During that brief interval, the second row of archers would stand up and fire into the crowd. This was repeated over and over again.

It was a massacre.

Eda felt a rush of blood surging through her veins. She squeezed the handle of the dagger and gently stabbed the sidewalk several times.

If the fighting hit the ground, would she take her place alongside the other warriors in battle?

Could she do it?

Eda had killed a man, a long time ago. It happened when she was still very young, several years after the war ended and everything was turning upside down in a world gone mad. This was before the curse, back when some of the more vicious men, roaming the streets in either large packs or as lone wolves, were raping and plundering at will, taking full advantage of the swift decline of the police and military influence. Losers became winners. Outlaws became kings. For those people, the end of the world was the greatest party there ever was.

She killed him in a city but she couldn't remember the name of it. It didn't matter.

Eda had been with Libby, one of several young women who'd taken the orphaned girl under her wing at the time. The man was a predator, like so many others. He'd followed them for at least two blocks before Libby leaned down and whispered in Eda's ear, telling her that she wasn't to panic but that they were going to start running fast. And Libby also told Eda not to look back.

They ran but they couldn't shake the guy off. He obviously knew the city well and they didn't. It was as if he knew every twist and turn his would-be victims were going to make before they'd made it.

He'd done this before. Many times.

They couldn't shake him off.

Eventually, he'd trapped Libby and Eda in a dark alley. The man had nasty facial burns running down one side of his face, probably from the war. He had long greasy hair and an ugly, jagged scar on the left side of his neck. He didn't say anything. Instead, he just cackled and marched forward like the attack was nothing out of the ordinary.

It was to be expected. Tolerated.

He pinned Libby to the ground and started beating her on the face and upper body. He went at this vicious attack with such a hot fury that it was hard to believe it wasn't personal, like somehow she'd wronged him in a past life. But Libby didn't black out. Throughout the assault, in which time seemed to stand still, she screamed at Eda, yelling one single world over and over again.

Run! Run! Run!

But Eda couldn't run away, even if she'd wanted to. She just stood there watching, her little legs paralyzed with fear.

She didn't cry.

The man pressed a large, filthy hand over Libby's mouth to shut her up. No doubt he wanted the kid to stick around for dessert.

Eda watched as he forced himself onto Libby. When he pulled down his pants, that's when she'd noticed the black-handled knife strapped around his leg with Scotch tape.

She didn't hesitate.

Eda ran over to where the man had Libby pinned to the ground. She grabbed the handle of the small knife and with all her strength, pulled it away, cutting through the tape in the process. That caught his attention. He turned around and in that moment, looked at Eda with the knife in her hand like she was the devil standing over him.

She might as well have been.

The man tried to get up but Eda was much faster than he was. As he moved, she stabbed him hard on the inside leg, one swift strike, and he yelped like wounded dog.

Eda pulled the knife out and backed away. A moment later, Libby got up and stood beside her. Eda's guardian was cut under the eye but it didn't look like she'd sustained anything too serious in the attack. They stayed there, watching the man in the alley wriggle around on the ground like a wounded snake. The blood flowed fast; it looked jet-black in the darkness. His face turned pale and all the fight went out of him along with the blood. It was only later that Libby explained to Eda about the femoral artery that was located in the leg.

The little kid had struck lucky.

In the days and weeks that followed, Eda never lost a wink of sleep over what happened in that alley. Her first kill, yes, but it was just another day in the wild years. Back then, people were doing bad things to each other all the time and sometimes for good reasons.

All that was a long time ago.

Eda stared at the dagger in her hand as the rain continued to crash down onto 42nd Street. Did she still have it in her? The ability to kill a man as easily as blinking – was it still there? She'd been living in the Complex for a long time, safe, wrapped up in community and in an environment that was well prepared.

That little girl – when Eda thought about her, it felt like she was thinking about someone else.

Many of the bandits lay dead on the road. The survivors, including the giant, had fled for cover at the side of the street, rushing inside the ransacked and empty buildings. Some of them had been hit and as they ran for their lives, Eda saw them clutching at a variety of wounds.

The horse had long since bolted along with the cart and the dead ambassadors tied to the back. The surviving bandits had no way out now except on foot.

Eda leaned her back up against the front an old Capital One Bank. For a moment, the carnage further down the street eased off. It was almost quiet again.

Then a voice yelled from afar:

"Come out and fight you cowardly bitches! Stop hiding behind your arrows."

One of the bandits stood in the doorway of a coffee shop, brandishing a short sword in the air. It was the giant. He waved the weapon back and forth like it was a signal to someone in the distance.

"We'll stay here all night and wait it out!" he yelled. His voice was high-pitched for such a big man – the sound so at odds with his imposing physical presence. "It'll take more than a few bitches to get rid of us. Cowards! Let's see you on the street, face to face with your swords in hand. What do you say?"

Eda heard the giant shout orders to the men at his back, most of who were hidden in that same coffee shop with him. She guessed that the archers' surprise attack had reduced the bandits to less than half their original numbers. A successful ambush but nonetheless, the surviving men were still up for a fight.

"Be careful what you wish for," Eda said, looking at the giant.

Another brief silence passed. Then a sharp voice cut through the night.

"SWORDS!"

It was Shay.

Eda watched as the archers called off their assault on the bandits. She saw them hurrying back along the viaduct – a long line of dark silhouettes moving under the cover of night. Soon she couldn't see them at all.

As the archers retreated, about twenty women in black rain cloaks marched out of the station entrance in single file. What Eda saw was the katana swords in their hands, the familiar single-edged blades with the distinctive curve of the samurai.

The warriors.

Eda's heart was racing with excitement.

The warriors took up their positions on the road. The tip of their swords pointed towards the bandits, who were by now shuffling out of the coffee shop and edging towards the battleground. They were bruised and battered but there was still a little swagger left in their step. As they approached the road, the men's restless eyes jumped back and forth between the warriors and the now empty viaduct.

But the archers were gone.

Lex was the chief warrior and she stood at the head of the small, female army. A former military veteran in her mid-fifties, Lex was the resident self-defense guru of the Complex. She was well over six feet tall, highly skilled with a variety of weapons, as well as in unarmed combat techniques such as Krav Maga. Her regular fencing classes were popular with the women but Eda had always held back from joining in. Group activities like that weren't her thing.

Maybe she'd been wrong to do that.

The giant stood at the head of the bandits with his sword drawn. He stared over at Lex and the warriors with cruel satisfaction in his black eyes. With a grimace, he pressed a massive, red-stained hand against a gaping wound under his left shoulder. He squeezed on the wound and a stream of blood spilled down the front of his rags.

"To hell with rebuilding the human race," he called out. "I say we empty New York of all these murdering bitches and after we're done, we march through this town and burn it. What do you say boys?"

There was an angry jeer of approval at his back.

The giant stabbed the tip of his sword off the wet road. It made a loud, clanging noise and he did it over and over again, building up towards a frantic, tribal rhythm. The others followed his lead and the sound of all those swords hitting off the road at once swelled into something terrifying and spectacular.

He turned around to face his men. Then after a long silence, he held his sword aloft and yelled a single word:

"CHARGE!"

Eda jumped back as if the bandits were charging directly at her. To her surprise, the warriors on the street didn't flinch at this sudden attack. They stood like statues as the enemy dashed forward with weapons raised and cries of bloody murder spewing from their hateful mouths.

It was happening. A battle – a real life and death battle was about to take place on the streets of New York. The history books were full of great battles, Waterloo, Trafalgar, Gettysburg and more. Perhaps Manhattan was about to add its name to the list.

Finally, Lex raised a hand in the air. She held it still for a moment, letting the men wear themselves out a little more.

Then she dropped it.

The warriors raced forwards in silence to meet the enemy.

From afar, Eda put her hands over her ears. The two small armies crashed into one another and the metallic clash of steel against steel felt like it was scraping off the inside of Eda's head. She'd never seen anything like this before. Even in the wild years, there'd been nothing like this.

Shay and several other women stood near the entrance to the station, watching keenly as the battle unfolded.

Lex and her warriors glided effortlessly through the battle like it was a dance. The men were undoubtedly bigger and stronger but it seemed like they were running solely on anger and raw strength. It was blunt force versus skill. Some of the bandits lost their footing on the wet road as they wielded the heavy short swords with clumsy abandon. Those that slipped, even just onto a knee, didn't have time to get back to their feet before a warrior's blade found them.

Lex and one of her soldiers had decided to tackle the giant. They took up position, one on either side of the big man, slicing up his massive torso and adding to his nasty collection of wounds. The giant roared in pain. The women were much faster and lighter on their feet than he was. He turned to launch a counter attack on Lex but as soon as he faced her, the other warrior ran the tip of her blade down his back in a vertical line, like she was marking him. The giant howled. If nothing else, he was brave and determined. He kept moving forward, trying to hack at Lex and then the other warrior. They led him on a merry dance, their feet skipping lightly off the surface of the road. Every now and then, one of the warriors would rush in and open him up somewhere new.

Eda watched, edging ever closer to the action. She was so focused on the fighting that she almost didn't hear the scream behind her.

She spun around. There was nothing but the dark road behind her.

Another scream.

Eda's thoughts turned to the two frightened gardeners who'd taken off earlier.

"Oh shit," she said. "What's happened?"

She turned back to the fighting on 42nd Street. It wasn't over by a long shot. The bandits were staging a comeback and they were sweeping forward, as if a second wind had spread across the ranks of surviving men. Some of the warriors in black were down, clutching at the stab wounds on their body.

Eda couldn't bear to turn her back on the battle. But she had to.

With the dagger in hand, she turned and ran back in the direction she thought the scream had come from. She took a sharp right turn, charging up the long, empty stretch of Lexington Avenue. The battle had inspired her. The blood was surging through Eda's veins and she was ready to do whatever had to be done.

But it was so hard to see. There were no night torches hanging off the buildings here like there were on Grand Central.

Eda kept moving through the darkness. She glanced back and forth down the side streets and through broken store windows. The heavy rain slammed against her face but she kept her hood down so that she could see better.

She approached 43rd Street, which turned off Lexington to the right.

Eda looked down that way and stopped dead.

She saw dark shapes on the road. Two of them were lying on their backs while the other, a big man with his sword drawn, stood over them.

The man struck the two women with the flat of the sword, one after the other. The blows landed with a painful sounding thud.

"Stop it!" a woman's voice cried out. "Please stop. Leave us alone, just leave us alone. My friend's badly hurt. You stabbed her."

Eda's blood turned cold. She recognized the voice of the Asian gardener.

"Shut up," the man hissed. There was another dull thud as he lashed out at the woman with his boot. "I stabbed you too, remember?"

"I think she's dying," the Asian woman said. "Won't you please just stop?"

Eda tiptoed down 43rd Street quietly. Her heart was pounding.

The attacker had to be one of the bandits – he was a dark skinned man of about fifty at least, dressed in tattered, soaking wet denims. He was extremely overweight and there was a thick mustache under his nose. Eda wondered if he'd fled 42nd Street after the archers had appeared. Had he stumbled across the gardeners as they'd tried to make their getaway?

The pale gardener wasn't moving. The bandit leaned over and said something to her, then kicked her, ordering the woman to answer. The Asian gardener cried out, begging him to stop the assault. She lifted her friend in her arms, as if trying to shield her from another, potentially fatal blow.

"What have you got for me?" the man said. "What have you got? Food, water, weapons – I need whatever you're hiding in this shithole that's useful. Give me what I want or I swear to God I'll carve you both into little pieces. You want to be my lunch? Huh?"

The Asian woman's protests were sluggish. Was she badly hurt too?

"Please believe me," she said. "We don't have anything."

The man lashed out with another kick but this one missed its target.

"Well I ain't going anywhere till you find me something," he said. "Get me some supplies bitch or I swear to God I'm going to turn this thing up a notch. You don't want that to happen, trust me."

Eda knew she had to do something. And yet she was paralyzed with fear. She could still hear the sound of the battle raging on 42nd Street, unsure whether the warriors from the Complex were winning or being massacred.

She kept out of sight, still gripping the dagger tightly. The weapon felt light in her hand, like it wasn't there anymore. What was wrong with her? Where was all the fight and the fire? She couldn't even call out – yell at the bandit to warn him off, to say something, anything, tell him that the warriors were coming.

Her voice was gone.

She was useless.

And how long before the bandit saw her lurking at the end of the street? How long before he turned his attention on her?

"What's going on?" somebody called out.

It was a man's voice. A different man.

Eda watched as a dark figure appeared in the distance up ahead. He hurried down from the opposite end of 43rd Street, making his way towards the bandit and the two women lying on the ground.

"What are you doing Pike?" the second man said.

The older man straightened up. He made a curt, dismissive gesture with his hands like he was swatting a fly off his face.

"Get the hell out of here boy," he said. "You haven't been with us long enough to ask me a question like that. Mind your own goddamn business."

The other man stepped forward and Eda recognized him immediately. It was the young man – the reluctant, baby-faced bandit with the mop of curly brown hair.

He stood there now, looking at the older bandit with an expression of pure disgust on his face. When he spoke, he did so with a peculiar, foreign accent.

"Are you crazy Pike?" he said. "Have you seen what's going on back there outside the train station? It's a massacre for God's sake. We should never have come to New York in the first place. We've got to get out of here. Now!"

Pike laughed. It was a cruel, mocking sound.

"And go where kid?" he said. "Back into that fucking desert? There's food and water in this city. Not to mention there's women here by the truckload. But I'll tell ya – if I'm going back out there I'm going to make sure I've got me some supplies first. Maybe a woman for the road too."

"You're insane," the young man said.

"Go away boy," Pike snapped. "You're getting on my nerves." He repeated the swatting gesture for a second time and turned his attention back to the two women on the road. He kneeled down in front of them, rubbing his hands together.

"You still with me ladies?" he said.

He poked the pale gardener in the ribs and she didn't move. Then he slapped the Asian woman on the back. She moved, but it was a feeble gesture.

"C'mon," Pike said. "I didn't hit you that hard."

"Pike!" the second man cried out. "Stop it. She's barely conscious for God's sake. What have you done to these people? Have you stabbed them?"

"Naïve boy," Pike said, looking behind him. "This is how you get people to do what you want."

He slapped the barely conscious woman hard in the face. It made a loud clapping noise that stung in Eda's ears and she felt physically sick.

The gardener shrieked and fell backwards beside her friend.

"Pike!" the other man yelled. "That's enough."

The bandit was about to lunge at the woman again, this time with the flat of the sword. But before he could do anything, the young man came up from behind and locked his arms around Pike's neck. He pulled the older man away from the two women.

Pike looked shocked by this sudden assault. He was so shocked that the short sword fell out of his hand and dropped onto the road.

"What are you doing you crazy bastard?" the bandit yelled. His voice was muffled under the choke.

"That's enough," the young man said. "You've done more than enough. C'mon, let's get out of here. We can go back to New Jersey – I know a place we can hide out there."

"Let go of me!"

Pike broke free of the young man's grip and lunged at him.

The two men fell to the ground. They wrestled furiously, rolling around on the wet concrete in a frantic struggle. As they fought, angry voices exchanged breathless insults. Pike managed to work his way on top of the young man and pushed his hands down onto the boyish face. His thumbs pressed forward, reaching for the eyes of his opponent. The young man cried out in terror. He leaned his head back to avoid being blinded. Then with a violent thrust of the hips, he shook Pike off and sprang forward, head-butting the old man hard on the nose.

There was a loud cracking noise.

Pike yelped in pain and put a hand to his nose.

Eda tiptoed along 43rd Street quietly. Maybe she could still get to the gardeners if the two men kept fighting. Maybe they were still alive.

Her fingers clamped tightly around the handle of the exotic dagger.

Could she do it? Could she still kill a man if she had to?

What about two men?

The fight between the bandits continued. The young man was on top now – he'd mounted Pike and both hands were locked around the fat bandit's neck in another tight, unrelenting choke. He cried out as he tightened the stranglehold. It seemed like he had no intention of letting go.

Eda watched from a distance, a hidden spectator in the shadows. It was the young man's eyes that frightened her the most. He didn't look like a killer and yet there he was, killing one of his own in order to help two strangers who might be dead already.

Pike's body stopped rattling in protest. His frantic struggle slowed down to an eventual, eternal halt. When it was over, the young man fell off the bandit's body and sat on the wet street, looking around in a daze.

Then he looked over and saw Eda. She was inching slowly up the street towards him, the sharp dagger in hand.

The man leapt back to his feet. His eyes remained glued to the dagger.

Eda noticed the sword strapped to his waist but so far at least, he'd made no attempt to unsheathe the weapon.

"I don't mean you any harm," he said to Eda. He held both hands up in the air as he spoke to her. With a sigh, he looked at the two gardeners lying motionless on the road.

"I'm sorry," he said. "I was too late."

Eda wasn't sure if the young man was trying to trick her. Was he playing games? Was he luring her in for a surprise attack?

"I'm sorry," he repeated.

They looked at each other in silence. Then, without another word, the young man turned around and raced back down 43rd Street as fast as he could.

Eda watched him disappear into the night like a ghost. When he was gone, she ran over to the gardeners and kneeled down in a cold puddle beside them. She pulled back their rain cloaks and saw multiple stab wounds on both bodies. There were numerous cuts on their faces too. The sick, twisted bastard. How long had he been working them over before Eda arrived? How long had they been screaming before she'd finally heard them?

She checked their necks for a pulse.

Nothing.

Eda jumped back to her feet and threw the dagger hard off the ground. There was a loud clattering noise but it didn't come close to cooling the fire that burned inside. She screamed briefly and then, not knowing what else to do, pulled the hood up over her head and closed her eyes.

She sat down beside the women again. As she whispered her apologies to them both, Eda felt the soft pitter-patter of the rain landing on her head.

5

Eda stayed with the two women for a long time.

She couldn't bring herself to leave them and as she sat there in the pouring rain next to the corpses, she lost track of the fighting and shouting noises that drifted north from the impromptu battlefield outside Grand Central.

But she couldn't stay there all night.

Eventually, after the rain had eased off a little and with no sense of how long she'd been sitting with the women, Eda dragged herself back to her feet.

"I'll come back," she whispered to the bodies. It was a hollow promise, but it was all she had.

The man called Pike was dead too. Although the young bandit had killed him, Eda had been the one to make sure of it. She'd dragged Pike's body to the side of the road and stamped on his head with the flat of her boot. She'd spat in his face and punched him all over for as long as her arms worked. But it was no good – even if the bastard's head had exploded all over the sidewalk, it wouldn't have made her feel any better.

Eda walked back to Lexington Avenue with a heavy heart. Every step she took felt like it was landing in a pool of thick mud that was trying to drag her underground. It was quiet now. The sound of clashing steel was gone, replaced by the gentle pitter-patter of the dying rainfall. There were no spirited battle cries to rouse hope or inspire fear. The only thing that drifted up from Grand Central now was a ghostly silence.

Eda turned the corner and looked over at the bloody mess that had formed outside the station. She clamped a hand over her mouth. There were bodies everywhere– mostly male bodies. They were sprawled out in a variety of gruesome poses, limbs frozen at impossible angles like a bunch of dead circus freaks on display.

Whatever private horror they'd seen at the end, it was tattooed in their wide-open eyes.

The giant was there too, lying flat on his back with his arms outstretched on either side. It would take at least another massive downpour to wash away all the blood that clung to his rigid frame.

Eda counted eight warriors down. She saw Lex walking across the battleground with several others, inspecting the bodies of her fallen soldiers in grim silence. Lex's face was a mask of black blood, but Eda had a feeling that most of the splatter belonged to the dead bandits.

"Eda. Are you alright?"

Eda spun around in a dazed shock. Somehow Shay had managed to creep up behind her and Eda, usually so sensitive to her surroundings, hadn't heard a thing.

Shay's hood was up. It had been pulled low over her face, shielding the older woman's eyes from view.

"Are you alright?"

Eda could only nod.

"You look like your legs are about to give way," Shay said. "Are you hurt?"

Eda looked down at her legs. It was true she could barely feel them – she might as well have floated all the way back down to 42nd Street.

"I'm okay," she said. "But..."

"But?" Shay said.

"There are two gardeners on 43rd Street," Eda said. "They're dead. I'm sorry, I don't remember their names."

Shay looked at the bloodstains on Eda's fingers. The rain hadn't quite washed everything away yet.

"Are you sure you're not hurt?" Shay said.

Eda looked at her hands and shook her head. She clenched her fists tightly together to hide the sight of blood.

She was lightheaded.

"It was so dark," Eda said. "I couldn't help them."

She wobbled on unsteady feet.

Shay grabbed a hold of her, pulling the younger woman into a tight embrace. Eda fell willingly into Shay's arms and buried her head in the older woman's chest. Shay's heart didn't sound like it was beating at all. How could she be so calm after everything that had happened?

"Thanks for letting me know," Shay said. "We'll pick up the bodies as soon as we can."

"Why did they do it?" Eda said, lifting her head off Shay's chest. She stepped back and brushed down the front of her rain cloak, which squeaked in protest. Eda felt like she was swimming in blood but there was only water on her clothes. "Why did they come here with two ambassadors tied to their cart?"

Shay pursed her lips. "They wanted to go backwards," she said. "They wanted to create a little patriarchal society of their own, to live in the past and do all the things they wanted. At our expense."

Eda pulled her hood up, dragging it forward over her forehead. It was as close to disappearing as she could get.

"Is it worth it Shay?" she asked. "Sending the ambassadors out I mean."

"That's the risk we take Eda," Shay said. "We could live here, keep ourselves to ourselves and no one would ever have to venture outside Manhattan again. We could accept the curse as final and live out the rest of our lives in peace. It's tempting. But I believe in what we're doing here. So do the ambassadors – they know the risks before they go out there and no one ever forces them to do what they do. And in turn, we know the risks in terms of what might show up on our doorstep."

"So it is worth it?" Eda said.

Shay's eyes lingered on the growing pile of corpses on the road.

"Don't know yet."

6

After the battle on 42nd Street, the women in the Complex were wary of who would show up next.

Still they tried to carry on as normal. The gardeners tended to the fruits and vegetables, to water storage and overseeing the distribution of supplies to the various occupied hotels. Lex's self-defense classes grew in popularity. Fitness training, swords and archery practice – there were women who hadn't picked up a weapon in their lives now showing an interest in these things. They'd seen the importance of learning how to fight first hand. If not for the warriors, the bandits would have taken over and they'd be as good as slaves.

But Eda wasn't interested in either the fitness classes or sword training. She took on a new role after the battle and one that suited her growing need for solitude, something that had become more important to her after the death of the two gardeners. With Shay's blessing, Eda became the official lookout for the Complex. She was their eyes. Every morning, she'd leave the Fitzpatrick hotel and walk down 42nd Street. She ventured far to the west as most of the men who came in arrived from that direction, probably having made their way into New York through the Lincoln or Holland tunnels.

Eda took up residence in a variety of lookout spots – usually on the upper floor of old stores, restaurants and coffee shops. She'd sit alone inside these empty buildings and sit by the window for hours, watching and waiting.

On most days, nothing turned up but the rain.

Eda didn't mind the nothingness or what other people might call the boredom of the job. She liked her new role. It was a useful job and thank God because it wasn't gardening or carrying supplies or doing any of the other mundane chores that kept the other women busy. She was no gardener and she was no warrior either – after what had happened with the two gardeners, Eda was convinced that all those years of soft living in the Complex had turned her into a coward. She wasn't that little girl who'd survived the wild years, not anymore. What was the point in learning how to fight if she lacked the guts? It didn't matter. She could be useful in other ways. Eda was still young and she had good eyes and ears. Her intuition was on point too. If something or someone showed up in Manhattan on its way to the Complex, she'd be the first to see or hear it.

Eda would stay away for days on lookout duty. She was in no hurry to get back to Grand Central and as long as she had supplies – food, water and books – in her backpack, there was no need to leave her post. She'd sleep in abandoned buildings, grabbing a few hours here and there throughout the day. When she was awake she'd perch on car roofs or stand on the top floor of tall buildings, staring out at an ocean of stillness.

One day however, the stillness moved.

On that day, Eda was doing squats close to Times Square. She pushed her body up and down while her eyes kept watch on a long stretch of road in front of her.

She stopped all of a sudden.

There was a speck of movement in the distance.

Something was coming towards her.

Eda grabbed the dagger lying at her feet. Slowly, she edged to the side of the road. Taking another look at the blurry shape up ahead, she took cover behind the grimy wreck of an old Ford and waited for it to get a little closer so she could take a better look.

A couple of minutes passed. Eda took a deep breath and peered out from behind the car. Now she saw what it was. Immediately, her tense muscles relaxed and a smile stretched across her face.

It was a dog.

Eda hadn't seen a dog in a long time and not knowing if this one was friendly, mad or riddled with the biting disease, she stayed hidden behind the car. But it was no good. About a minute later, she was peering out and having another look at it.

The dog trotted down the street at a brisk but leisurely pace. It was large and handsome, with a long black and tan coat that appeared to be in excellent condition. Its brown eyes perched over a long black snout and missed nothing. Eda wondered if it already knew she was there, hiding behind the car and couldn't care less.

Eventually, the urge to make contact proved too strong.

Eda got back to her feet in slow motion, holding her breath like she was underwater. With her heart racing, she stepped out from behind the car. Then, without looking at the dog, she strolled casually towards the center of the road where she'd been doing her squats.

Slowly, she glanced to her left.

The dog had stopped and it was looking right at her. Its tail was stiff and upright. Eda thought it looked more like a bronze statue of a dog than the real thing, such was its perfect stillness in that moment. What was it doing? What was it thinking? Eda figured there had to be two options running around in its mind right now – fight or flight. And she felt certain the big creature would choose fight. Any second now, it would come charging across the road towards her at a frightening speed, snarling and baring its sharp canines.

But she was wrong.

After a long and silent exchange between them, the dog turned tail and ran back in the direction it came from.

Eda's heart sank. A stab of loneliness went through her.

She returned to the Complex that night. During her report to Shay, Eda stated that she'd seen nothing of interest while on lookout. The next morning she packed some extra food into her bag and told anyone who was listening that she'd be on lookout for a few days. After that, she took off west along 42nd Street, going back to the exact same spot where she'd seen the dog, not far from where Times Square used to be.

The first day out she saw nothing. The dog didn't come back.

Eda had taken up residence in the shell of an old Foot Locker store on West 42nd Street. There was a plethora of advertising billboards on the opposite side of the street. Eda sat at the window, staring across at one of the images for a long time. It was a black and white photograph of two people, a black man and white woman. There was a guitar featured in the picture. Who were they? They must have been a big deal if they'd had their faces on billboards of that size. One thing was for sure – they looked happy. Music must have been quite something to make people smile like that. Eda had only heard singing before – she'd never experienced the sound of musical instruments like guitars even though she'd read about them, as well as pianos, trumpets and many others. A lot of the women in the Complex used to tell Eda that music was one of the things they missed the most.

It must have been quite something.

She tried to pass her time thinking about things like that. To take her mind on a journey somewhere nice. For the most part, Eda sat at the first floor window fighting off the drowsiness. She hadn't slept much for thinking about the dog.

God knows why she wanted to see it again so badly.

Why she *had* to see it.

Whenever Eda was on the brink of falling asleep she got up and walked around a little. Sometimes she counted her steps as she paced around the room. Foot Locker was like a bombsite. It had been ransacked a long time ago and now there was nothing but the occasional piece of upturned furniture and shards of broken glass on the floor.

After a while, Eda sat down at the window again. She nibbled on a little potato salad and watched the rainclouds gather in the sky.

The dog came back on the second day.

When Eda saw it, she pressed her face up against the glass. She felt a surge of energy shoot through her, like a flower in the sun. Outside the dog sniffed its way along the sidewalk, stopping occasionally to look up and check the surroundings.

Was it looking for her?

She grabbed some supplies, threw them in her bag and hurried downstairs onto the street before the dog reached Foot Locker. She didn't want to jump out on it this time and frighten it away.

As Eda walked outside, a gentle drizzle fell from the sky.

She pulled out a brown paper bag full of food from the backpack and placed it down on the road. Then she took a couple of backwards steps and sat down cross-legged on the wet road.

When the dog saw her it stopped and its tail went stiff like last time. Eda didn't call out or look at it in case she freaked it out. She did her best to look bored by the creature's presence. That wasn't easy because her heart was thumping and both her hands shaking.

The dog didn't run away but it didn't exactly come forward either. It kept still for a long time, watching Eda with exceptional patience. Its eyes were a mystery to her, hidden in the fog of its jet-black face.

Eda reached slowly towards the paper bag in front of her. As gently as she could, she opened it up and scooped out a chunk of potato salad with her fingers. Then she put it into her mouth. It tasted cold and wet but nonetheless she made a happy, contented noise as she chewed the food.

She could feel the dog watching her. When she looked over and made loud yummy noises, it tilted its head.

Eda dipped her fingers into the food and stirred back and forth. It felt disgusting and the rain getting into the box was only making it worse. When her hand was messy with food, she lifted it out and held it up, making sure the dog could see everything.

She had to repeat this act several times as the food kept slipping off her finger.

"C'mon," she whispered, holding her hand outstretched. "Are you hungry?"

The dog watched her for another minute. Just as Eda though it might be on the brink of trusting her, it turned and trotted away.

She was alone again.

The dog came back on the third day. It was raining harder this time but Eda didn't let the weather get in the way of what she was trying to do. When she saw it walking down the road at a steady pace, she hurried outside and went through the same procedure as last time of trying to lure it closer with food.

As she sat on the road, Eda kept her hood down. It was stupid to sit out in the rain like this for so long and her well-worn waterproofs were barely keeping her skin dry underneath. But it would all be worth it, if only the dog would come closer.

She sat there, pulling out chunks of wet salad, slipping them into her mouth and chewing slowly. After that, she'd grab some more and offer a finger out in invitation, beckoning the dog closer.

"C'mon," she whispered. "If I eat any more of this I'm going to be sick. And then you'll never come back."

The dog watched her for a while like it had before. It seemed unfazed by the heavy rain and Eda's heart leapt when it began to walk forward, edging closer to where she was sitting in the middle of the road.

She kept her hand out as it approached.

The dog lifted its nose into the air. The black nose twitched as it inhaled the scent of the food.

It came closer, leaning in with its face.

Eda felt its wet lips take the food from her fingers. She wanted to laugh out loud but knew that such a hysterical reaction would send the dog running off again. So she fought back the surge of emotion and kept silent, waiting until the dog had licked all five fingers clean.

"You want more?" she asked.

She reached into the bowl and worked the salad onto her fingers. Then she fed the dog for a second time until her hand was clean. It went back and forth like that for a while – Eda coating her fingers in layers of food while the dog stood beside her, waiting patiently for yet another helping.

Eda sat in blissful silence throughout. She hadn't felt this content in a long time.

Eventually however, the food ran out. By then, both Eda and the dog were soaking wet. Eda didn't mind – she could have sat there for hours.

The dog turned around and walked away. Eda wanted it to stay for a little longer but she didn't move. She let it go, certain this time that she'd see it again.

On Eda's fourth day away from camp, supplies were getting low. She didn't go back to Grand Central however, not right away. Determined to see her new friend again, she stuck around and when the dog showed up that afternoon, she gave it the majority of the remaining food. The rain had eased off, apart from a light drizzle that was more refreshing than bothersome.

After the final feeding session, Eda was able to stroke the dog on its back and she talked to it in a soft voice.

The dog, with a full belly, seemed to be enjoying the attention. At least Eda hoped it was.

"Where have you been?" Eda said, scratching the dog's ears. "Where did you come from?"

The dog sat down beside her and licked its lips.

"I know what you're trying to tell me," Eda said. "But it's like I said, I'm all out of food. Listen though, I'm going to go back to the station and get some more. I'll come back tomorrow, okay? Will you be here?"

The dog blinked slowly, its eyes heavy and ready for sleep.

Eda stroked its back for a while longer. While the dog snoozed, she stared down the long, empty road that stretched out ahead of them. Eda found herself thinking about Frankie. Had her old friend traveled down this same road when she'd left the Complex?

"I can't remember what it's like out there," Eda said to the sleeping dog. "I've been here so long, you know? What's it like now?"

The dog lifted its head and sniffed eagerly at Eda's fingers. It lapped up whatever meager traces of food lingered there.

"I told you," she said. "I'm all out, but I'm going to bring something back tomorrow. No potato salad though, I promise."

Eda sighed and climbed back to her feet. It was a long walk back to Grand Central.

The dog stood up and looked up at her with bright, friendly eyes.

"You'll wait for me?" she asked, shaking some of the water off her rain cloak. "Don't let me down now, I'm coming back."

She patted the dog gently one more time. Then she turned around and began walking east towards the Complex.

Eda heard the sound of light footsteps at her back.

She stopped and glanced over her shoulder. The dog was following her but when it saw her stop, it sat down again.

"What are you up to?" Eda asked. "Are you playing games?"

With a smile, she gestured towards their destination.

"Are you trying to say you want to come back with me?" she asked. "Back there? Back to the Complex?"

The dog got up and strolled over beside Eda. When it stopped, it leaned its muscular body up tight against her legs, as if signaling her to stroke its back again. Despite the fact that the dog was soaking wet, it felt warm pushed up against her. Eda knelt down and stroked its back gently, wondering how long this creature had been out there, wandering across the city on its own.

"Alright then," she said, standing up straight. There was a big smile on her face as she secured the backpack on her shoulder.

"C'mon dog. Let's go home."

"A dog for God's sake!"

Eda heard their voices from afar. Despite this, she kept walking towards Grand Central like it was just another day. The dog had other ideas. When it heard the disturbance pouring out of the station entrance it stopped dead and its ears pointed upright and forward. The tail was stiff and horizontal.

A small group of about eight or nine women was making its way towards Eda. There was a collective look of puzzled horror on all their faces as they approached tentatively.

"Easy," Eda said, kneeling down beside the dog. "I'll take care of this I promise. Please don't run away and please don't bite anyone."

The dog jerked backwards. It looked up at Eda, as if waiting to see what she was going to do in the face of this incoming threat.

"Stay," Eda said, stroking the back of his head. "That's a good boy. I'll go talk to them – just don't run off. Okay?"

She walked ahead to intervene with the mob.

"Slow down," she said, holding both hands up in the air. "You're scaring the poor thing."

A woman called Mia stood at the head of the protestors. Mia was a gardener, roughly in her mid-sixties, with a ridiculously long pencil-shaped neck. Every time Eda looked at Mia, she saw a two-legged giraffe in a yellow rain cloak. There was something about the old woman that Eda couldn't stand. She was a cold, stuck-up bitch and a sense of bitterness followed her around like a bad smell. Eda suspected that Mia had come from a privileged background and that she'd had it good once – very good.

"What's that *thing*?" Mia said, pointing at the dog.

Eda was waiting for the old woman to make the sign of the cross with her fingers.

"That thing's a dog," she said in a flat voice. She was tired – it had been a long walk back to Grand Central and all she wanted to do was go back to the Fitzpatrick and disappear into her room. An argument was the last thing she needed although it wasn't surprising considering what she'd brought back to the Complex with her.

Mia looked like she'd been poked with a sharp stick.

"Don't act stupid with me girl," she said. "Why is that thing here? Why did you bring a dog back to the Complex? Are you out of your mind? It's probably got rabies and ringworm and God knows what else it's carrying."

Eda glanced over her shoulder at her new friend. The dog was hanging back, watching events unfold with cautious eyes.

"He looks fine to me," Eda said. "In fact, he looks cleaner than some of the people around here."

Another woman, short and stumpy in contrast to Mia, stormed over. She took a closer look at the dog and her face creased up with repulsion.

"Oh this is bad!" she yelped. "What goes on in that head of yours Eda? I think all that solitude you've endured has finally driven you mad."

"Who'd notice around here?" Eda said.

"You brought a dog back!" Mia said, stabbing a needle-like finger at the dog from a safe distance. "And now you need to get rid of it. RIGHT NOW! You'll need to kill it or it'll come back. I don't care how you do it – drag it down a back alley and suffocate it, stab it in the neck with that dagger of yours, but whatever you do, get it out of here before it destroys our crops and spreads its disease."

Maybe it was the lack of sleep or the hunger that made Eda feel strangely lightheaded. But as she stood there listening to Mia go on, she felt a strong desire to burst out laughing. It would be worth it, just to see the look on Mia's face.

"I'm taking it to the hotel," Eda said. "He's staying with me from now on. And you can't stop me."

The two women at the head of the mob rolled their eyes. Eda watched as Mia's claw-like fingers curled into tightly clenched fists.

"Have you forgotten what happened here recently?" the shorter woman said. "We lost two ambassadors and eight warriors when the bandits attacked. Remember that? Everything we've worked so hard for was almost destroyed in the blink of an eye! And now you want to bring a disease-ridden animal into our home? Whose side are you on Eda?"

Eda felt her patience wearing thin.

"We need to be extra cautious from now on," the stumpy gardener said. "Everything you see here is hanging on by the slimmest of threads. We can't take any chances and now you want to bring something in here that will steal and destroy our crops and spread disease? What if those germs get to Helen somehow? What if she gets infected and can't have children because of you and your dog? You'll ruin everything!"

"I'm not sending it back," Eda said. Her tone was firm. "And I'm not killing it either. He's staying with me."

"This is not open for discussion young lady," Mia said. "As gardeners we have an important..."

Mia was cut off by a noise from behind.

Eda heard it too – it sounded like footsteps on the road. She glanced over the angry woman's shoulder to see what was coming.

It was Shay. She was walking towards the huddle of women, along with two companions on either side of her. Eda recognized Linda, Helen's chef, on Shay's left. And there was no mistaking the towering figure of Lex on the other side. Along with all her other roles in the

Complex, Lex was Shay's personal bodyguard, and Eda couldn't imagine anyone more suited to the position.

There was a smug smirk on Mia's face when she saw Shay approach the crowd of women. That didn't bother Eda as much as the look on Shay's face. The leader's eyes were grim and serious. She looked pissed off about something and Eda hoped that somebody hadn't already told her about the dog.

Eda couldn't bear the thought of Shay sending the dog away. Or worse – what if she ordered Lex to draw her sword and...?

"What's going on here?" Shay asked. Her eyes lingered on the dog for a brief second before returning to Eda and the pack of gardeners. "I could hear raised voices from halfway up Lexington."

Mia and the others stood slightly aside, opening up a narrow gap in the crowd that allowed Shay a better view of Eda and her newfound companion.

"Eda has brought a dog back with her," Mia said. "A mangy street mutt. Can you believe it Shay? She's supposed to be out there working, looking for danger and what's she doing instead? She's running around like a silly little child, finding pets to bring back to the Complex."

The woman's condescending tone tipped Eda over the edge.

"Shut up you old bag," Eda yelled. "What do you know about what I do on lookout duty? You wouldn't last five minutes out there. You'd probably cry if somebody pulled you away from your precious plants."

Mia gasped.

"Those precious plants give life to this community," she hissed. "I don't see you refusing the food we grow do I? If not for our crops you'd probably have eaten that dog the minute you captured him."

Eda and Mia exchanged tense looks. If Shay hadn't been there, Eda might have punched the old bat in the face.

Shay sighed and stepped in between Eda and Mia, pushing them both backwards a little to create space.

"Everyone just calm down," she said. "Can we do that please?"

Shay looked at Eda and then at the dog. There was a hint of a smile forming on her lips. That gray, serious expression that Eda had noticed just moments earlier was gone.

"There are worse things to fear in this world," Shay said, spinning around to face Mia and the other gardeners.

Mia's jaw dropped. Her face turned a ghastly shade of pale.

"What?" she said.

"It's just a dog," Shay said. "And it looks like it's in good condition."

"But it's filthy," Mia said, pointing at the dog once again. "Just look at it. Shay, you can't be serious about keeping that thing around here. What about our gardens? It'll be the ruin of us."

Shay looked at the dog again.

"I used to have three dogs," she said. "One of them looked just like that – a big German Shepherd male called Alfie. We used to take him and the other dogs to the beach with us on family vacations. Oh, Alfie loved the ocean. Didn't we all? My kids, they'd run into the water, splash around and make all sorts of noise. Sometimes they'd scream just like kids do when they're overexcited. But Alfie didn't understand that they were playing – he'd run down the beach, kicking up sand, and charge into the shallow water after them. He'd bite down on the arm of their t-shirt and pull on the sleeve. Or if they weren't wearing a t-shirt he'd gently lock his jaws around their arm. He thought they were drowning you see. All he wanted to do was protect them, to pull them back onto the beach. Alfie was a good boy."

There was a sad smile on Shay's face.

"But Shay," Mia said. Her hands were clasped together like she was praying. "Please, I appreciate your memories – we all have nice memories to hold onto but this isn't a..."

"Eda," Shay said, turning her back on Mia. "Will you make sure he doesn't go anywhere near the crops? Or the gardeners for that matter?"

"Of course," Eda said, nodding. "No problem."

"Consider the matter settled," Shay said. "The dog can stay. I'm sure he'll be a valuable member of our community."

Mia and the other women stood in stunned silence. But one look at Shay's resolute expression must have told them that an appeal was useless. With a violent snort of disgust, Mia turned around and stormed back towards the entrance of Grand Central. Her companions were close behind her.

Eda looked at Shay and smiled.

"So it's a boy?" she asked.

"*He's a boy,*" Shay said. "I've never liked people referring to an animal as 'it'. They're every bit as female or male as we are."

"Right," Eda said.

Shay walked over to the dog and crouched down beside him. There was a joyful and effortless smile on her face and Eda couldn't remember ever seeing her look like that before.

The dog stared back at Shay, its dark brown eyes both curious and unwavering.

"Definitely a male," she said, glancing up at Eda. "Have you ever seen a female with balls that big?"

Eda knelt down and had a look underneath. She giggled – she hadn't even thought to check down there. Up until now the dog had been an 'it', probably because she hadn't wanted to get too attached, just in case...

"They're massive," Eda said. "How could I have missed those?"

Shay got back to her feet. She nodded briefly at Linda and Lex who were silent spectators, lurking in the background. The expression on Shay's face darkened, as if she'd been reminded of something unpleasant.

Eda saw the veil close over the older woman's eyes again.

"I know you must be tired Eda," Shay said. "But there's something I need to talk to you about and it can't wait. Do you mind coming with us to the Waldorf for a little talk?"

Eda hesitated. All she wanted to do was take the dog back to the hotel. With any luck she'd sleep for a day or two without waking up in between. That was all she really wanted but after Shay had just spoken up for her in front of Mia, Eda felt like she was in no position to refuse the request.

"Is everything okay?" she asked.

Shay nodded. "C'mon. This won't take long."

They walked back along 42nd Street, heading east on the familiar route towards the Waldorf. Linda and Lex kept a few paces behind Shay and Eda who led the way, maintaining an uncomfortable silence as they walked. The dog stayed close to Eda.

It was late afternoon; the air was cool and the weather dry, at least for now.

They reached the Waldorf and began the long, arduous journey upstairs to the thirty-fifth floor. Eda felt a strange tingling sensation in her body as she climbed the stairs and it was only now that she dared to enquire about the nature of this unexpected visit to the hotel.

"So what is this anyway?" Eda asked, looking at Shay who was a few steps ahead of her. "What's going on? This is kind of freaking me out to be honest."

"Nothing to worry about Eda," Shay said, without stopping or turning around. "Nearly there."

By the time they reached the thirty-fifth floor Eda's legs were numb with exhaustion. After the long walk back to the station, combined with the hike up the Waldorf stairs, she was in desperate need of a rest.

Shay led the way down the corridor to the Presidential Suite. Lex and Linda took up the rear while Eda and the dog walked in between.

"Have you ever been in here before?" Shay asked. She paused, her fingers resting on the door handle.

"No," Eda said. She was pretty sure that Shay knew fine well she'd never been in that fancy apartment before. Few people in the Complex had ever set foot inside the Waldorf, let alone Helen of Troy's living space.

Eda looked at the dog.

"His feet are kind of wet," she said. "So are mine."

Shay nodded. "Of course," she said. "Don't worry about any of that. I've yet to encounter a mess in my life that couldn't be cleaned up somehow."

They walked into the Presidential Suite and Eda took a look around.

It was a grand sight, especially in comparison to her meager living quarters back in the run-down Fitzpatrick. This was something else altogether – a three-bedroom, three-bath den of luxury that looked as if it had bypassed both the war and the wild years and remained blissfully trapped in the world before. There was a foyer, a living room with a large fireplace, kitchen, dining room and a master marble bathroom that was impeccably clean.

"This is incredible," Eda said. "I've never seen anything like it."

She peered into the main bedroom – there was a massive king's size bed tucked into the far corner with fresh, cream-colored sheets that didn't have a wrinkle on them. Blue drapes hung from a large window beside the bed. The walls and ceiling were pale and spotless. This was Helen's bedroom and Eda was well aware that it was here that the grinning man and all the others discovered that the curse was real. That thought alone was enough to make Eda turn around and step back into the hallway.

"Where's Helen?" she said, turning towards Shay who was standing in the hallway with the other two women. "Is she out exercising?"

"Come back into the living room," Shay said. "We'll sit down and talk."

Eda felt a growing sense of unease stirring inside her. She followed Shay down the hallway and into a large room with a cream-colored couch with three fat cushions propped up on the backrest.

"Sit down," Shay said. "Please."

Eda didn't like the tone of Shay's voice. It was too formal, too polite.

At Shay's request, Linda and Lex left the room. They walked towards the kitchen, their long, lingering silence going with them like a shadow.

The dog lay down on a flowery rug near the couch. He was soaking wet, his paws and legs especially, but Shay didn't seem to care. Eda could only imagine what Mia would think if she could see the dog now, lying in the lap of luxury in the Waldorf Astoria.

The old bitch's head would explode.

"What's going on Shay?" Eda said. "Why did you bring me here?"

The older woman sighed.

"She's gone," Shay said.

Eda frowned. "What are you talking about?"

"Helen's gone."

"Gone?" Eda said. "I don't understand. Gone where?"

Shay walked over and sat down on the couch beside Eda.

"She ran away," she said. "She was out in the park exercising with Lex and some of the warriors yesterday morning. She told them she had to pee and she went somewhere private. It's happened before many times only this time she didn't come back. And despite our best efforts we couldn't find her. God knows we've tried but it's obvious by now that she doesn't want to be found. New York is big and empty – it's an easy place to get lost in."

Eda leaned back in the couch. Now she knew why they'd brought her to the Waldorf.

"I didn't see her while I was out there," she said. "You're right, it's empty out there. I didn't see anyone apart from the dog."

"I know," Shay said. "I'm sure you would have told me by now if you'd seen a young woman on your travels."

Eda bit down on her lip. She nodded slowly.

"So why do you think she did it?" Eda asked. "Why would she just up and run away like that?"

"It's hard to know what's going on inside another person's head," Shay said. "Helen was her usual cheerful self yesterday morning. There were no signs that she was planning to run away, at least not on the surface. To tell you the truth, I'm not angry with her – it's hard to blame her after everything she's been through."

Eda nodded in agreement.

"Do you want me to go look for her?" she asked. "I know the city well enough and I can try and tap into her mindset. Try and figure out where she'd go."

She didn't say it out loud but with the dog at her side, a one-woman search party sounded like quite the adventure. It was even better than being on lookout.

Shay shook her head. "No," she said. "That won't be necessary."

Eda shrugged and felt a surge of disappointment shoot through her.

"Then I'm not sure how I can help," she said. "I definitely didn't see anyone out there – no one at all, let alone the most beautiful woman in the world."

Shay smiled. She was staring at Eda, nodding slowly as if listening to some silent broadcast in the back of her mind.

"Eda," Shay said. "Have you still got all those books hidden away in the Fitzpatrick? Do you still read much?"

"Mostly," Eda said.

"History," Shay said. "That's what you like reading isn't it?"

"I guess."

Shay let out a long, whistling sigh. She looked around the living room with a sad smile.

"I wish some of the other women would take a leaf out of your book," she said. "If we don't learn from the past, how can we ever expect to build a better future?"

"I like reading," Eda said.

"And you gain so much from it," Shay said. "Reading not only expands your mind but it allows you to zoom out, to see the bigger picture from afar. And that's so important. In that sense, it offers clarity. And when we have clarity, when we've put enough distance between ourselves and any historical event, we always see that throughout human history, individual sacrifice, no matter how hard it might appear, has contributed towards the greater good of humankind. Indeed, humankind might have been lost without the noble sacrifice of the few."

Eda could hear a chorus of alarm bells ringing in her head.

"What's going on Shay?" she said.

There was a long pause.

"We have a vacancy to fill," Shay said. "I want you to become the new Helen of Troy."

Eda felt the room spinning around her. Even though she was sitting down, she grabbed a hold of the arm of the couch to stop herself from tipping over.

"Helen of Troy?" she said. "Me? Are you serious Shay?"

"Of course I'm serious," Shay said. "Do you think I'd bring you all the way up here if I wasn't?"

"But me?" Eda said, leaping to her feet. She began to pace back and forth across the room. "I'm not beautiful like Helen of Troy. Isn't that why men come here? To be with the most beautiful woman in the world?"

Her hands were shaking.

Shay stood up. "You have no idea how attractive you are to men because you haven't been around them enough," she said. "I know what men like and they'll like you. And besides your natural beauty, we have people, we have the tools, the skills to make you even more appealing."

"I don't want this," Eda said. "No way. I can't do it."

Shay stepped forward and took Eda's hand in her own. Then she led the younger woman back to the couch and they sat down.

"It's not as frightening as it might seem at first," Shay said. "In fact, it's rather exciting when you think about it. It's like an adventure."

Eda shook her head. "No."

"Of course it is," Shay said. "You'll live here in this suite like a queen. You'll never have to work or fight – you'll be taken good care of by all the other women who live in the hotel, whose sole purpose it is to look after you. You'll be given time outside to exercise every single day. Whatever you want you can have it. We'll bring all your books over from the Fitzpatrick and anything else you want us to collect. The dog can stay here with you too. You'll have to give him a name. Any ideas?"

Naming the dog was the last thing on Eda's mind.

"But I don't want to stay here," she said. "I...I like being the lookout – I'm good at it and it's an important job."

"It's not as important as being Helen of Troy," Shay said. "There isn't a position in the Complex that's more important than that."

Eda ran a hand through her long brown hair. It was still damp.

"But what would people say even if I did it?" she asked. "They'll notice that I'm gone."

"We'll make up a story," Shay said. "Now I don't mean this to sound cruel but no one out there in the Complex really needs Eda. Do you understand? Very few people in our community are irreplaceable in fact. And yet every single one of us needs Helen. We can't hope to tempt men back to New York unless Helen of Troy is here waiting for them."

"Men." Eda said. Her eyes drifted off into empty space. Sitting in that apartment, it felt like she was trapped inside a coffin, desperately trying to claw her way through the lid and back to the surface.

She couldn't breathe.

"Men..."

"Yes," Shay said. "Men."

"If I'm Helen of Troy," Eda said, "That means I'll have to..."

"Have intercourse?" Shay said. "Yes of course, that's what Helen does."

Eda looked at Shay. There it was – that blank, stoic expression on the older woman's face. Duty – that was all that mattered to Shay. Of course it was easy for her to be so cavalier about it because it wasn't her body that was up for grabs.

"I've never done it before," Eda said in a quiet voice. "Never."

"It was the same with Helen," Shay said. "Most of the younger women in the Complex haven't done it either and as for the older ones, they – we – haven't done it in a very long time. The urge just isn't there anymore. It's part of the curse."

"Shay," Eda said.

"Yes?"

"Do I have a choice here?"

Shay budged over on the couch and put an arm around Eda's shoulder. Eda felt her insides go rigid at the touch.

"I can't order you to do anything," Shay said. "I won't order you either. You're old enough to make up your own mind and of course, we'd never force anyone into taking on such an important task. It takes a special type of woman to do this. And if there's a special man out there who can defy the curse, with any luck Helen of Troy will become a mother – she'll give birth to the first child that's been born in our world for a very long time. How incredible. Don't you think?"

"A mother?" Eda said.

Shay stroked Eda's damp hair, gently twirling it back and forth in her fingers like an affectionate parent with a child.

"Everybody wants to be special," Shay said. "Just like the people in your history books Eda. You can be one of those people. You'll become a key figure in the story of human reconstruction. And who knows? Maybe someday when the new civilization is up and running we'll start writing books again. And if so, who else but the great mother of our postwar society will appear on page one of the new history books?"

Shay gently rocked back and forth with Eda in her arms, like she was trying to lull the young woman to sleep.

"Doesn't that sound wonderful?" she said.

8

Eda was grateful when they finally brought her books over to the Waldorf.

Seeing the women carry those boxes into the apartment, it felt like old friends arriving. At least with her books lying around the place, the glossy interior of the Presidential Suite would bear some resemblance to the sloppier bliss that Eda had known in the Fitzpatrick.

In her early days as Helen, Eda would sit around the suite in loose comfortable sportswear – baggy pants, old Nike t-shirts and sweaters that felt soft and brand new. She could wear whatever she wanted, as long as there were no men in town.

She went out early in the mornings with Lex and two of the other warriors for daily exercise. These workouts consisted mostly of light jogging and some aerobics in an area of Central Park that was kept tidy so it could be used as a private gym. There were yoga exercises too, performed on mats, which apparently helped to reduce stress and aid fertility.

Along with sticking to an exercise regime, Eda had to commit to Linda's nutritional plan. Unlike the early starts with Lex in the park, this part of Eda's new life was easy and even welcome. Linda was a wizard in the kitchen, using the crops provided by the gardeners – the finest of which were sent to the Waldorf – to create a variety of delicious meals. There were lots of hearty vegetable stews, as well as lavish, bulky salads and soups. With all the exercise and good food, Eda had never felt better, at least physically.

The rest of it was hell. There was even a woman who'd once been a nurse who showed up daily to chart Eda's body temperature – fertility awareness it was called. They had to know, as precisely as possible, when Eda was capable of conceiving a baby. It was invasive to say the least and Eda dreaded the sound of the nurse's voice in the apartment every day, calling out to her in that cheerful tone, like baby planning and all that crap was the best thing ever.

Most of all, Eda dreaded someone telling her that a man was in town. That was the big concern and it followed her around all day and night. On more than one occasion, she found herself wishing that America was already empty – that all the human males had died off and that was it, the end of people.

It was better than thinking about having sex with one of them. Better than thinking about seeing the curse in action.

"What if they're all gone?" Eda asked, sitting at the dining table with Linda one morning. She was pushing her fork around a breakfast salad bowl while rays of sunlight poured into the room through the large, open windows. It was, so far at least, one of those rare sunny days that occasionally found its way to Manhattan like a long lost friend returning for a brief visit.

"It's possible though isn't it?" Eda said. "That the men are gone."

Linda smiled but Eda saw through it right away. It was obvious that the chef didn't believe for one second that America had run out of men.

Neither did Eda.

"It's a possibility," Linda said. "Anything's possible I guess. We can't know for sure but if they're out there the ambassadors will find them sooner or later."

"How long since the grinning man showed up?" Eda asked. "And the bandits?"

"Been a few weeks I think," Linda said. "I'm not so good at counting the days anymore honey."

Eda nodded. "I hope the ambassadors don't find anything," she said, dropping her fork into a mound of green leafy vegetables. She looked up and felt her face turning bright red. It was the most honest thing she'd said since moving into the Waldorf. But it was perhaps a little too honest.

"I'm sorry," Eda said. "I shouldn't have said that."

Linda's face was expressionless.

"I wouldn't blame you if you wanted the ambassadors dead," she said. "Just between the two of us sweetie, if I was in your shoes, I'd probably be thinking the same things you are. You'd have to be crazy otherwise. The grinning man was a first class asshole and there's been plenty more arrogant sons of bitches like him. I sure as hell wouldn't want to go to bed with any of them."

Eda fell back into the stiff wooden chair. She closed her eyes and sighed.

"Every time I hear footsteps in the corridor," she said, "I think I'm going to be sick or pass out or something."

As she spoke, a large German Shepherd appeared at Eda's side. Its black nose trembled as it sniffed towards the food on the table.

Eda held up a finger.

"No more food for you Frankie Boy," she said. "You'll get fat living the soft life everyday."

"I didn't know you'd given him a name," Linda said, reaching down and giving Frankie Boy a pat on the back.

"Well I couldn't keep calling him dog forever," Eda said, wiping a little crust out of the dog's brown eyes.

"Handsome boy," Linda said. "Look at this gorgeous clean coat. Looks like you've had a bath or two."

"I think he kind of likes getting in the bath," Eda said. "Or maybe he just misses being out in the rain all the time."

"Yeah," Linda said. Her face took on a serious look. "Just remember Eda, he's taken to you well and all that but..."

"But what?"

"Well," Linda said, shrugging almost as if she was embarrassed. "Remember he's a wild animal at heart. He might act tame but he's a big boy – he could do some real damage to a person if he wanted to."

"That's why I like him," Eda said.

Linda laughed. "He goes out for walks right?"

Eda nodded. "Lucia takes him out twice a day," she said. "I've asked to do it myself but Shay won't let me, even thought she told me I'm not a prisoner here."

"Shay's a good woman," Linda said, gathering up some of the empty dishes in the middle of the table. "She's just looking out for you but also for the other women in the Complex. Those women can't see you – they think you're gone."

Eda nodded. "I never asked this before but…"

"Spit it out honey," Linda said.

"Well," Eda said. "It's been a few weeks since I got here, right?"

"Sure has," Linda said.

"I was just wondering," Eda said. "What did Shay tell the rest of the women about me?"

Linda's fingers danced across the table like she was playing fast piano. The chef tended to get fidgety when she hadn't had a smoke for a while. And for Linda, an hour was certainly a while. After breakfast, she'd no doubt head downstairs and outside onto the street for some cigarette and quiet time. It was a long way to go, especially with crappy lungs, but Linda was a committed smoker. The old world vices died hard for some.

"I'm surprised you haven't asked anyone that yet," Linda said. "I'd be dying to know what Shay said about me if I went missing."

Eda shrugged. "Shay always looks so busy," she said. "I didn't want to bother her and I wasn't sure that Lucia would even know because she doesn't spend much time over at the station. So I thought I'd try asking you instead, when the time was right."

"Guess it's only fair you should know," Linda said.

"Well?" Eda said.

"Well we had a gathering inside Grand Central about a week after your disappearance," Linda said. "Shay stood up and gave a pretty good speech – I'm telling you, that woman could have won an Oscar if she'd gone into acting before the war. Hollywood Shay – she almost convinced me. She pretty much told the women that you'd taken off overnight. That you'd just upped and ran away. No one looked that surprised to be honest. You're still young Eda. They figured you'd gotten bored hanging around with all us oldies. A lot of the younger ones have run away from the Complex before so it wasn't exactly a major shock. It's just something that happens."

"Frankie did it," Eda said.

"Right," Linda said. "Yeah, she was a lot like you – young, pretty and too goddamn curious for her own good. I hope she made it."

"Me too," Eda said.

She picked up her fork and started pushing the tomatoes and cucumbers from side to side.

"Can I ask a question Linda?"

"Shoot."

"If I wanted to walk out that door," Eda said, pointing a thumb over her shoulder. "If I wanted to walk downstairs, leave the Complex and never come back, just like Frankie – am I free to do that?"

"Oh Eda," Linda said, laughing softly into the back of her hand. "What do you think's going on here? You're not a prisoner. Do you see any bars or chains around here? You're as free as a bird honey."

Linda smiled. Then she stroked the back of Frankie's ear gently and looked over at the front door.

"Time I was heading out for a smoke," she said. "I'll clean up these dishes when I get back."

———

It was Lucia who delivered the bad news.

Helen of Troy's cleaner was, on an ordinary day, a cheerful old woman. She never stopped smiling and was always singing some Spanish ditty or another as she worked her magic around the apartment first thing in the morning. Added to that, Lucia always walked with a carefree light step. She was remarkably energetic for someone who was at least in her late seventies.

Not today.

Today the old woman looked grim and heavy as she sat Eda down on the bed. With a painful-looking smile, she stroked her thumb over the younger woman's cheek in a back and forth soothing motion.

"I'm sorry baby," she said in a croaky voice. "There's a man in New York."

Eda burst into tears right away. This sudden outburst surprised her as much as it must have surprised Lucia. It had been a long time. Eda had never been much of a crier but today it felt like she couldn't stop the waterworks.

She didn't want to either.

The two women sat on the bed in silence with Eda resting her head on Lucia's shoulder. Lucia stroked Eda's brown hair gently and whispered soft Spanish words into the younger woman's ear.

"I know child," Lucia said, after some time had passed. "Oh poor Eda, they shouldn't have asked you to do this. It's too much. What a burden for a young woman to carry on her shoulders, to have to see the curse in action."

Eda lifted her head up and wiped her eyes dry.

"I'll be alright in a while," she said. "No more men – that was a dream too big I guess. Anyway, who is he? Who is this man?"

Lucia made a loud, pig-like snorting noise.

"An old man of course," she said. "He's been here just over a week."

"A week?" Eda said.

"Yeah I know," Lucia said. "But Shay puts them in a hotel until you know..."

"Until I'm fertile," Eda said, nodding her head. "No point in sending them over if there's no chance of getting a baby out of it."

"That's right child," Lucia said. "It's the way of the world."

"Do you know anything else about him?" Eda asked.

Lucia shrugged. "One of the guards downstairs said he might have come up from Massachusetts or something like that. I don't know for sure. There are always a lot of rumors swirling around town every time another man shows up at the door. Most of them are rubbish but people talk, right?"

"What did he say about the curse?" Eda asked. "Shay asked him about it?"

"Don't know Eda," Lucia said. "Really I don't know. But if he's like all the rest of them I wouldn't hold out hope of any common sense coming out of his mouth."

"When's he coming over here?"

Lucia hesitated.

"Today," she said.

He arrived at the Waldorf later that afternoon.

As Eda's assistants helped her get ready, they kept her up to speed with his progress. After his arrival, he'd spent some time on one of the lower floors with Zahra, the hypnotist, undergoing a half-hour session known as the relaxation ritual. After that, he'd been taken somewhere else to clean up a little and have some time to himself before heading up to the thirty-fifth floor.

While the man was on his own, Zahra popped into the Presidential Suite to visit Eda.

"Look at you!" Zahra said, walking into the apartment with wide eyes and a large grin that showed off a set of dazzling white teeth. "Oh my God, Eda! You look amazing."

Eda was standing beside the wooden bookcase on the far side of the living room. Two of her assistants, Gillian and Nicola, were putting the final touches to her makeup. For the occasion, they'd put Eda into a white dress with a bright red floral pattern on it. Eda hated the dress – it felt like she was wrapped up in alien skin. The two assistants had picked it out for her, completely ignoring her protests about how disgusting it was. Gillian and Nicola said the summery dress was a perfect compliment to Eda's slim figure.

In the end, Eda had given up trying to complain.

Her long brown hair had been washed and hung loose over her shoulders. But the worst thing of all was the makeup they'd splattered all over her face – red lipstick, eyeliner and blusher. She'd seen pictures of clowns before and that's what she felt like now – a clown in an ugly dress.

They'd turned her into someone else.

Helen of Troy.

The clip-on earrings – two silver pearls – were also annoying the crap out of her as she fidgeted endlessly with them as Zahra stepped further into the living room.

"You look incredible," Zahra said. "Absolutely incredible. Oh wow."

Eda tried to smile but it wasn't easy with the two women still working on her face with brushes that tickled and God knows what else. When they sprayed a little perfume on her neck Eda thought she would puke for sure.

She looked across the room at Zahra, who was tall, dark and slim – the perfect Arab beauty of Middle Eastern fairy tales. Although she was about ten years older than Eda, Zahra would have made a perfect Helen of Troy. She had the looks. She had a great personality. So why hadn't Shay asked her to take on the role? Zahra looked like she could still bear children and on top of all that, she already lived in the Waldorf too – it's not like she'd have to move far to get her stuff into the Presidential Suite.

Maybe Shay had asked Zahra. And maybe Zahra had done the smart thing and said no. Hell no.

"Where is he now?" Eda asked.

"He'll be here in a moment," Zahra said. "Patience young lady."

"Did he do the relaxation ritual?" Eda asked

"He sure did," Zahra said. "This one's not quite the arrogant asshole that the last one turned out to be. That's my first impression anyhow."

"Why don't I get a relaxation ritual?" Eda said. "Don't I look scared enough or something?"

"You're not in danger," Zahra said in a calm voice. "This guy is. He's well aware of what happened to all the men who turned up here before he did. And while I appreciate that it's your first time and that you must be nervous Eda, the curse isn't a direct threat to your life. It kills men, remember?"

"What do they get out of the ritual?" Eda said. "At least give me some clue as to what it's all about."

"It just allows them to relax and become suggestible," Zahra said. "I start by encouraging them, telling them that they're going to sleep with the most beautiful woman in the world..."

Eda shuddered.

"...and that this will be the most pleasurable experience of their life," Zahra said. "They become fully immersed because I'm promising them pleasure after years of hardship, pain and loneliness. They want this. Not only do they want the sex, they want the glory that comes with it. Becoming the father of the new world is a big deal. It doesn't matter what or who they were before, this is their ticket to immortality. While I talk to them, the physical world shifts to the back of their mind along with the fear. Soon it's like they're under the spell of a drug. We concentrate on the high, the ecstasy of orgasm and the faith that yes, it still exists for us. With any luck, they come up here in a positive frame of mind. That's about the best I can do for them. And for you."

Eda heard footsteps outside in the hallway. She heard Shay's voice and another – a man's voice. They were getting closer.

"Kill me now," she said.

"You shouldn't joke about death," Zahra said. "I don't think it's appropriate right now."

"Who said I was joking?" Eda said.

Zahra signaled to the two assistants beside Eda and nodded.

"Our work's done here ladies," Zahra said. She pointed towards the spacious dining room behind them. "We don't want the poor man to see all of us standing here together like this. That would be quite intimidating and it's important that he stays relaxed. We'll go hide in the bedroom and once the coast is clear we'll sneak back out."

She winked at Eda.

"Good luck," Zahra said. "I have a strong feeling about this one."

"You'll be fine," Gillian said to Eda. "You look absolutely incredible."

She gave Eda a brief hug. The white and red flowery dress squeaked under the weight of the embrace. Nicola wished Eda luck too and then along with Zahra and Gillian, hurried out of the living room. Eda could hear the two assistants squealing with muted excitement as they ran off.

"Lucky bastards," Eda grumbled. "Don't trip up on the way out."

She glanced at herself in the antique silver mirror. There was a stranger, covered in face paint, looking back at her.

"What the hell are you supposed to be?" she said, screwing her face up.

At that moment, the door clicked open and Eda spun around. She stood tall and barefoot on the carpet, trying to summon the joyful demeanor of a summer goddess.

Shay's head appeared through a narrow crack in the doorway. She looked at Eda and a huge smile appeared on her face. Her eyes were glowing. The young woman's dramatic makeover obviously pleased her.

She opened the door further and walked into the room.

The man strolled in close behind her and his eyes lit up immediately when he saw Eda standing by the bookcase.

"Helen," Shay said, closing the door behind them. "May I present to you Mister George Mitford, from Virginia."

George Mitford stepped further into the living room. He was approximately in his mid-to-late sixties, a slightly overweight man whose large, leathery forehead glistened with a fine coat of sweat. Eda wondered if it was nerves or all those stairs in the Waldorf that were making him sweat so much.

He was dressed in a faded dark raincoat, one that stretched all the way down to a pair of zipped black boots that looked freshly scrubbed.

Mitford bowed slowly.

"Ma'am," he said. "It's a great pleasure to meet you at last."

When he lifted his head again, Mitford's eyes devoured every inch of the young woman he'd come so far to visit. His silver mustache twitched as he inhaled Eda's perfume. There was a flicker of bewilderment on his face, like he couldn't make sense of the foreign odor.

"So it's true," he said, wiping a layer of sweat off his brow. "You really are the most beautiful woman in the world. I can honestly declare that this long, arduous journey was worth every single step, and I say that no matter what happens next. Yes ma'am, I didn't think such feminine beauty existed anymore."

Eda forced out a smile. "Thank you," she said.

"You're welcome," Mitford said. He came closer, each step a loud clap of thunder. Eda noticed that the man's hands, hanging at his sides, were trembling slightly.

"What a sight this goddamn country is now," Mitford said, looking back and forth between Eda and Shay. He tugged at the collar of the white shirt under his coat like it was choking him. "Dust and skeletons. That's all that's left out there now."

"I can only imagine," Shay said. "Apart from the ambassadors, it's been a long time since anyone in the Complex ventured outside of Manhattan."

"That's about the smartest thing a person could do ma'am," Mitford said. "Just stay put and keep safe. I've trekked the length and breadth of this country and it's like walking around Hell and finding out that all the devils have deserted it. Well, most of them anyway. That goddamn war, I tell you. It took everything."

"Yes it did," Shay said.

Eda's heart was racing. She couldn't imagine being left alone in a room with this strange man, let alone having to get into bed with him.

"I guess it's up to us to do our duty," Mitford said, looking at Eda. "When I heard about what you gals were doing here in New York, my heart filled all the way up with hope. I'm being truthful now. I never thought I'd see it – an organized attempt to get the human race up and running again. To rebuild. Well, I'll be damned – maybe there's a chance for us yet."

He wiped his forehead dry again.

"This curse," he said, looking at Eda. "I don't know much about it and right now I don't give much of a damn either to be honest. We must do our duty, at all costs."

"Right," Eda said. "Duty."

She wondered if there was time to go to the bathroom and puke.

"And now for a brief fertility blessing," Shay said. She stepped into the center of the room and invited Eda towards her. Eda walked over slowly, taking Shay's hand in her own. Shay then reached over with her other hand, took Mitford's and placed it on top of Eda's. Eda flinched. Mitford's skin felt like a block of splintered wood. He was staring at Eda, still smiling but now that he was closer she could smell his hot breath blowing on her face. There was a hint of minty toothpaste on his breath and she wondered if someone had forced the old man to brush his teeth before coming up to the Presidential Suite.

Mitford kept licking his lips.

"Dear Universe," Shay said, closing her eyes. "Dear Creator, Dear Mother, Father and everything else in Nature. You know our deep desire for a child. To be forgiven for the sins of our savage and selfish past. Please forgive us now. Please lift the curse and bless this union between man and woman. Bless Helen that she may conceive today and bring forth a child into the world and with that child we'll begin to build a better future – a peaceful future. Hear this, our prayer oh Creator, oh Universe. Bless this coupling."

Shay opened her eyes.

Eda pulled her hand away from Mitford and took a step back.

"Well that was sure pretty," Mitford said, looking at Shay. His teeth were on show every time he smiled; they were mostly crooked and yellowing. "You don't hear nice words like that anymore. I never liked poetry much before but now, I appreciate it better I suppose."

"I understand," Shay said.

Mitford nodded. "Now before we go any further," he said, "I'm going to have to take a piss – excuse me, I mean take a leak. You got somewhere back there that I can go?"

Shay nodded.

"Down the hallway," she said. "On your left hand side."

"Thank you kindly ma'am," Mitford said, walking away. He glanced at Eda once more and she heard him whoop quietly under his breath.

"I'll be damned," he said.

Shay turned towards Eda once he'd left the room. The courteous smile that had lingered on her face since she'd walked in with Mitford was gone.

"Are you okay?" she asked. "How are you feeling?"

Eda shook her head. "I'm terrified," she said. "I don't know what I'm supposed to do here Shay."

"You're not supposed to do anything," Shay said, placing her hands on Eda's shoulders. "Let him do all the work and I promise it'll all be over soon. You don't have to go out of your way to please him Eda. It's obvious that he's overjoyed just to be in the same room as you. And so he should be."

"Let's just get it over with," Eda said, wincing. "God I hope he doesn't die on me..."

"One last thing," Shay said. She took her hands off Eda's shoulders and leaned in closer, lowering her voice to a whisper. "You must remember that if things do go wrong in there it'll be shocking. I'm sorry to say this but it'll be the worst thing you ever saw and you *must* be ready to face it. We won't be far away but brace yourself Eda. Be brave and stay calm. Do you trust me?"

Eda nodded. "Yes."

"Good girl," Shay said. "I'll see you when it's done."

Shay squeezed Eda on the arm and then walked out of the room. She closed the door quietly behind her.

It wasn't long before Mitford came back; it was almost like he'd been waiting for Shay to go before reappearing.

"She's gone then?" he said, looking around the living room.

Eda took a deep breath.

To hell with it.

She walked over and grabbed Mitford by the hand. Without

saying a word, she dragged him into the hallway and towards the bedroom.

"Well I'll be damned," Mitford said, laughing out loud. "I always liked my gals with a bit of urgency about them. Know what I mean?"

Eda pulled him into the bedroom and closed the door.

They stood in front of one another at the foot of the massive bed. The drapes were drawn, extinguishing all natural light from the room. There was only the faint glow of candlelight left. Gillian told Eda earlier on that it was supposed to look romantic.

"Take your clothes off," Eda said.

Mitford smiled and undressed like it was a race. As he clumsily pulled his coat and shirt off, Eda saw the man's large belly flop forward, the reddish-pink skin rolled out in all its fleshy glory. He pulled his pants off as quickly as he could too, almost losing his balance and toppling over in the process.

All the while, Mitford was breathing like he'd been running non-stop for days.

Eda just stood there, looking at his thing. He was visibly aroused and it looked so ridiculous standing up that Eda almost burst out laughing.

"Your turn," Mitford said. He pointed at Eda's summer dress.

She took it off gladly. The assistants had also put a bra on her, as well as a set of black lace underwear. She got rid of them and threw them across the floor. Then she stood in front of Mitford, naked, trying to project confidence, hoping that the dim lighting would hide the shaking in her hands.

Mitford whistled his approval as he looked her up and down. "My God," he said. "I've died and gone to Heaven."

"Don't joke about dying," Eda said.

How had she allowed herself to get talked into this? She should have been miles away on lookout duty. She should have been anywhere but here, masquerading as the most beautiful woman in the world.

"You want to do some of that foreplay stuff?" Mitford said.

Eda didn't hesitate. "Let's just get it over with," she said.

"Remember something George – this isn't about anything other than you putting a baby inside me, okay?"

It was her voice but it sounded like someone else talking.

Mitford threw out a quick salute. "Yes ma'am. Whatever you say."

Eda went over to the bed and slipped under the covers. She lay flat on her back and squirmed when seconds later, Mitford and his enormous gut climbed on top of her. She closed her eyes and winced as he put his thing inside her right away. Mitford wasn't wasting any time. He began thrusting back and forth like a crazed animal. Eda looked up and saw that his eyes were rolled back in his head and he was panting – it sounded like he was about to drop dead of exhaustion less than a minute in.

The bed squeaked, like it was laughing hysterically.

Eda took Shay's advice and did nothing. She just lay there, silent, feeling the strange, invasive sensation of a man inside her.

To hell with sex. Mother Nature could keep the damn thing. It hurt like hell and the pain was like nothing she'd ever felt before in her life. Mitford might as well have been taking a hacksaw to her insides the way he was going at it. The man was so far gone into the act that he looked like he was in a trance. He was a beast possessed by lust; he probably didn't even know his name at that moment. His brain was at the mercy of primal instinct – *keep thrusting, keep thrusting, keep thrusting.*

Mitford sped up, going back and forth while the bed, which had stopped laughing, now screamed like a frightened animal. His comical panting got louder and more intense with each thrust of the hips. Eda had never had sex before but instinctively she knew that this was it.

All of a sudden, the physical pain subsided. A cold fear came creeping underneath her skin.

The curse.

She tensed up, bracing herself for the end.

Mitford roared but it wasn't a cry of pain. There was nothing but pleasure in the old man's bright red, distorted face as he reached the end and shot his stuff into Eda's body.

"YES! OH FUCKING YES!" Mitford yelled.

He slammed a fist into the bed and hit it over and over again. "YESSSSSS!"

Eda was too stunned by the man's reaction to fully register the myriad of sensations within her body. She could feel the heat inside her, but the pain that she'd felt throughout the act had diminished, at least for the moment.

Mitford was still alive.

Eda looked up at him, her eyes bulging wide open. There was sweat all over Mitford's flabby body but still, he wasn't screaming. He was okay.

"Holy shit mister," she said. "You just beat the curse."

Mitford looked down, still breathing heavy and red in the face. There was a proud, defiant look in the man's eyes as he pounded a fist over his sweaty, glistening chest.

"Yes ma'am," he said. "I guess that makes me pretty damn special."

He laughed.

"You didn't feel any pain?" Eda asked. "Nothing at all?"

Mitford's boastful grin stretched further across his face. He was about to answer Eda's question when there was a loud thud behind them.

"What was that?" Eda said.

Seconds later, the bedroom door burst open and a crowd of women charged into the bedroom. It was a stampede of humans and they were racing towards the bed.

"What the...?" Mitford said, turning towards the door. There was a confused and frightened look on his face.

Eda sat bolt upright, pulling her legs out from under Mitford's body.

"What the fuck?" she yelled.

Shay was at the head of a group. They stormed into the bedroom in a fury and in those first few moments, Eda caught a glimpse of familiar faces everywhere – Lex, Linda, Gillian, Nicola and some of the warriors whose names she didn't know. There were about twelve women in total and as they marched towards the bed, Eda saw the weapons in their hand – large, gleaming butcher knives, held aloft over their heads.

Eda couldn't scream. She was frozen stiff with terror.

Mitford spun around as fast as his big body would allow. He held his hands up towards the crowd like he was surrendering.

"I beat the curse!" he screamed. "I beat the..."

The blades plunged into Mitford's exposed back, chest, arms, legs and face. He screamed and tried to fight back but Lex punched him hard in the jaw. The force of the blow sent Mitford's head rocking back like it had been dislodged from his neck.

He fell face first onto the bed.

Eda felt the hot blood spraying over her face as the pack of killers moved in for the finish. She screamed and leapt off the bed, falling onto the floor and crawling like a frightened animal towards the corner of the room.

"Stop!" she yelled, sitting up and pushing her back against the wall. "STOP!"

But the women kept stabbing Mitford. It was as if his every living breath was a personal insult. It was a shocking sight and yet Eda, for whatever reason, couldn't take her eyes off it. Even with her hands over her ears, she could still hear the slicing noise of the blades cutting into his flesh.

She thought it would never end.

Eventually however, the brutal slaughter came to a halt.

The killers stepped back from the bed. There was a strange moment of silence in which they all stared at the fresh corpse.

"Let's go," Shay said, signaling to the others.

The women moved fast, wrapping Mitford up in bed sheets freshly soaked in large, swelling patches of dark red.

"Keep the blood off the floor," Lex said. "Wrap him up tight. You know the drill ladies, c'mon."

Eda, bloody and naked, looked at the bedroom door. It was lying wide open. Instinctively, she sprang to her feet and made a run for it.

But then Shay was in front of her, grabbing Eda's arms and pushing her back into the wall.

"Eda," Shay said. Her voice was calm – shockingly calm considering what had just happened. "Eda, listen to me. It's over. You're okay. You're not in any danger I swear."

Someone – Eda didn't even register who it was – came over and wrapped a fresh bed sheet over her naked body. She was shaking from head to toe. Shay kept an arm around her, guiding Eda out of the bedroom and back into the hallway. Before they left the bedroom however, Eda took one last look over her shoulder and she saw the bloody sheets that covered George Mitford.

"No..." she whispered.

Shay stood with Eda in the hallway, gently stroking her hair.

"It's alright," the older woman said. She looked into Eda's eyes and smiled reassuringly. "It's alright."

"He beat the curse," Eda said in a quiet, choked voice. "And you killed him."

"I told you to brace yourself," Shay whispered. "Remember?"

Behind her, Eda could hear Mitford's body being wrapped up in the bedroom. There was a cold squelching noise as the damp bed sheets smothered the dead man's remains.

"Why?" Eda said, looking at Shay. "Tell me."

Shay rubbed a soothing hand over Eda's back.

"I can do better than tell you," she said. "It's time you came with us for a little walk Eda. There's something you need to see."

9

Eda felt numb.

She was sitting on the couch, watching two warriors carry the bloody sheets with Mitford's body wrapped up inside. They took it through the hallway and then out of the apartment but it would never be gone. Eda would be seeing that body bag in her dreams for a long time. And in the same dreams, she'd hear the fast slicing of the knives as they hacked at the dying man, over and over again.

Eda took a sip from the glass of water in her hand. She couldn't remember anyone giving her the drink but there it was. Linda was tucked up beside her on the couch, one arm wrapped around the young woman's shoulder. Linda had stayed close to Eda after Mitford's murder, helping her to get cleaned up, then dressed and finally escorting her back into the living room.

"What do they do with it?" Eda asked, pointing to the body bag as it left the apartment. "With *him*."

"They'll take it downstairs," Linda said, not looking at anything except Eda. "It'll get dropped into one of Lucia's laundry carts and after that, wheeled over to the East River."

"The East River?" Eda said.

"Yeah," Linda said. "That's the cemetery."

"Is the grinning man in there too?" Eda asked.

Linda nodded like it was no big deal. "They're all in there honey," she said. "Every last one of them."

Shay came back into the living room as Linda and Eda were talking. She looked at Eda with a warm smile, as if reassuring a frightened child that all the monsters in her bedroom were gone and it was safe to go back to bed now.

"Ready to go?" Shay said.

"Go where?" Eda said, putting her glass down on the table.

"The Roosevelt Hotel," Shay said. "It's not far from here."

"I know where it is," Eda said. Her voice was hoarse and scratchy, like she had the beginnings of a cold coming on. "But why are we going there? You told me once that the Roosevelt was a dump, that it got wrecked during the war and the wild years. That it wasn't safe."

"Yes I did," Shay said. "Everything will make sense soon Eda. C'mon, let's go for a walk."

Linda guided Eda gently back to her feet. Shay stepped forward and took over, locking an arm around Eda's shoulder and leading the way towards the double doors that were still lying open.

Shay glanced over her shoulder at Linda on the way out.

"You'll make sure everything's cleaned up?" she said. "Won't you?"

"Of course," Linda said. "It'll be like nothing happened."

Eda almost laughed. Almost.

In the hallway, Shay had a brief conversation with Lex while Eda stood off to the side, still in a daze. At the end of the conversation, Shay leaned over and whispered something in Lex's ear, most of which Eda couldn't make out.

Four words she did overhear:

Make sure they're ready for us.

Lex nodded and strode confidently towards the staircase. She opened the doors that led to the stairs and then she was gone.

"Are you ready?" Shay said. "We're taking the stairs too."

Eda lumbered forward. She hoped that her legs would hold up during the long walk to the lobby.

They walked downstairs in silence for the most part. From there, they exited the Waldorf and walked to the Roosevelt Hotel, which took up an entire block on Madison Avenue between 45th and 46th Street.

It wasn't raining but Eda kept her hood up nonetheless. The fresh air helped to revive her a little and she was glad to be out of the Presidential Suite.

They reached the 45th Street entrance to the Roosevelt about ten minutes after leaving the Waldorf. Eda didn't know much about this hotel except that it looked dull and listless, an exhausted building waiting for a wrecking ball to come along and put it out of its misery.

Shay led the way through the front door and into the lobby, which had soaring ceilings and marble columns. The first thing Eda noticed was that there was a lot of empty space inside the building – most of the furniture was gone, either stolen or destroyed years ago. Despite the apparent decay however, there was still a small hint of the Roosevelt's luxurious past inside the lobby. A short row of antique vases was lined up against the wall, some standing, others lying on their side, broken around the edges. A huge, dusty chandelier hung from the ceiling. This had been an impressive place once. Eda was sure of it.

Lex was waiting for them at the top of a small flight of stairs on the other end of the lobby. The steps led up to what looked like a small seated area with coffee tables and comfortable chairs.

There was a flicker of movement behind Lex.

"Are there people up there?" Eda said.

"Let's go take a look," Shay said.

As Eda got closer to the steps, she heard light footsteps on the carpet up there, followed by a muted shriek of excitement or two. These were strange, high-pitched noises that she didn't recognize.

"What's going on?" she said, looking at Shay.

"Nearly there," Shay said, putting a hand on Eda's back and guiding her forward.

They climbed the staircase towards Lex. The chief warrior, with fierce eyes and a curved katana sword hanging at her waist, looked like the guard of an ancient citadel who was about to refuse them entry.

"Hello Eda," Lex said. Her voice was clear and deep.

Eda stopped a few steps down from the top of the staircase. She nodded warily, still unable to see what was going on up there.

"Lex," she said. As she looked up she saw Mitford's murder all over again in Lex's eyes and flinched slightly, as if the cold had pinched her skin.

"There are some people who want to meet you," Lex said. "First things first though, you should brace yourself for a shock."

"Yes," Shay said from behind. "Take a deep breath Eda. Go up when you're ready."

Lex stood aside and Eda, with Shay tight at her back, reached the top of the staircase. She gasped out loud. There were about twenty or so women sitting around the tables and chairs, all looking at Eda with warm, welcoming expressions on their faces.

And children.

There were children playing at the women's feet. Dozens of them, running around, smiling and laughing like they didn't have a care in the world.

"Oh my God," Eda said, pushing down the hood of her rain cloak. She walked forward slowly, shaking her head.

"It's not possible," she said.

There were young children running or crawling across the floor on their bellies like big insects. Elsewhere a couple of babies slept, wrapped up tight in some of the women's arms. The older kids were non-stop movement. As Eda edged closer, she watched them playing together in small groups on a thick pile of brightly patterned rugs covered in toys to create an impromptu play area.

"Children," Eda said. "I haven't seen children in years."

She looked at Shay who was still standing close behind her. The older woman's eyes were locked onto Eda's and Eda could feel a scalding heat coming her way, burning through her head like hot lasers.

"This can't be happening," Eda said. "It doesn't make sense."

"But it is happening," Shay said. "Look at them. Your eyes aren't deceiving you."

Eda looked at them again. The children were so small and fragile. The women watched their every move like hawks and when the excitable kids crawled off the play rugs, the women would jump off their seat, call out the child's name and chase after them. They'd catch up with the runaway kid and wrap their arms around their little wriggling bodies, dragging them back to the designated play area.

This act was repeated too many times to count.

Eda noticed that some of the kids were playing in small groups. Others were content to sit by themselves, their attention focused on a toy of some kind – a truck, a doll or even an empty cardboard box. Others lay flat on their chests, drawing with colored crayons on blank sheets of paper.

"Jane?" Eda said. She was looking at a blonde-haired woman sitting at one of the nearby coffee tables. "Is that you?"

The woman waved over. "Hi Eda," she said.

Eda also recognized the dark-haired woman sitting beside Jane.

"Tammy?"

"Good to see you Eda!"

There was a polite smile on Jane's face as Eda approached the table with wide eyes. If Eda's memory worked right, Jane had been a gardener. She'd lived in the Grand Hyatt, one of the busier residential buildings in the Complex. Eda remembered Jane as a pretty, carefree young woman who was always laughing and smiling as she went about her work.

"It's so good to see you again Eda," Jane said. Her eyes were still bright blue but when she smiled now there were more lines on her face. "You look great."

"You too," Eda said. "You look well."

"You made it over here at last then?" Tammy said. "Congratulations." She was bouncing a chubby young girl off her knees in a playful up and down rhythm. The kid looked like a giant beach ball with legs and she had the same blackish-brown colored hair as her mom.

As Tammy smiled at Eda, the kid did likewise.

Eda waved at the little girl.

"You guys live here?" she said, looking at the two women. "But didn't you...?"

Eda quit in mid-sentence. She turned back to Shay.

"Alright," she said. "What's going on? What is this place?"

Shay strolled over and waved at the little ball-shaped kid bouncing on Tammy's knees.

"This won't be easy for you to hear," she said, leaning closer to Eda. "But you do need to hear it. Just remember this Eda – you're not alone. All of the women sitting here went through exactly the same thing as you're going through now. Look how happy they are."

Eda shrugged. "What are you talking about Shay?" she asked. "Just spit it out whatever it is. It feels like my head's about to explode."

Shay jerked a thumb at the people gathered around them.

"All of these women," she said, "were once Helen of Troy."

Eda's brow creased, confusion mounting alongside a sudden surge of anger.

"What?" she said.

"Up until now," Shay said, "you thought there was only one Helen before you. In truth, there were many."

Eda looked back and forth across the room. Most of the women had taken their eyes off the hyperactive children for a moment. Now they were looking over at Eda, a sympathetic expression etched onto their faces. It was as if they understood the whirlwind of confusion spinning around in her mind at that moment.

"Jane went missing," Eda said. "It was a couple of years back, I remember it well. So did Tammy. And..."

"All the women here went missing," Shay said. "At least that's what we tell the rest of the Complex – that they've run away out of the blue. Have you ever noticed that it's always our youngest and most attractive women that disappear? The other women, they dismiss these vanishings as acts of reckless youth. Everyone knows that the lust for adventure is strong with young people, right?"

Shay gently took a hold of Eda's arm. She led Eda on a brief lap of the play area over towards a pretty young woman who was sitting at a table alone, slightly apart from the others. She had long black hair and at first glance, it looked like she was wearing a bed sheet with armholes.

She welcomed Eda with a tired smile.

"Eda," Shay said, "this is Rachel."

"Hi," Eda said.

"Hello," Rachel said, wiping her eyes. She looked like someone who just moments earlier had been on the verge of falling asleep.

Shay looked at Eda with a knowing smile. "Well?" she said. "Do you recognize Rachel?"

Eda looked at the young woman again and shook her head.

"No," she said. "Should I?"

"She worked with the gardeners for a while," Shay said. "In fact, I believe she used to help out your old pal, Mia the dog-hater."

Rachel laughed softly. "Oh how I miss that snooty old bitch," she said. "She was a real slave-driver, nothing was ever good enough for her."

"Yeah I think I remember you now," Eda said. "Weren't you the young girl who went missing about six months ago? I think I remember Shay talking about you at one point."

"That's me," Rachel said. "Shay offered me a new job and I took it –that's the way I saw it anyway, sort of like a promotion. Live in the Waldorf or put up with Mia's bullshit in Grand Central. That's a no brainer right there if you ask me."

"As you can see," Shay said, "Rachel is young and very beautiful. When the previous Helen – Natasha – fell pregnant, Rachel was a natural choice to take over. Rachel was Helen directly before you took up the role Eda. She's expecting, in case you hadn't noticed under all those loose clothes she's wearing."

Shay placed a hand on Rachel's belly.

"How are you feeling today?"

Rachel shrugged.

"I'm okay," she said. "Apart from being a little tired here and there I'm fine." She looked at Eda. "I had a short career as Helen – it was over before it began I guess. Damn shame, I liked living in the Waldorf too. But it's not so bad – the girls here pamper me day and night, bringing me food and whatever I need whenever I need it. They've done everything but put me in bubble wrap like I was a china doll."

"That's still to come," Shay said, smiling. "Just you wait and see."

Eda scratched her head. "You were Helen before me?"

"Yeah," Rachel said. "I sure was."

Eda pointed to Rachel's belly. Even under the baggy tent-like clothes she thought she could see a slight swelling poking out.

"The grinning man?" Eda said. "He did that?"

"Yes he did," Shay said. "Turns out he had good reason to be confident after all."

One of the women came over and handed Eda a tall glass of water. Eda mumbled her thanks and drained the glass in one gulp.

"Feeling better now?" Shay asked.

"I wouldn't go that far," Eda said, wiping her mouth dry. "I don't get it Shay. You've got all these Helens hiding out in here and they're either knocked up or they're full-blown mothers. What the hell is this place?"

"Let's go sit down," Shay said. "We'll talk some more."

They went over to a vacant table.

Eda sat down in a soft chair and leaned her back up against the wall. When she closed her eyes she saw the blood all over again. She saw the controlled fury in Shay's eyes as the door to Helen's bedroom was kicked open. And now, with all the kids laughing and playing on the floor around them, Mitford's murder was starting to feel like a nightmare slipping to the back of Eda's mind.

But it happened. It *did* happen.

"What's going on Shay?" she said. "What is all this?"

"The future," Shay said. "This is a nursery and it's where human civilization, which was nearly lost in the End War, will begin to grow again."

"But why did you kill Mitford like that?" Eda said. "What was *that*?"

Shay looked around the room with a blank expression.

"It might be hard for you to grasp at the moment Eda," she said. "But there's still evil in the world. It's out there and I'm determined that these children will be raised in peace, far removed from the influence of the old world. You ask me what this is – this is what starting over looks like. You have to clean up the mess in an empty house before you start building a new home there."

"The curse is a lie," Eda said, staring into empty space. "The ambassadors send men here not to breed, but to die. That's what the Project is, right?"

Shay's eyes were cast down, fixed on hands that were clasped tightly together on the table. It looked like she was praying.

"You're too young to remember the End War," she said. "But I'll never forget the things I saw. And all of it driven by greed and blood-lust, which has always existed in the hearts of certain types of men. It's these men who come to New York looking for Helen. The world fell apart and there were no trials to punish them for starting a war. *The* war. What we're doing, it's justice."

"It looks like murder to me," Eda said.

"Justice," Shay whispered. "Better late than never."

"You're killing the existing male population off," Eda said. "Luring them to New York and using Helen as bait. And with any luck, they put a baby in Helen before they get hacked to pieces. Jesus, you kill them and use their sperm to add to this nursery. I'll admit, it's one hell of a plan Shay but it's still murder."

"You're a smart girl Eda," Shay said. "You've seen them. They come to New York like conquering heroes and that's exactly how we want them to feel. They deny the curse, knowing that their bodies are working just fine. It makes them feel special. They think they're different to all the other men. They feel like kings, like the chosen one. Is it any wonder, in a world where so few men are left, that so many of them still choose to come here? It's because they want to feel alive again. To feel strong, to feel good about themselves."

Eda shook her head.

"It's a hell of a bait," she said. "But it's not the only reason you came up with the curse. Is it?"

A smile emerged on the older woman's face.

"You *are* a clever girl Eda," she said. "Go on then."

"The rest of the women in the Complex," Eda said. "If there's a curse then they don't ask any questions when all these men disappear, right? The men die and it's because of the curse. Tell me, are you ever going to tell them the truth about what you're doing? About the Helens? About all these kids?"

"Maybe," Shay said. "But only when our children are older. And let's be honest – by then will it matter? A lot of those women out there won't be around to see it. They're old and they're happy the way they are. Why rattle their world at this point?"

"There must be other children out there," Eda said. "If there's no curse, you know what I mean?"

"I don't worry about that," Shay said. "There aren't enough people out there for me to worry about it. Listen to me Eda – life is here. Growth is here. The future is *here*. This is a thriving community and unlike the rest of the human scraps out there we're organized. This will endure. Eventually, when our children have grown up, they can venture out there and see if there's anything left. They'll carry the values of peace with them – values that were instilled right here in the Roosevelt. From there, we can build a new world. It'll take a long time and I won't be around to see it flourish but it's enough just knowing that we'll survive. What more can we do in such dreadful circumstances?"

Eda glanced over at Rachel. The young mother-to-be had fallen asleep in her chair.

"You make it sound so noble Shay," she said. "And maybe it is, apart from the fact that you're lying to everyone in the Complex. Killer orgasms, Jesus. I guess we'll believe anything if we're frightened or desperate enough."

Shay pointed towards the staircase. "There's one more thing I want you to see," she said.

"What?" Eda said. "I'm not sure how much more I can take today."

She heard the sound of someone walking upstairs. At the same time, all the other Helens and even the children had gone quiet.

"I think you should turn around and take a look," Shay said. The way she said it, it was enough to persuade Eda to look over her shoulder.

A young woman stood at the top of the stairs, carrying a sleeping infant in her arms.

"Hello Eda."

Eda jumped up to her feet and clamped a hand over her mouth.

"Frankie!"

Eda couldn't move for about five seconds. Her body was a mess of mixed signals. She didn't know whether to be overjoyed or outraged at the woman standing in front of her. Then she ran to the stairs and threw her arms around her old friend, doing her best not to smother the sleeping child in the process.

"Eda," Frankie said, whispering in her ear. "Oh thank God. I've missed you so much."

Eda held onto her for a long time. She was too happy to cry and yet the tears came anyway. Now she knew what tears of joy were and what that felt like.

Eventually she broke free and stepped back, her mind in a daze. Frankie looked exactly like she remembered. Her dull blonde hair was loose around the shoulders and her skin was still the same flawless shade of alabaster. She looked beautiful, but older somehow in a way that Eda couldn't place.

The little girl in her arms was a miniature replica of Frankie.

"You didn't run off then?" Eda said. "Jesus Frankie, you'll never know what that did to me."

Frankie looked down at the floor, clearly embarrassed.

"I'm sorry Eda. I begged Shay to let you know but it's a pretty big secret, right? I guess you understand that now. As far as anyone in the Complex is aware there's only ever been one Helen of Troy living in the big Waldorf castle. Shay couldn't risk anyone else knowing."

"And you got pregnant," Eda said. Her head was spinning. The fact that she was standing there talking to her long lost friend was incredible. And she had a kid too for God's sake. "I can't believe it Frankie – you're a mother. You!"

Frankie nodded.

"It didn't take long before I was knocked up," she said. "It was the second man that I slept with – a real asshole, I was almost glad when they..."

Eda lowered her voice. "Killed him?"

Frankie looked at the sleeping child in her arms and shrugged.

"Today was your first time then?" she asked Eda.

Eda nodded. "First time for a lot of things," she said. "But yeah, that too. I can still feel his blood on my skin. I think I can even smell it too."

Frankie rocked the sleeping child back and forth.

"I hear you," she said. "With any luck you conceived today and that's it – you'll never have to go through all that again. You're fertile right? That means there's a good chance. It won't take too long for your body to tell you if there's a baby growing in it. And hey, you know what the best thing is? If you get pregnant you'll come and live here too – won't that be great? We'll get to spend all day together raising our kids side by side. Who would ever have thought it, huh?"

Eda tried to smile.

"You like it here?"

Frankie laughed, a little too hard to sound convincing. "Yeah of course."

Eda's hand fell to her belly. It was strange and terrifying to think there might already be a tiny seed of life growing inside her.

"So now you know Eda," Shay said, walking over to the two young women. "The rest of the women in the Complex would never understand what we're doing here."

"Yeah," Eda said.

Frankie turned sideways on, showing off her daughter's peaceful face as she slept. Eda reached over and stroked the girl's soft hair. It felt like silk running through her fingers.

"She's gorgeous," Eda said. "She looks just like you."

"It's worth it," Frankie said. "These kids we're bringing up right here, they're the future."

"That's what everyone keeps telling me," Eda said.

"It's decision time Eda," Lex said, still standing at the top of the stairs like a giant guard. Her green eyes burned a hole through Eda from afar. "Are you with us?"

"You have to make a choice." Shay said. "Right here, right now. Will you remain among us as Helen of Troy and play your part in building a better tomorrow? Will you work with us towards creating a peaceful future? The price of true, lasting peace is always blood. Can you handle it Eda?"

Eda exchanged tense looks with Frankie. Then she turned back to Shay.

"What if I say no?"

"Then you're banished," Shay said. "You take your chances out there in the desert with the rest of the human dirt. We need team players here in New York. You understand, I'm sure."

All eyes were on Eda.

"Are you with us?" Frankie said, looking deep into Eda's eyes.

Eda sighed. "I'm with you," she said in a quiet voice.

Shay hurried forward and wrapped her arms around Eda in a tight, choke-like embrace. Lex's gesture of approval consisted of a curt nod from the stairs. Elsewhere, the ex-Helens clapped their hands as if there was something to celebrate. Some of the older children clapped along with their mothers.

After the applause had died down, Eda turned back to Frankie. She threw her arms around her old friend, burying her face in the warm skin of the woman's neck.

She whispered softly in Frankie's ear.

"I hope I'm not pregnant."

10

It had been weeks since the killing of George Mitford.

The murder itself had slipped into the dark corners of Eda's mind. There were no nightmares, despite the horrific brutality of the act that she'd witnessed that day. Mitford's bloody and terrified face, along with the high-pitched shrieking noises he'd made as he begged for his life, had stayed away from her dreams.

A new horror had replaced the Mitford killing and it was a much more prolonged nightmare, something that Eda couldn't wake up from, no matter how much she wanted to. It was her life as Helen of Troy. She was becoming numb to the routine – to the same things happening at the exact same time every day. Seeing the same faces all the time. In the morning, Eda would get up early and exercise with Lex in Central Park. After that, she'd come back to the hotel and eat whatever Linda had prepared for breakfast. For the rest of the day, her time was her own but the options were limited to say the least. When Frankie Boy came back from his morning walk with Lucia, Eda would curl up on the bed or on the couch with the dog and a book. Only lunch and dinner broke up the rest of that day's monotony.

Most of the time she wanted to go out, alone. But she knew what they'd say if she asked. Too risky. The other women in the Complex couldn't see her and so on and so on.

She was a prisoner.

Eda's heart would beat faster every time she heard footsteps in the hallway outside the apartment. But there had been no other men since Mitford, thank God.

One of the things that drove her crazy was that some of the women in the Waldorf had started calling her Helen. They'd slipped it in there as a joke at first but it was a joke that grew into a habit and a habit that spread like a virus. Eda was having none of it. She wouldn't respond to anyone until they called her by her real name. Even so, she could do nothing about it when they called her Helen whilst talking to each other. And they did.

Has Helen had her lunch yet? Is Helen back from her workout? Put those books back in Helen's room will you?

Despite the struggles, there was one thing to celebrate. Eda wasn't pregnant. As time passed, she became clear on one thing – she didn't want to have a dead man's baby inside her. In fact, she didn't want to become pregnant at all. Not ever. While she'd been overjoyed to see Frankie alive and well in the Roosevelt, Eda didn't want to end up like that, moving from one prison to another like all the other Helens.

The Frankie she knew and loved was gone – it was a hard thing to accept but Eda had felt it strongly in the Roosevelt, standing beside her old friend. The old Frankie had been every bit as restless as Eda. She would have balked at the idea of being trapped in one place with a baby. Thinking back, Eda would recall how the two friends had often tramped the boundaries of the Complex together, peering towards the unknown and daring one another to trek further, to go explore the dangerous secrets of New York.

And it had been Frankie's plight, perhaps more than anything else, that had inspired Eda's final decision.

She was going to escape.

Had to escape.

She had to get out of New York before another man came along and put a baby inside her. But of course, Shay wasn't just going to let

Eda walk away from the Waldorf anytime soon. Eda was Helen, Helen was Eda and she would be until she became pregnant. It's not like there was a clear-cut replacement waiting in the wings either – the younger, prettier women in Manhattan were already few and far between. It was hard to envision where the next Helen would come from and until that decision *had* to be made, Shay wasn't about to let a perfectly good candidate walk away.

So it was escape or nothing.

That morning, Eda lay on the bed with Frankie Boy at her side. She'd just come back from a light run with Lex and it was still early in the morning. As Eda stroked the dog's head gently, she listened as Lucia swept the floor elsewhere in the apartment. The old woman was singing a Spanish ballad to herself and the music was accompanied by the monotonous rhythm of the brush fibers stroking the wood as she cleaned.

Eda waited. She knew Lucia would come to her sooner or later.

She looked at Frankie Boy who was still sleepy. The dog opened his eyes and looked back at her.

"I'll ask her today," Eda said. "I'm not putting it off anymore."

Frankie Boy's black nose twitched. Then he closed his eyes again.

Eda looked at the door, waiting for Lucia to poke her head through the gap. Her fingers clutched the soft bed sheets and she squeezed tight.

"C'mon," she said.

When Lucia eventually showed up, brush still in hand, she was her usual cheerful self. She was whistling a new song now, the melody more upbeat than the mournful ballad of earlier.

"Good morning child!" Lucia said. "How is the great and beautiful Helen of Troy today?"

She walked over and kissed Eda on the head. Then she rubbed Frankie Boy's back vigorously, the dog responding to this by rolling onto his back and exposing his underside to her. Lucia obliged with a quick belly rub.

"And Linda always says to watch out because you're a wild animal," Lucia said, talking to Frankie Boy in a silly voice. "That you could turn on any one of us at any moment, huh? What does she know Frankie Boy? Huh? What does she know?"

Nobody in the Complex had a bad word to say about Lucia. During her time as Helen, Eda had found out only a little snippet of information about the cleaner's past. She knew that Lucia came from a large Mexican-American family and that she'd had nine children, as well as a husband and a small menagerie of pets before the war. Everyone she'd ever loved was gone, taken by the war or the wild years. Eda wanted to know more – to ask how Lucia had survived but of course it was a delicate subject. She felt intuitively that underneath all that surface laughter, the old woman was nursing a broken heart, one that would shatter into a thousand pieces if poked too harshly by the wrong questions.

Lucia was about to start wiping down the surfaces in the bedroom when she looked at Eda. Her smile faded.

"What's the matter with you today child?" she asked, hurrying back over to the bed. "You look pale, almost dead. Have you got a fever or something?"

She put a hand on Eda's forehead.

"You feel normal enough."

"I'm not sick," Eda said. "At least not in that way."

Lucia sat down on the bed beside Eda. She wiped her hands on the white apron that she was wearing over her clothes. Afterwards, she looked at her hands and sighed.

"My God," she said. "I used to have such beautiful hands."

"What's wrong with them?" Eda asked. She looked at Lucia's hands, which were dark brown and heavily wrinkled.

"They're old," Lucia said without missing a beat. "Never mind. What's all this about child? What's going on in that head of yours?"

"I need to ask a favor," Eda said. "It's a big one. Real big."

"Of course," Lucia said. "What do you want me to do?"

Eda hesitated.

"Help me get out of here," she said.

Lucia threw a sudden glance towards the door, as if somebody might be out in the hallway listening in on their conversation. But there was never anyone else in the apartment during cleanup time. Not even Linda.

Lucia reached out and took Eda's hands in her own. Behind them, Frankie Boy rolled over in the hope of getting another belly rub.

"You're having a bad day?" Lucia asked. "Right? You woke up feeling lousy, I get it. It happens."

Eda shook her head. "It's more than just a bad day Lucia," she said.

She squeezed hard on the old woman's hands. "I have to get out of here," she said. "But I need your help to do it."

Lucia's eyes widened. She shrank back a little.

"You can't be serious," she said.

Eda nodded. "Will you help me?" she said. "I can't do this anymore. Living in fear, waiting for the next man to come along, knowing that he's going to be murdered in cold blood and maybe when he's still inside my body for God's sake. This isn't right what's going on here Lucia. Please help me."

Lucia shook her head.

"Oh Eda," she said. "The only way out of the Waldorf is when you're with child. You agreed to this, remember? What would Shay think if she could hear you now."

"Shay told me I wasn't a prisoner," Eda said. "But that's not true is it? Otherwise I could just get up and walk out of here right now."

"Of course you're not a prisoner," Lucia said. "But..."

"But what?"

Lucia hesitated, like she'd changed her mind about what she wanted to say next.

"Why do you want to escape from all this good easy living?" she said. "You have everything you'll ever need here. They treat you like a queen and you should be enjoying every second of it while it lasts because you won't be Helen of Troy forever."

"A queen?" Eda said. "This is a prison cell Lucia."

"Eda," Lucia said, letting go of the younger woman's hands. "I care for you very much dear child, but please don't talk like this. It's silly and dangerous. Don't even think about this anymore, okay?"

Eda shifted closer to the distressed-looking cleaner.

"Look," she said. "I've got an idea and no one will ever know you were involved. I promise."

But Lucia kept shaking her head.

"Don't do this to an old woman," she said. "I'm begging you Eda, drop it now and we'll just get on with our lives as normal. Please."

"You take the dirty sheets downstairs, right?" Eda said. "You've got that huge laundry cart stashed somewhere on the first floor – I've seen how big it is. I could fit inside easily."

"Eda..."

"Listen to me please," Eda said. "If I can get out of the apartment and run downstairs without being seen by the guards, you could wheel me to the back door in the laundry cart. Nobody would look twice at you pushing that thing around, right? Get me to the Lexington Avenue exit and I'll do the rest. Nobody will ever know you helped me."

"*I'll* know," Lucia said. "Shay's been good to me over the years and you're asking me to stab her in the back."

"Shay's using you," Eda said. "She's using every single one of you and no one sees it."

"What are you talking about?" Lucia asked.

"Look," Eda said. " I don't have time to go into it now but let's just say that Shay's utopian dreams aren't as noble as she likes to make out okay? Now will you help me or not? I'm begging you for God's sake Lucia."

"There are always guards on the first floor," Lucia said. She was still shaking her head, as if denying this conversation was taking place. "Warriors – not anyone I'd want to mess with, even in my prime. You know the guards are always down there because Shay doesn't want any of the other women in the Complex sniffing around here. You'll be caught. *I'll* be caught."

"You won't," Eda said. "Look, the apartment doors aren't usually locked are they?"

"Of course not," Lucia said. "There's no need to lock them.

Nobody gets to the thirty-fifth floor unless they're meant to be here. That's what the guards are standing downstairs for."

"Right," Eda said. "So I sneak out and run downstairs. I'm a fast runner, I can do it in good time and I'll make sure the guards don't see me. As long as I don't bump into anyone on the stairs it's a walk in the park. Right? All you have to do is park the laundry cart at the bottom of the stairs and wait for me and Frankie Boy to jump into it."

"Frankie Boy?" Lucia hissed.

The dog tilted his head at the sound of his name.

"You're taking the dog with you?" Lucia said. "What are you trying to do to me? Get me killed?"

Eda grabbed Lucia's hands again and squeezed down.

"He'll be quiet," she said. "I guarantee it. Please Lucia, don't leave me in here like this. If I don't go crazy first I swear to God I'm going to end up killing myself or something."

"Don't say that," Lucia said, looking both angry and hurt. "Don't ever say that. One of my boys, Erik, he…"

Lucia shook her head and fell silent.

"I'm sorry," Eda said.

"I know child."

"I just mean that one way or another I'm getting out of here," Eda said. "I'm not going to be Helen of Troy anymore. Not for them, not for anyone."

Lucia made a strange noise – a quiet, exasperated shriek that sounded like someone was letting the air out of her for a split second.

"Nobody's ever asked for anything like this of me before," she said. "The other Helens were good girls who got on with the job. *Querido Dios!* I knew you were going to be trouble the first time I set eyes on you Eda. You've got that look in your eye, I've seen it before."

Lucia looked long and hard at Eda. It felt like a lifetime passed before the old woman spoke again.

"I'll push the cart to the back door," she said. "After that Eda Becker, you're on your own. And let me give you a friendly piece of advice – when you get out, don't ever look back. Don't ever come back because they'll skin you alive for this. I feel like skinning you alive myself!"

Eda threw her arms around Lucia and then she jumped off the bed and did a happy dance. Frankie Boy stood up on all fours and started to bark, his tail wagging furiously.

Lucia's eyes lit up.

"You see?" she said. "What if he does that when he's in the laundry cart?"

Eda clicked her fingers until the dog piped down.

"Quiet Frankie," she said. "Now!"

Frankie Boy stopped barking and lay down. His brown eyes were locked onto Eda.

Lucia shook her head as if she was caught in an anxious trance.

"Oh child," she said. "Why?"

"Don't worry about it," Eda said, stroking Frankie Boy's ear gently. The dog rolled over once again, looking for belly rubs.

"He'll be quiet," she said. "I swear."

11

The escape plan was simple.

In terms of detail and preparation it wasn't going to take much effort to get things moving. Eda had to get downstairs, jump in the laundry cart with Frankie Boy and after that, Lucia would push her through the hotel to the Lexington Avenue door. After that, Eda and Frankie Boy would get out of the cart and run like hell before 'Helen's' absence was discovered. And in a building full of women whose lives revolved around Helen, it wouldn't take long before someone noticed she was missing.

It wasn't complicated. But it required a lot of nerve on Eda and Lucia's part –something that Lucia constantly referred to as 'balls'.

A couple of days before the planned departure, Eda began cramming supplies into her backpack. She went into the kitchen and took as much as she could – leftovers, fruit, vegetables – anything that fit comfortably into the bag but not too much that it would look like someone had stripped the apartment clean of food. She also took two large stainless steel water bottles out of the pantry and filled them up from the water tub.

On her way back to the bedroom, Eda stopped by the bookcase and put a couple of books in the bag too. History books.

As she packed the books, Eda saw herself running down Lexington Avenue, putting miles between herself and the Complex. She could feel the raindrops on her head again.

It felt glorious.

The following morning, Lucia walked into the apartment early as usual. She went into the bedroom where Eda was recovering after her workout and pressed her back up tight against the door as if she was trying to stop an intruder from breaking in. The old woman was breathing heavy, like she'd been working out alongside Eda in Central Park that morning.

"Are you sure about this?" Lucia said. "You've only got one day left to change your mind child. I suggest you think this over again very carefully."

"Lucia," Eda said, sitting up in bed. "It's happening and for the millionth time, it's going to be okay. If you keep your mouth shut after I'm gone you'll be fine."

"I'm not thinking about me," Lucia said. "I'm thinking about you Eda. You have no idea what's out there do you? We're all gathered here together in Manhattan for a reason – safety in numbers, survival and companionship. Have you thought about what your life's going to be like once you're out there?"

"I'm thinking about tomorrow morning," Eda said. "That's all."

Lucia clasped her hands together and sighed. She might have been saying a silent prayer but her eyes were open and still focused on Eda.

"Okay then," Lucia said. "I tried but you're a stubborn creature. It's like talking to a brick wall except I'd get more sense out of one of those."

"Tomorrow then?" Eda said.

"Tomorrow," Lucia said, shaking her head sadly. She lowered her voice to a whisper and crept closer to the bed. "You've definitely got a day off from working out?"

"Yeah," Eda said. "Lex says I've earned it."

"Right then," Lucia said. "I'll knock three times on the door first thing. That's my signal, telling you I'm on my way downstairs to get the cart. And I can do those stairs pretty fast for an old woman so you'd better get moving. When you're about to leave the apartment, triple check that no one else is in the hallway. When you're on the stairs, if you hear someone coming up, turn around and run back here as fast as you can. We can always try again later. Got it?"

"Got it," Eda said. "Thanks Lucia."

———

The next morning Eda woke up early.

She'd slept surprisingly well considering how nervous she'd been before going to bed for the last time as Helen of Troy. Pulling open the drapes, Eda looked out onto a dull and gray morning, one that was hovering on the brink of heavy rain.

It was perfect.

The tight knot in her stomach was gone. She felt light on her feet, lightheaded even; it was as if her body was spilling over with energy.

As she'd done many times, Eda sat on the bed and visualized the journey out of New York. In her mind, she saw herself walking along that long, empty road, surrounded on either side by old cars and empty buildings. She could feel the rain on her face and it was cold.

The vision felt so real that the nerves kicked in all over again.

"You'll be okay," she said, opening her eyes and looking at Frankie Boy. "You'll be fine. Nobody will see us."

Frankie Boy was fast asleep on a thick pile of blankets on the floor. When Eda spoke to him, he lifted his head briefly and then went back to sleep.

Eda pulled her backpack out from under the bed. She checked the things she'd packed over the past couple of days, making sure that everything was still there. When she was satisfied, she slid the bag back under the bed, knowing that she'd check it at least another five times before Lucia finally knocked on the door.

She went into the kitchen. There was a basin of cold water sitting in the sink and Eda scooped some of the icy liquid up, throwing a handful over her face to shake off any lingering grogginess. After that, she picked at a little leftover vegetable stew sitting on a tray on the countertop, eating slowly and mechanically. The food was cold and unappealing but it was no time to be fussy. She had to put something in her stomach ahead of the journey and as well as that, she didn't know when she'd be eating again.

When she'd had enough, Eda went back to the bedroom and got dressed. She dug deep in the closet and found her old clothes – *Eda's* clothes – at the back. With a smile, she put on the khaki pants, a black sweater and wrapped the old maroon rain cloak around her, zipping it up tight to the neck. It had been a long time since she'd worn these clothes. Now that she had them on, Eda was beginning to feel like herself again.

Frankie Boy jumped onto the bed, came over and licked Eda on the face.

"Hey," Eda said. "Remember me now? Do these clothes remind you of the day we met?"

She patted Frankie Boy on the head, then dropped to her knees and grabbed the backpack from under the bed. She checked the contents once more and then threw the bag over her shoulder.

"C'mon boy," she said. "We're all set. Let's go stand at the door. Lucia will be here any minute now and I don't want to be somewhere else when she knocks."

She walked towards the front door of the Presidential Suite. Frankie Boy followed close behind.

Eda's heart was racing as she stood in the living room waiting for Lucia to show up. She was leaning up against the double doors, fists clenched at her sides. Doubt after doubt crept into her mind. Doubt about the sanity of this undertaking. Doubt about Lucia – what if she didn't show up?

Frankie Boy sat next to Eda, mouth open and with his tongue hanging out.

"C'mon Lucia," Eda said, gently pounding on the door with the side of her fist. She needed to use the bathroom again but couldn't leave the door in case the old woman showed up and she missed the signal.

The bathroom.

That was another thing Eda would have to get used to out there. No fancy bathroom anymore. No water pots for taking a shit in, no lid to cover up the nasty smell and definitely no assistants to come along and dispose of her waste in the East River.

She wasn't a queen anymore.

"What if she's had second thoughts?" Eda said, looking at Frankie Boy. She felt the hair on the back of her neck standing up. Lightheadedness washed over her. If this delay went on for much longer there was a good chance she might pass out on the floor.

"What if Shay found out?" she said. "What if she got to Lucia? Do I run? Do we make a run for it now Frankie Boy?"

Eda pictured Lucia in her hotel room further down the corridor, handcuffed to the sink and being grilled for details about their escape plan. In Eda's mind, a terrified Lucia was begging Shay for mercy, blaming everything on that disobedient and ungrateful Helen of Troy, the little bitch who'd forced a frightened old woman into betraying the Complex.

Eda leaned up against the wall.

"Oh shit," she said.

It didn't matter. She could make a run for it anyway. To hell with Lucia's help. To hell with the laundry cart. She could do it – take her chances downstairs, try to slip past the guards and make a run for the back door.

The dagger was in the front pocket of her bag, within easy reach.

But you're too scared to use it, remember?

There was a noise outside in the corridor.

Eda almost jumped out of her skin. She heard a door closing somewhere in the distance. It was a quiet noise, like whoever had closed the door was trying their best to be as discreet as possible.

She heard light footsteps coming closer.

Frankie Boy's ears were up. He stood on all fours, staring at the door.

Eda held up her hand. "Quiet Frankie Boy," she said. "Remember our deal, okay?"

The gentle knocking, when it came, was followed by a whisper on the other side of the door.

"Eda."

"Lucia! Thank God."

Eda almost yanked the door off its hinges but that would surely have alerted everyone else on the thirty-fifth floor. Fortunately she managed to regain control of herself and taking a deep breath, she turned the handle and pulled the door open gently.

Lucia was standing in the hallway. There was a blank expression on her face.

"Okay," Eda said, with a curt nod. "Twenty minutes. I'll be down in twenty minutes. Just make sure the cart is easy to access from the stairs. Alright?"

But Lucia shook her head.

Without saying anything, the old woman walked through the gap in the doorway, past Eda and into the apartment. When she turned around, her brown skin looked pale yellow and there was a haunted look in her eyes.

"Lucia!" Eda said. "Say something for God's sake, you're scaring me."

Lucia was staring at the floor.

"Shay is coming over to see you," she said.

Eda's jaw dropped.

"Does she know?"

"No," Lucia said. "That's not it."

"Well c'mon," Eda said. She could feel a real panic rising up inside her now. Her forehead felt like it was burning up. "I'm getting out of here before she shows up. C'mon Lucia, what's the matter with you? Is the laundry cart where it's supposed to be?"

Lucia shook her head.

"I'm sorry Eda," she said. "It's off."

Eda felt like she was drowning.

"What are you talking about?"

Lucia's gaze still lingered on the floor and it was annoying the hell out of Eda that the old woman wouldn't look at her. *Couldn't* look at her.

"What is it?" Eda asked. "Spit it out for God's sake!"

"There's a man," Lucia said in a quiet voice. "There's a man in town."

She might as well have slapped Eda in the face with a metal bat. As Eda stood there, the words sinking in, she could feel the hope suffocating inside her.

"No," she said. It was all she could say.

"I have to go now," Lucia said, walking past Eda towards the double doors. She stopped in the hallway and turned around. There was a sad smile on her face.

"I'm so sorry child," she said. "He's been here a few days I think. It's your fertile time now isn't it? Damn it – we should have paid attention to your cycle. I know we haven't seen a man in a long time but we should've been smarter, more aware – if only we'd done this a few days ago or..."

Eda reached out and grabbed Lucia by the arm. It happened so suddenly that it was like watching someone else do it.

Lucia yelped in pain. "Let go!"

"This is happening," Eda said. "We're going to go now. We're going to run downstairs together before everyone else gets up and moving around. Okay? I'll wait on the second floor while you go down and wheel the cart to the stairs. Please Lucia, don't give up on me."

Lucia managed to free herself from Eda's grip.

"It's too late," she said "Everyone is already up and about so you'd better get your mind right child. The others will be here soon to tell you the news and to help you get ready. Forget about escape Eda. All you can do now is make the best of the situation. Now I'll be coming in soon to clean up before he gets here. Let's just forget this ever happened, okay?"

She walked away.

Eda stood by the door, listening to the old woman's feet tramping down the hallway floor. Lucia was walking towards the storage room where all the cleaning materials were kept.

Eda turned around and walked back into the living room. Her eyes roamed the empty opulence of the Presidential Suite and she was too numb at that moment to hate it. It felt like Lucia had shut the cage door and Eda was still trapped inside.

She managed to walk back to the bedroom where, after putting her bag under the bed, she sat down on the floor in a daze. Frankie Boy came in behind her and dropped back down on his blankets.

It wasn't long before Eda heard the front door open and then Linda's voice called out to her from the living room.

"Eda!" she said. "Are you there?"

Eda buried her face in her hands for a couple of seconds. Then she got up and walked into the living room, trying to add a fake spring to her step. Linda was there, along with Gillian and Nicola. They were all smiles this morning. Eda did her best to act surprised when Linda told her that a man was coming over to the hotel. If the women picked up on Eda's sense of crushing disappointment, they didn't show it.

A few minutes later, Shay entered the apartment.

"Good news," she said, walking inside with a smile. "We've got one."

Eda nodded. "So I heard."

Shay looked at the other assistants and there was a flicker of disappointment in her eyes. Then it was gone again. "Of course," she said. "Well it doesn't matter who gets to tell you I suppose."

"Where is he now?" Eda said.

"Downstairs with Zahra," Shay said, "He's about to take the relaxation ritual. Don't worry Eda, you've got plenty of time to get dressed and polished up. Nicola and Gill are wizards at this – they'll make you even more beautiful than last time."

Shay pointed to Eda's stomach.

"I've got a good feeling about this one," she said.

Eda turned away. She couldn't look at them anymore or they'd see it in her eyes for sure.

"Where did he come from?" she asked, pretending to wipe a spot of dust off the seat of the couch.

"New York apparently," Shay said. "The ambassadors had nothing to do with this one. He said he arrived in the city a short time ago."

Eda thought briefly about telling Shay outright that she didn't want to do this anymore. That she wanted nothing to do with this man. But she couldn't do it. Perhaps deep down, she dreaded the thought of hearing Shay telling her what she already knew.

You cannot leave.

As Shay and Eda talked, Nicola and Gillian were walking back into the living room with several outfits in hand. They laid the dresses on the couch and flattened them out for all to see. The two wardrobe assistants then scurried back and forth like insects, bringing out shoes, underwear, make-up and everything else they needed to turn Eda into Helen of Troy. Their work ethic was admirable – both Gillian and Nicola were in their late forties and they always looked so glamorous. They were the rare type of women who still used make-up on their faces on a daily basis. They only wore clothes that had been looted from designer stores or the most expensive apartments.

And of course, they were a pair of brutal killers.

"Pick your dress," Nicola said, shooing Eda's attention away from the window and towards the pile of clothes lying on the couch.

Eda shrugged. She knew fine well it would be Nicola and Gillian picking the dress like they did last time. And with Shay in the building, she would no doubt get final approval.

"Just pick something and put it on me," Eda said. "I'm not in the mood to make any decisions."

In about forty minutes, Eda had been transformed into Helen of Troy.

The two wardrobe assistants escorted her from the bedroom back into the living room. She stood alongside them like a fashion model, waiting for Shay to bring the man into the apartment.

Eda turned towards the mirror and took in the reflection. Much to her surprise, she actually quite liked the dress that Gillian had chosen for her – a slick V-neck black evening dress that complimented her hourglass figure. The face paint was mercifully less thick this time around, although her lips were still too red.

She looked towards the window again. How far away would she have been now? If only she'd jumped into that laundry cart yesterday.

She turned back to face the door. As she did, she caught a glimpse of Frankie Boy trotting through the hallway.

"What's he still doing here?" she said. "I thought he was going out for a walk with Lucia. He can't be here while...you know?"

"Lucia got held up with the cleaning," Nicola said, dusting down Eda's dress at the back. "Maddie said she was going to do it but I think she's feeling a bit sick today. Maybe she postponed it or called it off altogether. Don't worry about it, we'll lock him in the bathroom or something once you lovebirds go into the bedroom."

"Can't someone else take it out?" Gillian said. "No offense Eda but that mutt stinks of serious filth. It's a wild animal and it belongs outside."

Eda was about to respond when she heard Shay's voice in the corridor. And a second voice, a male voice.

"Stand with your back straight," Gillian said, doing a final inspection of Eda. "You're a pretty girl Eda but your posture is honest to God shocking sometimes. You're more like the hunchback of Troy."

Nicola giggled. "That's mean Gill."

Eda paid no attention to them. She was staring at the door, her eyes wide and unblinking. When it finally opened, Shay walked in with a serene smile on her face. The man followed, just a few paces behind.

Eda gasped under her breath.

It was the same man who'd been with the bandits that night. The one with the boyish features and curly black hair who'd killed Pike on 43rd Street after the mean old bandit had killed the two gardeners.

He was back, standing there in the Presidential Suite of the Waldorf Astoria.

He was wearing the same clothes that Eda remembered from that night – faded dark jeans and a brown jacket with military patches on the breast and running down both arms. His feet shifted uneasily on the floor. Either he had to use the bathroom or he was terrified. There was no recognition in his eyes when he first looked across the room at Eda – if he remembered her at all from their first encounter he was hiding it well.

"Helen of Troy," Shay said, "may I introduce David. David is from...?"

"New Jersey," David said. "Although after the war I traveled around with an Englishman for some time – that's why my accent might sound a bit funny to you."

David looked at Eda. A shy smile crept across his face.

"I've never seen such a beautiful woman," he said, gesturing towards Eda. "It's true what they say about you."

"Helen is the one," Shay said, her face glowing with the pride of a mother looking at a newborn child. "It was always going to take someone special to persuade Mother Nature to lift the curse. To forgive us."

"Yes," David said, nodding.

Eda tried her best to smile.

"Will you excuse us for a second please?" she said, looking at David. "I just need to talk to Shay about something – it's kind of an embarrassing subject and...sorry it won't take long, I promise."

David nodded. "Of course," he said. "Uhh, where do you want me to go?"

Eda turned to the two assistants who were still hovering like flies at her back.

"Nicola, Gill," she said, clicking her fingers just to annoy them. "Would you mind showing David around the apartment for a few moments. Perhaps he'd like to use the bathroom or maybe he's hungry or thirsty. You'll take care of him, won't you?"

The wardrobe assistants exchanged irritated looks.

"Go on girls," Shay said. "Do as she says."

After Gillian and Nicola had left the room with David, Shay approached Eda and took in her second makeover with a quiet round of applause.

"You look stunning," Shay said. "I'm not just saying this but you might actually be the prettiest Helen yet, I mean that. So what's wrong? You're nervous right? Well let me tell you, the second time is the hardest because you know what's going to happen. But I promise Eda, it'll get easier from here on in. All the Helens said it gets easier after the second time. And who knows? Today might be your day to conceive a child. Remember that when it gets tough in there."

Eda pointed a thumb over her shoulder.

"Are you sure you want to kill that man?" she said. "He's about the same age as me and that means he was only a boy during the war – a baby most likely. Does he really deserve to die for the crimes of older men?"

"I've thought about that," Shay said. "But he's been out there with them. Unfortunately David now carries the same ignorance and blindness in his heart as they do. We can't take the risk of letting him live – of letting *their* thoughts live through him."

Eda didn't take her eyes off Shay.

"Okay," she said, nodding slowly. "I just wanted to make sure but there's one more thing."

"What?" Shay asked.

"I get to kill this one," Eda said.

A hint of suspicion flared up in Shay's eyes.

"Say that again please."

"Let me kill him," Eda said.

"Why?" Shay asked. "Why do *you* want to do it?"

"Because I recognize him," Eda said. "Don't you?"

Seeing Shay, the sharpest mind in the Complex, look as confused as she did in that moment was a rare thing indeed.

It was beautiful.

"What are you talking about Eda?" Shay said. "Do you know that man? Do I know him?"

"I do," Eda said. "He was with the bandits when they came here and tried to take over this place. He's one of the survivors."

Shay's eyes darkened with rage.

"Are you serious?"

"There's more," Eda said. "He's the one who killed the two gardeners on 43rd Street that night. He would have killed me too if I hadn't gotten away. Thank God he doesn't recognize me in all this make-up. Listen Shay, I should have killed him that night for what he did, but I was too scared. I guess I froze. Well I'm not scared anymore. I want to be the one who does it. Call it delayed revenge if you will."

Shay stared at Eda in silence for a moment. Then slowly, she opened her rain cloak to reveal a faded-looking brown sheath hanging from her belt. She flicked open the sheath with her thumb and pulled out a large kitchen knife with a razor sharp blade.

She extended the wooden handle towards Eda.

"You make the first cut," she said. "You've earned that much. We'll be nearby. After you cut him, we'll come in and finish it with you. We can share the revenge."

"Deal," Eda said, smiling. "But I can't use that knife – you keep it. I work better with my own weapons. I'll use my dagger, like I should have done that night."

"As you wish," Shay said, replacing her knife back in the sheath.

"Will you get Lucia for me?" Eda said. She glanced over her shoulder, as if she'd heard distant voices getting closer. When no one walked into the living room she turned back to Shay. "The old woman has moved my stuff when she's been cleaning the bedroom. It's in there somewhere but I can't find it."

"Just use my knife," Shay asked. "What difference does it make?"

"I need to be comfortable with this," Eda said. She looked deep into Shay's eyes as she spoke and didn't blink. "It's Eda, not Helen who's going to kill this man. You understand? I don't need my dagger, I *want* it."

Shay's face was as hard as granite. Her eyes were dark and empty.

"You're absolutely sure?" she said to Eda. "It's not easy to kill a man. And it'll stay with you, long after we put the body in the river.

I'm telling you now, everything about it will stay with you. It'll haunt your dreams."

Eda nodded her head.

"I killed a man once," she said. "A long time ago. And I slept just fine."

12

Eda breathed a sigh of relief as Shay closed the door behind her.

With any luck, Shay would be gone for at least five minutes and maybe a little longer if Lucia wasn't in her apartment. It wasn't much but it was better than nothing.

Eda spun around as David walked back into the living room a moment later. Gillian and Nicola must have gotten bored or maybe they'd felt uncomfortable spending time around a man they were about to murder. Either way, they'd sent him back alone.

He looked around with a curious expression.

"Is she gone?" he asked. "I thought I heard the door closing."

Eda knew the time for small talk was over. She hurried over and grabbed David by the wrists. The bewildered look on his face as she held onto him implied that he wasn't sure if the rough stuff was part of the mating ritual or not. But then he looked at Eda and his expression turned grim, no doubt mirroring the look on her own face.

"Are you okay?" he asked. "What's wrong?"

"We don't have long," Eda said, lowering her voice. "Look David, this isn't what you think it is. They're going to kill you."

David's face turned chalk white. "What? They're going to what?"

"They're going to kill you," Eda said. There was no way of sugarcoating the bad news and even if she'd tried it would only have wasted more time. "They're going to wait till we have sex and when it's done - well, put it this way, you won't be around long enough to find out whether you put a baby in me or not."

David took a couple of wobbly steps backwards, his hands up in the air as if he was calling for a timeout.

"Why?" he said.

"Shay's killing them," Eda said. "The men from the old world. Anyone who had a hand in the End War."

David's face was a sickly gray color.

"Men from the old world?" he said. "But I was only a child during the war. I lost my family, I lost everything..."

"Keep your voice down," Eda said. Her eyes darted back and forth across the apartment; she knew that somewhere nearby, the assassins were sharpening their knives.

"I was only with the bandits a couple of weeks," David said, doing his best to stay quiet while he pleaded his case. "I'm not one of them. Surely you can tell I'm not like they were. There were a couple of survivors after the battle and when they fled the city I chose not to go with them. I stayed here to regroup. Can't you see? I'm not one of them and I'm not a man of the old world."

"It doesn't matter anymore," Eda said. "You've been out there amongst them. You've lived with them and maybe you even killed with them for all I know. You're guilty as far as Shay's concerned."

"That's bullshit," David said. His voice shook with fear.

"We don't have time to discuss it," Eda said, glancing back towards the double doors. "You have to trust me on this. I know you're not like the other bandits and I know you're not an asshole but Shay doesn't and that's why they're going to kill you. That's all that matters right now."

"How do you know?" David said. There was a puzzled look on his face. "How do you know I'm not like the other bandits? Or that I'm not an asshole?"

"We've met before," Eda said.

David squinted his eyes. It was like he was trying to peel back the make-up on Eda's face and look straight through her.

"What?"

"You don't remember me," Eda said. "Do you?"

He shook his head. "No," he said. "But I can't imagine how I'd ever forget someone like you."

"After the battle on 42nd Street," Eda said, "you killed one of your own. A guy called Pike. He killed two women, remember now?"

David leaned in closer. His eyes were bulging and his mouth hung open.

"You?" he said. "The girl with the knife? That was you?"

"Yep," Eda said.

"But you look so different..."

"We don't have time for this," Eda said. "Look here's the deal. Life as Helen of Troy isn't all it's cracked up to be so I'm working on a plan to get us out of here. Both of us. You probably saved my life that night and I figure I owe you one."

"Working on a plan?" David said. "How about this one? How about we open the door and start running the hell out of here right now?"

Eda shook her head. "Because we wouldn't get very far," she said. "You're surrounded. *We're* surrounded."

"So what do we do?" David said.

Eda was about to answer when she was cut off by the sound of footsteps in the corridor.

"Shit," she whispered. "Okay David, you're going to have to trust me from here on in. Whatever you do, follow my lead and play along. We'll have our chance to run the hell out of here, I promise."

David swallowed hard. He was about to say something when the door to the Presidential Suite swung open. Shay walked in, followed by an anxious-looking Lucia.

"Are you two getting along?" Shay asked.

"Of course," Eda said, spinning around to face the two women. She was smiling.

"Yes," David said. Eda could still hear the trembling in that strange, foreign accent of his. "Helen of Troy is as charming as she is beautiful."

Eda laughed and gazed demurely at the floor. She looked at David, then walked over to the two women and lowered her voice.

"Shay," she said, "would you mind keeping David company for a second? Lucia and I won't be long."

Before Shay had a chance to answer, Eda turned around and giggled softly as she looked over at David.

"It's embarrassing," she said. "Lucia is my cleaning lady and she's moved my tray of scented candles. Now I can't find them anywhere."

David nodded. He stood on the other side of the room like a block of stone with arms. "And they're important to you?" he asked.

Eda grinned. "I need them," she said. "You know, for atmosphere and stuff."

"Do what you need to do," David said. "I want you to be comfortable."

Eda noticed his hands were shaking at his sides. She hoped that if Shay saw it, and Shay didn't miss much, that she'd put it down to nerves about the curse.

"I just want this to be perfect," Eda said. And with that she threw a stern look in Lucia's direction. "Why do you keep moving my things and not putting them back where you found them? Haven't we had this discussion a hundred times before?"

Lucia's jaw dropped.

"I..."

Shay walked over to David. "I guess the most beautiful woman in the world is allowed to have it whatever way she wants," she said. "Wouldn't you agree?"

David flinched. It looked like he'd just brushed up against a row of jagged thorns.

"Absolutely," he said. His voice was flimsy and nervous. He looked at Eda like an animal from behind the bars of a cage, his eyes longing to be set free. "Take your time Helen, I'll still be here when you get back."

Eda smiled. "I won't be long," she said. "C'mon Lucia, follow me – where the hell did you put my candles?"

Eda took Lucia's hand and dragged the old woman towards Helen's bedroom. They didn't talk until they were inside and the door was firmly shut behind them.

Lucia still looked baffled.

"What is this?" she said. "What was all that about with the candles? Did I miss something?"

Eda marched over and leaned her head towards Lucia.

"The plan goes ahead," she whispered into the old woman's ear. "That man out there is innocent. He saved my life the night the bandits came knocking at our door."

Lucia squinted her eyes. She took a step back.

"Are you crazy child?" she said.

"No I'm not crazy," Eda said, still keeping her voice down. "To tell you the truth Lucia, sometimes – like right now – I feel like I'm the only sane person in New York. I'm leaving."

"I can't help you Eda," Lucia said. "We've talked about this already. I won't. It's too late."

There was a part of Eda that loved Lucia. She'd lost count of the number of times the old woman had sat down with her on the bed when Eda was feeling trapped in the Waldorf, and cheered her up with endless stories and songs from the past.

But she had to forget all about that now.

Eda grabbed Lucia by the shoulders and dug her fingers in deep. Lucia winced under the pressure and tried to shake Eda off.

"Keep quiet," Eda hissed.

"Let go of me!" Lucia said. "Have you lost your mind?"

"You're going to help me," Eda said. "Those crazy murdering bitches out there are about to stab an innocent man to death. He doesn't deserve to die like that. You had sons before the war, didn't you Lucia? For God's sake, imagine it was one of your boys who showed up here thinking he was doing a good thing. How would you like it if Shay and all the rest of them hacked him to bits? Well?"

"My boys are all dead," Lucia said. "Don't try and play mind games with me girl."

Eda nodded.

"Okay then, she said. "How about this? I'm going to tell Shay that you came up with an escape plan for me. I'll tell her it was all your idea – the laundry cart, escaping out the back door, everything! She knows that you had daughters of your own and I can tell a good story if I have to – why wouldn't a sweet old woman feel sorry for a sad girl who felt trapped? And why wouldn't she want to help that sad girl by offering to break her out?"

Lucia's eyes fixed on Eda with something close to hatred. That's if the sweet old cleaner was even capable of such a feeling.

"You little bitch," she snapped. "Shay's not stupid. She'll never believe any of that nonsense."

Eda jerked a thumb towards the door.

"Who do you think she'd prefer to believe?" she said. "Who does she need more around here? Helen of Troy or the cleaning lady? Even if she doesn't believe me, she'll never really know for sure. She'll never be able to trust you again Lucia. Tell me, how long do you think you'd last out there if you got banished?"

"After everything I've done for you," Lucia whispered. Her eyes brimmed with tears.

Eda felt a stabbing sensation of guilt in her heart. This was killing her but it was too late to stop now.

"For God's sake just help me," Eda said. "Don't let them butcher an innocent man in here today."

"It's impossible," Lucia said, running a hand through her frizzy gray hair. "Shay's in there."

"There's still time," Eda said. She took her hands off Lucia and glanced at the bedroom door. If they took too long, Shay would start getting suspicious.

"Look," she said. "Here's how it works. Linda told me that when there's a man in here with Helen, all the killers gather in the bedroom on the opposite end of the apartment. As soon as they hear all the sex noises, that's their cue to creep towards the living room. From there, they start edging towards this room. When the man's finished, that's when they storm in and butcher the poor bastard. You see Lucia? They've got a routine and we can take advantage of that."

"I don't see how them having a routine makes any difference," Lucia said.

"It gives us a window of opportunity," Eda said. "A small one but it's better than nothing. David, Frankie Boy and me – we can sneak out of the apartment before the killers move from the other bedroom into the living room. As long as they don't hear anything, you know, the sex noises, they'll think we haven't started yet and they'll stay on the far side of the apartment."

"And what about the two warriors in the lobby?" Lucia asked. "If they see you..."

"We stick to the original plan," Eda said, cutting in. "After you leave here, you go straight down to the first floor and wheel the cart to the foot of the stairs. Make sure it's the big one. Tuck it into the wall, don't block the stairs or someone might move it. You take Frankie Boy with you too – if anyone asks you're taking him for a walk. Me and David, we'll be down as quick as we can, we'll jump into the cart and you'll push us to the back. You think you'll be able to push it if there are three of us in there? It's going to be heavy. Real heavy."

Lucia looked like she'd aged ten years in five minutes. But there was stubborn defiance in her eyes as she looked at Eda.

"I've been working all my life," she said. "You should have seen the things I did before, during and after the war. Don't you worry about me Eda Becker. I can push a laundry cart from one side of the hotel to the other with ten people inside if I had to. I'm far from done yet in this world."

"So you'll help me?" Eda said. This was it – they'd run out of time. It was now or never.

Lucia stared up at the pale ceiling.

"I had daughters as well as sons you know," she said. "God rest their souls, all of them One of them was a lot like you Eda – a stubborn little smart-ass who wouldn't take no for an answer. Okay then.

I'll do it for my Isabella who would have liked you and told me to help you. I'll put the laundry cart at the bottom of the stairs. God help us."

"Thank you," Eda said, almost crying with relief.

It was back on.

A few moments later, they were back in the living room. Shay and David were standing near the bookcase, not talking and pretending to look at books. Shay smiled at Eda and Lucia as they returned, although Eda detected a hint of impatience in her eyes.

David's face was chalk white. He looked like he was already dead.

"Find what you were looking for?" Shay asked.

"We got there eventually," Eda said.

"Sorry about that," Lucia said, looking back and forth between Shay and David. "I'm old and I forget where I put things sometimes. Anyway, excuse me folks will you? I'll go take Frankie Boy out for a walk and get him out of here. Come on you crazy dog. You want to go for a walk with Lucia?"

The big German Shepherd rushed into the living room, his tail wagging furiously. Eda grabbed his leash off the hook next to the door and handed it to Lucia with a nod.

"See you guys later."

Lucia returned the nod and left with Frankie Boy.

"I think we've kept this poor man waiting long enough," Shay said, stepping into the center of the room. "Shall we proceed with the fertility blessing?"

"Of course," Eda said.

Shay brought the young man and woman together and spoke the words. Eda didn't listen to a single one of them. She was imagining the forthcoming escape and the feel of the rain on her head all over again.

The fertility blessing didn't take long.

"Good luck," Shay said, her face glowing like a priestess who'd just conversed with the divine spirit. She walked to the door, glancing over her shoulder at Eda and David, who were still touching hands in the center of the room.

"See you when it's over," Shay said. And then she closed the door gently behind her.

Eda and David dropped hands as soon as she was gone. David was about to say something but Eda pressed a finger to her lips. She shook her head and pointed further inside the apartment. David seemed to understand – there were killers hiding somewhere inside the suite, and even if it seemed like they were alone, they weren't.

Eda took his hand again and they walked towards the bedroom. Once inside, she closed the door behind them. She made sure that it didn't click fully shut though.

"Helen," David whispered. "I can't stay here, not knowing what they're..."

"Don't call me Helen," Eda said. "My name's Eda. And right now we have to wait for a few minutes. Let them clear the hallway outside – Shay will come back into the suite through one of the adjoining hotel rooms – it's like a secret passage that means she doesn't have to go through the front door. Let them all gather in the other side of the apartment. We've got to get the timing just right or we're going to screw this up."

Eda sat down on the bed and took off her heels. Then she stood up and began to unzip the tight evening dress from the back.

"What are you looking at?" she said, catching David's eyes on her body. "Nothing's going to happen. If it does, you're dead. Remember?"

David turned around and faced the door.

But he couldn't stand still for long. It was like he was standing barefoot on a carpet of hot coals.

"What are we waiting for?" he said. "Please, I'm feeling very claustrophobic right now."

"I told you," Eda said. "Timing. I have to be sure that Lucia's had enough time to get downstairs and move the cart. Try not to freak out alright? As long as we're quiet, Shay and the others will stay on the other side of the suite. Unless they mess with the routine of course..."

David looked horrified. "What are you talking about?"

"Nothing," Eda said. "Forget it."

She threw the black dress on the bed and pulled out her sweater and khakis from the bedroom closet. She put them on and then wrapped the rain cloak over the top, zipping it up tight.

"Second time lucky," she said, looking down at her old clothes.

Eda grabbed her backpack and fastened it over her shoulders. Then she picked up her boots and tucked them under her arm.

"Take your shoes off," she whispered over to David. "We're going to have to sneak out as quietly as possible."

David did as he was told.

Eda unzipped the backpack at the front and pulled out her dagger. She brushed her finger over the sharp blade and promised herself that she would never come back to the Presidential Suite. Whatever happened, her career as Helen of Troy was over.

Eda pointed to the empty scabbard hanging off David's belt. "Where's your sword?" she asked.

"Downstairs," he said. "I wasn't allowed to bring it up with me."

"But you kept your scabbard on?" Eda said.

"It's kind of hard to take off," David said.

Eda smiled. "I hope you're a fast runner."

She tiptoed across the bedroom. Opening the door slowly, she peered towards the living room. The apartment appeared to be deserted.

Eda turned and nodded at David, silently mouthing 'let's go'.

They crept into the living room.

As they approached the white double doors of the Presidential Suite, Eda felt the panic monster waking up inside her. A barrage of potential problems hit home like a sledgehammer – the most immediate being the thought that Shay had locked them into the apartment.

It was a terrifying thought. If they *were* locked in, it was over.

Eda's forehead burned with endless streams of hot sweat. Her entire arm was trembling as she reached for the door handle.

It turned freely.

She almost cried out with relief as she pushed the door open and stepped out into the corridor with David close behind her.

So long Helen of Troy.

It was a small victory but it was far too early to get carried away.

The corridor was empty, thank God. Eda closed the door over but made sure it didn't click shut. As she started walking away, Eda could almost hear the group of assassins breathing from somewhere inside the apartment.

How long before impatience forced them to abandon the routine and start moving towards the bedroom?

They made slow progress down the corridor. Eda and David's feet gently kissed the worn-out Waldorf carpet and yet their caution wasn't enough to prevent the occasional squeak leaping out of the floorboards. It sounded like a warning alarm, like the hotel had betrayed their trust. When this happened Eda and David would halt their advance. Eda stared at the white walls, not daring to blink in case someone lurking behind those walls heard it. As they started walking again, Eda expected those big double doors behind her to suddenly swing open. Shay's enraged voice would chase the runaways down the corridor, ordering them to 'STOP'.

And then all hell would break loose.

Eventually Eda and David made it to the top of the staircase. It felt like they'd been creeping down the corridor for hours. It was another small victory. They even exchanged a brief smile with one another as they slipped their shoes back on.

Eda looked down the first set of stairs. It was a long way down but at least she'd get to run. And as long as the staircase was empty they had a chance. Even if it wasn't, there was no turning back now.

Eda and David charged downstairs as fast as they could. They didn't talk, they just ran all the way with only a brief stop halfway down to catch their breath. Eda's arms and legs were burning but it wasn't enough to make her slow down. Nothing was. Her heart was thrashing in her chest, exhilarated and terrified by the escape. She had to keep going. They could rest later, somewhere safe, somewhere far away from the confinement of the Complex.

Her thoughts returned to the thirty-fifth floor. What was going on up there now? Had Shay and the others discovered the empty bedroom?

Were they already on the stairs behind Eda and David?

Eda turned the last corner of the staircase and she almost screamed with joy when she saw the laundry cart parked at the bottom step. As she raced downstairs towards the cart with David close behind, Lucia appeared as if she'd been waiting in the shadows all the time. An excited Frankie Boy walked on the leash at her side, his tail wagging as he tried to get closer to Eda.

Lucia looked at the exhausted escapees. She pressed a finger to her lips.

"There are two guards posted at the front door," she said. "Lucky for us, it looks like they're staying there instead of wandering around. They're probably making sure that no one else gets into the building while there's a man in here. C'mon you lot, get in the cart before I drop dead of a heart attack."

"Thank you Lucia," Eda said. She leaned over and kissed the old woman on the cheek.

"Get in!" Lucia hissed. "For God's sake."

Eda grabbed a hold of Frankie Boy and with David's help, they lifted him into the cart and lowered him onto a thick pile of bed sheets and pillowcases. The dog tried to climb back out immediately but fortunately he didn't bark. Eda jumped into the cart to calm him down and Frankie Boy quickly settled.

David looked at Lucia and then at the cart.

"Will you be able to push this with all three of us inside?" he said.

Lucia looked like she was about to slap him in the face.

"Get in there," she said. "We've been through this already. Listen to me sonny boy, I was pushing heavier weights than this way back when you were a tiny little itch in your daddy's pants."

David nodded and climbed into the cart.

It was a tight squeeze and they curled up inside as best they could. As the cart began to move, Eda grabbed a handful of bed sheets and towels and flung them over their heads, hiding them from view if anyone were to look in. Frankie didn't like that. He wriggled back through the sheets towards the surface and scratched at the side of the cart.

The dog began to whine gently.

Eda grabbed a hold of him and buried her face in his coat.

"Quiet Frankie Boy," she whispered. "Please. That's a good boy. We'll be outside again in a second. You'll feel the rain on your head and you can run as fast as you want, I promise."

Eda felt the strange sensation of movement as the wheels turned underneath them. Lucia was covering the ground quickly, no doubt desperate to get it over with.

David lay curled up on the floor of the massive cart, his body as still as a corpse.

Eda tried to resist the panic monster. It was still there whispering in her ear, telling her that Lucia had cracked under the pressure and that she wasn't taking the runaways to the back door – instead she was wheeling them to the front door where the guards and Shay would be waiting with swords and handcuffs. It would be sweet revenge for Lucia after Eda had pushed her too hard in the apartment.

No matter how much Eda resisted the voice, it wouldn't go away.

Frankie Boy let out another soft whine.

"Shhh," Eda said.

Eventually the cart stopped.

Eda's fingers were wrapped around the handle of the dagger. She'd fight them to the end if she had to because she was never going back. That was never going to happen.

Somebody pulled the sheets away to reveal the three escapees underneath. Eda looked up, knife in hand, and saw Lucia's leathery brown face peering down into the cart. The old woman's forehead was drenched in sweat.

"Out," Lucia said. "Quickly!"

Eda stood up and with David's help, lifted Frankie Boy out of the cart. They jumped out after the dog.

Eda threw her arms around Lucia, kissing her on the cheek and forehead multiple times.

"I'm sorry I was such a bitch to you upstairs," she whispered into the old woman's ear. "You've been good to me Lucia. You and your songs and stories are about the only one thing I'll miss about all this."

Lucia cupped Eda's face in her hands. "Good luck child."

Eda looked at her. As much as she wanted to get away, she hoped the old woman would get away with helping them. Eda didn't want to think about the consequences of Lucia being caught.

"Thank you Lucia," she said.

"Yes," David said. "Thank you. I'll never forget this."

Lucia's hands slid down Eda's face and dropped at her sides. She then turned back to the cart, grabbed the handles and turned towards the runaways one last time.

"You don't have time to thank me you idiots," she said. "Run for your life. Go on! Get the hell out of New York and don't ever come back because as sure as it's going to rain outside today, they'll be coming after you."

13

Eda, David and Frankie Boy ran down Lexington Avenue as fast as they could. They didn't look back, not once.

Rain fell hard from a gloomy sky. The clouds were fat and puffy, lingering over New York like a supernatural fog. When Eda looked up that way, she had the strangest feeling that the fog was descending towards them.

Frankie Boy barked as they ran. To Eda's ears, it sounded like a cry of pure joy and she laughed out loud with him, sharing in the feeling of one who'd bolted from the jaws of a trap that had once seemed so final, into the arms of a second chance.

The city stretched out for miles, opening up to the three runaways like a pair of welcoming arms. They ran past a liquor store, the wreckage of the old Marriot Hotel, countless restaurants and store-fronts that the rats had taken over since the end of the wild years.

Eda had seen all this in her dreams. She'd seen this journey down Lexington Avenue over and over again. Now it was here.

"C'mon Frankie Boy," she called out. She'd stopped laughing now, realizing that it was still far too early to celebrate. The dog had stopped to sniff something near the edge of the road.

"Frankie Boy! Hurry up!"

Eda turned around to go fetch the dog from the sidewalk. She saw something that stopped her dead.

"They're chasing us!" she called out to David.

Eda's blood ran cold and she strained her eyes, peering through the crashing rain for a better look at what was coming.

She saw the towering figure of Lex and two other warriors, sprinting towards Eda as if their lives depended on it. A little further back, Eda could see the dim figure of Shay. She was running too but it was obvious that she was struggling to keep up with the impossible pace that Lex and the two warriors had set.

Shay was running – that's how badly she wanted to get Eda back. It wasn't enough just to give orders to Lex and then to sit back and wait. She had to get involved.

Eda watched them coming towards her, distorting the perfection of her dream. Behind Shay and the warriors, the Chrysler Building loomed large on the New York skyline like a futuristic space rocket waiting for take off.

Four in total, at least for now. More warriors would be dispatched soon. It was that important – Helen of Troy had escaped after all.

"C'mon!" David yelled over to her. "Keep running for God's sake. We've got a lead on them."

He ran over to Eda's side and stared down the road at the small posse coming after them.

"Oh no," he said.

There was a look of terror in David's eyes and he began to pull on Eda's arm, dragging her away, tipping her slightly off-balance in an attempt to encourage her legs to start moving again.

"Let's go," he said. "Eda! We can outrun them."

Eda's head was spinning but she turned around and tried to run at David's side like he wanted her to. She was a little faster than he was and quickly slipped into the lead but even then, with the cold air crashing against her face like an invisible wave, something didn't feel right. Frankie Boy seemed to pick up on this too; he'd been running at the head of the pack just moments earlier but he'd stopped again and was staring intently down the street at their pursuers.

Eda slowed to a stop and took a deep lungful of air. She turned around and with hands on hips, faced the direction they'd just come from. They'd made good ground in their initial dash from the hotel – the Waldorf was a mere speck in the distance.

It had been a good effort but it was obvious to Eda now – running wasn't the answer.

"What are you doing?" David yelled, slowing down and coming over to her. "We're nearly out of here."

"No," Eda said, shaking her head. "We're not."

As she stood there, waiting for them, Eda recalled a pocket-sized book of inspirational quotes that she'd taken from a bookshop in Times Square several years ago. It wasn't her usual type of reading material but something had compelled her to pick it up. Now, as Eda stood under the cold rain, one of those quotes leapt out from the back of her mind.

The best way out is always through.

"Jesus!" David screamed. The power of the rain wasn't enough to cover up the panic spilling into his voice. "Keep running! C'mon Eda!"

"No," Eda said again. She looked at David and shook her head sadly. "They think I belong to them and they're just going to keep coming and coming. We can't outrun Lex. And besides for God's sake, I've done nothing wrong."

"Are you thinking about fighting them?" David said. "These women are killers – you know that better than anyone. You know something else? Those bandits I came to New York with were no slouches in fighting department and those women destroyed them. You can't win."

Eda walked over to Frankie Boy, knelt down and buried her head in his wet coat. The smell of dog and wet rain combined was beautiful. "It's back to the old days boy," Eda said, lifting her head up and looking into his chocolate brown eyes. "You're on your own but I'm glad I got to know you. Real friendships are a rare thing."

She kissed him on the head and stood up straight.

"Go!" Eda yelled, trying to shoo him away. "Run. Get out of here."

Frankie Boy didn't budge.

"Please," Eda said. "Just go! I don't want them to hurt you."

She looked over at David.

"That goes for you too," Eda said. "This isn't your fight David. Why did you come back to the Complex anyway? Why didn't you just take off after the battle?"

"And go where?" David said, holding both arms out so that his body formed a cross shape. "I knew there were people here. I guess I didn't want to go back out there into the desert alone. 'Cos that's what it is out there Eda – it's a desert and it's fucking depressing."

"But you have to go back there," Eda said. "And whatever you do David, don't ever come back to New York."

Eda let the backpack slide off her shoulder. She unzipped it and pulled out the dagger.

She pointed it at the four women in the distance.

"If I can just get to Shay," she said.

David rushed over beside her. Streams of rainwater poured down his boyish face. His bottom lip trembled but he nodded like he finally understood what Eda had to do.

"Well I'm not running either," he said.

Eda smiled and looked at him. She pointed to the empty scabbard hanging off his belt.

"Bet you wish you had that sword now don't you?"

David looked down at the scabbard and smiled.

"So what now?" he said, as they both stood there watching Lex and the warriors catch up with them. "We just stand here in the rain and wait to get killed?"

"No," Eda said, looking at David. "That's the stupidest idea I ever heard. Why bother waiting?"

With the dagger in hand, Eda charged down the road.

She heard David yelling after her. She heard Frankie Boy barking too, all of these sounds merged with the gushing rain to form a single mosaic of chaotic background noise that she tried to blot out.

Further down the street, Lex roared a deafening command and

the two women running alongside her suddenly picked up the pace, sprinting at full speed, moving past Lex and towards Eda.

Their samurai swords were drawn.

Eda didn't even think about slowing down. She was dead already in her mind and everything in between now and then was just a bonus. If anything, she ran harder, determined to show Lex and the warriors no fear just like the Viking berserkers that she'd read about in the history books.

The best way out is always...

Eda crashed into the nearest warrior at full speed. As she'd been running, she'd braced herself for impact, knowing full well that she wasn't going to back out of a collision. But it still felt like jumping into the side of a giant tower block. Eda's aggression took the warrior by surprise. The katana sword flew out of the woman's hands and she fell backwards, landing badly on the road with a painful groan. Eda went down with her and for a moment it was a wild scramble to see who would recover first. But Eda was the quicker of the two. Almost as soon as she was down, she regained control and seconds later found herself climbing on top of the stunned warrior.

In that moment, Eda Becker was herself again.

She raised the dagger and held it high above her head. Time stopped. Even the rain seemed to have frozen in mid-air as if what was about to happen would do so outside the boundaries of reality. Eda couldn't see the warrior underneath her anymore – the woman's face was a blur and it was like there was a revolving gallery of images where her features were supposed to be. The images moved in reverse and flipped past quickly, going from the everyday sights that Eda had known in the Complex – Grand Central, the Fitzpatrick, then onto Shay, Lex and Frankie, and finally the pictures went all the way back to the wild years where her earliest memories lingered.

The last thing she saw was the burned man trying to rape and murder Libby in that dark alley.

Eda stabbed the warrior in a vicious frenzy of strikes. It was like the adrenaline surging through her had given her superpowers and she struck fast, faster than anyone else in the Complex could ever have believed she was capable of.

The warrior screamed but it was the burned man's voice that Eda heard.

Or maybe it was George Mitford's.

She stood up and backed away from the dying warrior. The dagger was still locked in Eda's hand and a steady waterfall of dark blood dripped from the blade onto her boots.

Eda could hear Frankie Boy barking in the background.

The warrior lay on her back, drowning in blood. Her fingers grasped at the myriad of fresh holes in her neck and upper body, trying to fix something that couldn't be fixed. She let out a loud and wet choking noise, convulsed violently and then stopped.

There was a fierce clanging at Eda's back.

She spun around and saw David wrestling with the second warrior. They were down on the wet road and David's fingers were clamped tightly over the women's wrist as he fought for control of her sword hand. With his other hand, he threw a series of wild punches at the woman's face. After about ten blows in a row, one connected flush on her chin. The warrior's head wobbled and David seized the opportunity by ripping the sword out of her grasp.

He didn't need to turn the weapon against its owner. The warrior had already blacked out and she lay still on the road with her arms stretched out at the sides.

David leapt back to his feet with the sword in hand. He looked over and saw the dead warrior at Eda's feet.

His mouth hung open.

"Oh Jesus," he said.

He was about to say something else but stopped. A finger pointed over Eda's shoulder.

"Look out!" he screamed.

Eda turned around.

Lex charged towards her, the tip of her sword pointing directly at Eda's throat. There was a murderous rage burning in the chief warrior's eyes. At that moment, it didn't look like she was the slightest bit interested in bringing Eda back to the Waldorf alive to resume her career as Helen of Troy.

David leapt forward with sword in hand, intercepting Lex before she could get to Eda.

There was another loud clang as the two swords clashed. Lex advanced on David, swinging relentlessly and grunting with rage. She towered over the man by at least five inches. As she attacked with a level of skill that looked effortless, she pushed him backwards.

David remained composed on the back foot, parrying and dodging Lex's attack. He was obviously good with a sword but was good going to be enough against the best killer in the Complex?

Eda glanced further down the street and saw Shay coming through the rain like a nightmare. She wasn't running anymore. She was walking with a chilling confidence in her stride, as if certain beyond all doubt that she was going to reclaim Helen of Troy.

Meanwhile David lunged at Lex, trying desperately to turn the sword fight around in his favor. But Lex dodged his every blow with ease. It was like she knew every move David was going to make before he did. With a neat step to the side, she threw a sharp knee that connected flush with his groin. David groaned and doubled over but somehow managed to stay on his feet. While he was bent over, Lex threw a vicious left uppercut that toppled the young man like a falling building. He writhed around in a fresh puddle of rainwater, clutching at his groin. Blood streamed from a deep gash beside his right eye.

Lex stood over him.

She took the hilt of the sword in both hands. Slowly, she raised the weapon over her head, the tip of the blade pointing at David's heart.

The warrior laughed.

"Better late than never," Lex said.

Eda took advantage of this short delay. She charged at Lex from behind, slamming into her and wrapping her forearm around the warrior's thick neck. Lex staggered forward under the impact but she managed to remain upright with Eda glued to her back in a piggy-back position.

As Lex fought to stay on two feet, Eda jerked back and forth, using both arms to try and sink the choke in deeper.

It felt like she was trying to strangle an oak tree.

Frankie Boy's barking increased in volume and intensity. But Eda couldn't see the dog anywhere. It was like he was invisible and she couldn't help but worry that one of the other warriors might have gotten to him while she'd been on the ground.

"Get off me you little bitch!" Lex yelled. "I'll fucking kill you."

The two women grappled furiously with Lex still carrying Eda's weight on her back. Eda's dagger was locked in the fingers of her right hand but it was useless while both arms had committed to securing a chokehold. If she loosened her grip now in a bid to bring the dagger into play, the freakishly strong Lex would undoubtedly seize the opportunity to throw Eda off her back.

It was a grueling stalemate, one that seemed to last forever.

Soon, Eda's arms were like two lead pipes attached to her body. The adrenaline was wearing off and exhaustion was setting in.

Lex must have felt the younger woman start to fade. All of a sudden she dipped to her knees in a low squat, held it there for a second before springing upwards like a big cat leaping through the undergrowth at its prey. This sudden motion sent Eda hurtling over the warrior's head and for a moment she was flying like a bird through the air.

She landed on her back and the impact rattled her insides. As Eda lay there, fighting to regain her senses, she heard loud feet splashing through the puddles and coming over towards her. She yelped as someone grabbed her by the hair.

There was an explosion of pain.

"Let go!" Eda cried out, trying to unlock Lex's grip on her hair.

"You ungrateful little shit," Lex said. "After everything we've done for you, this is how you thank us?"

The chief warrior tugged harder and Eda felt like she was on the brink of being scalped. She screamed in agony and as Lex kept yanking on her hair she was forced back up onto her feet. Once she was upright, she saw the hateful look forming on Lex's face. The warrior let go of Eda's hair all of a sudden and her entire body snapped forward with a vicious punch that landed clean on Eda's temple.

Eda felt the lights go out for just a second. There was a flash of bright and beautiful colors dancing before her eyes.

She felt her body slam off the ground as she dropped onto the road. When Eda looked up, there was a blurry shape towering over her. The image slowly cleared and it was Lex, stepping forward with both hands gripped around the handle of the samurai sword.

She was smiling.

"It was a good try Eda," she said. "But it's over now and I mean over. You're a danger to everything we're trying to build here. You're not going back to the Waldorf – you belong in the East River. Don't worry, we'll put your boyfriend in with you."

At that point, Eda heard a voice yelling in the distance. It sounded like Shay.

"No!" the voice yelled. "Lex, don't kill her!"

Lex glanced over her shoulder and shook her head.

"Not this time Shay."

While the warrior was looking behind her, Eda twisted around so that she was lying on her front. Her fingers grasped at the road as she began to crawl down the rain-soaked street in a bid to get away.

But she was like a slug in the rain.

Lex stepped forward and pressed the flat of her boot on Eda's back, pinning her tight onto the road.

"So long kid," she said. "You could have been one of the great ones."

Eda's face dropped into a shallow puddle and she spat out a mouthful of rainwater. Then she closed her eyes and braced herself for the end. She'd fought them at least and even though it had never been about winning, Eda didn't feel ready to die.

Not yet.

She waited. But the blade didn't touch her.

From where she lay face-first on the ground, Eda heard a faint gasping sound. It was enough to make her spin around and just in time to see something charging towards Lex – a lightning fast streak of black and brown that shot through the air, leaping over Eda like she was a hurdle on a track and crashing into the chief warrior, throwing her off her feet and onto the street where she landed badly.

Eda managed to lift her head slowly off the ground. Before she saw anything, she heard Frankie Boy snarling and growling, sounding at last every bit like the wild animal that Linda always feared he was. She saw Lex's sword lying on the road just a few feet by her side. Then she lifted her head further and caught up with the action. Frankie Boy's assault on the warrior was vicious and blurry. His jaws lunged and snapped at Lex's face over and over again. When he wasn't going for the face, his sharp teeth ravaged the hands that Lex held up to defend her face.

This wasn't a warning attack. Frankie Boy was trying to kill her.

Eda heard both Shay and David shouting from afar. She couldn't make out what either one of them was saying. One thing Eda did understand though – she had to get a hold of Lex's sword before Shay did.

With a yelp of pain, she pushed herself onto two unsteady feet. A sharp knot twisted in her side and she felt a stream of hot blood run down the side of her mouth. Eda tasted it and then wiped her lips dry.

Shay was about fifteen feet away from the sword. She was racing towards the weapon with remarkable speed for an older woman. Her face was one big giant grimace. But Eda, although hurt, was much closer. She bent down and after fumbling around for a second like a blind person, she locked her fingers around the hilt.

She straightened up and pointed the blade at the advancing Shay.

"Too late," Eda said.

Shay stopped dead. Her face shriveled up with a look of crushing disappointment.

David picked up the sword that belonged to the warrior that Eda had killed.

As she stood there, Eda glanced over Shay's shoulder and strained her eyes towards the horizon. There were more warriors racing down Lexington. No doubt Linda or someone else back at the Waldorf had rallied the troops and now here they were, coming to aid the recovery effort, to reclaim Helen of Troy for the Complex or at the very least to make sure Eda Becker ended up in the East River.

"Get it off me!" Lex screamed. "Get this fucking monster off me!"

The warrior's face was a mask of blood. Her shredded hands threw a barrage of defiant punches at Frankie Boy's head but it seemed like the dog had a brick for a skull. He was impervious to Lex's blows and he continued to snap his jaws and open her up a piece at a time. Eda felt luckier than ever now that he'd chosen to befriend her that day on West 42nd Street.

"Call him off," Shay said, looking at Eda. Her voice was desperate. "Eda. Please! He'll listen to you if you call him."

Eda left the older woman hanging for a second.

"Why should I?"

Shay stood there, helpless and pleading with her eyes.

"Please," she said. "We'll talk about this but right now get him off before he kills her."

Eda nodded slowly. She turned to her left.

"Frankie Boy!" she yelled. "Frankie!" She walked over towards the struggle, clapping her hands loudly.

"Enough!"

But Frankie Boy ignored her. He had a fierce grip on Lex's forearm and he was shaking his head back and forth, as if trying to pull it clean off her body.

Eda dropped her sword at David's feet. She hurried over and taking a deep breath, reached down for Frankie Boy. She wrapped an arm around his neck and gripped his underside, making sure her face was out of biting range.

"Don't bite me boy," she said. "C'mon let's go."

She pulled the dog off the bloody and battered Lex.

But Frankie Boy struggled and came back in, lunging at Lex's neck once more, perhaps sensing it was his last chance to finish her.

But Eda secured her hold on him again and pulled him out of range. His jaws connected with thin air.

Eda looked down at the dog. His mouth and teeth were stained red. His tail was stiff and pointing up at the grey sky.

He looked happy.

"Take him," she said to David.

David looked worried. "What?" he said.

"Take him," Eda said, bringing Frankie Boy over. "He won't hurt you. It's just for a second while he calms down."

David lowered the two swords he was carrying onto the road. He knelt down beside the big German Shepherd and tentatively took over from Eda, wrapping his arms around the dog.

"Easy boy," David said, his voice trembling. "Take it easy."

Eda picked up one of the swords. Then, looking at Shay, she strode over to Lex and pulled her by the hair until the chief warrior was up on her knees. Lex gasped but she didn't have the strength left to protest further.

"Does that hurt?" Eda whispered in Lex's ear.

She pressed the blade against Lex's throat.

At the same time, David tentatively uncoiled his arms from around Frankie Boy's middle. The dog lay down on the road, licking its bloody lips, and seemingly uninterested in going after Lex again.

David picked up the two remaining swords and staggered forward, pointing the weapons at Shay who surveyed the situation with a blank expression.

"Congratulations," Shay said, lowering the hood of her red rain cloak. She lifted her face towards the rain. "You fought well."

"Thanks," David said, edging closer to her.

"What a pity it wasn't enough," Shay said. She turned around and jerked a thumb at the pack of warriors in the distance. "As you can see, the cavalry is coming. And you can't beat them all, not even with the ferocious Frankie Boy at your side."

She looked over at Eda.

"You belong here with us," Shay said.

Eda pressed the blade tighter against Lex's throat.

"Didn't you say in the Roosevelt that you'd banish me if I refused to be Helen of Troy?" she said. "Well I refuse."

Shay cackled with laughter.

"It's too late to refuse," she said. "You made the decision to become Helen and there's no going back once you've said yes. You don't leave the Waldorf until there's a baby growing inside you. You're being selfish Eda. Think about it – that's one more life, a great man or woman to incorporate into our future society. Have you forgotten why we're doing this? We're doing this to save our species and all you can do is think about yourself."

"Why are you still pretending?" Eda said. "Why are you still making out that this – all *this* – is about the glory of rebuilding the human race? That's bullshit. I know you Shay and I know what the real goal is here for you."

"What are you talking about?" Shay said. "This is..."

"Knock it off for God's sake," Eda said, cutting in. "I'm not stupid or blind Shay. I was there. I saw the look in your eyes when you stuck the knife in Mitford's back. My God, I've never seen you look so alive. Never. Now compare that to when you were looking at those kids in the Roosevelt – at your future utopia. The great dream! You know what I saw then? Nothing. If anything Shay, you looked bored."

Shay's eyes lit up. "Eda..."

"Murder," Eda said. "Simple old fashioned murder. That's what Shay's Project is all about. You're using all of us – the gardeners, the warriors, all the Helens – to run one big giant factory of revenge that serves no one but you. Right? You lost your family in the war – your husband, kids, your dogs and all those nice vacations at the beach. Gone. The war took everything from you and you're angry about it. You're so angry that when you survived, you dedicated the rest of your life to getting revenge on those responsible. You can't kill all those men by yourself though right? So you built the Complex to do it for you. Don't pretend that this place is about life Shay – that's an insult to all the ambassadors and warriors that died for you. The Complex is all about death and revenge. *Your* revenge."

Shay stood like a statue with the rain streaming down her face.

"The Project *is* a noble cause," she said.

Eda glanced down at Lex who was floating in and out of consciousness every couple of minutes or so. Right now it looked like she was out but Eda wasn't taking any chances – she kept the blade pressed tight against the warrior's throat.

"Noble?" Eda said. "Is that how you sleep at night? You try to convince yourself that it's all about the kids?"

Eda peered over her shoulder. The other warriors would catch up with them soon enough. There were about ten of them in total closing the distance, still running at a fast pace and with their curved swords drawn and ready. Eda was only too aware of how these women were going to react when they saw the state of Lex and the other two.

"You're Helen of Troy," Shay said. She was also looking back at the reinforcements on the horizon. "Come back with me now. You have no choice in the matter."

Eda shook her head. "You're going to let me go."

"No," Shay said. "That's impossible."

"You have to let me go," Eda said, "If you don't I'll make sure all the warriors know the truth about this place. I will. Everyone here loves you Shay because you've given them a purpose – they think they're working towards something bigger than themselves and it keeps them going from day to day. The gardeners are clueless – they still think there's only one Helen and that the curse is real, but at least they've got a dream to beat the curse. That's why they get up in the morning and work so hard. The warriors at least know the truth about Helen but they're still in the dark too – they think that little utopia you've got going on in the Roosevelt is the end goal. Bullshit! Shay's revenge is the only end goal there ever was. What do you think they'd say if they found out that you're using them?"

"They would never believe you," Shay said. "And you know it."

"I'll make them believe me," Eda said. "If it's the last thing I do and it just might be. I might not be very convincing as Helen of Troy but I'm damn good at persuading people, even you."

"What do you mean?" Shay said.

"Do you really think I give a damn what knife I use to kill some-one?" Eda said. "That's ridiculous. And yet back in the hotel I made you think I did. That's why you left the room to go fetch Lucia while I told David the truth. Remember?"

Shay laughed softly. She exchanged silent glares with Eda and it felt like a long time passed before she finally said something.

"Maybe we can work something out," she said.

Eda squinted her eyes.

"Like what?"

Shay sighed. She blinked rapidly like there was a stinging pain loose in her eyes.

"I want you to become an ambassador," she said. "You can leave New York and still be a part of the Complex. I want you to walk across this country Eda and see for yourself what they did. You don't ever have to come back here, on one condition."

"What?" Eda said.

"If you find any men who fought in the war," Shay said, "you send them to New York. You send them to Helen of Troy."

Eda's brow creased. "You want me to send men here?" she asked. "To their death?"

"They carry too much darkness with them," Shay said. "And that makes them unsuitable." She raised the hood of her rain cloak and her stoic features were hidden once again. "That's the best offer you're going to get Eda."

14

Eda and David walked west along Lexington Avenue.

The rain had at last eased off and the blanket of thick clouds that had looked so permanent was now breaking up nicely. Somewhere up ahead, in between those blue pockets of sky, an unknown America was waiting for them.

Frankie Boy trotted briskly at their heels, a silent four-legged shadow.

The three travelers passed by a long line of familiar faces gathered on both sides of the street. All the assistants, including Linda, Gillian, Nicola and Lucia, were there, blank-faced and detached. The warriors were there too, still seething about what had happened to Lex and their two comrades. Fortunately for Eda, after striking a deal about becoming an ambassador, Shay had dissuaded the warriors from killing Eda and the others on the spot.

The hatred clearly lingered in the women's eyes.

It was there on Lex's face too. She was still bloody and dazed but she was at least back on her feet. At that moment, it looked like a stiff breeze would decapitate her. Eda even found herself pitying the woman a little. Lex had been unconscious at the end and as far as Eda was aware, she still had no idea that she was, like so many others, a pawn in Shay's elaborate revenge plan. Maybe Lex wouldn't have cared to know anyway. Would anyone? The women in Manhattan had a home, a familiar routine and a safe environment to live in. The truth was perhaps an inconvenience they were better off without.

The modest farewell ceremony had been arranged in a hurry. It had to be kept as quiet as possible because the majority of the other women in the Complex, those who still believed in the curse, couldn't know that it was taking place. As far as they were concerned, Eda Becker had skipped town a long time ago.

Eda had protested the ceremony; it seemed a ludicrous suggestion considering what had just taken place. And yet Shay insisted on it anyway. All the ambassadors were given a farewell ceremony on their way out of town. It was tradition. Mostly however, Eda suspected that Shay wanted to show the others that Eda wasn't really leaving the Complex.

She was an ambassador now. She was still one of them.

Shay was waiting for them at the end of the line. She stepped out to meet the wary-looking travelers.

A long, tense look was exchanged between the two parties.

"Farewell," she said. "Safe journey to you all. I expect to hear your name on the lips of future visitors Eda."

Eda lowered the hood of her rain cloak. There was still a dull ache throbbing on the side of her head where Lex had punched her.

"I might not find anyone," Eda said.

"You will," Shay said, a half-smile on her lips. "You have no idea what's waiting for you out there. One day, you'll realize what you left behind here Eda. And you'll be sorry."

Shay stepped aside, allowing space for the three travelers to move on.

As they left the Complex behind, Eda's eyes darted back and forth towards the commercial and residential buildings. Was it really over? She couldn't help but look out for the tip of a wooden bow poking out of an open window. She listened for the sudden, high-pitched whooshing noise of an arrow let loose.

Would she feel the sensation of something sharp impaled in her neck? Any second now...

Eda didn't say anything to David. For the most part, they walked in silence.

After about thirty minutes of walking, Eda stopped and turned around. A long stretch of empty road rolled back for miles, flanked by towering skyscrapers and car wrecks that blemished the streets like litter.

It *was* over.

She stood there, letting it sink in.

"Are you okay?" David asked,

"Yeah," Eda said, as a few light raindrops landed on her head. She was alright, but there was still a tight knot in her guts that reminded her this wasn't going to be the happy ending she'd hoped for.

"An old friend of mine is still trapped back there," she said. "I liked it better when I thought she'd run away. But I guess she's made her choice."

David looked back in the direction of the Complex. He nodded thoughtfully.

"And you've made yours," he said. "No regrets, right?"

"None," Eda said without hesitation.

She turned around and along with her two companions, set off towards the dark ruins of postwar America.

The fog of a gloomy afternoon closed in around them.

Eda shivered and glanced over at David as they walked. She could see the same fear on his face that she felt in her heart, but it was too late to doubt. They had nowhere to go back to.

They could only go forward.

THE END

THE SINNERS (AFTER THE END 2)

For Bill...

1

"Shut up," Eda whispered. "Just shut up, will you?"

David's voice came back at her – a faint vapor of familiarity drifting across the darkness. Somewhere in the close confinement of the tunnel, his whisper turned into a shout.

"What did you say?" he said. "Eda?"

Eda shook her head. She knew he couldn't see her but she did it anyway.

"Nothing," she said, staring into the pitch-black.

"Were you talking to me?" David said.

Eda shook her head again. "No."

"But what...?"

"Forget it David," she snapped. "I thought I heard something that's all. Let's get moving, alright? This place is...never mind, let's go."

"Sure."

Eda kept walking. It wasn't the first time she'd imagined footsteps or voices on her tail and it wouldn't be the last either. Ever since they'd set foot in the Lincoln Tunnel things hadn't felt right. A permanent unease had lingered amongst them like an uninvited companion. Where was the relief Eda had been hoping for? She was out for God's sake. Where was the happiness, the joy at breaking free from New York? Damn it. Wherever the elation was, it wasn't in the tunnel alongside the travelers. But there *was* something else in there, Eda was sure of it on a purely instinctive level. In the absolute silence, she could hear it breathing, just a few paces behind her. Walking when she walked. Stopping when she stopped. Sometimes she felt a gust of breath blowing on the back of her neck.

But whenever she investigated, there was nothing there. Nothing at all.

It was the darkness playing tricks with her mind. She had to keep telling herself that over and over again, repeating it like a mantra.

The alternative was to go crazy.

Thank God they were more than halfway through the one and a half mile long tunnel, which was located under the Hudson River. This creepy underwater bridge, shrouded in darkness, would transport them from Manhattan, New York, to a place that David apparently knew well, somewhere called Weehawken, in the old state of New Jersey.

"Frankie Boy?" Eda said. "Are you still there?"

Silence.

"Frankie?" she said, a hint of panic creeping into her voice. "Don't wander off for God's sake. Not in here of all places."

Then she heard it. The sound of the dog's paws skipping over the roadway towards her. A light tap-tapping, accompanied by the repetitive sniffing noise Frankie made as he took in some new, unfamiliar scent in the air.

"Good boy," she said. She reached down and found his back. It was a tiny oasis of warmth inside the icy tunnel.

"How long David?" she asked.

"We're nearly there," David said. His voice sounded further away, like he'd kept on walking while Eda had waited for Frankie Boy to catch up.

"I think this place is getting to me," Eda said. "It's like some giant haunted cave, don't you think?"

"Try to relax," David said. "Take slow, deep breaths. It's just the tunnel playing tricks with your mind. I was the same the first time I came through here and I did it alone. Not being able to see two inches in front of me – it nearly drove me bonkers."

"Bonkers?" Eda said.

"Yeah, you know. Mad. Crazy. Off my head."

"Never heard that one before," Eda said.

David laughed and it felt like the tunnel was shaking underneath them. "I grew up with an Englishman remember," he said.

"Yeah," Eda said. She wasn't in the mood to talk about David's hybrid accent or his upbringing. "Well I'm right on the edge of goddamn bonkers. How long?"

"You just asked me that," David said.

"Yeah?"

"Not long to go," David said. "Hopefully no more than fifteen minutes if we keep a steady pace. Trust me, it's worth it if we keep pushing on and don't think too much. We're nearly out. And once we are, New York and the Complex will feel like a bad dream."

Eda groaned. Fifteen minutes. It might as well have been fifteen days.

They kept walking.

About a minute later, Eda heard David curse up ahead as he walked into the back of yet another abandoned car. It wasn't the first time either one of them had had a collision. There were a lot of cars sitting in the tunnel in silence, like a fleet of ghost ships from a distant era. Eda imagined that people back then, not knowing what else to do, had driven into the tunnel to hide from the madness of the city. Now their vehicles were still here, cloaked in darkness. Sometimes Eda caught a glimpse of an impending trunk at the last minute and barely avoided a collision. Mostly she knew nothing about it until she'd walked into the metal and taken the hit. Pain took a backseat to frustration. It was something else to slow her down. Afterwards, Eda would use her hands, feeling her way around the car, trying not to think about what might still be inside.

That was easier said than done.

Judging by the stale rot that permeated throughout the tunnel, they were walking through a giant, underground graveyard.

There were patches of occasional debris under their feet. As Eda and David stepped over these, a sickening crunching sound filled the air. It was a blasphemous noise. Eda had by now climbed over a small mountain of bones and if the ghosts of all those car owners were still in the tunnel then surely she'd pissed them off big time.

It was enough to make her walk faster.

When the light of the exit finally appeared up ahead, Eda groaned with relief. Throwing caution aside, she hurried outside and reveled in the gray, overcast sky that greeted them. They both stood there for a while, basking in the dull light of either late morning or early afternoon.

It had been a long day so far.

"Thank God," Eda said. She ran a hand through her long dark hair. Despite the cold she'd felt inside the tunnel, her forehead was hot and damp with sweat.

There was also a dull pain throbbing around Eda's temple. That was the spot where Lex had punched her. Her jaw ached too. That brutal struggle in Manhattan was still fresh in body and mind and despite what David had said earlier, it would be a long time before Eda could simply pass it off as a bad dream.

At the very least they were out of New York. That was official.

"Alright," Eda said, adjusting her eyes back to daylight. She looked over at David, who was no longer just a voice in the tunnel alongside her. His wounds from New York added up to no more than a few minor facial cuts. He was smiling, clearly in good spirits.

Frankie Boy strolled ahead, his black tail wagging gently back and forth.

"I think you're in the best shape out of all of us," Eda said, looking at the dog. "Talk about not giving a shit."

She turned back to the gaping jaws of the Lincoln Tunnel – three black holes, toothless and bleak, that dared to invite them back to New York. Above each tunnel, a huge advertising billboard looked down at the travelers. The images on each billboard had long since faded into insignificance.

"Let's go," Eda said.

The road led uphill into Weehawken. There were more cars sitting on the road as it curved steeply away from the Lincoln Tunnel entrance. At first glance, it looked as if this pack of vehicles had just emerged from the New York side and had paused for a moment before continuing on into New Jersey. But in reality, these rust-covered carcasses had been lying there for years. Going nowhere.

Eda didn't get too close.

"So this is home for you?" she asked David as they walked up the hill.

"Yeah it is," David said. "Not Weehawken specifically but New Jersey. I've moved about over the years but somehow I always end up coming back home. It's like a magnet. It pulls me in and I guess..."

"Frankie!" Eda said, cutting David off.

The big German Shepherd had strayed too close to the abandoned cars. Although it was unlikely there was anything to fear – at least anything that was alive – Eda didn't want to take the chance that someone else, someone who wasn't just a pile of dust and bones, was waiting inside one of the vehicles to ambush the newcomers. Dead bodies were harmless in comparison to the living.

Even though they'd left the Lincoln Tunnel behind, Eda still had the strange feeling that she was being watched. As she climbed the hill into Weehawken, her claustrophobia had morphed into a sudden attack of agoraphobia.

She walked faster.

"Are you alright?" David asked, catching up with her. "You look a little bit pale if you don't mind me saying."

"I'm just getting used to things," Eda said. "I thought a change of scenery would be easier than this."

"You'll be alright," David said.

Eda looked at him as she walked at speed. "So where do we go from here?"

"I know a place where we can lay low for a few days," he said.

"Once we get there we can put our heads together and come up with a long-term plan."

"What is it?" Eda asked.

David smiled. "It's my quiet place," he said. "Somewhere green, without a ruined car or a smashed window in sight."

"Sounds good to me," Eda said. "Is it far?"

"There's a bit of walking involved. But it'll be worth it, I promise."

"Alright then," Eda said. The thought of a long walk didn't bother her, not as long as it was taking them further away from New York. A quiet place sounded just right.

The rotten scent that Eda had encountered in the tunnel lingered in the air. It was like the breeze was coated in decay; now it followed them like a shadow.

They made their way onto a large road, which the signs called the 495. After that they walked west for about an hour. Eda's legs became tired quickly but the thought of David's quiet place encouraged her to push past the fatigue, to say nothing of exhaustion. The quiet place had turned into a fabled paradise in Eda's imagination. It was glorious. Nothing she saw along the way of a shattered world could discourage her from the ideal of perfection that awaited them.

They walked slowly, veering off the 495 and traveling through a town called Secaucus. It felt small compared to the enormous skyscrapers of Manhattan but despite superficial appearances, the emptiness inside was identical. Broken-down vehicles lined either side of the street, some of which had the driver and passenger side doors lying open, as if inviting further investigation. Eda declined the invitation.

Shattered glass peppered the sidewalk. Eda stepped over the gleaming, crystal-like shards and was immediately reminded of the crunching noises she'd heard inside the Lincoln Tunnel when she'd walked over the bones of the dead.

Eda noticed that David's initially brisk pace was slowing down too. His feet looked like they were sinking into the road with each step.

"You getting tired?" Eda said. She hoped he'd say yes.

David nodded but he kept his eyes on the road ahead. "I forgot how far it was to the quiet place from the tunnel."

"The adrenaline is wearing off," Eda said. "I know the feeling. Hey, how about this? Maybe we should rest somewhere in between here and your quiet place. There's no rush to get there, right? It doesn't have to be this afternoon. It doesn't even have to be today when you think about it. Not unless this quiet place of yours is moving."

"Yeah okay," David said. "We'll keep moving for now and stop in a little while. Okay with you?"

"Sure," Eda said.

They walked through Secaucus and at the edge of town, came to a long bridge that crossed over a broad, dark blue river. Once they were standing on the bridge, Eda knew that they'd found a good place to stop. She felt safe up there. It was the elevation – standing atop the bridge, Eda and David were high above all the houses and cars and everything else of the old civilization that stretched out for miles on either side of the river. Nothing could touch them on the bridge. It was like standing on the roof of a skyscraper in New York, safely out of reach of danger.

Looking down, the water was calm and tempting. But Eda would never go in to cool off, not even on the hottest of days. She knew that large rivers such as this one had been used as mass graves during the war years. Below the surface, the riverbed was fat with human remains. The surface, so blue and appealing from afar, would smell old and rancid.

The water level was high at the moment and Eda wondered how many times this particular river had spilled over its banks and rampaged through the empty town with no spectators to witness it wreak havoc upon the neighborhood. Even if it flooded today, Eda, David and Frankie Boy would be safe up on the bridge.

"What about here?" Eda said, calling out to David. "This is the best hotel I've seen so far in all of New Jersey."

"Here?" David said. He looked around, seemingly unconvinced. "You don't want to cover a little more ground before we stop?"

Eda shook her head. "We've got food, water and blankets," she said. "It's safe up here. I say we sleep and recover a little and then start up again early in the morning. Your quiet place – it isn't going anywhere is it?"

"You really want to stop here?" David said.

"Yeah," Eda said. Her eyes roamed over the bridge and nearby surroundings, and she was yet again assured of its strategic advantages. They wouldn't find anything better than this. Anything safer. "If we stop in the middle it offers us a great vantage point. We can see for miles on all sides and if anyone or anything shows up to say hi, we'll see them before they can get close."

"Still think we're being watched?" David said, smiling.

Eda shrugged. "I need to sit down," she said. "Fully digest everything that's happened today. You know?"

David nodded. He slid Eda's backpack off his shoulder and held onto it by a single strap. They'd taken it in turns to carry the bag so far; it contained all their supplies, a modest bundle of food and water and amongst other things, two rolled up blankets, which had been fastened to the front.

They walked to the middle of the bridge and sat down on the road. Eda put her back up against the sturdy, stone barrier and sighed with relief.

David ran a hand back and forth over his tired calf muscles. "I'll never get up now," he said.

"No need to get up," Eda said. "We rest. Start again in the morning."

They ate the leftovers that Eda had taken from the Waldorf Astoria. Before the hastily assembled farewell ceremony, Eda had helped herself to as much food as she could carry – enough for a few days split between the two humans and Frankie Boy.

She offered some cold vegetable stew to Frankie Boy who devoured it in seconds. Then she poured out a small bowl of water, which she set down on the road.

Conversation was sparse. Exhaustion settled into their bodies and minds and when the small talk began to dry up, no one went out of their way to prolong it. Both David and Eda lay down on their blankets. It wasn't much of a bed but as far as Eda was concerned it was a slice of heaven on Earth. She would sleep well here.

"Wait till you see it," David said. His voice was sluggish as he drifted off. He was looking up at the gray sky that shielded the stars from view. "I should never have left the quiet place. Everything's so much better there. You'll see..."

"Then why did you leave?" Eda said. Her eyelids were closing over fast.

"Itchy feet," he said. "Curiosity. Adventure. The usual. Same things that always get me into trouble."

A minute later, David was snoring lightly. Eda rolled over onto her left side and saw Frankie Boy curled up beside her on the blanket. The last thing she did before falling asleep was slide her dagger out of the crumpled backpack. After that, she closed her eyes, wrapping her fingers around the handle and laying the weapon flat against her chest.

———

In the morning they had a quick breakfast, gathered their belongings and set off towards the quiet place.

Eda felt refreshed after the long rest. As they traveled in a westerly direction, she set a swift pace that David matched stride for stride. There was a renewed sense of purpose in the traveling party now that the horrors of New York had faded ever so slightly further into the background.

Frankie Boy walked a short distance ahead, probing the surroundings like a well-trained scout.

After about six hours on the road they reached the city of Paterson. Paterson looked like it had been hit by a bomb and of course it had many times over. But walking through the city, Eda thought the destruction looked fresh – like it could have happened yesterday. Nobody had tried to rebuild over this since it happened. Debris of all kinds – bricks, stone and glass – were scattered all over the streets and sidewalks. The burned out shells of cars were everywhere, some of them skeletal and barely upright.

David stopped in the middle of the street. There was a strained expression on his face as he spun around, taking it all in.

"I remember this," he said. "When it happened. All the noise and confusion – the shouting and screams. The worst screams you could ever imagine Eda. It all happened right here."

"You lived in this city?" Eda asked.

He looked at her with an embarrassed smile.

"Think so," he said. "I can't remember to tell you the truth. All I remember is running with a gang of street kids in a place that looked just like this. A big city in New Jersey – how could I forget the name?"

"I grew up in a city," Eda said. "I don't remember what it was called either."

David sighed. "They were right when they called it the wild years," he said. "The things I saw Eda. I've never been so scared in all my life and yet I had to act tough if I didn't want to be one of the victims. There was no way I could have kept that up for long. It would have worn me down sooner or later."

"You got out?" Eda said.

"Yeah," David said. "Thank God, one day someone found me. He took me and some of the other kids and got us the hell out of here. He saved our lives. Took us somewhere better."

He looked at Eda.

"Can I ask you a question?"

"Sure," Eda said.

"Are you really going to do what Shay asked you to do?" he said. "Are you going to become an ambassador for the Complex, find men and lure them to their death in New York? I mean, it's none of my business but why should you? You're free of those women now – you can do whatever you want without having to satisfy Shay's bloodlust."

Eda shook her head.

"I don't know," she said. That was the truth. She hadn't really stopped to give it much thought since leaving Manhattan. "I'm not going to go out of my way to look for anyone. But at the same time, if I ever meet some gaping asshole who deserves it then why not? It's an ugly way to die, that's for sure."

David nodded. He pointed to the backpack on Eda's shoulder.

"Want me to carry that for a while?"

"Nah," Eda said. "I'm good."

"How are our supplies?"

"We're not going to starve or die of thirst just yet," Eda said. "But we'd better think about topping up soon or we just might."

David's eyes fell on the road that led west. "We're close to our destination."

"So tell me," Eda said. "What exactly is this quiet place of yours? You're not giving much away you know."

"I'm not?"

"No."

David laughed, jerking a thumb over his shoulder.

"There's a massive stretch of wetland that way," he said. "It's like a big wooded swamp, that kind of thing."

Eda shrugged, which made David laugh again.

"It's about as far from New York City as you can imagine," he said. "There's a beautiful river that runs through it, trees, flowers, and things growing like that. Great Piece Meadows – that's what it was called before the war. I call it my quiet place. It's not like anything we're walking through right now. Not like Paterson or New York. In the quiet place, everything looks just like it did before everything happened. You'd never even know there'd been a war. Nature takes care of you in there. There's deer. Rainwater. It's got everything you'd ever need to survive."

They traveled west out of Paterson and onto a long stretch of blacktop highway with surprisingly few vehicles on it. It wasn't long before Eda saw a vast ocean of trees looming in the distance. This blurry, mirage-like vision was every bit as inviting as the bright blue river of Secaucus. This time however, Eda was going to take up the invitation.

After walking for another twenty minutes straight, they came to a small, winding road that ran parallel to the highway. David led them along this road until gradually they began to enter the wetlands of Great Piece Meadows.

But before the swamp took over completely, the travelers passed by the remains of a few shack-like houses. These tiny abodes were lined up neatly on both sides of the road, the last hint of old civilization to be found in the region. From there, the path into the swamp narrowed further and the trees got larger and closer. For Eda, it was like walking into a different world and so far at least, it felt welcoming in a way she'd never encountered before. New York, Paterson and all the concrete skylines in her mind began to recede slowly, figments of a dream fizzling out in the morning sunshine.

Muddy puddles leaked out of the lush greenery and spilled onto the road. It was as if the swamp was trying to escape from itself, one tiny piece at a time.

"Great Piece Meadows," Eda said, stepping over one large trail of mud. "So this is it? This is your quiet place?"

There was a smile on David's face. His eyes drank in the environment, filling him up.

"You can see the appeal right?" he said. He stopped and held up a hand. "Listen. What do you hear?"

"Nothing," Eda said.

"Exactly. Best sound you'll ever hear."

"Uhh, sure," Eda said. "It's different, I'll give you that much. And right now, anything different is good."

David kept walking. "Don't worry," he said. "You'll like it here."

It was a while before either one of them spoke again.

Eda peered into the swamp from the road. She couldn't see anything in between all the trees and the long, overgrown grass. It looked like the Meadows didn't want to be found.

"You really lived in there?" she asked.

"I sure did," David said. "It's not quite as empty as it looks from out here on the road. There are a lot of animals living in the Meadows. There's life everywhere you look, even if you can't see it at first. I have weapons stored away – bows, knives. I've got plenty of traps too. We can..."

"Shit!"

Eda jumped when Frankie Boy started barking. She knew that bark, fierce and frightened all mixed into one head-splitting noise. It was a warning. The dog's body was as stiff as a board, the tail erect. He was facing the swamp head-on, barking at a blanket of trees and jungle grass.

Eda crouched down beside him. Her heart sped up as she stared into the swamp.

"What is it Frankie Boy?" she said. "There's nothing there."

David stepped over beside them and Eda straightened back up. They stood side by side, frozen on the narrow path, staring into the swamp because they knew that Frankie Boy wasn't barking at nothing. But they couldn't see anything, just a dense blanket of foliage swaying back and forth to a gentle breeze.

"C'mon boy," Eda said. She patted Frankie on the back several times, hoping he'd snap out of it. "Let's keep walking. We'll go..."

Eda was interrupted by a rustling noise in the distance. Like something big pushing through the trees.

They heard the distinct sound of twigs snapping under feet.

"David?" Eda said. "Is that a deer?"

David shook his head. "I don't think so."

Eda looked harder, not allowing herself to blink.

There was something there, directly up ahead. A man's face had appeared in a small gap in between a couple of bloated tree trunks. He was looking at them through the gap, staring at the travelers with a calm, unblinking expression. The man was so perfectly still that Eda thought she might have been looking at a statue. And then he moved. It was like watching something step out of a dream and set foot in the material world – a two-dimensional image slowly coming to life in the three-dimensional realm.

More twigs snapped.

The man came through the Meadows, gliding towards them like a phantom.

And he was smiling.

2

The man was dressed in a brown and green camouflage jacket and matching pants. His black boots, along with the rest of his clothes, were drenched in layers of age-old mud. Eda's first impression upon seeing the manner of his clothing was that he was a former military man. Looking past the clothes and more at the man however, she suspected that wasn't true. It was pure instinct. Eda still retained memories of the street platoons from the wild years, just before they lost control of the streets to the mob. They were big, scary looking men and women. To a frightened little girl they were like giants and Eda used to spend hours watching them patrol the streets in their khaki-colored tight tops. She recalled their obscene biceps bulging underneath the sleeves as they clutched onto their semi-automatic weapons with grim determination.

The most frightening thing of all about the soldiers was the blank, robotic look in their eyes. It was like a uniform stare that had been programmed into every single one of them. Whatever they'd absorbed in those dead eyes, it wasn't pretty.

The man in the swamp didn't have that killer look about him. He was a bag of bones. Emaciated. It looked like a stiff breeze would knock him off his feet and keep him down for days.

As he walked towards the road, Eda and David kept perfectly still.

The man's skull was bald, at least on top. In contrast, lank gray hair spilled down from the back and sides, flowing beyond his shoulders. His appearance was odd and incomplete – it looked like he'd been interrupted while shaving his head and that he'd never gotten around to finishing the job.

"Hello friends," he said.

He was still walking forward, very slowly.

"Don't be alarmed. I mean you no harm."

He held up both hands like he was surrendering to the travelers. His voice was nasally and he possessed a distinct accent. The accent wasn't unlike David's but then it wasn't quite the same thing either. Eda imagined that from now on she'd have to get used to hearing things like that – different accents, new words – if she was going to travel the country.

David nudged her on the forearm.

"Look," he whispered. "Behind him."

There were five other people standing where the bald man had first appeared. They might as well have materialized out of thin air. There were three men and two women, all in either their forties or fifties. Eda noticed they were all dressed in the same camouflage clothes as the bald man. Likewise, their hands and faces were freckled with mud.

They came forward, staying close behind their leader. Moving at a careful pace, they approached the edge of the narrow road where Eda, David and Frankie Boy were waiting. Eda felt uneasy at this slow motion welcoming committee. Watching these people slip through the cracks in the swamp, it was like witnessing the emergence of a long lost humanoid species that had been living apart from the rest of the world.

Eda tilted her head back and inhaled. There was a pungent, not unpleasant odor in the air. It was the smell of dirt after heavy rain.

"Welcome to our home," the bald man said.

He stepped onto the road and glanced briefly in both directions, as if checking to see if there was anyone else catching up.

Eda took a closer look. The man's skin was an unpleasant, withering gray. This combined with his skeletal frame and bug-like eyes, gave him the appearance of a freshly reanimated corpse. When he looked at Eda, it took everything in her power not to turn away.

He pointed a finger at her, then at David and Frankie Boy.

"Three souls," the bald man said with a trying-too-hard smile. His canine teeth were crooked and long. "Is that all?"

Eda nodded. "We're travelers, just passing through."

The man raised a wild-looking eyebrow. "Passing through here? In the Meadows?"

"Yeah," Eda said. "Why not?"

"What brought you down here?" he asked.

Eda couldn't think of an answer. David wasn't in a rush to speak either.

"Food?" the bald man said. "Did you come here because you wanted to hunt game on our land?"

David glanced at Eda and then turned back to the man.

"*Your* land?"

"Yes," the bald man said. "*Our* land."

"Okay," David said. " Well then, I've spent some time out here before, on and off. I suppose we came back to rest and to hunt a little."

"And yet no bow that I see," the bald man said. He was pointing back and forth between Eda and David. Eda wondered if the pointing would ever end. Every time he did it, she felt like she was being stabbed by a pocketknife.

David shook his head. "No," he said. "But I have other tools hidden in the..."

"And the dog of course," the bald man said. Now he was pointing at Frankie Boy again although he kept his distance. "Yes, yes. I'd say that creature right there is your best chance of catching a meal in this swamp of ours. The animals are plenty, but they're sly and they know how to survive. But I dare say that dog would make a fine hunter."

"A fine hunter," Eda said. "Sure."

The bald man clapped his hands together in one resounding strike.

"But there's no need for you to hunt," he said. "Or the dog. You can eat with us and that's not something we're offering to just anyone these days. But I trust people of your generation. I trust them far more than I would strangers of my own. You were children when it happened. You know nothing of the corruption that led up to our demise."

He smiled.

"What I'm saying is, that I'm willing to help you if you are of course willing to trust us."

It was David who spoke.

"Excuse me," he said. "But how long have you been living here? I've never seen anyone else in the Meadows before. I always thought it was deserted."

"Most of us have been in here since the wild years," the bald man said. His large, swollen balloon eyes expanded as he looked intently at the younger man.

"I always thought I was alone in here," David said.

"Or perhaps just left alone," the bald man said. "Hmmm? It's a big place the Great Piece Meadows and there's room enough in here for those who are peaceful and non-threatening to our particular way of life. But there are so few visitors these days that we don't really encounter alternative viewpoints. And we're quite happy with that."

Eda glanced back down the long stretch of road. The highway wasn't too far away, not if they turned around and started walking now. The quiet place wasn't as quiet as David had thought it was. Bad luck. Maybe they were better off sticking to the roads and trying to find somewhere else to lay low for a while.

"Come with us," the bald man said. His small flock of companions stood a few feet behind him, lined up in a neat row. They were all smiling. All silent.

"Stay a few hours or spend the night if you wish," the man said. "Eat and rest. You're more than welcome. The end of civilization doesn't mean we have to forget good manners. Right?"

David looked at Eda.

"What do you think?" he asked.

There was no point in pretending.

"I don't think so," Eda said. She blurted the words out and was well aware of how blunt it sounded. After an awkward pause, she looked at the strange man and the others. The camouflage posse. They were so uniformly polite and attentive in response to her bluntness. She struggled to find the right words – to articulate how uncomfortable she felt in a way that wouldn't cause offence.

"Thank you for the offer though," she said. "But maybe we should just keep walking. Take advantage of the weather while it's dry. What do you think David?"

David hesitated. "Sure," he said. He glanced back and forth between the strangers and Eda. "If that's what you want. Although…"

"What?" Eda said. This time it was her tone, not the words that were blunt.

David pointed to the backpack hanging off Eda's shoulder.

"Supplies *are* low," he said. "We only took a few days worth of food and water out of New York with us, didn't we? Maybe it's not such a bad idea to…what I mean is, maybe these good people wouldn't mind helping us out in terms of refilling our supplies. We can always hit the road later today or tomorrow, you know?"

Eda nodded. It was a mechanical gesture.

"Yeah."

With a nod of the head, the bald man gestured into the woods behind them.

"We have plenty of food," he said. "You're more than welcome to share a meal with us. And we can certainly spare some supplies for your onward journey, be that later today or in the morning or whenever you wish to depart."

He looked at Eda.

"You have nothing to fear from us young lady," he said. "We're merely survivors of a great disaster, just like you and your friend. We are a shy community here. Very shy. We're a peaceful people and I suppose you might call us religious of sorts – we stay deep in the woods, we worship our god and avoid the lingering madness of cities and towns. Everything we need is here. Right here."

The other strangers came further forward. Now they stood along-side the bald man, forming a camouflage line. In the process, a small channel opened up in between them that led into the swampy background.

It was an open door. It was the invitation.

"My name is David," David said. He stepped forward and then turned back to Eda. "And this is Eda. We've come from New York. And we gratefully accept your offer of hospitality."

The bald man lowered his head in greeting.

"My name is Frank Church," he said in a quiet voice. "But for as long as I remember people have called me Baldilocks."

"Baldilocks?" Eda said. "Are you kidding?"

The man chuckled and pointed to the top of his perfectly round, gleaming skull.

"It's not hard to guess why is it?" he said. "Bald head, long hair at the back and sides – of course. Very clever, yes? Of course, it was designed as an insult. It was done to mock me. But for some strange reason my friends, I kept the name. Now I wear it like a badge of honor. Why? It reminds me that nothing lasts forever – that what we fear is but a fleeting shadow. All the jokers are dead. Yet I'm still alive."

He laughed, as if suddenly aware that he'd lapsed into a speech. But even as he laughed, Eda saw a hint of anger flare up in his eyes and she noticed how it lingered there, long after he'd stopped talking.

"Forgive me my young friends," he said. "Sometimes I get lost in my own head."

3

Eda, David and Frankie Boy were taken further into the swamp.

It felt like they were entering a lost realm, something secret that shouldn't have existed anymore. This was the greenest place that Eda had ever seen or imagined. Easily. Central Park was one thing but the towering New York skyline was so overwhelming that it would never let Eda forget that the park was a blip, a mere oasis of green encased within a concrete giant.

Great Piece Meadows.

It was both a beautiful forest-like structure and a grimy sea of swampland. As they walked through it, the sky was mostly clear but as always the threat of rain was never far away. Eda kept her head down, trying to get used to walking over the soft and squishy surface of the swamp floor. She heard the loud sucking sound of feet being pulled out of the mud, a constant reminder that the terrain had taken a heavy soaking recently.

They were deep inside the swamp now. It was a brown and green maze and it was hard to tell exactly how the camouflaged strangers could so easily navigate their way through such a dense landscape and one that was an endless mirror image of itself. But they were doing it. Eda had a feeling these people could probably find their way around the swamp with their eyes closed.

"We're close to the river," David said, calling out to those at the front of the line. "Aren't we? Maybe a little too close?"

"Don't worry," Baldilocks said. He glanced over his shoulder at the travelers. "Our camp isn't located anywhere near the water. The constant flooding means we have to keep a respectful distance at all times. As you know, the rain comes hard. It's almost spiteful in its attack. In all our time here though, it's never been enough to make this place inhospitable. In fact, the swampy conditions are a blessing of sort – they keep other people away. Mostly."

He smiled and turned back to the front.

They hiked west for another twenty minutes and eventually reached the camp. What Eda saw there far exceeded her expectations.

The strangers had built their home inside a massive clearing. It was essentially a tiny village in the heart of the swamp. There were two rows of wooden huts scattered on either side of the settlement, adding up to about forty buildings in total. A narrow lane ran in between the two rows, just like a regular street, only this thoroughfare was built of grass and mud instead of asphalt or concrete. And the traffic was human.

Eda noticed wooden number plates hanging from a piece of string on each door. The numbers had been scrawled in childish handwriting with red paint.

The cabins themselves were about twelve by fifteen feet at most. They'd been built on a sturdy foundation of two fat, stumpy pillars poking out of the dirt. The cabins had gable roofs and had obviously withstood the elements for many years, providing shelter for this strange little community that had set up home in a harsh environment that couldn't have been anything other than challenging at the best of times.

Eda took it all in, nodding in silent appreciation. They'd chosen a good spot, keeping their distance from any obvious signs of washout and erosion, which were both indicators that moving water had run through the area. The village had also been built on a slightly elevated region of the Meadows and there were sloped areas on all sides, which would provide runoff after rainstorms.

As Baldilocks and his companions returned to camp with the visitors, people began to emerge from their cabins to take a closer look. The human traffic on the road, carrying supplies and buckets of water, stopped what it was doing too. Gradually, several people walked over to greet the visitors; they were smiling and some of them were even clapping their hands as if Eda and the others were long lost friends who'd returned home after a long absence.

The camp was full of people of all ages – mostly in their middle to later years but there were some teenagers and a scattering of younger children too. Eda still hadn't gotten used to the sight of young people, not after all the time she'd spent in New York swallowing Shay's lies about the curse. It was refreshing to see youth on display, even if they were still in the minority. Everyone in the camp had camouflage jackets on, although these came in a multitude of shades – bright green with brown, muddy brown with pale yellow stripes and many other varieties.

Eda and David were led over to a long, communal wooden table at the edge of camp. Two benches ran down either side and to keep the rain off the table, a four-legged canopy had been erected.

The visitors sat down. Almost immediately, people began bringing out large plates of food and placing them in front of the two guests. Eda glanced at the offering with interest. There was some sort of reddish brown meat, as well as several plates of vegetables. Water jugs were set down on the wood with a hearty thud. Somebody poured a glass for Eda and she thanked the server and then drank it down quickly. She was thirstier than she'd realized. She drank a second glass, then filled a spare bowl and lowered it down to Frankie Boy, who was at her feet.

"Eat, drink and rest my friends," Baldilocks said in his strange, musical accent. "Welcome to our home in the Meadows."

"Thank you," Eda said, looking around. "I like what you've done here. It's impressive."

Baldilocks bowed in gratitude.

"We've made plenty of mistakes along the way," he said. "Boy did we ever. It took us a few attempts to find the right spot to settle down. There were two other sites before this one but we got flooded out each time. We learned – learned what we needed to do to keep the water away. Now it's perfect."

Eda jabbed a thumb towards the villagers. "Did everyone come from the city?"

"We were all city people once," Baldilocks said. "But not anymore. These days we call ourselves the Children of Nature. The Children, for short. What we shared and still share was a common goal of escape from the city. The emphasis, ever since the war, was to get away from those urban hellholes – the polluted towns and cities and everything and everyone that was ever associated with the war. We chose to start again here, to return to a simple life dictated by the basics. And thanks to the Great One, we've been blessed with the opportunity to do that here in the Meadows."

Eda's ears pricked up. Great One? Was he talking about God? She recalled some of the women back at the Complex who spoke about God and how some of them used different words to refer to what sounded like the same thing. But Eda had never heard the term 'Great One' before.

It piqued her interest, but she said nothing.

"How many people are here?" David asked, tearing into a slice of dry meat. He sat forward, his elbows propped up on the table. Eda noticed that he was enjoying the constant attention of the people around him, as well as the food and what felt like an atmosphere of muted celebration, inspired by their arrival.

"Seventy-four in total," Baldilocks said. "There were more of us originally but we've had more deaths than births over the past five years. Such is the way with an older population."

A tall, slim woman brought over yet another large water jug and placed it on the table. But this woman, instead of retreating backwards like the other servers, sat down on the bench beside Baldilocks. She smiled across the table at Eda. Her long hair was white – it was the whitest hair that Eda had ever seen before. Not gray, but the color of fresh snow. Eda couldn't tell whether it was real or dyed. She still looked relatively young – in her late forties at most.

"Drink up," the woman said. "You must be thirsty after your long journey."

"Thank you," Eda said, reaching for the jug and pouring out another glass for herself. She checked Frankie Boy's bowl and topped it up.

"You're welcome," the woman said. Her voice was deep, almost masculine in tone. "What's your name?"

"Eda."

Eda offered her hand and the white-haired woman reached over the table and shook it. She didn't even look at David.

"I'm Number 10."

Eda screwed up her face. "Number 10?"

Baldilocks sat watching the two women, laughing softly to himself.

"Of course," he said. "How strange it must seem to an outsider."

"Just a little," Eda said.

Baldilocks pointed to the villagers. Those who weren't occupied elsewhere stood within earshot of the table, ogling the visitors with their eyes.

"There are no names amongst us," Baldilocks said. "Not anymore. Myself excluded of course."

"Why not?" Eda said.

"We rejected them," Baldilocks said, turning back to the table. His tone was lazy and matter-of-fact. "And now we reject everything about the past. Everything. Our old names have no relevance to our new lives."

Eda put her empty glass down on the table. She scoured the banquet with her eyes and although she was hungry, none of the food tempted her.

"Why didn't you give up your name?" Eda said, glancing at Baldilocks.

"I did," he said. "Frank Church was my name. I rejected it because it has no meaning for me anymore. But I wear my new name with pride. You see I'm the joke that lived through the End War. I was the clown, the one who wandered the streets holding up a sign and warning them what would come. I *knew* it would come. What did they do? They spat and called me many names. But I always hated Baldilocks the most – the jokers really took to that one back in the day. Oh yes they did. How the world turns, hmmm?"

David took a break from eating.

"How have you survived in here for so long?" he asked, wiping tomato juice off his chin. "I mean, with so many mouths to feed. It must be hard going."

It was Number 10 who answered.

"Simplicity," she said. "Like the animals, we ask for no more than what is necessary to survive. We live off what he provides for us. We have water and we hunt a minimal amount, always looking for the weak, old and sick animals. We have a few vegetable gardens – it's not much but it's enough."

"Yes," Baldilocks said, nodding along to every word. "And we are thankful for your safe arrival my friends. Despite our retreat from the outside world it's good to know that there are still some people out there. Young people especially. The uncorrupted."

Eda's eyes darted back and forth between Baldilocks and Number 10. As they spoke, she could hear boots squelching in the mud behind her as the Children went about their business.

She took a deep breath.

"Who is the Great One?" Eda asked.

The table fell silent. Eda noticed David looking at her with a mildly troubled expression, making her wonder if she'd committed a grave error. Then he went back to shoveling food in his face with all the enthusiasm of someone who hadn't eaten in a week.

Baldilocks took a sip of water and placed the glass on the table. He ran a finger back and forth around the rim in concentration.

"The Great One is Uncle Sam," Baldilocks said. "He's the one who spoke to me in the past and forewarned me of the End War. He's the one who speaks to me still."

"God?" Eda asked. She spoke in a whisper. "Are you talking about God?"

Baldilocks shook his head.

"The God you speak of abandoned us a long time ago," he said. "You can't blame him for that. We fell too far and so he closed the door on his creation for good. However, he left behind an empty throne and before long there came another to deal with the mess of humankind. This other was brutal in his tactics."

Baldilocks pointed towards the ground.

"He lives down there."

"He lives in the dirt?" Eda said.

"There's a place near here," Number 10 said. "That's where he resides in darkness. With any luck he'll stay there and let us live out our lives in peace. The End War was like a giant meal for him and he's satisfied, at least for now. But it's up to us to keep him satisfied. We must *keep* him satisfied. To love, respect and fear him. That way, we might turn his wrath away from Earth and he'll go back to whatever dark corner of Hell he first crawled out of."

Eda glanced at David. He looked like he was only half-listening to their hosts, such was the level of food distraction in front of him.

"How do you keep him satisfied?" Eda said.

"We go to him," Number 10 said. "To the place where he lives – a giant crater near Fairfield. Biggest you ever saw. We go there and we give thanks, amongst other things."

"That's it?" Eda said. "You just go there and say thanks."

"Like I said," Number 10 said. "Amongst other things."

Baldilocks ran a hand over his skull, sliding it through the dirty gray hair that sprouted from the back and sides.

"Do we sound like mad people?" he said. "Of course we do. But you're quite young both of you – I don't imagine you remember much about the war."

David shook his head. "Just the aftermath."

"The wild years," Baldilocks said. "A second End War of sorts, only we were fighting amongst ourselves that time."

Eda pointed to the villagers. "What did all these people do before the war?" she asked. "Jobs and things?"

"We were all kinds of people," Baldilocks said. "Some of them carrying water buckets over there were once big shots in Paterson and Jersey City. They made a lot of money, had families, two cars and a nice house. Their lives fit nicely into that old world model. The American Dream. They paid their taxes and put their trust in the governments and authority figures. Not for one minute however, even at the height of the pre-conflict crisis, did they believe that the war would happen. They put their trust in the wrong people. While I was on the street, a homeless bum telling them the truth, they listened to the people they trusted, the ones that wore expensive suits while they lied."

His upper lip curled into a snarl.

"And you?" Eda said. "Who were you?"

"I was nobody," Baldilocks said. "I was an English immigrant, an outsider from the get-go. In later years, I was the madman who walked the streets of Jersey City with a sign that said 'The End is Nigh'. I did that day and night. I used to carry another sign too and it said that 'Uncle Sam will be the death of us all'. They didn't realize that I knew. I *knew* what was coming."

Baldilocks pointed at a curly-haired man who was carrying a large plastic container towards one of the cabins.

"Number 28," Baldilocks called out. "Who was I before? Before all this?"

Number 28 stopped what he was doing and looked over towards the communal table. All of a sudden he roared with belly laughter. It was an enormous sound, enough to make Eda jump slightly in her seat.

"I remember," Number 28 said, yelling back over. "Crazy Baldilocks, that's what we used to call him. What *I* used to call him. Used to laugh at him on my way to work every day = the mad bastard going up and down the street, holding up his sign. I used to see groups of kids sitting on the wall on the opposite side of the street from where he patrolled. They were all laughing at him but they were too scared to get close. The local loon, that's what he was. You were only what back then? Twenty-five? Thirty?"

Baldilocks managed a feeble nod.

"The way they used to look at me..."

Number 28 walked over and his fat hands fell on the table.

"Turned out we were the crazy ones," he said. "One day I saw it with my own eyes – the war this mad bastard had been predicting for years. The same war that all the suits said would never happen. And Baldilocks walked out of that war unscathed, not a scratch on his face. When we were all homeless, he had this look on his face that said I fucking told you so and he was right – he did fucking tell us so and what did we do? We laughed at him for it."

"For those of us who survived," Number 10 said, leaning forward on the bench, "it was a wake up call. There was no ignoring him after that."

Baldilocks watched the others intently as they spoke. His lips moved, as if he was repeating their words silently to himself.

Then he turned back to Eda.

"They were dropping bombs all over Jersey," he said. "Newark, Jersey City, Paterson, Edison – and not one of those places played any sort of strategic role in the war. Not one. When the bombs came, when there was no more help from the outside – that's when they realized that I was more than just a street bum. Their overlords didn't care about them. They couldn't help them and like I always said, the end *was* nigh. Savings, a big house and a fancy car meant nothing. The bombs, Jesus Christ, they were hitting everything and everyone and nobody even knew if it was *their* planes or *our* planes dropping them. I guess, it didn't matter if you were on the ground."

Eda shifted uncomfortably in her seat.

"People began to listen to him at last," Number 10 said. "I was only a kid back then but it was like I grew up overnight. Holy shit, everyone's childhood ended all at once. My mom was the only other survivor in my family. She apologized to Baldilocks like everyone else. Well if I'm being honest, she downright begged for forgiveness and asked what the hell she was supposed to do next to keep me safe.

When Baldilocks declared an exodus out of the city, nobody hesitated to go with him."

"It was Uncle Sam who proposed the exodus," Baldilocks said. "I was merely the vehicle through which the message was communicated."

"Why here though?" Eda asked. "Why a swamp?"

"I knew the Meadows well," Baldilocks said, pouring himself another glass of water. He topped up Number 10's glass too. "My family moved to Jersey City from London when I was around ten years old. My dad used to bring me here fishing and hiking – he was a real outdoorsman and some of my happiest memories are of this place. I felt safe here. I still do."

David looked at Baldilocks.

"How did you know?" he asked. "That it was going to happen. What I mean is, why did you start carrying those signs before the war?"

Baldilocks stared back at David.

"A long time ago," he said, "when I was a young man, I heard it for the first time. It was an incredible experience – a voice whispered in my ear. Like a dream. It told me that we were a cursed species and that a time would come when Uncle Sam would wreak havoc upon the world. Unless of course, they repented. I tried to warn people but nobody repented."

"So Uncle Sam lives under a giant crater?" Eda said. "He's full up now?"

Baldilocks narrowed his eyes and looked at Eda. He looked like someone who was checking to see if the other person was making fun of them.

"Why don't you let us show you where he lives?" Baldilocks said, chuckling quietly. "See it for yourself, hmmm? I know what you both must be thinking. Who the hell are these crazy people living in the middle of the swamp? You must think us mad."

Eda didn't want to stay there much longer, let alone go visit their god. But she couldn't think of the words to get out of it.

"Spend the night here," Baldilocks said. "We have a few cabins spare and you're more than welcome to sleep and rest up after what must have been a strenuous journey from New York. First thing tomorrow, we'll show you where Uncle Sam lives. Trust me, it's like nothing you've ever seen before."

"I don't know," Eda said, shaking her head. She caught a glimpse of the dense swampland that surrounded them and felt a sinking feeling inside. Even with David's knowledge of the Meadows, they were at the mercy of their hosts when it came to finding their way back to the road. "I think maybe we should be..."

"Is it far?" David asked. He was looking at Baldilocks.

"Not too far," Baldilocks said. "We go to Fairfield via the river. We've got some wooden canoes tied up on the bank not far from here. It's rather a pleasant journey you'll find."

"But we should really get going," Eda said, looking at David. "Don't you think?"

Her voice felt like a whisper that wasn't being heard.

Baldilocks responded first. "Of course," he said. "Do what you think is right Eda. Don't listen to us rambling on and on. You're more than welcome to fill your bag with supplies on the way out. We'll take you back to the road if you'd like to get moving now. Are you sure we can't tempt you? It's quite safe here I assure you. We can show you where Uncle Sam is tomorrow and then we'll drop you off on the highway no later than noon. Last offer, going...going..."

David's eyes lit up. There was a hopeful smile on his face that turned Eda's stomach.

"Sounds fascinating," he said. "I'd quite like to see this crater."

"You really want to?" Eda said to David. "Don't you think we should be...? You know? Moving on."

"I'm curious that's all," he said, dividing his attention between Eda and their hosts. "Live a little Eda. You won't find anything like this in a book, that's for sure."

Eda sighed and leaned her elbows on the table. The sigh sounded like a whistle escaping slowly through her lips.

4

That night, Eda, David and Frankie Boy slept in one of several vacant cabins located at the far end of the village.

They'd been taken there not long after the conversation had dried up at the communal table. The visitors were left with some food and drink and a mountain of blankets. After that, the Children left them alone for the rest of the night. The plan was that they would meet up at breakfast the next morning and from there they'd be taken to Uncle Sam's crater near Fairfield. The one that David so badly wanted to see.

The cabins were sparse in terms of interior decoration. There wasn't much room for anything except two handcrafted beds inside, which took up the majority of space. Eda threw her blankets onto the bed, leaving a spare one for Frankie Boy, which she dropped onto the floor and crumpled up a bit for him. Frankie Boy took up the offer, grateful to have somewhere quiet to curl up and close his eyes. The noise of camp had exhausted him as much as it had Eda.

For the rest of the day, Eda and David lay on their beds. Eda's limbs felt like they had lead weights inside and she didn't think she could move again, even if she'd wanted to. Fortunately she'd paid a visit to the bathroom – behind a bush – before climbing into bed.

Afternoon turned to evening. The light in the forest flickered out gradually as Eda listened to the strange noises coming in from outside. The Children began to move into their cabins and loud conversations fizzled to silence. The occasional spurt of birdsong lasted long into darkness. The space in between, that was filled by the listener's imagination.

"They're trying to convert us," Eda said. She was unsure of whether David was asleep or not. "You know that right? You get what they're trying to do here?"

She heard him turn over on the bed.

"What did you say?" he asked. His voice was lazy and sluggish.

"The Children want us to join them," Eda said. "They want to turn us into Uncle Sam worshippers just like they are. Why else would they be so keen to take us to this crater where their god lives? Or is it meant to be a demon?"

There was a short pause.

"Nah," David said. "You're imagining it Eda. They're weird but they're harmless enough, don't you think? We'll be back on the road by tomorrow afternoon."

"I hope so," Eda said. "What's with all that Uncle Sam crap anyway? Do these people really worship a giant hole in the ground? They don't seem that crazy to me."

Another pause.

"I guess so," David said. "I quite like them. I can't believe I've never ran into them in here before."

"Listen," Eda said. "Here's the plan. We'll grab supplies off these guys first thing in the morning. Fill up the bag till it almost bursts. After that, we go with them to look at this hole in the ground that they love so much. We act impressed, we're polite and all that but we don't stay too long. Right? We'll tell them we need the daylight and that we've got to keep moving. Hopefully we get that in first and they'll realize there's no point in asking us to join their cult."

"Right," David said. "Any idea where we're going next? We could go find the weapons I've got hidden in the swamp. What do you think?"

Eda's eyes remained glued to the ceiling.

"I want to get out of the swamp," she said. "Let's just get back to the road, okay? See what else is out there."

They fell asleep soon afterwards.

The next morning, after a light breakfast, a small party set off towards Uncle Sam's crater. About fifteen of the Children, led by Baldilocks and Number 10, accompanied Eda, David and Frankie Boy through the swamp and on the trail that led back to the road. From there they walked east, parallel to the large highway that Eda, David and Frankie Boy had traveled out of Paterson on.

Eda's boots and khaki pants were covered in mud. Her rain cloak wasn't much better off. It was fast becoming tiresome having to wrestle her feet out of this hostile terrain every second or third step. Nature didn't want her here. That suited Eda – she didn't want to be there either. The swamp was sending a clear message to the city girl – *get the hell out.*

The Children didn't seem to notice the difficult conditions anymore. With their camouflage clothing, they glided through the swamp, blending into the scenery effortlessly. It was like they'd always been there, like their ancestors had lived in the Meadows for a thousand years before them.

They came to a halt on the banks of the Passaic River. The river was a wide stretch of dirty brown water that meandered for about eight miles through the swamp lowlands of New Jersey. The trees hung low here, stooping over as if reaching towards the surface of the water for a drink.

Five upturned canoes sat at the edge of the water. The canoes had been secured on the riverbank with rope, tightly wrapped around the nearest, sturdiest tree trunk. The rope was taut. It looked ancient and exhausted, but in times of flood it had probably worked wonders in terms of preventing the boats from drifting away.

The canoes appeared to be in good condition. They were made of wood and each one possessed a well-rounded hull with five planks showing on either side. They were hardy-looking vessels with the scars to prove it.

Some of the Children rolled up their sleeves and after untying three of the canoes, they began to push them into the murky water. Baldilocks, Number 10 and a few others jumped into the lead boat. One of the men picked up a couple of single bladed paddles off the floor. He handed one to another passenger and the two paddlers began to direct the tiny vessel over the river.

Eda, David and Frankie Boy were escorted into the third canoe with two other women. Eda didn't know their numbers. She didn't ask.

The canoe drifted gently onto the shallow water, following the two leading boats. As instructed by one of the women, Eda and David sat on the bench in the middle with Frankie Boy slouching at their feet. The women sat at front and rear of the canoe, sandwiching their guests while they paddled further away from the riverbank.

It was Eda's first time on a boat and yet despite the strange sensation of land receding behind her, she enjoyed the sensation of the canoe gliding along the Passaic. It felt light and unreal, like movement inside a dream. The trees that lined the edge of the bank resembled huge and ancient beings, leaning closer, hoping to hear a secret pass from the travelers' lips.

"The river must flood a lot," Eda said, looking at how close the water level was to the land. It wouldn't take much for the Passaic to spill its banks.

"We stay away when it floods," the black-haired woman at the front of the canoe said. Her voice was stern, like her expression. "You want to survive here? Rule Number One. Respect the environment."

"Yeah," Eda said. As far as she was concerned, Rule Number One was applicable anywhere.

They traveled northeast on the Passaic, mostly in silence.

A chorus of screeching sounds filled the sky. Eda looked up and watched a flock of large white birds flying by – she'd never heard or seen anything like it before. It was like another world. Eda had read something once about the River Styx – the river in Greek mythology that acted as the boundary between the Earth and Hades. She imagined that sailing down the Styx was much like this, cruising downstream in the Passaic, accompanied by an extraordinary feeling of isolation.

In the lead boat, Baldilocks was sitting on the center bench, deep in conversation with Number 10, whose silky white hair blew backwards in the breeze.

The little armada moved at a swift pace. After moving north it dipped south again and sailed underneath a couple of highways, leaving the Meadows altogether and coming out into a sedate, urban setting. A short while later, it came to a stop in the place that the Children called Fairfield.

The three canoes pulled into the edge of the riverbank. The Children disembarked quickly, stepping out onto a bed of lush grass that was a far cry from the sludge-like terrain deeper inside the Meadows. The paddlers dropped the paddles inside the canoes. After dragging them further onto land, they turned the boats over and headed inland.

Eda stepped onto the riverbank, followed by Frankie Boy. David was lagging a few paces behind.

"Did you enjoy that my friends?" Baldilocks asked, turning back to his guests. "No matter how many times I make that journey it never gets old. Hmmm?"

Eda and David both nodded.

"I always find the river to be a wonderful source of contemplation," Baldilocks said. He was looking at Eda. "Really clears the mind."

"I suppose," she said.

"But as wonderful as that was," Baldilocks said, "it's nothing compared to what you're about to see. Are you both ready?"

"Yeah," Eda said. She forced a smile onto her face. "Ready."

"Let's go see this thing," David said.

There was little talking after that. Eda and David played along, adapting to this mood of hushed reverence that the Children had adopted on their way to the crater. It was as if they were walking on sacred ground.

Eda and David followed at the back of the group. They walked through a forest-like stretch at first, consisting of a thick wall of trees and an explosion of overgrown foliage. After a few minutes, this led them onto a tiny, secluded street. A faded sign told them the street was called Riverside Drive. There were several small houses, mostly one-story buildings peering out from behind a jungle of long grass in the garden.

With Baldilocks and Number 10 leading the way, the traveling party walked up the driveway of one of the houses, jumped a short wooden fence at the back and then from there climbed up a short, grassy incline that eventually brought them onto a long, winding stretch of empty road.

"Uncle Sam," Baldilocks said, stepping ahead of the group. He was pointing straight ahead, beyond the road.

Eda took one look and her jaw dropped.

"Oh my God," she said. "You've got to be kidding me."

David stepped ahead of her, shuffling forward like a sleepwalker. He went ahead of all the others too, including Baldilocks.

"That's...that's incredible."

Even Frankie Boy, who'd been enjoying the hike at a leisurely pace, stopped dead when he saw it. The dog let slip a low growl and then he fell silent, staring off into the distance, mesmerized like everyone else.

Baldilocks stepped out ahead of the pack again. Then he turned around and faced his audience. His brow creased as he nodded his head slowly.

"This is where you'll find him," he said. His voice was quiet, like somebody was sleeping nearby that he didn't want to disturb.

Eda couldn't take her eyes off it.

It was a giant crater. It was the biggest thing she'd ever seen and probably ever would see in her life. The small party stood about a hundred meters away from where the rim of the monstrous hole began. And from there it stretched back as far as the eye could see. Eda imagined that a long time ago, a giant had knelt down here and scooped a massive chunk of the world away with a shovel. How many millions of tons of earth had been displaced in its creation? It was at least a couple of hundred feet deep. The diameter was perhaps as much as a thousand feet.

The Children began to file across the road towards the crater. Eda only moved when David nudged her gently on the arm. They followed but their steps were tentative, as if wary of getting too close.

"What could do such a thing?" Eda whispered to David.

"Something a little stronger than that dagger you've got strapped to your waist," he said.

Eda didn't laugh. Instead she touched the hilt of the dagger, which hung from her belt under the rain cloak. Somehow it comforted her.

Baldilocks took large, exaggerated steps towards the crater's edge. His arms were spread wide open like he was greeting an invisible friend. The other Children were close behind and together they walked down a steep, rocky hill that brought them down to the lip of the crater. Baldilocks was the first to arrive. He stopped and turned around, watching the others catch up with him. Then he noticed that Eda, David and Frankie Boy were still hanging back on the road.

"Come down my friends," he said, calling up to them with his hands cupped over his mouth. "Uncle Sam has no plans to disturb us today."

"That's reassuring," David said. And then in a louder voice that Baldilocks could hear, he cried out:

"It's that big bloody hole that worries me though."

"Oh yeah?" Baldilocks said. "What about the big bloody hole?"

"I've heard things about the bombs that made holes in the ground like that one," David said. "Stories. They weren't ordinary bombs, were they? There were other risks."

"You're talking about radiation," Baldilocks said. "Aren't you?"

"I am," David said. "How do you know it's safe to stand so close to that thing?"

"I don't," Baldilocks said. The question appeared to bore him. "What I do know is that we've been coming here for years and there hasn't been one instance of radiation poisoning amongst the Children. Okay? Look at the trees over there my friend and remember the flowers we saw on our way here today. Life grows on in Fairfield. Maybe it wasn't a nuclear bomb at all. Maybe it was. Why worry about it now? If it's dangerous, you're already exposed."

Eda and David exchanged worried looks.

Baldilocks beckoned them closer.

"Tread quietly friends," he said. "He's right underneath us. Sleeping, but always aware."

Eda and David looked at one another. David made the first move, lifting his leg over the metal barrier and slowly descending the rocky hill that led down towards the crater. Eda followed, keeping close to Frankie Boy in case he bolted in the wrong direction. At the moment that was any direction. Most importantly, she didn't want him getting too close to the edge of that hole. She had no intention of getting close herself.

Damn it, she thought. To hell with Uncle Sam, whatever it was supposed to be. God, demon or delusion. Eda's most pressing concern lay ahead of her. How would Baldilocks and his followers take it when Eda and David rejected the inevitable offer to join the Children? They'd brought them to the crater for a reason – to see it up close. Perhaps Baldilocks thought the crater's magnificence would clinch the deal. No such luck. Eda hoped things weren't about to get ugly in swampland but the old man didn't strike her as someone who took bad news well. Not in the slightest. At the very least, Eda and the others would be cast out into the Meadows with no guide to lead them back to the road.

A trickle of sweat ran down Eda's forehead. She wiped it away quickly before anyone noticed.

The Children gathered somberly around the hole. Their feet were so close to the edge that it felt like someone was twisting Eda's insides into tight knots when she looked at them. How could they stand there like that? Staring down into its jaws. One misstep, one heavy gust of wind or a dizzy spell later and they'd be goners.

Eda stopped at the bottom of the steep slope. She was about twenty feet away and that was near enough as far as she was concerned. She kept a firm hand on Frankie Boy's back, squeezing harder on the coat to deter him from approaching the bizarre scene unfolding nearby.

When David saw Eda stop, he did the same.

"I know what you're thinking," he said. "What the hell are we doing here? Sorry, I never thought it would be like this. Hey, at least the crater's impressive, right?"

"Yep," Eda said, talking through gritted teeth.

The Children held hands with one another. They stood in a straight line with Baldilocks in the dead center. By now, he no longer appeared interested in Eda and David. Eda was grateful at least that Baldilocks hadn't summoned them over. The thought came to her as she stood there that along with David and Frankie Boy, she could make a break for it. Maybe steal one of those canoes and get back to the highway. It wasn't far from here. She could almost feel the blacktop highway under her feet again, wide open spaces on either side, and nowhere in the world she had to be.

But Eda decided against it. Just a little longer. Let them hold hands and stare into the hole. Sing songs, do whatever it was people like this did. Hopefully they wouldn't ask anyone to convert until they got back to camp and by then, Eda would be a long way from that hideous chunk of missing earth.

"It's time!"

Baldilocks dropped the hands of the people standing beside him. Slowly, he raised both arms and held them out in a straight line, pushing his fingertips a few inches over the edge of the crater.

"Great One," he called out. His voice trembled with awe. "Uncle Sam. Thank you, oh thank you for watching over us, your Children, as you do. Thank you for delivering us from harm every day and allowing us the room to be better. Thank you for the food and the water that sustains our simple existence far from the maddening past. Please accept our daily gratitude for everything you do. For allowing this cursed species to repent."

"Thank you Uncle Sam," the crowd murmured as one.

"We will never forget," Baldilocks said, taking a step back. "And we will forever be your Children."

"Amen," the crowd said.

A long silence followed. The Children's heads remained bowed and their eyes tightly closed. It was like every one of them was engaging in a silent dialogue with Sam.

Baldilocks was the first to break away. He turned around and walked over to Eda and David with a stern expression.

"Now you know," he said.

Eda's posture stiffened up. She sensed it coming any second now.

Will you join us?

But it didn't happen. Baldilocks didn't ask them to join the cult, at least not yet. Without another word, he began walking back towards the road. The Children followed in single file. Eda noticed their solemn-looking faces – their eyes were still partially closed as if they were locked in a trance, but there was something else happening. A muted chant. One word, over and over again, drifting out of their midst like smoke from a fire. Eda couldn't quite make it out at first but as they got nearer, she caught it. One word. It had a hypnotic and sinister rhythm, slow at first and then as it went on, it sped up towards it climax.

"Sam."

"Sam."

"Sam."

"Sam-Sam-Sam."

5

Silence accompanied the three boats on the return journey. It felt like a sacred one so Eda, although full of questions, didn't break it.

As the canoes floated along the Passaic River, she visualized what would happen once they reached land. Back to camp, pick up their bags and start walking, with or without an escort. After what she'd seen at the Fairfield crater, Eda was beyond caring whether any of the Children were willing to show them the way out.

With any luck, Baldilocks and the others would see how eager their visitors were to leave. Then they'd abandon their attempt to convert anyone.

And once they'd left, Eda, David and Frankie Boy would be back on the highway by early afternoon at the latest. It would give them a few hours of daylight to walk, to put a few miles between themselves and Great Piece Meadows.

Baldilocks was sitting in the lead boat again. His eyes stared straight ahead as the canoe plowed its way down the center of the river and back towards the Meadows. A gentle breeze blew on what was left of his hair. It danced wildly, like pieces of old string attached to a skull.

Even the birds were silent on the way back.

When at last they reached the riverbank near the camp, the Children secured the canoes to the trees and turned them upside down, locking the paddles inside. All the while, the icy silence lingered, much like the plague of biting insects that followed them everywhere. Eda swatted the mosquitoes away. They always came back.

They trudged back to the camp where the rest of the Children were going about their business – carrying supply bundles back and forth, food preparation, sword sharpening and other routine tasks.

Eda hung back a little. While the others walked ahead, she reached out and grabbed David by the arm. She squeezed tight. Without looking at her, David nodded as if he understood the message. They had to get out of there and preferably before the uncomfortable question – *will you join us?* – arose. Nobody else said anything about them leaving. That meant it was up to them to bring it up first. Eda could see some of the Children bringing out plates and spreading them out across the communal table in preparation for lunch.

She shook her head. All offers would be refused. Politely.

"Let's get the bags," Eda whispered. She elbowed David gently in the ribs. "C'mon."

Eda's heart was racing and yet it was true the Children hadn't given her any reason to feel so uneasy. They seemed like good people – they'd taken the strangers in, fed them and offered them a comfortable bed for the night. They meant no harm – they only wanted to show off their god and yes, perhaps to convert Eda and David into Uncle Sam worshippers. But they must have thought that was the right way to live and if so, it was a kindness on their part to invite others along for the ride. There was nothing malicious going on. It was how they coped with the past and as Eda knew, anybody who'd survived the End War was grateful to be alive. Gratitude manifested itself a number of different ways. So they worshipped a hole in the ground. So what?

The swamp was harmless. She had to stop thinking that it was a giant net with no discernable exit.

David stood like a wooden board beside her. He bit his lip, chewing on it like he was trying to draw blood.

Eda sighed. She knew it was up to her to be the impolite guest. "Okay," she said. "Well, thanks for everything. I guess we'd better hit the..."

Nobody paid any attention to her.

Eda cleared her throat and tried again. A little louder this time.

"Hey," Eda said, not speaking to anyone in particular. Her eyes skipped back and forth, not wanting to single anyone out. Doing this, the little community turned into a blur. It was easier that way.

"I guess we'd better get going," she said. "Don't want to miss out on all that daylight. You know?"

Countless faces turned to look at her. The blur collapsed and she was met by a wall of blank expressions.

"Sorry," Eda said. What the hell was she apologizing for? "We've got a lot of walking to do and I think we'd better start covering some of that ground while we can."

Still, nobody said anything. They just looked back at her like she'd dragged a rotten carcass into camp and dumped it at their feet.

Eda didn't give a damn about picking up supplies anymore. All she wanted was the backpack on her shoulder and the feeling of movement again. To get out.

She turned to David for support.

"Right?" she asked.

But David said nothing. He was as white as a blizzard. Was he experiencing a private nightmare – the slow, churning dread of what they might do to him if he didn't pledge his loyalty to the Uncle Sam cult? Was he, in his mind at least, back at the crater, standing at the edge and looking down?

Whatever it was, it had rendered him useless.

"Yeah so we'll just get our bags and be on our way," Eda said. She'd already started towards the little cabin they'd spent the night in. Unfortunately it was at the far end of the village and she'd have to pass through the crowd to get there.

Frankie Boy walked faithfully at her side. She didn't know if David was behind her or not.

"Thank you for your hospitality," she said. She could feel them looking at her. Looking *through* her.

Baldilocks stepped forward, separating himself from the crowd. He blocked Eda's route towards the cabin. When she tried to walk past him, he moved with her, cutting her off once again.

"Not just yet," he said.

Slowly, he turned around and walked through the crowd. The Children parted for their leader like he was pushing them back with magic powers.

Baldilocks looked at Eda. Then he pointed to the communal table.

"Please sit down," he said. "This won't take a moment."

Eda glanced at the table and sighed. This is it, she thought. Conversion time. She threw a desperate look towards David who'd caught up with her at last. His eyes darted back and forth between Baldilocks and Eda. The way he looked, it reminded Eda of a phrase she'd read about once – *like a rabbit caught in the headlights*. Eda made a mental note to kick David's ass later. It was his call to follow the Children into the Meadows. He'd been the one who wanted to see Uncle Sam's crater. And now he was leaving it to her to sort out the mess they were in.

Fucking men.

"We have to go," Eda said.

"Just a moment," Baldilocks said. His voice was so quiet that she could barely hear it. "It's better if you sit down while I talk."

Eda knew there was no way around it. She walked over to the table and sat down with a disgruntled sigh. Frankie Boy lay down on the grass while David stayed on his feet, standing directly behind where Eda was sitting on the bench.

"Some water please," Baldilocks said, calling out to the crowd.

The Children's leader sat down opposite Eda and a painful silence passed until the water arrived. Baldilocks thanked the server, picked up the jug and poured out three glasses. He pushed two of them across the table towards Eda and David. David reached over and snatched his glass, draining it in one gulp like he wished it was something stronger. After that, Eda could hear him breathing behind her; it sounded like he'd just woken up from a nightmare in sweat-soaked sheets.

Eda was thirsty but she didn't touch the water.

"What do you want to say to us?" she said, looking at the man across the table. She would do her best to keep it polite.

"I took you to the crater today for a reason," Baldilocks said. As he spoke, he swirled the water in his glass around and stared at it. The dizzying motion of the liquid held his attention for at least ten long seconds. "I took you there to show you who we are. And now that you know, I have a question for you. Do you think we're crazy?"

"No," Eda said. "They way you live here, it's admirable. I respect what you've done."

"I wouldn't blame you," Baldilocks said, "if you thought we were a bit bonkers. Everyone who knew me in Jersey City thought I was mad. Stark raving mad. Most of them are either dead or they came here with me begging for forgiveness."

Baldilocks took a long drink of water. Then he slammed the glass down hard on the table.

Eda flinched, but tried to keep her composure.

"I don't think you're mad," she said. "And we're very grateful that you would consider us worthy of joining the Children and staying here with you. But the truth is, I've just left New York after being there for a long time with another community. I'm just not looking to settle down with anyone right now. I want to keep moving – no disrespect intended. Now, we'd like to leave and get back to the road. That's okay, isn't it?"

Baldilocks laughed. But it didn't last long and as the laughter subsided, his eyes hardened into two blocks of stone.

"Did I ask you to join us?" he said. "Did I?"

Eda pushed her glass away. Then she got up to her feet.

"C'mon," she said, directing the comment at David behind her. "Let's get our bags. Let's go Frankie Boy."

Eda began to walk away. Then she stopped dead.

About ten of the Children were trudging across the muddy road in the heart of the village. They were walking towards the communal table, all of them carrying short swords with a bright silver hilt and distinct leaf-shaped blade.

She heard a noise to her left.

On the other side of the table, another ten Children approached, all of them with swords in hand. And a mean look in their eyes too.

"You're surrounded," Baldilocks said. "Don't try anything silly now. It's a waste of energy, hmmm?"

Eda unsheathed the dagger from her belt anyway. She looked at the Children closing in on both sides, daring them to come closer.

"What's going on?" she said. "You won't let us go?"

Baldilocks shook his head. "There's really no need for this is there?" he said. "I hate violence. Really, I hate it."

He held up a hand. The Children on either side halted their advance and slowly, they lowered their weapons.

"We'll talk this over like adults," Baldilocks said. "It's for the best."

"Talk what over?" Eda said. "Just let us go. Okay? You can't hold us captive in here when we've done nothing wrong. Have we offended you or something? Are you afraid that we're going to tell someone out there about your home? Well we're not. It's none of our business anyway. David, Frankie Boy, let's go."

Eda stepped over the bench and backed off, still facing Baldilocks and his chilling, blank expression. She moved a few paces away from the communal table. Then she bumped into something sharp and stopped dead, her hands shooting up into the air automatically.

David was standing behind her.

The tip of his sword was pushing into her back.

Eda felt a rush of dizziness. "What the fuck?" she yelled.

David put a hand on Eda's shoulder and spun her around. He reached out and snatched the dagger out of her hand before she knew what was happening. He quickly tucked the weapon into his belt and then stared at her for a couple of seconds. His left eye twitched nervously. Eda saw regret in there, or at least she thought she did.

"What are you doing?" she asked. Her voice was tame, almost unrecognizable in its shock. "David! What the hell are you doing?"

"I'm sorry Eda," David said. "This isn't easy for me. But the Complex isn't the only community of survivors that sends out ambassadors to do a job. Only here in the swampland, we call them Seekers."

Eda shook her head, unable to stop.

"David...?"

He took a step closer.

"Back in New York you were smart enough to realize that I wasn't one of the bandits," he said. "It's like I told you, I met them here in Jersey on their way to New York. What I didn't tell you was that I went with them because I was Seeking. I was trying to single one of them out, lure him away from the pack and bring him back here. Of course, things didn't go to plan. But I stuck around New York because I knew there were other people – your people to be exact. I knew I'd find someone in the end."

"You dirty bastard," Eda said. "After what I did for you. I saved your life."

Baldilocks waved a dismissive hand in the air.

"Enough," he said. "We don't care about the details anymore. All that matters is that the Seeker has brought one last soul to us. You've done well Number 47."

"Thank you," David said.

"Number 47?" Eda said, gawping at David.

David leaned in closer. "Remember that Englishman I told you about? The one who raised me after the war?"

"Jesus," Eda said, turning back to look at Baldilocks.

No wonder David had been so quiet and unassertive over the past couple of days. So useless. He'd been biding his time, the son of a bitch.

Eda glanced at the tip of her dagger poking out of David's belt. If his sword hadn't been in the way, she would have made a grab for it there and then. After that, she'd stick it in his throat without hesitation.

"This wasn't easy for me," David said. "I like you Eda, I really do. All I can say is try to think of the big picture here. This isn't a community of crazy people like you think it is – we're trying to repair the damage of human history. We're trying to fix things because listen to me, Uncle Sam is real and he's right underneath that Fairfield crater. He's real and he can do whatever he wants with us whenever he wants. He's already wiped eight billion people off the face of the planet for God's sake. And how many are left? A few thousand? Less? If we don't appease the Great One, there's no way back for the human race."

"Sit down Eda." It was Baldilocks. "Please."

Eda glanced at Frankie Boy. The dog was leaning up against her, oblivious to the unfolding disaster.

"Sit down," Baldilocks said again.

Eda sat down on the bench. David stayed close behind her like an armed guard watching over his captive.

Baldilocks leaned over the table and Eda heard his camouflage clothes creaking. Either that or it was the old man's bones. There was a manic glint in his eyes as he spoke.

"We *have* to do this," he said, his fingers digging deep into the wood like he was hanging on for his life. "But take it from me Eda, nobody takes any pleasure in the act. I promise you."

"Just let me go," Eda said. "Please."

Baldilocks edged back into his seat. He shook his head.

"Everyone here remembers the *horror* of those years," he said. "The sheer horror of it. What they saw, the loved ones they lost and the manner in which they lost them. We're hanging on by a thread Eda. We're at his mercy, you, me, everyone. So, we do as he asks of us. Four souls a year – that's the price of peace."

Baldilocks was smiling again. It was like there was a switch going off inside the man, taking him back and forth between light and darkness.

"We're so happy to see you here," he said, staring into his empty glass. "Now all the pieces are in place for this year's ceremony."

Eda shook her head. "No."

"Don't try to fight it," David said. He put a hand on Eda's shoulder and she shook it off. He was standing so close behind her that Eda had to resist the urge to elbow him in the gut or somewhere even more painful. It was only a fraction of what he deserved.

"Just accept it," he said. "It'll be so much easier for you."

"This is bullshit," Eda said.

"With any luck," Baldilocks said, getting to his feet, "this year will be the last time we have to perform the ceremony. Uncle Sam told me from the start that this wouldn't be forever. Hopefully, we've repaid our debt and we can move on."

At that moment, Number 10 walked over to the table and sat down beside Baldilocks. She poured a glass of water and pushed it across the table towards Eda.

"Now you know," she said. "There's no longer any need for pretense."

"Tomorrow will be the day," Baldilocks said, walking around the table and stopping next to David. Now they were both standing behind Eda. "We'll delay no longer. Number 47, take the Sinner away and put her with the others."

"Let's go," David said. "Eda?"

He put a hand on Eda's shoulder for a second time and she flinched. His fingers felt like razorblades scraping against her skin.

"Number 47?" she said, looking over her shoulder. "I always hated that number."

"It's nothing personal," David said.

"Save it," she said, getting up to her feet.

Eda looked over towards the crowd. They were hovering in the distance, a sea of eyes staring back at her.

"It's a hole in the ground for God's sake!" she said. "You're going to kill me because a hole in the ground told you to?"

Baldilocks signaled to David.

"Take her away," he said. "And make sure she gets something to eat."

6

Number 10 escorted Eda to the hut where the other prisoners were kept.

The hut was about a hundred meters north of the village. It was a tiny building, surrounded by dense swampland and almost hidden by the trees, like a secret hideaway.

While Number 10 had led Eda out of camp, David had distracted Frankie Boy with scraps of food. The poor dog still believed that David was on their side. It was enough to make Eda wish that treachery had its own unique scent. If so, if Frankie Boy knew what was really going on, he would have ripped David, aka Number 47, to shreds.

It was a nice thought.

There were two guards standing outside the hut. They stood to attention as Number 10 appeared, leading Eda through the challenge of angry branches and mud puddles. The hut looked so small – it was more like a miniature storage facility in the middle of nowhere. There was one pentagonal window on the side of the hut, which would at least allow the early afternoon light to trickle in.

One of the guards opened the door. Eda was ushered inside and she ducked her head as she passed through the small doorway. A musty odor shot up her nostrils. The smell of dirty clothes. Inside, three people were sitting on a wooden floor, which was partly covered by a pile of worn out blankets. There was a man and a woman on one side, both in their mid-to-late forties, and an older man, perhaps in his sixties or even older, on the other. As the door opened they all looked up in unison and Eda saw the flash terror in their eyes. The old man looked at Eda and then sighed. He possessed a mop of curly white hair and a large white beard that covered his neck. The beard was peppered in brown specks of dirt and as he raised his hand to block the light that flooded in through the open doorway, Eda saw that his fingernails were caked with dirt.

"Now we have four," Number 10 said. She gestured a hand, signaling to Eda to take her place on the floor beside the others. "I've got a few things to do elsewhere. But I'll be back soon to explain what happens from here. Try to stay calm, this'll all be over soon."

Nobody said anything.

Number 10 stepped outside and the guards pulled the door shut behind her.

Eda sat down in between the couple and the old man. As she did, she heard the sound of someone twiddling a key in the hut padlock outside. Voices faded into the distance.

"Welcome to Hell," the old man said, looking at Eda. He offered his hand across the gap between them. "The name's Murphy. Joseph Patrick Murphy. Most folks call me JP. From Albuquerque, New Mexico."

Eda shook his hand. The skin felt coarse enough to be a dangerous weapon.

"Eda Becker," she said. "From...New York, I guess."

The man and woman on the other side of Eda were less forthcoming than Murphy. Nonetheless, after a moment or two, the woman smiled even though it looked like smiling was the hardest thing she'd ever done. She reached out a hand to Eda.

"I'm Becky," she said. "This is my husband Mike."

Eda took Becky's hand, then she offered her own to Mike. Mike took it but it was like shaking hands with a feather. It didn't take an expert to see that Mike was in bad shape. He was wearing a red shirt, unbuttoned all the way down to the waist. His ribs were poking out and his skin was a rotten dark yellow. As he sat on the floor, he was rocking back and forth on the floor ever so slightly. There was a blanket draped over his shoulders.

Eda shifted around a little, trying to find a spot on her own blanket that didn't feel or smell like stale puke. Something that looked like a cockroach crawled slowly towards a large ceramic plate in the corner of the room. There were a few crumbs left around the edges of the plate.

"So where did they find you Eda Becker?" Murphy said. He sat up, alert and interested. Eda heard his joints crack as he moved.

"New York," Eda said. "I guess they found me in New York."

Murphy nodded. "Man or woman?"

"Man," she said. "I saved his life – biggest mistake I ever made."

"Damn right," Murphy said, chuckling.

Eda glanced over at the disheveled couple to her right.

"What happened to you guys?"

Mike and Becky sat close, brushing up tight against one another. While Mike only had on a shirt and pants, Becky wore a thick water-proof jacket that was zipped up all the way to her neck. Every thirty seconds or so, she would glance at Mike with a concerned expression, as if keeping track of his condition.

"We were on the road," Becky said. "Heading back east. We're trying to get back to Boston, Massachusetts. Mike had a twin sister there once, long before the war."

"*Has* a t-t-twin sister," Mike stammered. "Has."

"Sorry babe," Becky said. "Has. They were separated as kids when their folks divorced. Mike traveled west with his mom. The sister stayed in Boston with her dad who apparently was a real asshole. Then the war happened and yeah...it's a twin thing I think. Mike's just gotta know...he's gotta know if she's still there."

"She's alive," Mike said in a croaky whisper. "I know she is."

"Why'd you wait so long to make the trip east?" Eda said.

"There were a few reasons," Becky said.

She ran a hand through her shoulder-length blonde hair. When she was done, Becky looked at her hand and cringed.

"When the time was right though," she said, "we set off and it was alright you know? It wasn't the great hardship I thought it would be, trekking across the country. We had food, we had water. You can always find somewhere to sleep. We hardly saw anyone on the road either – a couple of caravans migrating south, but that was it. Then we got to Jersey. We ran into someone not far from Paterson. A real nice woman, polite and considerate – you'd never suspect she was a loon agent from a cult in a million years, know what I mean? We'll feed you, she said. Give you water. Well that skinny little bitch found us at the right time. We were low on supplies and based on our earlier encounters with people on the road we were willing to trust her."

Murphy leaned his head over. As he did so, Eda could feel the man's hot, rancid breath blowing on her skin. He was wheezing, like his body was broken somewhere inside.

"Where did you folks say you came from again?" he asked. "Iowa?"

"Illinois," Becky said.

"Right," Murphy said. "Midwest."

"Illinois?" Eda said. "Isn't that like really far away?"

"Yeah I suppose," Becky said, taking Mike's hand in her own. With her other hand, she rubbed his forearm back and forth in a reassuring manner. Mike kept on staring at the floor with blank eyes.

"We were so close," she said. "So close to Boston and to finding out about Pam. As you can see, Mikey's taking it quite bad. This sort of confinement doesn't help either."

"Yeah you almost made it," Murphy said. The man's voice, a natural foghorn, dropped to a whisper. "Curse these damn sons of bitches. They're a devious mob – they send out the young ones with the innocent-looking faces. You see them on the road and there's no fear. No threat, no harm. You even hope after all that nothingness you've walked through that you might have met someone normal again. Jesus Christ, ain't that the truth? Someone good. What they're doing is taking advantage of desperate, hungry people. They reel you in and the next thing you know, you're here. And for what? The bastards haven't told us anything yet! Uncle Sam. A ceremony. What the hell does that mean anyway?"

"I don't suppose you have any news of Boston?" Becky said, looking at Eda.

"Sorry," Eda said. "As far as I know, there's no one left in a lot of those big cities."

They sat in silence.

Eventually, Becky turned back to Eda.

"So what about you?" she said. "What were you doing when they found you?"

"Getting away from somewhere," Eda said.

"Whatever it was," Murphy said, "it probably doesn't look so bad now. Right?"

Eda shrugged. "I don't know."

She watched the cockroach go to work on the leftovers.

"Where's home?" Becky asked. "You didn't sound too sure when you said you were from New York."

"I don't know exactly," Eda said. "It was a big city, not New York, but I don't remember what it's called. I left town with a small caravan when I was still a kid. Eventually I ended up alone again, and that's when I went to New York."

"Yeah you gotta keep moving," Murphy said. His back was pressed tight against the wall. "That's how I ended up so far from New Mexico. Movement – it's the only thing that keeps you alive anymore."

"There has to be something else," Becky said. "Something out there, somewhere..."

Murphy shook his head. "Maybe it's best you never reached Boston in the end."

Voices approached the hut. The four prisoners stopped talking and sat up straight. A faint whimper spilled out of Mike.

The door opened and Number 10 walked inside, leaving the two guards standing at the door. From outside, Eda thought she could hear a light rain tapping on the roof.

Number 10 wiped down the front of her camouflage jacket.

"Is everyone okay?" she said, looking at the four prisoners lined up on the floor. "I know, it's a stupid question."

She walked further into the hut.

"So now that we're all here," Number 10 said, "I'm going to tell you how this thing works. First of all, let me apologize to the three people who've been stuck in here for almost two weeks already – we've kept you in the dark, well quite literally at times. But the reason I haven't said too much is because I don't like having to explain this thing more than once for starters. But also, we think it's better if you don't know too much. Especially sitting in here all day and night. Anyway, now we're four. That means we're ready to go."

"Please tell," Murphy said. "I'm dying to find out."

Number 10 looked along the line of people on the floor.

"From now on, you four will be known as the Sinners."

There was a moment's silence, broken by the sound of Murphy's low-pitched laughter.

"The what?" he said.

"Sinners," Number 10 said, ignoring the misplaced hilarity on Murphy's part.

"W-w-what does that mean?" Mike said. He battled hard to get the words out and Murphy's crude laughter came to an abrupt halt. Stringing a simple sentence was like a Herculean task for Mike. The least anyone could do was be quiet so he could be heard.

Becky squeezed Mike's hand. "Yeah," she said. "What does that mean?"

"It means that tomorrow we make our annual offering to Uncle Sam," Number 10 said. "Sinners. That's what we offer him. We need four people to take on the role of Sinners and I'm sorry, but that's where you guys come in."

Murphy struggled up to his feet. His old bones snapped and he groaned like somebody was twisting a knife into his back.

"Fuck you," he said, breathing heavy. "Let me out of here, I'm sick of this shit."

The guards at the door heard Murphy jump to his feet. In unison, they spun around and took a couple of steps inside the hut, their hands on the hilt of their swords. Eda didn't like their vacant, machine-like eyes. It looked like they were bored and would welcome a little violence.

"Sit down," Eda said. "For God's sake."

"Yes," Number 10 said, staring back at Murphy. There was no fear in her eyes. "I'd do that if I were you."

Murphy glared at the two guards with pure hatred. He got the message however and as the fire in his eyes cooled, he sat back down again.

"Like I said," Number 10 continued, "there are four Sinners. Each one of you will have an individual role to play during the ceremony. These roles are as follows: President of the United States, the Mayor of New Jersey, Bank Manager, and Joseph Church, brother of Frank Church, aka Baldilocks."

Eda's brow creased and she glanced at the others, who looked equally as confused.

"What are you talking about?"

"Baldilocks is on his way over here to designate each role," Number 10 said. "You'll get a little more information when he shows up."

Eda sat up, her back leaning against the wall. She rubbed her hands together and watched the dust fly.

"Can I ask you something?" she said, looking up at Number 10. "You seem like quite a smart person to me. Do you really believe that a demon called Uncle Sam lives under that crater in Fairfield?"

Number 10 stared hard at Eda. Then she broke off the eye contact and began pacing around the hut. Her feet sounded like two hammers pounding off the wood.

"I'll tell you what I believe," she said. "I believe that man went through hell every day on the streets of Jersey City, trying to cure civilization of its blindness. Nobody listened to what he had to say back then. Nobody had time, including my parents. He called it."

Number 10 stopped dead. Her eyes stared into unseen horror, as if she was living the childhood nightmare all over again. Eda knew that look only too well. She'd seen it on the face of countless survivors.

"I lost my dad in the war," Number 10 said. "My mom and me, we had nothing and Baldilocks forgave us, even after all the crap we'd put him through. Don't you get it Eda? He forgave all the people who laughed at him, just like that. He showed us a way to safety."

Number 10 clicked her fingers.

"This is a great man we're talking about."

"He helped you out and that's great," Eda said. "And so now you believe everything he says, right? He talks about a demon called Uncle Sam and it's just accepted without question? You know that Uncle Sam...you know it was originally used to symbolize the..."

Number 10 held up a hand.

Eda stopped talking.

"This will be the final sacrifice," Number 10 said. "The last ever. Trust me, we don't like doing this – we're not monsters. I'm not a monster."

Murphy cackled to himself in the background.

"You're riding full speed on the crazy train," he said, pointing a finger at Number 10. "There's nothing mystical going on around here. This is cold-blooded murder you're talking about. Nothing less."

At that moment, Baldilocks appeared at the door. It was like he'd popped up out of nowhere. He was carrying four black garment bags with a zipper up the middle.

"Congratulations," Baldilocks said, stepping past Number 10. He walked over to Mike and Becky and dropped two of the garment bags on the floor. Mike's body trembled like a candle flame in the breeze.

"Hello Mike," Baldilocks said. "You my good man will be the Mayor of Jersey City. Let me tell you about him – his name was Tom Johnson and he was a *horrible* man. Nothing personal, okay? You're nothing like him Mike. It's just a part you're playing. Johnson was an adulterer, drug addict, a liar and a cheat, and yet apparently that was okay with the public because he was a handsome man too. He had that sickening charismatic charm that made people ignore his flaws.

In fact, they loved him all the more for his crimes. *Oh it makes him so... human*. That's how stupid people are Mike. *Were*."

Baldilocks spat into the corner of the hut. It was an unexpected shower for the hungry cockroach. Then he pointed to the case lying at Becky's feet. At the same time, Mike flinched and Becky wrapped her arms around him.

"It's okay," she said, whispering into Mike's ear.

"You my dear," Baldilocks said, glaring down at Becky, "are the Bank Manger. To be exact, you are the bank manager of Chase in Jersey City. Oh what a specimen of humanity she was. There was one winter I remember it well – the weather was bad. The temperature had dropped to ten degrees and I was homeless at the time. I had no one to turn to – no friends, no family, nothing. I saw this woman on several occasions – she was always dressed in a black suit, wearing pants like a man's suit, and she was walking into the bank everyday like she was queen of Jersey. So confident, so self-assured. I don't know what compelled me to do what I did – maybe I still believed in human decency back then. But I was desperate..."

"I know the feeling," Murphy said, cutting Baldilocks off. "Hey mister, if you want to see a little human decency in the world then why don't you start showing it? Huh? Think about it."

Baldilocks didn't look at Murphy. His focus remained on Becky.

"One morning I went over to her," he said. "This smartly dressed woman. I introduced myself as Frank Church from London, England. She smiled at first, I remember that. I was hopeful. She said her name was Jane Mooney and that she was the manager of that particular branch. I told her about my situation and then I did it – I asked this woman for help. And do you know what her response was? She giggled into the back of her hand. Now don't get me wrong, it wasn't a malicious gesture. She wasn't deliberately being cruel or anything like that, I have no doubt. No, it was more of an embarrassed laugh and I have no doubt that later that day she told the story of our encounter to her friends around a beautiful dining table in a warm, luxury apartment on the Waterfront. She brushed me off politely. But I could see it in her eyes – how eager she was to get in out of the cold.

The worst thing was that I saw myself through her upper middle-class eyes. And it drove me crazy. I never asked anyone for help again, not ever."

Baldilocks stepped to the right and dropped a case at Eda's feet.

"You're the President of the United States," he said. "Congratulations Eda. How do you like that?"

"Fuck you."

Eda waited for the story – for all the reasons why the President was included on this angry old man's hate list. But Baldilocks had already moved on to the next Sinner. He was standing over Murphy now and he tossed the last black bag onto the old man's lap.

"And you?" he said. "You've got a very special role. You're going to play the part of my dear brother Joe. We had our differences to say the least, my brother and I. He even tried to have me committed at one point. That was before he disowned me and cut me off. But I'll never forget dear old Joe. I hope he died well in the end."

Baldilocks smiled at Murphy.

"Hey isn't that your name too? Joe? Joseph? Well, looks like you get to keep it tomorrow."

"Your brother?" Murphy said. "A bank manager? The President and a mayor? This is your personal kill list huh? Let me tell you something Frank fucking Church. This doesn't sound like someone whose hand is being forced by the supernatural. This sounds like someone venting. Pure and simple."

Baldilocks shook his head. "You're wrong," he said.

He looked at the four prisoners with a sad smile. Behind him, Number 10 was backing off towards the doorway.

"Get some rest Sinners," he said. "Food and drink will be brought to you shortly. We'll start out early tomorrow for Fairfield."

Baldilocks and Number 10 walked out of the hut. The guards closed the door behind them and locked it, leaving the four prisoners to sit in the murky, cold silence of the afternoon. The only thing Eda could hear at that moment was Mike's nervous breathing. The poor guy, he was in for a rough night.

Weren't they all?

7

The next morning, Eda and the other three prisoners were dressed.

A man and a woman – Eda didn't catch their numbers – came into the hut not long after sunrise to help the prisoners put on the outfits that Baldilocks had left for them. It had been a long night inside the hut as Eda had suspected it would be. She'd dozed for an hour or two at most but the close confinement with three strangers, the weird sounds coming from the swamp and of course, the thought of what was to come – that was more than enough to disrupt anyone's night. There had been other noises inside the hut – mostly this was Murphy's ridiculous snoring, as well as a scattering of muted conversation between Becky and Mike. Somebody wept at one point.

Eda almost welcomed the dawn when it finally came.

The two numbers had brought with them a light breakfast of dry meat and some salad scraps for the prisoners. Nobody ate a thing.

The garment bags were opened. Four black suits, dusty and wrinkled were pulled out.

Eda allowed the numbers to dress her. Her only protest was a contemptuous expression that she wore throughout. She undressed first, taking off her rain cloak and her other clothes while the men in the hut – at Murphy's insistence, not Eda's – were forced to look the other way. Eda thought this gesture, this clutch at chivalry, was ridiculous. They had bigger worries going on.

They put a white shirt and pants on her first. Then came the suit jacket. It felt heavy, like one more burden to carry and on top of that, it felt like someone else's skin taking over Eda's body. She watched as one of the numbers put on the tie, turning and pulling until the knot was tight up against the collar of her shirt. She couldn't believe that people used to put themselves through this shit. Putting on a tie felt like punishment enough.

Eda was allowed to keep her boots on. She was thankful for that at least.

When they were all dressed, the prisoners were taken back to the main camp. They walked through a forest of glue-like sludge to get there, moving in single file with the guards and two numbers marching on either side of them. Overhead, a miserable blackish-gray sky threatened to unleash rain.

The four prisoners weren't the only ones dressing up for the big day. The Children had taken off their filthy camouflage rags at last. Now they were dressed in what Murphy might have described as their murder clothes.

As Eda walked back into camp, she saw the small community, all of them dressed in long gray cloaks that looked like a cheap bathrobe. A snake-like belt was looped around the waist. The cloaks stopped at the knees and the legs were naked down to the shoes or boots that covered their feet.

They also wore masks over their faces. It looked like the skull of an animal, long and narrow at the snout, like a wolf. Black straggly hair fell down from both sides of the mask. The craftsmanship was clumsy, almost child-like, and yet it was the amateurishness of the design that chilled Eda's blood. She felt sick as the horde of Children turned around to witness the prisoners' return. They peered at the captives through the tiny eye-slits in their dog heads. Nobody spoke.

Eda looked around for Frankie Boy. No sign of him.

The crowd of dog-heads parted, opening up a narrow channel in the center. Somebody walked through the gap, approaching the prisoners.

This person was wearing a different sort of mask. It was made of rubber and it was a caricature of an image that Eda had seen before. It was the real Uncle Sam, the one who'd become a symbol, a personification of the now defunct American government. The mask consisted of an old man's face with white hair and long chin whiskers for added decoration. There was a top hat on his head in the colors of the old American flag, the stars and stripes. Eda wondered if any of the Children were aware of what the mask was supposed to represent. She didn't get it. Most of them were old enough to remember the real Uncle Sam. Or had they forgotten already?

Eda recognized the straggly hair spilling down either side of the mask. Baldilocks had also spurned the cheap-looking gray robes sported by the rest of the cult. He had something else going on, something much more colorful. He wore a matching blue coat with red and white striped lapels. The front of the suit stopped at the waist but at the back, a long tail ran down to his calves. The pants were black and white striped. It was a garish outfit but it went perfectly with the Uncle Sam mask.

Baldilocks walked towards the prisoners. His bulbous eyes burned through the eyeholes of the mask.

"Sinners," he said. His voice sounded metallic, smothered under the disguise. "It's time to repent."

Somebody lunged at him from the group. It was Becky. The guards grabbed a hold of her before she could get close to the cult leader. Becky wriggled, trying to break free of her captors. She clawed angrily at the mask but was well out of range.

"You crazy son of a bitch," Becky yelled. "What are you doing to us? We're not sinners for God's sake!"

Her outburst was sudden and violent. She lunged at Baldilocks again and two more dog heads appeared on either side to restrain her.

"This is murder!" she cried out. It was a plea to sanity but nobody in the crowd was listening or wanted to listen.

"Murder!" Murphy yelled, joining in. "Murder!"

"Bind their wrists," Number 10 said, pulling the dog mask up over her head. She walked up and stood at Baldilocks' side. There was an anxious look in her eyes. "Let's get them to the canoes. Quickly."

The prisoners' arms were forced behind their back. Their wrists were bound together with rope.

Just before they were led away, Eda searched for a glimpse of David in the crowd. She knew the bastard was hiding behind one of those ugly masks. If only the Children would do her a favor and grant her a last minute request. If they did, Eda knew what she'd ask for and she also knew that she'd never get it.

Baldilocks pointed back and forth along the line of prisoners. Then he turned to the crowd of dog masks gathered behind him.

"Behold the Sinners," he called out. He sounded like a preacher, like he was half-singing, half-talking to the crowd. "The President of the United States. The Bank Manager. The Mayor. And my brother. Their black hearts will not beat for much longer. With good fortune my friends, this will be the last time we – the Children of Nature – are called upon to perform this act. Let us hope that the next time Uncle Sam whispers in my ear, he'll tell me that it's over. That he's satisfied."

Number 10 pointed to the crowd.

"To the boats," she said. "The first twenty-five people only as well as the Sinners. The rest of you wait here. Two of us will come back with the canoes in a short while. When we're all together at the crater, the ceremony will begin. C'mon, let's start moving this thing out."

Some of the Children began to walk through the swampland, making their way towards the banks of the Passaic.

Eda and the prisoners were taken with them.

As they walked, a low-pitched chant emerged from the crowd. Someone was beating on a drum and with each jarring thud, a single word came from their lips:

Sam.

Sam.

Sam. Sam. Sam.

The chant continued all the way to the river.

The prisoners were placed in the first and second boats. Two prisoners in each one. Soon a small fleet of canoes pushed away from the riverbank and set off towards Fairfield. Eda closed her eyes, unable to escape the soundtrack of her impending doom.

Sam.

Sam.

Sam. Sam. Sam.

"Bye Frankie Boy," Eda whispered.

The canoes arrived at the Fairfield riverbank.

After the Children and the prisoners had disembarked, two of the dog masks in the lead boat hooked the vacant canoes together with rope and then set off, herding the empty fleet back to the Meadows to collect the next load of Children. Eda figured it would take several trips before all of the Sam worshippers were present in Fairfield. And they *would* all be there. Nobody, not man, woman or child would miss the annual sacrifice.

The Sinners were led to the crater. Nobody spoke, but every one of the Children chanted.

Sam.

Sam.

Sam. Sam. Sam.

Would it never end?

Eda felt numb inside. Hope was slipping away. But it *was* hopeless. It felt hopeless. Along with Murphy, Mike and Becky, she was escorted on the short hike to the edge of the bombsite. Eda's stomach lurched as she got nearer. She cast her eyes into the mouth of the crater and finally understood how someone might think it was alive. It was like balancing on the lip of a hungry monster. It wasn't a straight fall down to the crater basin – the edges sloped downwards at an impossibly steep angle and went on like that for hundreds of feet, all the way to the bottom. It was a brutal thing to contemplate.

Peering down, Eda saw numerous dark specks scattered across the basin. There were also bright paint-like dots, most likely bones.

Instinctively, she tried to take a step. Eda bumped into one of the

Children whose stubborn refusal to move told her there was nowhere else to go. The only way out was down.

A long wait followed. The rest of the Children arrived in phases while the prisoners were forced to remain teetering on the brink of the Fairfield crater. A light drizzle fell at one point and Eda lifted her face to the sky, allowing the cool spray to comfort her.

After arriving, the Children wearing dog masks began walking around the edge of the giant hole, taking up position on the outskirts. They moved in silence and when they reached their destination they turned to face the prisoners.

Eda looked to her right. Becky was taking slow, labored breaths. For some reason the Children had positioned Eda in between Mike and Becky and she didn't know if this was deliberate cruelty on the part of their captors or just an unfortunate accident. It didn't seem to matter to Baldilocks or the Children that they might want to die standing side by side. As it was, Becky and Mike stood with their heads bowed. Every now and then they'd glance past Eda at one another, smile bravely, and then lower their eyes back to the dirt.

To Eda's right stood Mike and then Murphy. Murphy, who was a big bear of a man, had shrunk to half his original size. He was silent now but throughout the canoe journey he'd hurled abuse at his captors. It was his last stand, a fit of anger and fear, manifested in every curse word under the sun. Now all his bravado was worn out. Uncle Sam's crater had already devoured his soul.

The other boatloads arrived.

The last of the Children came through the small firs at the edge of the road. A hint of after-rain sunlight sparkled on the leaves, illuminating the green. The Children walked towards the crater, once again in silence. There was no need to say anything – everybody had been here before and they knew what to do. The dog heads took up position on the outskirts and they stretched far and wide, forming a crude semi-circle that shadowed the rim. Some of the dog heads were no more than blurry specks on the horizon, not much bigger than the debris that littered the bottom of the blast hole.

Sam.

Sam.

Sam. Sam. Sam.

As the crowd chanted, the red, white and blue masked figure of Baldilocks approached the prisoners. His step was slow, painfully slow. While the mask glared at the unfortunate four, he pulled a small dagger out from underneath his coat. Eda shrank at the sight of the dagger – an inwardly curved blade of about eight inches with a bone handle.

"Get away from me," Murphy groaned. He was snarling at the wind. Not looking at anyone or anything.

"Great Spirit," Baldilocks roared, his face pointing at the sky. "Uncle Sam. Please accept this, our sacrifice. We give you these four Sinners. And we beg of you, not to ask too much more of us. We are not killers. Let this be the last time, if it pleases you."

Baldilocks turned towards a small crowd of dog masks at his back. He offered the dagger to one of them.

"Number 30," he said. "You were the first of the Seekers to deliver a Sinner to us this year. I give you the blade. Will you take it?"

The dog head came forward and took the dagger.

"I'll take it," said a low-pitched male voice.

Number 30 walked over to Murphy with a violent swagger. Eda watched him stop in front of the old man, their faces just inches apart.

The dog head raised the dagger and began sawing at the soft rope that bound Murphy's wrists. Murphy's arms fell to the side, limp and exhausted. His proud eyes were old and worn out.

Number 30 stood upright, saying nothing. Eda had a feeling that the masked man was reveling in the slow torture of his victim. That he was drinking in Murphy's fear, becoming more powerful in his mind. Maybe it's what he had to do to finish it.

Murphy began mumbling incoherently to himself. Eda looked over and saw an outpouring of regret in his eyes, pushing everything else, even fear aside. Murphy had spoken in the hut about movement, about travel, as a way of keeping alive. Now he couldn't move an inch.

This was the end of the road, the end of all movement, and he knew it.

Number 30 inched closer. He put the tip of the dagger to the old man's throat.

"I don't deserve this," Murphy said. He shook his head back and forth.

Sam.

Sam.

Sam. Sam. Sam.

"Joseph Church," Baldilocks cried out. "My beloved brother. You are the first Sinner. Go down into the hole and confess to Uncle Sam."

"My name's Mur..."

Number 30 slid the blade across Murphy's throat while the old man was still talking, cutting from one end to the other. Murphy's words morphed into a gasp. His eyes swelled in horror, his hands reaching towards his neck.

Eda cringed at the sound of flesh being sliced open. She thought she felt hot droplets of blood spray onto her face.

Murphy gagged violently. Eda couldn't help but look over and she saw a blackish-red waterfall running down his neck, soaking the white shirt collar. Number 30 took a step back as if he wanted to watch the old man for a moment. Then he came forward again and pushed Murphy into the mouth of the crater.

Eda heard him rolling down the crater like a boulder. Was he dead already? Or was he still conscious? God, she hoped he was dead.

It was a long time before the hole was silent.

"Number 42," Baldilocks said. "The second of the Seekers to deliver."

Number 42, a tall figure, stepped out of the crowd and with a quick bow of the head, took the dagger from Number 30.

"Thank you," a husky woman's voice said.

Number 42 approached a petrified-looking Mike. Mike had squealed like a frightened child when the dagger cut Murphy's throat open. Now his eyes were closed. His body shook like it was in the grip of mid-seizure. He'd already pissed himself, a last act of rebellion that would stain his death garment.

Becky's head leaned down the three-person line. She called out to Mike, loud enough for everyone to hear.

"I love you Mike. It's going to be okay."

Eda tried to duck her head out of the way. She wanted to step aside, to allow the lovers to get closer, but there was no room to move. Even at the end, the Sinners were denied their dignity.

"B-B-Becky," Mike said.

Number 42 cut the rope around Mike's wrists.

Sam.

Sam.

Sam. Sam. Sam.

"Find my sister," Mike cried out. His eyes strained down the line, pleading with Becky. "Please. Get out of here, go to Boston and find Pam. Tell her I..."

"Mayor Tom Johnson," Baldilocks called out. "You are the second Sinner. Go down into the hole and confess to Uncle Sam."

"I love you!" Mike said.

Becky screamed, a wild-high pitched protest. "No!"

The sound of Mike's throat being sliced open was so close that it sounded like it was happening inside Eda's head. Number 42 stepped back, blood dripping off the blade. Mike doubled over, staggered backwards like a drunk and then fell into the hole. It happened so fast that Number 42 didn't even get the chance to perform the coup de grâce – to push him in. At least Mike took that away from her at the end.

The last thing Eda heard was a watery, gurgling noise. Mike sounded like he was trying to scream underwater.

Then he was gone.

Becky screamed over and over again.

Eda charged with wrists bound at the dog heads blocking her path. She didn't get far before they pushed her back. Becky tried to run too and Eda didn't know if it was rage, survival instinct or whether the woman was desperately trying to escape so she could fulfill Mike's dying but impossible request of her. The Children restrained Becky too, blocking all routes of escape. She hopped about wildly. One of the guards locked an arm around Becky's waist, stopping her from tumbling backwards into the crater prematurely.

"Mike!"

"We're now halfway through the ceremony," Baldilocks said. His eyes were burning through the slits in the mask. "Only the President of the United States and the Bank Manager remain. And then mercifully, it will be over."

Baldilocks glared at Eda, but his words addressed the crowd behind him.

"Number 47," he said. "The third of the Seekers to deliver."

Eda's body lapsed into a state of icy, rigid terror. She was about to die and for a few seconds, couldn't move a muscle. Couldn't breathe. She doubled over, burying her face in her hands, squeezing until the tendons in her arms felt like rope. Her guts churned like a typhoon.

She wanted to puke...was going to puke.

Then it passed. Eda straightened up, raising her chin in the air.

Another dog head took the dagger. The masked figure walked up to Eda, minus the detached swagger of the others. The blade in his hand was still dripping fresh blood. It was the darkest, reddest blood Eda had ever seen.

A familiar set of eyes peered out from behind the animal mask.

"David," Eda said. "So that's how it works, huh? You get to make the kill on the big day."

The dog head said nothing.

"Not as easy as it looks," Eda said. "Is it?"

He came closer and cut the binding on her wrists.

"Don't have the guts to look me in the eye David?" Eda said, loud enough for everyone to hear. She thrust her face towards the dog snout and David flinched like a shell-shocked man hearing gunfire in the distance. His eyes blinked furiously. She felt both rage and fear seeping out of his skin.

"After what I did for you in New York?" Eda said. "And you can't even look at me?"

"President of the United States," Baldilocks said.

Sam.

Sam.

Sam. Sam. Sam.

"Fucking coward," Eda hissed. "I can't believe it. I'm going to die at the hands of a fucking wimp from New Jersey."

When Baldilocks spoke again, Number 47 held up a hand.

"One moment," he said.

Number 47 pulled the dog mask over his head. That familiar, boyish face had never looked so old.

"Well well well," Eda said. "Look who decided to show up."

"You want to look in my eyes?" he said. "That's what you want? Okay then. You're right – I owe you one after New York. If that's what you want then I'll give it to you. It's not going to make it any harder for me to do this Eda. You're still going to die."

David glanced over his shoulder at Baldilocks. There was a curt nod, a signal for the old man to continue.

"President of the United States," Baldilocks said.

David walked forward. He put the dagger to Eda's throat and she couldn't help but gasp at its jagged bite. Hot blood smeared on her skin, dead men's leftovers. She couldn't believe David was going to kill her like this. It didn't matter that she'd saved his life in New York. He had to do it.

Baldilocks waited a moment before continuing.

"Go down into the..."

A sudden noise cut the old man off in mid-sentence. It sounded like the air being sucked out of a beach ball at lighting speed. At first, Eda thought it was her dying shriek but putting a hand to her throat she realized she wasn't bleeding.

David was staring at her. *Through* her. He took a couple of drunken steps backwards.

His shoulder jerked up and down, a violent spasm beyond his control. His face sagged horribly. With a groan, he reached a hand towards his head and it crashed clumsily off the back of his neck. He didn't give up there. His fingers probed further, reaching past the shoulder; it was like he was looking for something that he couldn't find. Something on his body.

Slowly, he turned around to look at Baldilocks.

That's when Eda saw it.

There was an arrow in David's back.

8

The Children pulled off their dog masks in a hurry. Frantic fingers clawed at straps and when the masks were removed, Eda saw a blurry wall of shocked faces looking at David. Their wide eyes twitched in disbelief. It was as if their minds couldn't digest the sight of an arrow embedded in the young Seeker's back.

All of a sudden, Eda heard a lone scream. Frightened murmurings. Mass confusion burst forth around the bombsite like water through a paper dam.

Eda spun around and saw the Children standing at the edge of the crater. They were looking over in Eda's direction, too far away to get a grip of what was happening. Did they even know they were under attack? Eda's question was answered when the Children started jumping around in manic half-circles of terror.

She strained her eyes. The gleam of distant swords winked back at her.

"What the hell?" Eda said. "What are they...?"

The Children were attacking one another.

Loud footsteps crashed towards Eda. Coming from behind.

Eda spun back to the front and saw a pale-faced David staggering towards her. A wretched groan spilled out of the man. His right arm was folded over at an impossible angle, hanging above his shoulder like he was still trying to reach the arrow in his back. To get it out, like somehow that would stop the pain. Now the arm just hung there, useless and frozen.

He looked like a ghost already.

"Help me," he said.

Eda watched him drop to his knees in a crumpled heap. Sweat gushed off his yellowing forehead. With a look of disdain, Eda turned back to the crowd of dog heads gathered around the crater in the distance. They *were* attacking one another. Eda's face creased up in confusion. It was like there was madness in the air, turning brother against brother, sister against sister. The screams were frequent; they were high-pitched and cut like a knife.

"What's going on?" Eda said.

Was there a rogue faction at work within the Children? A pack of rebels attacking their own kind?

"Eda!"

It was Becky's voice.

Eda battled through a foggy trance and came back to the present moment. She looked to her right and saw Becky's panicked eyes staring back at her. Becky held up her wrists and Eda saw that she was still bound with rope.

She moved towards Becky but as she did so, David – who was back on his feet – almost crashed into her. He was a runaway boulder with arms and legs. Just inches away from Eda, from the edge. Eda saw the dazed look in his eyes and his arms reached for her still, like she was his only chance of staying afloat in deep water.

Eda caught a glimpse of the sacrificial dagger lying on the ground where David had dropped it. She dodged his wild advances, knelt down and picked it up.

"Help me," David whispered. "Please Eda...I'm..."

Eda tucked the dagger neatly into her belt. Then she smiled, reached out and placed her hands on David's shoulders, helping to keep him upright. His eyes lit up and a faint smile formed on his bluish lips.

"It'll be okay," she said.

"Thank you," David said. "Eda, please listen to me. I'm..."

Before he could finish, Eda spun David around so that his back was facing the crater. There was no strength left in the man – it was like dancing with a child's doll as far as Eda was concerned.

"It'll be okay," she said.

It only took the slightest bit of effort for Eda to push him backwards. David's eyes ballooned with terror as he tumbled over the lip of the crater.

He rolled down the side at tremendous speed, barreling his way over a vast empire of hard, occasionally jagged rock. Pieces of David flew up in the air, like water spurting from a geyser. It was the slow explosion of a man. At the bottom, the bones and bloody flesh of his predecessors awaited him.

Eda took a step back from the crater's edge. As she did, she dragged Becky alongside her and used the dagger to saw off the rope around the other woman's wrists. Becky sighed with relief and shook her arms free. Now she looked over the hole, taking in the strange sight of the Children fighting amongst themselves. She looked at Eda and shook her head. Eda shrugged and glanced over at the action yet again.

She stopped dead.

"Oh shit," Eda said.

Her blood ran cold. Eda walked to the edge of the crater, as far as she could go and then she stopped. All the chaos fell silent in her mind. The world blurred at the edges as her eyes locked onto a weapon, currently being wielded with savage intent by one of the rebels. Even from a distance, Eda could see that it wasn't a short sword like the ones she'd seen the Children carrying back in camp.

It was a katana sword. A samurai sword.

She looked back and forth, panic leaking like blood through an arterial wound. The rebel faces became instantly recognizable. The truth hit hard. It wasn't the Children attacking other Children.

"It can't be," Eda said.

"What are you talking about?" Becky asked. Her voice was a

distant murmur, something lost in the fog of confusion swirling around in Eda's head.

Eda staggered back from the edge, unable to trust her sense of balance.

She was looking over at the towering figure of Lex – the female giant who stood head and shoulders above almost everyone else. Lex moved like a ballet dancer, spinning gracefully, moving in and out of range while hacking mercilessly at as many Children as her sword could reach. She slashed once, twice then kicked her helpless victims down into the hole.

All the while, she was getting closer to Eda.

Their eyes met from afar. Lex's face was an angry tapestry of cuts and bruises – a reminder of the damage she'd accumulated in New York courtesy of Frankie Boy. The expression on the chief warrior's face was even angrier than her wounds.

Lex strode forward with hate in her eyes. A huge man in a dog mask leapt in front of her wielding a short sword. Lex greeted the swordsman with a kick in the chest and that was enough to send him down to Uncle Sam, dog mask still attached to his head.

Eda's hands were clamped to the top of her head. Her mouth hung open. "Why?" she said. "I left. They let me go for God's sake!"

Becky grabbed Eda by the arm.

"We need to get out of here," she said. "You and me. Now!"

Eda was too stunned to respond. In the distance, Lex charged forward, even as she continued to cut down the swathe of Children who tried to fight back valiantly. They probably thought she was going for Baldilocks. Eda knew better.

There were about twenty of the New York warriors in total. It wasn't much but Eda knew firsthand the damage that just a handful of those women were capable of.

Becky pulled Eda's arm again and this time Eda relented. They turned and ran towards the steep hill that led towards the road. As they raced forward, Eda removed the small sacrificial dagger from her belt, where it was at risk of cutting her, and put it into the inside pocket of her suit jacket.

Shrill screams pierced the air.

Eda and Becky charged up the hill. Eda's legs were still paralyzed with shock, not quite functioning at full speed, but Becky didn't stop dragging her in a bid to make haste.

"C'mon!" Becky yelled. "Keep going Eda."

Eda staggered forward like an ambitious toddler who hadn't quite mastered the art of walking, let alone running. Finally, her legs warmed up to the task. Near the top of the hill, she turned around and caught a glimpse of Baldilocks on the outskirts of the crater. He was bouncing on his feet like a madman. Yelling orders. When he saw Eda and Becky making a run for it, still dressed in their sacrificial suits, he pointed uphill and screamed like a man whose property was being stolen in front of his eyes.

His voice soared above the sound of clashing steel. "They belong to Uncle Sam! Bring them back. Bring them back!"

"To the boats," Becky said. She pointed across the road to the row of short firs that led to the river. With any luck, five canoes would be waiting beside the water.

Eda slammed her arm against the other woman's chest.

"Hang on a minute," she said.

"What?" Becky said, looking at Eda like she was crazy. "Wait for what? We need to go."

"That first arrow," Eda said. "It went into David's back. It must have come from the trees over there. What if the archers are still hiding in there and we're running straight towards them?"

Becky tapped Eda on the shoulder. "You mean those archers?" she said.

She pointed towards a huddle of three warriors standing about thirty feet away from the crater, crouching and firing arrows into the crowd of Children. They were advancing towards Lex and the others, moving away from the trees.

"They spilled out after the first shot," Becky said. "I think the coast is clear."

"But there might be more," Eda said, looking warily at the foreboding wall of firs.

"We're going to have to take that chance," Becky said. "Come to think of it, how do we know these girls aren't on our side? They just saved our lives didn't they?"

"Trust me," Eda said, shaking her head. "They're not on our side."

Becky tilted her head.

"You know them?" she asked.

Eda nodded. "This isn't the right time to talk about it."

Eda and Becky tackled the steep incline and crossed the winding road. They jumped the metal barrier and pushed through the fir trees, coming out by the genteel ghost houses on Riverside Drive. From there, they pumped their arms and legs, running eagerly to the river like two aquatic creatures floundering on dry land.

They trampled through the mini-forest at the edge of the riverbank.

"Shit!" Becky yelled, looking towards the water.

The canoes were drifting away. They were moving in an easterly direction at a very slow pace with the nearest one about ten to fifteen feet from the bank. Three paddles floated gently on the calm surface of the Passaic.

"Fuck! Fuck! Fuck!" Becky said, punching at the air. She glanced over her shoulder to see if anyone was coming after them yet.

"It was the warriors, " Eda said. "They must have ambushed the Children's camp after we were gone. I guess they traveled down on the last boatload, then probably killed whoever brought them here and didn't secure the boats."

Somebody screamed in the background.

"Jesus," Becky said. "We need to get out of here."

She looked at Eda with a hopeful expression.

"Can you swim?"

Eda bit her lip. "I swam once when I was young," she said, "In a river much smaller than this. Actually I wouldn't really call it swimming."

Becky raised an eyebrow. "What would you call it?"

"Drowning."

Becky managed a weak laugh. She pointed to the nearest canoe.

"We just need to reach that one okay?" she said. "You don't need to be a genius to figure out that a lot of people are going to be coming after us Eda. If we can't get to one of those canoes, we're screwed."

"Yeah," Eda said in a flat voice. "I know."

A pause.

"You can do this," Becky said.

Eda stared at the dirty brown water.

"Sure."

With that said, Becky leaned forward over the riverbank. She took several deep breaths and then dove headfirst into the Passaic River. There was a light splashing noise – it sounded like a bird dive-bombing the water. A few seconds passed. Eda began to panic, to suspect that something had grabbed Becky under there and pulled her down into the dark depths.

A head popped up out of the water. Becky twisted into position, then her arms cut through the surface as she swam towards the nearest canoe.

She stopped halfway and turned back towards land.

"C'mon!" she called out to Eda. "It's alright."

Eda glanced over her shoulder to see if anyone was coming yet. Warriors, Children – they would show up sooner or later on the river-bank. Nothing yet. Then she turned back to the water, heart racing, and with sheer force of will, blocked out all memories of her near drowning incident as a child. The panic. Being pulled down into the darkness. The certainty of death, it never happened.

Her mind locked onto the position of the boat on the water. Then she took a deep breath, followed by another. Slowly, she leaned forward over the grassy bank and stared at the unwelcoming river.

"I can swim."

Eda closed her eyes. Then she dove into the water and in contrast to Becky's landing, it sounded like another Uncle Sam bomb crashing into the Passaic.

A rush of cold filled Eda's body. She found herself in an alien world with very little visibility. Her mind barked out a series of hundred miles per hour commands – *don't panic, move your arms, kick!*

At the same time, a small, frightened voice reminded Eda that she couldn't swim. And the voice wouldn't go away. What was she doing in a river for God's sake? Nothing – neither reassurance nor panic could prevent her body from sinking now.

Eda moved her arms and legs. She did what she thought was right – plowed and kicked with her limbs and yet it only made things worse.

A deep churning noise filled her head. The river was inside, choking her.

Panic slipped away after a moment or two. If this was drowning then it wasn't as bad as Eda had always imagined it to be. Not if she stopped fighting and just let go. Surrender. It wasn't cold, in fact it was warm and comforting somehow. Everything would be over, including her worries. No more warriors. No more Uncle Sam.

Let go. Let the water fill your lungs then.

And yet something wouldn't let go. Eda found herself clawing relentlessly through the water, reaching for the surface again. Reaching for daylight. Her fingers grasped at the cold liquid like it was a piece of rope she could use to pull herself back up.

There was a sudden jarring sensation. Space and time ceased to exist and for a few moments, Eda was outside of herself. Watching herself drown. Then something hard bumped into her and brought her back. Now it felt like she was floating instead of sinking.

And then she broke through the surface, gasping for air. It was like waking up from the worst nightmare she'd ever had. The murky light of the sky was right there over Eda's head again, having replaced the dark, grotesque roof of the river.

She was in the middle of the Passaic River and there was a canoe floating immediately to her right. Becky was in the water and she was pulling Eda towards the boat. She had one arm wrapped around Eda's waist and the other was dragging through the surface, bringing them closer to the boat.

"Climb up," Becky said, when they reached the side of the canoe. She was gasping for breath as she spoke. "Grip the edge and push yourself over."

Eda reached up but in her panic, she pushed the boat instead of grabbing a hold of it. The boat bobbed away from the two women, daring them to try again.

Becky cursed, then pulled them closer. Eda coughed relentlessly.

"Reach up and grab the edge," Becky said. Then a new panic filled her voice. "Jesus Christ. Eda...those women, they're at the edge of the river. They're coming after us. C'mon, please. I need you to grab the edge of the boat Eda. Holy shit!"

Eda heard a splashing noise in the distance. When she turned her head the other way she caught a brief glimpse of the warriors swimming towards the other boats, which were about fifty feet away from where Eda and Becky were.

Eda reached for the canoe again.

The boat swayed towards her too fast and it knocked her off balance. With hope fading, she tried for a third time and with Becky's help, Eda hurled herself into the canoe with such force that she landed on the wooden base with a yelp.

Becky climbed into the boat effortlessly and grabbed the paddle. There was only one in the canoe.

"Oh shit," Becky said, looking over her shoulder. Her eyes were alight with terror. "What did you do to those women Eda? What the hell did you do?"

Eda sat upright, coughing ferociously.

"Long story," she said in a hoarse voice.

She glanced over her shoulder.

The warriors were swimming towards the other canoes – an abandoned fleet of four that were scattered further up the river. Eda counted around nine or ten warriors in total, including Lex. The chief warrior cut through the surface of the Passaic like her life depended on it.

"Can you row this thing?" Eda said, turning to Becky.

Becky nodded, keeping her eyes on the river.

"Fortunately that's one thing I can do," she said. "Don't worry about it – I'll get us out of here."

Becky paddled hard, plowing the wooden stick through the water in long, deep strokes. The canoe took off at an impressive speed. Eda felt a wave of fresh hope rising up inside, but she didn't allow herself to get carried away.

"I swear to God Mike," Becky said. "I'm going to Boston. I'm going there for both of us and I'll find Pam, dead or alive."

As Becky talked to herself, Eda could smell the river all over their clothes. It smelled like shit and dirt and puke all wrapped into one foul super-odor. It was in her throat too; she could taste the Passaic like she was still in it.

"I hate this swamp," she said.

She coughed again, keeping an eye on things at their back. Further downriver, the warrior pack had already climbed into one of the vacant canoes, leaving the other three to drift. They'd overloaded the boat, which with any luck would slow them down.

Eda was about to inform Becky of this when some of the Children appeared at the riverbank. There were about thirty at least. Most of them had pulled their gray robes off and Eda could see their camouflage colors once again, blending in perfectly with the earthy shades of the Meadows.

Eda couldn't see Baldilocks. She imagined him back at the crater, still hopping like a man trapped on hot coals, yelling orders, demanding that Uncle Sam's Sinners be captured and brought back to face justice.

Seconds later, one by one, the cult members dove into the river. They made it look graceful and effortless, like they were returning to their natural habitat.

When they surfaced in the water, the Children began to swim towards the remaining canoes.

9

Becky was a strong rower. As well as her natural skills with a paddle, the adrenaline rush fueled body and mind, giving her that extra surge of emergency power to push the canoe through the water with superhuman strength. This, along with the head start they had over their pursuers, both the warriors and Children, gave Eda and Becky a fighting chance.

Eda sat next to Becky while land flashed by on either side. While Becky kept her eyes out front, Eda concentrated on the progress of their pursuers. The warriors' canoe was an angry dot on the horizon. Their overcrowded boat, powered by a single paddle was betraying their ambition. As for the Children, Eda couldn't see them but she knew they'd also have overloaded the three canoes and would have a hard time of building speed. With any luck, both parties would impede the other's progress, buying the two Sinners time to escape.

From a distance, Eda could see two of the archers up on their feet, pointing their bows to the sky, shooting arrows at something behind them. Eda heard a cacophony of angry shouts, battle cries in the distance.

That's it, she thought. Kill each other.

She turned back to the front, at least a little relieved.

"Where are we going anyway?" she asked.

Becky shrugged.

"Back to camp?"

"Is that a question?" Eda said, looking at the other woman.

"Guess not," Becky said. She was breathing in a slow, deliberate manner. It looked like she was fully in control of herself and Eda was impressed by her composure. She wondered briefly about Becky's past but this wasn't the time for a get to know one another discussion. There would be time for that later.

"If we can get back to the Children's camp," Becky said, "I might be able to find my way back to the Two Bridges Road."

"The Two what?" Eda said.

"It's a road north of the Children's camp," Becky said, with a quick shake of her head. "That's all I know. It's a long shot but if we can find that road we're back in business. And by back in business I mean we're out of the Meadows and home free. Some of us anyway..."

Becky's eyes glistened. Survival instinct had pushed grief aside, at least for now.

"You know where we get off here?" Eda asked.

Becky pursed her lips and took a long and intense look at their surroundings. "For the Children's camp?"

"Yeah," Eda said. "This damn swamp – it all looks the same to me."

"I think so," Becky said. "It's a little cove-shaped bay on the river, right? There's a bunch of trees overhanging the water and there's one of them in particular that looks like it's almost horizontal. You could lie on your back and sunbathe on that mother if you wanted to."

"I remember it," Eda said. The horizontal tree that Becky was talking about was pretty distinctive. Its gnarled, purplish-blue trunk extended from the bank, leaning towards the water in a gravity-defying manner. When she'd first seen it, Eda had imagined lying on that trunk and letting her arms slide down to caress the cool water.

"Keep your eyes peeled," Becky said. "We can't be too far away. We're getting out of here, alright? If it's the last thing I do I'm going to find that Two Bridges Road, walk the rest of the way to Boston and I'm going to find Pam."

Becky's entire body was trembling.

"Pam is Mike's twin sister?" Eda said. "Right?"

"Yeah."

"What will you say to her?" Eda said. "If she's...alive."

"I'll tell her that Mike never forgot about her," Becky said. "Because he never did. He never stopped loving or missing his sister. Twins, damn it. I'll tell her that he was on his way back to Boston to find her. And I'll tell her why it took us so long, I'll tell her about little..."

Becky stopped. She made a loud, hacking noise that sounded like she was clearing something stuck in her throat.

"About little what?" Eda asked.

Becky's face was a block of stone.

"Just keep your eyes peeled Eda," she said. "Okay? We can't afford to miss that little harbor."

They sat in silence. Eda was overjoyed to see no sign of either the warriors or the Children behind them. There was only an empty view stretching out at their backs, and it was hard to believe in that moment that Eda and Becky weren't the only two people in the swamp. Under other circumstances, it would have been a blissful journey through a forgotten, unspoiled world.

The Passaic River was a permanent chocolate brown color. Tall trees stooped over the edge of the riverbank, their image barely reflected in the dull surface of the water. As Eda sat in the canoe, searching for the Children's harbor, she realized that the entirety of the Meadows consisted of mostly two colors – green and brown. It was like she was traveling through a watercolor scene painted by an artist from the nineteenth century. Eda had seen those types of paintings in the old Met museum in New York. She'd always marveled at how she could smell the damp earth just by looking at them.

"No sign?" Becky said, glancing over he shoulder.

"Nah," Eda said. "They've put too many people in the boats. With any luck they've overturned. I don't know if the warriors have ever done this kind of thing before. Not much call for canoeing skills in the middle of Manhattan."

"So who are these women?" Becky said. "What did you call them – warriors? What the hell are they doing here in the swamp chasing you like this?"

"I think they want to take me back to New York," Eda said.

"No shit."

"It's either that or they've come here to kill me."

"What did you do to them?" Becky asked. "Are you a runaway or something?"

"No," Eda said. "They let me go. I was free to walk and I walked. It doesn't make any sense for them to come after me like this. Haven't really had a chance to ask them and I don't want to for that matter."

Becky took another look downriver. With the coast clear, she held her paddle arm aloft, stretching her exhausted muscles and taking deep lungfuls of fresh air. She wiped a pool of sweat off her forehead and closed her eyes.

"Hell of a workout," she said.

"I'll paddle for a while," Eda said.

Becky opened her eyes and shook her head. "It's not as easy as it looks," she said. "I just need a minute and..."

But Eda reached over and snatched the paddle out of Becky's hand before she could finish the sentence.

"Don't be a martyr," she said. "I can do it."

Eda budged over, swapping places with Becky so that she was at the far side of the boat. She gripped the wooden handle and plunged the paddle into the water, using long, deep strokes like she'd seen Becky do. Right away she realized it *was* harder than it looked. Much harder. The canoe swayed to the side, no longer under human command. Eda was taking it closer to the riverbank.

"What the...?" Eda said.

Becky didn't say anything. She sat poker-faced, not moving.

Eda squeezed the handle tighter, stabbing the water angrily in a bid to correct their course.

She stole a worried glance behind her. A barrage of voices drifted up the river like a rolling fog. Men and women's voices – all intermingled in one dissonant roar, coming closer.

"I fucking hate boats," Eda said, plowing the paddle through the water. There was little grace in her stroke and the canoe continued to rebel against her touch. "I hate rivers too. And I hate swamps most of all. If I make it out of here Becky, I don't ever want to see any more boats, rivers or swamps in all my life. I'm making that promise to myself here today. I'm a city girl damn it."

Becky gently lifted the paddle out of Eda's hand. They switched places and she resumed her position as rower.

"*When* you make it out of here," she said. "Thanks for the break Eda."

Becky corrected the runaway canoe and a few minutes later, sat bolt upright on the bench. It was like she'd sat on something sharp.

"I see it!" she said. She poked an elbow into Eda's arm. Eda looked up and saw a tiny little bay tucked into the edge of the riverbank. The familiar hanging trees leaned far over the edge like old friends waiting for the two women to return.

"Thank God," Eda said. "At the very least I get to feel dry land under my feet again. If only I had time to get out of this goddamn suit. It's soaking wet."

"I don't think we've got time to change," Becky said.

"Yeah," Eda said. "I know. I'll settle for finding Frankie Boy. God, I hope he's alright."

Becky steered the boat towards the water's edge. Although she was sweating and breathing hard, her eyes were bright. She'd needed that boost of finding the harbor. Eda felt the same. And although they still had a lot of running to do before they found the Two Bridges Road, they were at least a long way from the rim of Uncle Sam's crater.

"Listen," Becky said, jumping out of the boat first. She turned around and offered a hand to Eda. "We gotta be careful. Your friends stole the Children's costumes but we don't know if they killed everyone. Some of them might be on the loose around here."

"My bet?" Eda said, taking Becky's hand and stepping onto dry land. "They're all dead. Lex and the warriors wouldn't leave any prisoners behind, not if they could help it. Mercy isn't exactly their style, you know?"

Eda and Becky hurried through the swamp back to the Children's camp. When they got there they found bodies lying everywhere. It wasn't a surprise but that didn't make looking at the bloody aftermath any easier. The corpses were scattered throughout camp, their camouflage clothes stained with patches of dark blood. As well as men and women, Eda saw one dark-haired little boy of about eleven lying in a grotesque pose, limbs pointing in a multitude of directions. He looked like a doll that an angry child had tried to break. Cloudy pale blue eyes stared lifelessly up at the sky.

"Oh shit," Becky said. She was staring intently at the dead boy.

Eda clamped a hand over her nose and mouth as if the air was toxic.

"These bitches are savages," Becky said, creeping closer to the boy. An army of flies danced gleefully around his fresh corpse. "Fucking heartless savages. Look what they did to him."

"They'll do the same to us," Eda said in a flat voice. "If they find us. Frankie Boy! C'mere dog."

A strange, high-pitched barking noise from deep inside the swamp stopped both women in their tracks. It wasn't Frankie Boy, but whatever it was it didn't sound welcoming.

"What the hell was that?" Becky said. "That wasn't a dog, was it?"

"No," Eda said. "That's not Frankie Boy. God knows what else is out there."

Looking around, Eda crouched down beside a small pile of bodies. She gagged on the foul odor of decaying flesh and with a grimace, picked up two short swords lying next to the death mound. Then she stood up and offered one of the swords to Becky.

"You any good with one of these?" she asked.

"I'm good with a paddle," Becky said. There was a reluctant look on her face.

"Take it anyway," Eda said, forcing the weapon into the woman's hands. The swords were heavier than they looked and the weight would take some getting used to. "We might need it if we run into whatever's barking out there. And if we miss that, we've always got the warriors and the Children to worry about. At the very least, you'll look more frightening with a sword than with a paddle."

They heard voices in the swamp. Somewhere close by.

Becky's face was as white as snow. "We have to find that road," she said.

Eda nodded. "I know."

A sudden snapping noise to Eda's right made her jump. Something was coming towards them, stalking them across fallen branches on light feet. For a second, she thought they'd blown it – that they'd waited too long and now the warriors or the Children had caught up with them and that was it – game over. It was either back to New York or throat slit and tossed into the Fairfield crater. Little wonder then that Eda almost cried out with relief when the beautiful sight of Frankie Boy came bounding through a wall of bushes.

"Frankie!"

When he saw Eda, the German Shepherd ran across the clearing towards her, ears down and tail wagging. He looked as overjoyed as Eda felt.

"Thank God," she said, kneeling down and burying her face in the black and tan coat. It was damp and yet it smelled divine.

"Eda for Christ's sake!" Becky said. She was looking across the clearing towards the happy reunion. Her eyes ballooned with fear, as if she was expecting a horde of murderous, sword wielding women to barge through the foliage at any second.

"Right," Eda said. "C'mon Frankie."

They moved fast.

It wasn't easy going, making their escape through the Meadows. On multiple occasions, their feet became weighed down in the black oozy mud. At times Eda felt like she was running on the spot. The landscape was rugged and the swamp, very much a living thing, wanted them to fail. Eda pushed through. She saw the empty road in her mind and felt the joy of standing there with the world and all its doors wide open. The road was opportunity and freedom.

Surely it was only a matter of time. It was just ahead of her, always.

The odd chink of sunlight stole past the clouds and it made the grass look like long strands of white crystal. Now and then, Eda and Becky would stumble upon the remains of a dirt path, forged by feet from the old world. These disappearing pathways were a reminder that people, such as Baldilocks and his father, had once visited the Meadows for recreation. Eda thought it madness to come to such a place to relax. There were other reminders of the past too. At one point, Eda saw an overturned table and chairs, withering to the point that it had become one with the landscape. Eda tried to imagine them, the people of yesteryear, sitting by the riverbank, drinking tea and laughing. The picture in her head wasn't clear. It seemed too far-fetched.

Becky slowed down a little and Eda, whose legs were surprisingly fresh, took the lead.

About a minute later, she stopped dead. She pointed a finger ahead, noticing as she did that her hand was trembling.

There was something up there – something in between a tight row of river birch trees.

And it was looking at her.

"You see that?" she said. "Becky, do you see it?"

It was the Uncle Sam mask. There it was, peering out at the two women from in between the narrow gap in the trees. Hideous and grinning. Long strands of stringy, gray hair spilled down from the back and sides of the mask.

Eda thought she could hear him laughing. She staggered backwards and her boots made a loud squelching noise underneath.

"Baldilocks!" she yelled. "I see you."

Becky caught up with her at last.

"What is it?" Becky said. Her shoulders sagged wearily and she gasped for breath. Frightened eyes searched the landscape, trying to find the source of Eda's outburst.

Eda was still pointing towards the gap in between the two river birches. She was like a statue, frozen in terror.

There was nothing there.

Eda dropped her arm, shaking her head.

"I don't see it," Becky said. "I don't see anything at all Eda."

"It was there," Eda said.

"Are you alright?" Becky said, looking at Eda with a concerned expression. "There's no one there Eda. How could Baldilocks be here if he didn't even get in the canoes with the others? There's no way that old bastard could get in front of us."

Eda ran a hand through her damp hair. She was well aware of how crazy she must have seemed in that moment. *Loco*, as Lucia back in the Complex would say. "Thought I saw something."

"You know what it is?" Becky said. "It's this place. It's fucking with us."

"I guess."

All of a sudden, a deer bounded out from behind a large bush up ahead. It was a big animal and it skipped away in the opposite direction, trying to get clear of the three intruders who'd appeared in its territory.

Both Eda and Becky shrieked.

Frankie Boy charged after the deer, barking furiously. Eda watched the dog take off with a look of horror in her eyes.

"Frankie!" she hissed. "No!" She ran after the dog but he was gone before she could even get started.

"Come back Frankie!" Eda said, slowing to a halt.

"Forget it Eda," Becky said. "That dog's got a mind of his own. You can't stop him doing what he wants."

"Shit," Eda said. She looked into the wetlands, trying to pry him back with willpower alone. But Frankie was gone.

"Where the hell are we?" she said. The rancid smell of the river drifted up from her suit, choking Eda quietly. It was a constant reminder of almost drowning.

As far as Eda was concerned, they were trapped in a giant green labyrinth. One that didn't want to let them go.

"Are you sure we're going north?" she asked Becky.

Becky shrugged. "I think so," she said. "When Mike and I first got here, Baldilocks gave us a tour. We came up this way first. Baldilocks said this was their hunting grounds. And you know what that means right? It means they know this place well. A hell of a lot better than we do."

"That's just great," Eda said.

Becky nodded. "What the fuck have we done?"

"It's too late to turn back," Eda said.

Her eyes darted back and forth across the rugged terrain. She was still keeping an eye out for Frankie Boy, hoping he'd come back at the last minute.

"We'd better keep going," Becky said. "We can't be too far away now. Right? I mean, how big can this place be?"

"Sure," Eda said. "We're close."

At that moment, the Two Bridges Road felt like a long way away. Eda sensed it and she was sure that Becky did too.

A noise up ahead.

It sounded like someone walking on fallen branches.

Eda looked towards the huddle of birch trees where she'd imagined seeing the Uncle Sam mask a few minutes earlier.

There was something there. There *really* was something there.

"Oh Christ," Eda said. She lowered her voice to a whisper. "Becky. Over there."

"Holy shit," Becky said.

It was a man.

He stepped out from behind the trees, dressed in a camouflage jacket and matching pants. It wasn't Baldilocks but it was one of the Children. He was an older man, perhaps sixty with a full head of gray hair and fat cheeks that sagged into jowls. His eyes were an intense, otherworldly blue. There was a short sword in his hand and Eda saw a splatter of blood on its distinct, leaf-shaped blade.

"Uh-oh," Becky said.

Eda guessed he was a survivor – perhaps the only survivor from the warriors' attack on the Children's camp. Had he fought to the end with his people? Or had he run away, deserting everyone including the dead boy?

"You're the Sinners," he said. His voice was unpleasant, like a bite inside the ears. He acted as if Eda and Becky's presence was a personal insult. With a fat finger, he pointed to their suits, the purpose of which he must have known. "You've been chosen. You can't leave Uncle Sam hanging like that or he'll...no, no, no. It'll never be over unless you go back."

Becky's sword arm hung limp at her side. It was like she'd forgotten the weapon was there and as the man talked, she backed off.

It was Eda who stepped forward, brandishing her sword in the air. The steel was heavy and nothing felt good or familiar about it. It was like wielding a skyscraper. But it was all she had and she had to at least make sure she looked comfortable with the blade. If she could scare the old man off they might avoid an unpleasant, not to mention time-consuming confrontation.

"You're in our way mister," she said. "Look, we don't want any trouble. Just let us go past and we'll pretend like we never saw one another."

The man approached Eda slowly. His eyes burned with blue fire.

"You belong to Uncle Sam."

Eda's hands were shaking but she came forward with false bravado. The warriors and the Children were on their tail, probably not far behind, and they had to get past this man. Quickly.

"You could just go," she said. "Forget all this Uncle Sam crap and take off. We both know it's not real, don't we? There doesn't have to be any more blood spilled today. We saw what happened in camp back there. That must have been hard..."

To her surprise, the man smiled. "You must be joking little girl."

"No," Eda said, her brow creasing in a mix of anger and frustration. "I'm not. Let us go or you're going to end up like them. Dead in a swamp."

A look of indignation flashed across the old man's face. He raised his sword and walked towards Eda at a terrifyingly rapid pace.

Eda glanced over at Becky. She was frozen to the spot, feet

trapped in the mud, her eyes locked onto the sword in the man's hands.

"It's going to be alright," Eda said, nodding at her.

She turned around and charged forward. Her opponent wasn't smiling anymore. As Eda rushed in with sword aloft, the man wheezed in horror. His already wrinkled face aged twenty years in a split second. Eda realized now that he'd been trying to psych her out all along and that the last thing he wanted was a fight.

Too late.

The swords made a loud clanging noise as they clashed. The old man did his best to fight back but it quickly became apparent that he was no fighter and that he probably hadn't held a weapon in years. His swing was slow and clumsy. Predictable. Eda pushed him backwards, using a combination of speed and skill and brute force. Had she been fighting one of the warriors, her limitations with the short sword would have been exposed. Fatally. Fortunately what she had was enough for this encounter.

The man's defense became non-existent as his arms tired. After a feeble attack, he left himself wide open. Eda saw it, leapt forward and with lightning fast speed, slashed the tip of the blade across his ample waist like she was trying to spill his insides onto the dirt.

He shrieked and dropped to his knees. The sword tilted to the side, then slipped from his grip.

Eda took a step back and surveyed the damage while she caught her breath. The man was bleeding out badly from the middle. He snarled like a threatened animal, touching the wound repeatedly to confirm that it was real and then he let go, knowing that his escape from death earlier that day had only been a temporary reprieve. His face was eerily calm.

"Let's go Eda," Becky said. She was behind Eda now, tugging on her arm like she wanted to pull it off. "For God's sake."

But Eda knew they couldn't leave, not yet. The old man was still conscious. And when the warriors or the Children showed up he'd be capable of giving them information about the two Sinners. At the very least he'd confirm their presence in the hunting grounds.

The man grunted. His blue eyes were on Eda, as if he could read her mind. Unlike Becky, he knew what she had to do next.

"You should have let us pass," Eda said.

"You can't escape," the old man said through a coughing fit. His face was a sickly shade of white. "Nobody escapes."

Eda took a long, deep breath. She tightened her grip on the hilt. Then she charged forward and with all the strength she could muster, buried the sword deep in the man's chest. There was a loud ripping noise, like the sky being torn in half. The blade cut through him like his skin was paper. The man screamed, just for a second but it was enough of a primal roar that it sent a barrage of shivers down Eda's spine.

Eda stepped back. She watched him, panting like a dog on a hot day, gasping loudly before at last he fell over and curled up into a ball.

More wheezing. Eventually he stopped moving.

Becky approached the corpse in slow motion. Her shoulders were heaving, her breath out of control. "You killed him," she said, turning back to Eda. She spoke quietly, as if they were intruders on sacred ground. "Holy shit."

Eda hurried over, knelt down and began hurling leaves, sticks and dirt over the body. Anything she could find. She worked relentlessly and alone. When the remains were hidden, she got back to her feet.

Eda reached for the collar of the shirt. Her fingers pulled at the tie, searching, wrestling back and forth until the knot was loose.

At last, she could breathe.

10

Eda and Becky fought their way through this hostile maze, through Great Piece Meadows, as best they could. Wooden limbs, extending out of fat trunks, and spear-like branches, made a grab for them as they hurried past. The swamp floor devoured their legs up to the knees at times. These muddy trenches were becoming more common the further they went into the hunting grounds. As a result, valuable energy was expended in the basics of movement. The rewards were pitiful.

It didn't feel like they were getting closer to anything that mattered. Everything was a repeat of what they'd just battled through moments earlier. It was as if the landscape was constantly imitating itself to fool them. To drive them mad.

They were slowing down too. There was a muggy heat enclosed within the swamp and it was robbing them of oxygen.

Because of the slow pace, Eda noticed something that she hadn't seen before. It was something that broke the unchanging rhythm of the monotonous environment. More importantly, it was something that allowed her to hope again. The trees were marked, at least some of them were. Marked with shapes. At first, Eda didn't pay too much attention to it but when these landmarks kept showing up time and time again, spaced twenty or thirty feet apart, she realized it wasn't just random swamp graffiti. It had to mean something.

There were only two shapes – circles and triangles. Crude carvings in the heart of the trunk. And there was always just one shape per tree. Each marked tree had a twin nearby, about ten feet away, standing parallel to the other. The next set of markings, thirty feet further north, would feature a different shape from the previous set, but it was essentially the same thing over and over again – two trees running parallel, with a wide gap in between. There was clear design on display. And as time went on, Eda became convinced that she was looking at a trail on the Meadows' floor.

"You see that?" Eda said.

Becky had been quiet since the old man's death. As she looked at the nearest set of marked trees, she cleared her throat.

"Shapes? Oh yeah, I see them."

"I've been thinking about it," Eda said. "Wanna know what I think? It might be some kind of mapping system designed by the Children. Or maybe it was put there by the people who came here before the Children – you know? We've seen tables and chairs and other things left over from the past. People used to come here all the time before the war. How did *they* find their way around? Don't you see Becky? I'm talking about directions. That right there might be our way out of here."

"A map?" Becky said.

"Why not?" Eda said. "You've got to admit, it's pretty easy to get lost in here and..."

She was about to say – *let's face it, we're probably lost already* – but decided against it.

"Look at it Becky," Eda said. She could hear the enthusiasm in her voice again. Despite this, the two women kept their distance from the carved trees, cautious spectators hovering in between faith and skepticism.

"I see the carvings," Becky said. "But what makes you think it's a map?"

"Not a map so much," Eda said. "More like road signs."

"I still don't see it," Becky said, shaking her head.

"You've got two trees with markings," Eda said. "In each set there are always two trees with either circles or triangles. A narrow path runs straight through the middle, you see that? It's kind of beaten down but it looks like a trail. You go through that and then it's a short walk to the next set. I don't know Becky, it looks to me like it's leading somewhere. Go through the trees and you're following the route."

"But where?" Becky said. "If that *is* a route marked out, where's it taking people?"

"Two Bridges Road?" Eda said. "Why the hell not? We're going north aren't we?"

Becky looked at the markings again. She scratched her arm, leaving an angry red patch. "Maybe we're just seeing what we want to see Eda."

"Maybe," Eda said. "But maybe not."

"And the circles and triangles?" Becky asked. She tilted her head to the side a little. "Why the different shapes?"

Eda sighed. "Who knows?" she said. "Maybe they got bored. Who cares as long as it takes us to the road?"

"I guess it could be a path," Becky said. She sounded a little less doubtful.

"I think the Children made it," Eda said. "The grass looks kind of beat down in between the trees, doesn't it? That's a fresh trail if you ask me. Think about it. It only makes sense they use some sort of mapping system to find their way around this place. They've probably got them all over the swamp."

"So do we follow it?" Becky said. "I guess we've got nothing to lose right?"

Eda held up a hand. She strained her ears, certain that she'd picked up on voices behind them.

"Warriors," she said quietly. "They're catching up."

Becky shook her head slowly. Her haggard features suggested a cocktail of emotions – fear and exasperation. There was something unnerving about being the centerpiece of an enduring, determined pursuit. About being hunted. But it was annoying too, it was damn annoying. Why couldn't they just leave her alone?

"Okay," Becky said. She put a hand on Eda's shoulder and squeezed. "We follow the Children's map. Right?"

Eda nodded. "We don't have a choice," she said. "Not if we want to get out."

They walked quickly towards the marked trees. As they did they heard that eerie high-pitched yapping sound again – the one they'd heard back in the Children's camp. It was closer this time, even though it still sounded like it was deep inside the Meadows.

"That's a scary fucking noise," Becky said, glancing in all directions. "But I think I've figured out what that is. It's a deer barking – apparently they do that you know."

"Sounds like he's telling us to run faster," Eda said.

"Yep," Becky said. "That's exactly what he's saying. Wanna know why? He lives in the hunting grounds and he knows only too well what happens to the hunted when they get caught."

At that moment, Frankie Boy came trotting through the dirt. He had a panting grin on his face.

"You little bastard," Eda said, stroking him behind the ears. "You're having the time of your life in here aren't you? Hey guess what? We might have found a way out of this shithole at last. You ready to run?"

She leaned closer and Frankie Boy licked her on the face. His stale breath almost knocked her dizzy.

"Jesus," Eda said, recoiling backwards. "What have you been eating?" She wiped her face dry of dog spit.

"Let's hope this trail doesn't lead us back to Camp Crazy," Becky said. "That would just about finish me off I reckon."

She walked towards the marked trees. Despite her words, her stride was confident.

"Alright," she said. "Deep breaths. Here we go."

Becky led the way, running in between the first set, two triangles about fifteen feet apart. Eda followed close behind. Frankie Boy took his own route, running on the outskirts of the trees.

They set a swift pace.

The next set of marked trees, two circles on the trunks, appeared up ahead. Becky glanced over her shoulder and grinned at Eda. It was a big grin, full of hope. Her eyes were alight and Eda knew that Becky could see the tall skyline of Boston again, just up ahead.

"We're getting out," Becky roared.

Eda smiled.

Becky charged through the gap in between the circled trees. Seconds later, an explosion of noise made Eda stop dead in her tracks. Like she'd crashed into a brick wall. At first she didn't know what was going on. In a split second, everything happened. She'd heard a vicious, metallic crunch followed by the worst scream ever.

It was Becky.

"AGGGHH!!"

Her leg was caught in a steel-jaw trap.

"No!" Eda yelled, running over to her. "No, no!"

She dropped to the dirt and her hands frantically probed the trap. It had been nailed into the earth but to secure it further, a long piece of metal chain had been fastened around the base of a tree trunk. Most of the trap was buried under a mound of grass and dirt. Now it returned to the surface, victorious and with prey.

"Fuck," Eda said. A single tear ran down her cheek. "This isn't happening."

Becky's face was horribly contorted as she looked down at the damage. She'd dropped the sword when the steel jaws had shut around her lower leg. Now she fell onto her backside, both hands clawing helplessly at the trap.

"Oh God," she hissed. Her face was scorched red with pain.

Eda realized their mistake, far too late. It wasn't a map they'd been following after all. And it wasn't road signs either. They were on a hunting trail and those carved shapes on the trunks weren't indicating the route to the Two Bridges Road. The markings pointed to where the Children's hidden traps had been set. It was a miracle that Eda and Becky hadn't triggered the first set of markings they'd raced through just moment before this one. Maybe some of the traps didn't work anymore. Maybe they were just old.

It didn't matter. Not now.

Eda crouched down beside Becky, an arm locked around the woman's shoulder. Her knees sunk into the spongy surface of the swamp.

The serrated jaws had clamped down tight around the ankle. The trap's jagged teeth had pierced through Becky's suit pants and the initial struggle after it was triggered had only made the wound angrier.

"Becky," Eda said, placing a hand on the woman's back. It was soaking wet. "Don't worry, I'm going to get you out."

Becky was on the brink of hyperventilating. She gripped her leg tight with both hands while Eda probed at the trap, searching for the release trigger. There had to be something – a lever or a switch that would open the jaws. She pulled and pushed at everything she saw. Not a damn thing worked. The chilling thought came to Eda that maybe the release lever was broken. After all, the first trap hadn't sprung. Maybe this one was partly broken too. For all Eda knew, these traps had been out here for months, years maybe.

"This fucking thing..." Eda screamed. It felt like her head was about to explode. She pulled at the jaws with all her strength but they were razor sharp and clamped tight. Her arms felt like they were going to snap. Several minor cuts had opened up on her hand.

Becky looked at Eda, tears flooding down her cheeks. Her shoulders sagged to the dirt.

"It's over," she said.

Eda shook her head. She gritted her teeth, not taking her eyes off the trap.

"I'm getting you out of this," she said. "Don't worry about a thing Becky."

She jumped up to her feet and picked up one of the swords lying on the dirt. Gripping the handle tight, Eda hacked furiously at the metal chain fastened around the tree.

"Eda," Becky called over. "Stop. Just give it up."

But Eda didn't stop. She kept chopping at the chain like a madwoman. Hoping for a miracle to show up.

Clink-clink-clink...

"You're wasting time!" Becky said. "Eda, you have to give it up now. NOW! Even if you somehow got the trap off my ankle I won't be able to run."

"Then I'll carry you," Eda yelled. "I'll carry you out of here if I have to."

She looked at Becky and saw a look of resignation in the other woman's face.

"You have to keep running Eda," Becky said. "This thing, it's not over for you, not if you keep moving. Remember what Murphy said about movement – it's what keeps you alive, right? That's never been truer than right now."

"I can get it off," Eda said, glaring at the chain.

She raised the sword over her head. Becky intercepted the strike with a scolding tone, sharper than any blade.

"No," she called out. "It's over Eda – it's over. All you're doing by staying here is killing yourself. And I sure as hell don't want you to do that."

Becky winced with pain as she spoke. Her skin was a ghoulish white and her breathing was slowing down.

Eda looked at Becky and dropped onto her knees in frustration. Frankie Boy walked in and out, ears down and looking at Eda intently, seemingly confused by the energy going around. Or maybe he already knew what Eda didn't want to accept.

Eda hurried over to Becky's side once again. Her eyes scoured the trap, searching for the answer to an impossible question. Going over old ground, she pulled at anything that might have been a lever.

It was a dead end.

Becky wiped her face dry of tears and sweat. It looked like she was trying to make herself presentable for what was coming. She reached out and grabbed Eda's hand, giving it a squeeze. In that single gesture, Eda felt the woman's strength fading.

"Maybe you'll get to Boston someday," Becky said. "You'll go back east. Right?"

Eda nodded.

"Well," Becky said, swallowing a mouthful of pain, "if you ever bump into a woman called Pam Burton in the south end, tell her that Mike tried to find her. Tell her about me too, I only wish I could have met her. Who knows? Maybe she's checked out already and the reunion with Mike has already happened. But if somehow she's still alive...I know, I know, it's a long shot, but just tell her that Mike and I, we had a daughter. We called her little Pam. Will you do that?"

"You had a daughter?" Eda said.

"Once," Becky said.

"That's why you waited so long before traveling east?"

Becky nodded. "Little Pam was the fragile sort," she said. "Too fragile for the old world let alone this fucked up version. I'm surprised but thankful we had her as long as we did."

Eda didn't ask what had happened. Knowing wouldn't make it easier for anyone. Instead, she looked at the trap again, still pushing and pulling, hoping for a last minute reprieve.

Becky squeezed Eda's hand again. "You need to go now," she said.

"I can't leave you like this," Eda said. "How the hell am I supposed to leave you like this?"

"Go!" Becky said. She pulled her hand away from Eda.

Eda shook her head stubbornly.

"Listen to me," Becky said, sitting up a little. "That bastard Baldilocks only wins if he gets all four of us. That's why you've got to make it out of this swamp. You have to beat him. You have to get away from the Children, from the warriors. Somehow you've got to keep going."

Becky reached for the handle of the short sword lying next to her. Groaning, she held the weapon aloft. "Fuck me, this is heavy."

Eda threw her arms around Becky and held on tight. To her surprise, Becky's skin felt cold already.

"I'm sorry," Eda whispered into her ear. "I'm so sorry."

"Find the road," Becky said. She patted Eda's back three times, like a mother to a child.

Eda got back to her feet, leaving Becky stranded in the mud. Becky looked up and smiled. She rubbed Frankie Boy's head as he came over for a visit.

"Get out of here," she said. "Both of you."

Eda stood there, all out of words and empty comfort. With a curt nod, she turned around and ignoring the voice of her conscience, set off through the swamp, pumping her arms and legs with violence.

Everything shut down – it was what she had to do. She had to become an unfeeling monster.

Eda's exit built up to a tremendous speed. She ignored the obstacles – the long limbed trees, the sharp branches and the black glue-like surface that tried to slow her down.

She had to get out.

Frankie Boy ran at her side all the way. Thank God, he didn't bark as they accelerated through Great Piece Meadows.

11

Frankie Boy charged ahead of Eda. He stayed well clear of the marked trees like he had first time around but now he was telling her to do the same. But although she avoided the booby traps, there was no skipping over the fact that Eda was lost. She was so lost that she might as well have been wearing a blindfold.

After losing track of how long she'd been running for, Eda slowed down to a stop. The Meadows' consistent landscape – the trees, grass and mud – surrounded her on all sides. No matter how far she ran, it felt like the scenery would never end. There was no way she could ever outrun it.

"Where the hell are we?" she said, doubling over and trying to catch her breath. She'd pushed her body too hard trying to get away from Becky. Her heart was pounding. Her lungs burning up.

Frankie Boy trotted forward. He caught a whiff of something in the air and disappeared through a wall of greenery.

"You're leaving me again?" Eda said, watching him go. She straightened up, still breathing heavy. "This isn't a good time Frankie Boy."

Eda wiped a trickle of sweat off her brow. She was alone.

An almighty roaring noise in the distance made her jump. It came from somewhere else in the Meadows – somewhere far enough away that Eda didn't have to worry too much. She spun around and her eyes fell upon a barrage of maple trees about a hundred feet back. Eda looked over that way, listening closely. She heard loud voices – male and female. The pounding of feet on the ground, shaking the world. It sounded like a horde of barbarians running rampant through the swamp.

Then she heard it – the familiar clash of steel on steel.

Before she knew it, Eda was creeping towards the noise. Going back in the direction she'd just come from. Somewhere in her head a voice screamed in protest. This was her chance to get away.

But Eda ignored the voice. She had to see it.

After a five-minute walk, she crouched behind a row of birches. Very carefully, Eda peered through the foliage, down a steep slope that tumbled to a massive clearing. A skirmish was taking place. The Children and the warriors, having already collided at the crater and on the Passaic, were now squaring off for a third time in the heart of the swamp.

Eda watched with fascination.

Despite the overcrowded canoes coming out of Fairfield, it looked like everyone had made it back to the Meadows. The Children outnumbered the warriors by about three to one on the battlefield. It should have been a massacre but the warriors, while fewer in number, had a lethal combination of skill and savagery on their side. Their stamina was solid too and Eda knew they would fight all day if they had to. Literally.

The women stood their ground as a swarm of camouflaged figures encircled them.

The Children charged in recklessly. Eda's head rang with the sound of clanging steel and battle cries as another wave of fighting commenced. From her vantage point uphill, it didn't look like anyone was winning the second skirmish. There was a blur of close quarter fighting and it didn't paint a clear picture of how things were going. The Children were nothing more than a blunt instrument, crude and inelegant in their assault. They took some losses as they closed the distance. But they *were* getting through. They were a stubborn mob, clearly intent on revenge for the ambush at the crater. And if their strategy was to overwhelm the warriors with sheer volume there was every chance of success, albeit at a great cost to their numbers.

Eda felt an outburst of relief. Her enemies were killing each other and it was beautiful to watch. Their screams and dying shouts were poetry in her ears. In order to get what they wanted, both the Children and the warriors had to get past one another.

That was proving too much for either side.

Eda retreated backwards, scolding herself for wasting time when she should have been running. But now she could at least run with the knowledge that her pursuers wouldn't be coming after her anytime soon.

She looked around for Frankie Boy. No sign of him anywhere.

"Damn it," she said.

Eda heard a noise to her left. Her first thought was that Frankie Boy had come back to her and she turned to greet him with a smile. She would tell him about the battle – tell him that they had a chance of getting out.

It was Lex.

The chief warrior stood tall like a bloodstained mirage. She was fifteen feet away and without saying anything, she began to close that distance. Twelve feet, ten feet. And then she stopped. She wore a black vest top and matching pants. Her white skin shone with a thin layer of perspiration.

"Going somewhere?" Lex said.

Eda's body shook. She didn't know if it was shaking inside or out. Probably both.

Slowly, she glanced downhill towards the battle.

"Shouldn't you be down there?" she said. "Fighting alongside your soldiers?"

Lex stole a brief glance at the battlefield. There was no emotion on her face.

"I came here for you," she said, turning back to Eda. "Only you."

"But they're losing," Eda said, nodding towards the clearing. "They're outnumbered. Without you they'll..."

Lex shook her head.

"They're doing their job," she said. "They're loyal soldiers and they do what I tell them to do. Today I told them to get those freaks out of the way so that I can look for you undisturbed. Don't worry about them Eda. Bringing you home is all that matters. Dead or alive? That's up to you."

Eda gasped for air. She took a step backwards.

"Why?" she said, outraged as well as fearful. "Why the hell are you chasing me all over this swamp Lex? Shay let me go. Remember? I'm an ambassador for the Complex and you're running after me like all that means nothing. Like we didn't make a deal."

Lex's lips curled into a smile.

"Did you really think I was okay with that?" she said. "Don't you know me Eda?"

"Shay let me go!" Eda snapped. "That has to mean something, even to you. I'm an ambassador for God's sake."

Lex pointed to Eda's damp, mud-soaked suit. The soggy garment clung to Eda's body like glue.

"You don't look much like an ambassador to me," she said.

The battle cries in the background grew louder. A woman screamed and it was like a pair of claws scraping down the inside of Eda's skull.

"They need you down there," Eda said. "They're going to die."

"Where's your dog?" Lex said.

Eda shrugged while her eyes darted back and forth across the rugged landscape. Thank God, Frankie Boy was nowhere to be seen. Whatever he was chasing, Eda hoped that it had taken him far away. Lex was ready this time. Damn it, she wanted to fight the dog again. Crazy bitch. Her body was covered from head to toe in the blood of slaughtered Children. It still wasn't enough for her.

"Leave the dog out of this," Eda said. "You never answered my question. Why are you doing this?"

Lex smiled and stretched up to her full height, well over six feet tall. Her bones snapped like whips cracking. Overhead, a solitary beam of sunlight crept through the gray sky, enhancing the murderous gleam in the chief warrior's eyes.

"Who do you think has the power in the Complex?" she said. "Who controls the warriors?"

Eda shook her head. "You're not as smart as Shay."

"Maybe not," Lex said. "But smart's not the same thing as power. Is it?"

"What are you talking about?" Eda asked. "Why can't you just answer the question for God's sake? Tell me why you came after me?"

Lex took a step forward.

"Once your little farewell ceremony was over," she said, "I had some quiet time with Shay back in the Waldorf. I informed her that it couldn't end like that. You humiliated me Eda and every time people look at my face I can see it in their eyes. They know. Sometimes I even see pity in their eyes. No, no, no. Only your death can make this right – you and the dog."

"Shay let you come after me?" Eda said. "After an ambassador? I doubt that very much."

"Yeah," Lex said. "Shay wasn't happy but guess what? I pulled rank and she knows she can't afford to lose the warriors. Like you said, she's smart. Not long after that, we hit the road and we were right behind you Eda. We followed you all the way to this godfor-saken swamp. We waited too long, should have hit you before you disappeared in here. What the hell were you thinking about walking into this place?"

"I knew someone was following me," Eda said. "Right from the start, I knew."

"Yep."

Eda's fingers curled around the hilt of the short sword. The grip was unwelcoming and she knew in no uncertain terms that she couldn't beat Lex. Taking out the old man with an unfamiliar weapon was one thing. Lex was another thing entirely.

But what choice did she have?

"It doesn't have to be that way," Lex said, pointing at Eda's hand on the hilt. "Although I admire your spirit."

"What do you mean?" Eda said.

"I want to take you back to New York alive," Lex said. "And in return for coming back, I'm willing to give you a swift, albeit public execution."

Eda glanced towards the clearing. The fighting raged on, as fierce as ever.

"You want the warriors to see me die," she said. "Right? You *need* them to see it. Is that the B-team down there today? Is the A-team waiting in New York for you to bring me back? For the big revenge ceremony?"

Lex wagged a finger back and forth.

"You should be more grateful," she said. "I saved your life back there at the crater. That would have been a *horrible* way to go."

"You saved my life so you can kill me."

"I can give you so much better."

"The East River?" Eda asked. "Is that where you're going to put me?"

"You always were a smart girl," Lex said, grinning. "Sure. That's where you'll go when it's over."

Lex took another look around, as if expecting someone else to turn up.

"But before any of that," she said. "I really want to find that dog of yours. I want you to see what I'm going to do to it."

Eda pointed the tip of her short sword at Lex. Her arms trembled under the weight of the weapon.

"This conversation's over."

Lex looked at the weapon with robotic contempt. "You want to fight me?" she asked. She opened her arms out wide. It was an invitation to violence.

Eda didn't say anything. She took another subtle step back, opening up a little space in between them.

"Well why not?" Lex said, bouncing on her feet like a boxer. There was a cold, half-smile on her lips. "I think it's fair to say I'm not at my best right now. I'm cut. I'm still beat up from New York. You're a good fighter Eda, much better than I thought. There's fresh blood on that sword of yours, I can smell it. Who knows? Maybe you'll finish me off this time."

A bird squawked overhead and it sounded like mad laughter.

"No," Eda said in a quiet voice. "I don't want to fight..."

She glanced upwards at the warrior. Slowly, her eyes moved beyond Lex; it was a subtle maneuver but Eda did it in a way that Lex couldn't fail to miss.

She stared over Lex's shoulders, looking at nothing but swamp. In her mind however, she saw Frankie Boy creeping up on all fours. He was coming to the rescue yet again.

Eda smiled, imagining it so vividly that it had to show up on her face.

Lex's body stiffened. Eda knew what she had to be thinking in that moment. That Eda was trying to play her, that Frankie Boy was at that moment, just inches away. And for all the warrior's bravado, she had to be at least a little bit afraid. She should have been terrified of Frankie Boy after what he'd done to her in New York. It couldn't just be the wounds on Lex's face and hands that were still fresh – the dog had almost killed her.

Eda looked at Lex. Then over her shoulder again, towards the imaginary beast coming up from behind.

Lex spun around and drew the katana from her scabbard. "C'mon you fucking dog," she yelled. Ready for war, all she got was empty space.

Eda charged past while Lex's back was turned.

"Bitch!" she heard Lex call after her.

Eda didn't look back. She raced over the mud and grass, trying her best to make sure that she didn't take one wrong step. If she slipped now it was over. But she had to throw caution to the wind, abandoning everything else for the sake of speed.

Lex tore after her. It sounded like an angry winged goddess on her tail. Supernatural speed. Feet like thunder plowing through the dirt.

"Get back here! I'll kill you."

The threats were getting closer.

Eda knew she couldn't outrun Lex. After everything that happened, her body screamed for mercy. The engine was exhausted and slowing against her will.

Thrown into a state of intense, trance-like focus, Eda rediscovered the markings on the trees. Circles. Then triangles. They went past in a blur. She wondered if the warriors had made the connection yet. Had they triggered one of the traps?

Had they lost someone like Eda had?

She groaned, in between gasping for breath. It was her only chance of giving Lex the slip. It was also very likely a suicide mission. In order to lead Lex through the booby-trapped trees, Eda knew the price she'd have to pay. She'd have to lead the way.

Victory and failure, it was in the lap of gods. Eda would either end up like Becky or she'd sentence Lex to the same grisly fate. But what if it was Eda's leg caught in the steel trap? What would Lex do to her if she couldn't open the trap? Would she hack off the limb and drag Eda, bleeding and deformed, out of the swamp and back east to New York to face a public revenge?

Lex was gaining on Eda. She had to be close enough now that she'd follow Eda through the marked trees. Not close enough however, that she could reach out and grab Eda before triggering the trap.

Eda saw the shapes carved onto the two trunks. Triangles.

This was it.

She gritted her teeth and with a final burst of acceleration, charged through the hunting trail. Eda hurdled over a little mound of earth piled up in the center of the pathway. She landed with a jarring thud but stayed upright.

She was through.

Lex's feet crashed over the soft ground behind her. She was so close that Eda thought the warrior had already escaped the trap. Any second now, Lex's hot breath would touch Eda on the back of the neck. Then the hand would reach out and...

There was a thick snapping sound. It wasn't the ordinary sound of twigs snapping underfoot in the Meadows.

Lex roared in horror.

Eda turned around. At the same time her feet kept moving, survival instinct pulling her backwards. She caught sight of a thick branch to Lex's left. This branch hauled up a large net of rope concealed under the swamp floor, smothered in leaves, dirt and fine sticks. The net ascended quickly, wrapping itself around Lex and lifting her about ten feet above the ground.

The katana fell out of her hands on the way up.

"NO!"

Lex hung in midair, peering through the bars of her rope cage. With all her strength, Lex tore at the net but it was too sturdy to give way. She didn't stop there – she thrust an arm through the net, clawing at Eda from above. A deep growling noise spilled out of the woman, perhaps involuntarily. It sounded like a wild bear caught in the trap.

"Eda. Get me out of this and we'll talk, I swear."

Her fingers wrapped themselves around the rope and she tried once again to tear it apart like it was paper.

Eda walked tentatively closer.

She bent down and picked up Lex's sword and looked at it. It was much lighter than the short sword. It would make a fine weapon.

"Leave it!" Lex snarled, extending her arm through the net, crooked fingers yearning for the blade. "Don't you touch that. Don't you dare take my sword!"

Eda stared at the wriggling figure caught in the rope net. Despite feeling dizzy and sick to the stomach, she allowed herself a smile.

"You should have stayed in New York," she said.

12

Eda left Lex hanging in the trap without a second thought.

Still carrying both swords, she ran about a hundred meters in a direction she hoped was north. Lex's angry insults faded into the background. When she arrived at a small clearing, Eda dropped the short sword onto the dirt. She took a long look around and when she was certain that she was alone, she fell onto her knees and buried the weapon under a mound of shallow earth.

She stood up again, a little too quickly. Dancing on wobbly legs, Eda took several deep breaths and waited until the dizziness passed. How long had she been on the move now? How much had happened? Looking at her hands, Eda saw they were black with dirt. Her clothes smelled foul. She couldn't remember the last time she'd felt dry.

With a self-motivating, primal grunt, Eda set off with the katana in hand. The memory of Lex swinging in the net had at least renewed her spirits, which had been flagging after the loss of Becky. The Children and the warriors were preoccupied with each other.

She had a chance.

If only she knew where the hell she was going.

Eda's eyes roamed the vast expanse of wetlands. As well as

looking for a way out, she was still searching for Frankie Boy who'd gone missing again. But the dog, wherever he was, was in no rush to be found. He'd made himself at home in the Meadows and why not? Eda had noticed a spring in the German Shepherd's step ever since they'd left the urban world behind. The thought occurred to her that Frankie Boy wouldn't want to leave all this green stuff when the time came. If it came to a choice between Eda and staying in the swamp, what would he do?

A surge of loneliness swept over Eda, so powerful that it almost knocked her off her feet.

"Frankie?"

The air was damp and rotten and it had the effect of making Eda feel like she was still trapped underwater. Still drowning.

She looked over to her right and saw a flicker of movement behind the trees. A face. Then it disappeared behind the green barrier.

"Who's there?" Eda said.

Was she imagining things again?

She stood frozen, her feet trapped in the spongy surface underneath. Eda stared towards the trees, not blinking, gripping the handle of the samurai sword with both hands.

Was it Lex? Could it be?

No. There was no way Lex could have escaped from the net so quickly. Not unless one of the other warriors had found her and released her. But that would have been a miracle in itself – surely all the warriors were dead by now.

There was a loud rustling noise.

"Come out!" Eda yelled. Her eyes jumped back and forth, trying to cover all sides. "I know you're there. I see you."

There was short pause. A meek voice called out from afar:

"Don't hurt me."

Light footsteps on the swamp floor.

A young man stepped out with his hands up. He was no more than a boy really, about sixteen or seventeen at most, dressed in tattered camouflage clothing. His scruffy red hair was soaked with sweat and his cheeks were ablaze with a hot, flustered pink.

"You won't hurt me?" he said.

"That depends," Eda said. "You can put your hands down."

He lowered his hands.

"So what are you doing...?"

As Eda spoke, she heard something to her left. Rustling. The crackling of the ground as it betrayed whoever was trying to move unnoticed. At first, Eda thought it was an ambush – that the boy had others of his kind lurking in wait, waiting to pounce on her.

Eda's knuckles turned white as she squeezed the katana hilt. Adrenaline coursed through her veins.

"Come out you bastards..."

She groaned with relief when the big German Shepherd crept out of the bushes. It looked like a wild animal slithering out of the belly of the swamp. He didn't look at Eda. Frankie Boy was all business, stalking the boy, moving forward in a low crouch, so low that his underside brushed off the dirt. Half-lizard, half dog.

The boy whimpered at the sight of the black beast.

"No! No! No! Please. Don't let it hurt me."

His hands were up over his head again. Two large, frightened eyes darted back and forth between Eda and Frankie Boy.

"Call it off," he begged.

Eda did nothing at first. Opportunity had distracted her.

Now she stepped forward, all set to play the role of the white knight, albeit one dressed in a sacrificial black suit.

"Frankie!" she said. Eda's tone was firm. She made a loud clapping noise, once then twice.

"Frankie Boy. Stop it. Come over here."

She had no idea if the dog would listen to her. Why should he? There was no ownership in the relationship between them. It didn't matter how many times people referred to Frankie Boy as 'her dog', he was a free spirit, one that did as he pleased.

But Frankie *was* listening to Eda. His ears pricked up at the sound of her voice, his brown eyes mellowed and he raised himself back to a standing position. His looked back and forth between Eda and the teenage boy. Then he sat down, like a bodyguard looming in the background.

The boy exhaled with relief. With a trembling hand, he wiped the sweat off his pink face.

"Who are you?" Eda said. She pointed the tip of the katana in his direction, making sure he didn't get too comfortable.

"Number 64," he said.

"You don't have a proper name?" Eda said.

"That *is* my name," he said, sounding offended. "What's wrong with it?"

"Never mind," Eda said.

She noticed glimmering droplets of water running down one side of his face.

"Is that...?" she asked. "Are you crying?"

Number 64 wiped the back of his hand over his face. Violently. Sweat and tears intermingled, beyond his control. As he rubbed his face dry, a sudden explosion of birdsong erupted above their heads.

"My dad's dead," he said.

"What?"

"My dad is dead."

Eda jerked a lazy thumb over her shoulder.

"Back there?" she asked. "In the fighting?"

Number 64 nodded. "Most of them are dead or dying," he said. "It was a massacre back there. There were no winners."

"How'd you get away?" Eda said.

"I ran," the boy said. He looked irritated by the question and shifted restlessly on his feet. "I'm a coward, okay? I ran away before any of those women could butcher me like they did my dad."

Eda lowered the sword, very slowly. "Sounds like the smart move to me," she said. "That's what I would have done."

Number 64 stared at her. There was a long silence, like he was waiting for the punch line.

"You mean it?"

"Sure," Eda said. "It's kind of stupid dying when you don't have to. Right?"

Number 64 brushed a clump of sweaty hair off his forehead. In turn, he wiped the damp hand off his camouflage pants.

"Yeah."

"Where are you going now?" Eda asked.

The boy hesitated. "I don't want to be here anymore," he said, lowering his voice. "All of this, living in the Meadows and hiding away from the world – I'm done with it. I'm finished with Uncle Sam and with Baldilocks."

"You're done with Uncle Sam?" Eda said. "Is that what you mean? He won't be too pleased about that, will he?"

"My father worshipped Uncle Sam," Number 64 said. "I don't. Where was Uncle Sam today when my old man needed him? Huh? Where was Baldilocks for that matter? To hell with it. I just want to get out of here and start afresh. Uncle Sam won't miss me."

Eda pointed the sword north.

"Are you going to the Two Bridges Road?" she asked.

Number 64 nodded. "Yeah. Of course, where else?"

Eda's heart was racing. As long as she could trust the boy, this was the way out of Great Piece Meadows that she'd been looking for. This was it. She'd earned a break for God's sake, and here it was.

So why did she feel lousy?

Her thoughts were never far from Becky. That tortured face, the one that would never see the Boston skyline, was a constant companion. Eda knew that she'd have to live with it for the rest of her life. Awake and in dreams. And not just the face, but the knowledge that she'd left Becky to die in that terrible situation. That was a shadow that would follow her through darkness. And it was something she could never fix.

"The other woman," Eda said, staring hard at Number 64, "the one I ran with."

"Bank Manager," Number 64 said.

"Her name was Becky," Eda snapped. "Don't call her Bank Manager.

"Sorry."

"Did you see her back there?"

Number 64 nodded. "I saw her."

An icy chill ran down Eda's spine. "And?"

"The warriors got there first," he said. His matter of fact tone disgusted Eda. "Man, they did some terrible..."

Eda held up a hand. But it was the fierceness of her eyes that told the boy to shut up.

Fortunately he took the hint.

"It's not right," Number 64 said, looking at his feet. "What goes on in here. I've always known it. A lot of people know it I think but after the war, everyone is so scared of what's out there that they just take it. Not me, not anymore. I'm leaving."

"Why don't the others leave?" Eda said. "If they know it's wrong."

Number 64 shrugged lazily. "Baldilocks always says the same thing – this year might be the last year. It's nearly over and yet it never is. In the meantime, people are safe."

Eda was only half-listening to the boy.

"I'll show you how to get to the road," Number 64 said. "That's what you want right? As long as you let me go I'll take you wherever you want. What do you say?"

Number 64 glanced at Frankie Boy, his eyes expanding with terror. "Well?"

But Eda couldn't answer.

"We'd better get moving," Number 64 said, looking towards the murky sky. "Daylight's wasted, you know. We've still got a lot of ground to cover and it gets dark real quick in here."

"Wait a minute," Eda said, shaking her head.

"What for?" Number 64 said, sounding impatient. "Do you want to get out of here or not?"

Eda couldn't believe what she was thinking.

"Where is he?" she said. "Where's Baldilocks right now?"

"He's back at the crater," Number 64 said. He was edging backwards, eager to get moving. "He's waiting for the Children to bring you and the Bank Manager back so he can finish the ceremony. There's no way he'll leave until Uncle Sam gets what he wants."

"All those Children he sent to bring me back are dead," Eda said. "Except you. Right?"

"Yeah," Number 64 said in a quiet voice. "So?"

"Your dad's dead," Eda said. "And all Baldilocks cares about is the ceremony. What's that about huh?"

The boy looked like a ghost – like he was about to throw up.

"How many people are with him at the crater?" Eda said. "How many of those fuckers are still alive?"

"About twenty," Number 64 said. "Or thirty maybe, I've lost track. We're almost wiped out you know, wiped out in a single day. It's unbe-lievable. We're done."

"They're not done until he is," Eda said, speaking through clenched teeth.

The boy took a step backwards, like she'd verbally shoved him.

"You want to kill Baldilocks?"

Eda heard the words spoken out loud. *Kill Baldilocks*. The same thing she'd been thinking moments earlier. When Number 64 said it, it sounded so real.

"He's been using you all this time," Eda said. "Listen to me – I know someone just like him back in New York. She uses people for selfish reasons too. People like her and Baldilocks, they're taking advantage of people's fears, twisting them so tight that people lose sight of the truth. I couldn't do much about it in New York, but maybe I can do something this time around. With your help."

Number 64 looked at Eda with child-like fascination, as if she was someone from another planet.

"You know these hunting grounds," Eda said, gesturing to their wild surroundings with the sword. "You know them like the back of your hand, right?"

The boy looked warily at Frankie Boy. The dog was sitting nearby, blocking off the nearest exit.

"Can you get me back there without being seen?" Eda said.

"Back where?" Number 64 said.

"To the crater. To Baldilocks."

"Oh c'mon," Number 64 said. His pink cheeks were sizzling hot. "You don't really want to go all the way back to Fairfield do you? Are you crazy? Think about what you're saying lady. We're almost out of here. We're not that far from the Two Bridges Road. That's where I'm going."

"Not until you've helped me do what I have to do."

Number 64 stared at the sword in Eda's hand. "Help you kill him?"

"Don't overthink it," Eda said. "Just listen. I'm your prisoner and you're taking me back to the crater to finish the ceremony. If you play by that script, we're good. But if you pull any tricks I'll tell Frankie Boy to rip your throat out. And you know just by the way he's looking at you that he wants to do it, don't you? His appetite is legendary. All I need to do is give the word."

Number 64 clasped his hands together.

"Don't do this," he said. "Going back there, it's suicide. If we run now we'll be out of here by..."

"C'mon," Eda said, shouting over his desperate pleas. She turned around and faced the direction she'd been running away from. "Let's get moving."

"I can't do this," Number 64 said.

But Eda couldn't see him. He was a weak voice from behind, begging for reason.

"You can," Eda said, waiting for the boy to catch up and start leading the way back to camp. "And you will. Won't he Frankie Boy?"

The boy stuck to his word.

Perhaps he was scared about what Frankie Boy would do to him if he misbehaved. Or maybe, and Eda thought this the more likely scenario, he was a decent kid at heart. Despite being brainwashed from birth, Number 64 seemed to possess an inherent sense of right and wrong. And just maybe, he knew a twisted mess when he saw one.

He led the way back through the swamp. They were traveling south now, moving at a steady pace. Two Bridges Road was fading into the distance behind them. But Eda let all thoughts of the road go, a new vision having replaced the one that had fueled her so far.

She marched a few paces behind Number 64, staying close but not too close. Eda was drawing on the last of her energy reserves, but she had to keep a little something behind for the crater.

"You know where you are?" she asked the boy.

"Of course," he said.

They pushed through a vast expanse of overgrown land. Trees, grass, mud – no matter how far they went the swamp remained a colossal net of repetition. Number 64 escorted his two companions off the beaten track where there were fewer clearings. The wildness and hostility of nature was amplified here. Bigger. Fortunately however, there were no markings on the trees, which meant no traps.

They made it back to the Children's camp in good time. As soon as they arrived, Eda hurried over to the empty cabin where her backpack was stored. She found the bag and brought it back to the communal table where she proceeded to help herself to whatever food she could find, tossing it into the backpack for later. She picked up one of the large jugs and topped up her water bottle. As far as supplies went it wasn't much but it was enough to get started. Enough to get far away from Great Piece Meadows.

As Eda took care of practical concerns, Number 64 was kneeling beside the dead boy. Wiping a tear off his cheek, Number 64 reached out and closed the boy's eyes gently.

"Ready?" Eda said, walking over. She was aware of her insensitivity, but there was no time for grief, at least not now.

Number 64 slowly rose to his feet. The weight of the world sat on his shoulders.

He looked at Eda and nodded. His eyes then drifted over to one of the little wooden cabins. There was a pale, haunted expression on his face. Eda turned to see what he was looking at and she saw his number hanging off the door. There was another number there too. Number 14.

"We'd better get going," Eda said in a quiet voice.

"Yeah," Number 64 said. "And I don't ever want to come back here."

He led her to the riverbank where only two canoes remained upturned on the grass. The others were gone, probably drifting downriver. It didn't matter – they only needed one to carry them back to Fairfield.

Number 64 pushed one of the boats into the water. He grabbed a paddle and jumped in, as did Eda and Frankie Boy. Eda sat on the wooden bench, trying to ignore the doubts settling into her mind. What the hell was she thinking? What if Number 64 tried to tip her into the water? Did he know she couldn't swim? She glanced over at him. There was no contempt in his eyes. He didn't look fearful or bitter that Eda was forcing him to do something against his will. If anything he looked empty. Like a machine, simply obeying orders. And if he was plotting something, he was keeping it well hidden.

The canoe traveled down the Passaic River. East towards Fairfield.

Eda hoped this was her last time on the water. The near-drowning incident was fresh in her mind and she could still taste the rotten Passaic on her lips.

The voyage to the crater was somber. Only the squawking birds that flew over the boat made any noise. On occasion, Eda closed her eyes and drifted off a little, not quite sleeping but landing somewhere in between that and wakefulness. In this trance-like state she saw Becky's mangled limb caught in the steel trap. She saw the blood. She heard Becky groaning as Eda pulled on the broken lever over and over again. And yet no matter how hard she tried, it wouldn't release the trap.

Eda opened her eyes and saw only the river. Felt the boat skimming gently across the surface. She'd left her there for God's sake. Frightened and alone. How could she have done that? Why hadn't Eda at least offered to...finish it? At the very least she could have spared Becky further pain and...

No.

She couldn't. And thank God, Becky had never asked it of her either.

When the boat reached Fairfield, Eda disembarked quickly. With sword in hand, she strode forward with a renewed sense of purpose. There were no doubts about turning back from the Two Bridges Road anymore. She was supposed to be here. Righting wrongs, hoping it would fill the hole inside.

Number 64 struggled to keep up with Eda's rapid pace. Together they hurried through the wall of trees that led towards the winding road.

As they got closer to the road, Eda heard Number 64 lagging behind. She stopped and turned around to check on him. There it was – the conflict brewing in his blue eyes. Now that he was closer to the sacred site, it was like he realized what was going on. What was *really* going on. The inner voice of his former self had to be causing resistance. Here he was, helping this woman, this stranger, to kill his false god.

"Are you okay?" Eda asked.

Number 64 licked his lips and winced, like he'd tasted something bitter. He nodded slowly.

"Are you really going to...?"

"I'm going to do the right thing," Eda said, moving closer to him. Frankie Boy stood in between, watching this quiet interaction with interest. "But I need you to help me. Okay? If this is going to work, if we're going to stop all these people dying then we're going to have to trust each other. Think you can do that?"

Number 64 swallowed. "I think so."

"Don't lie to me," Eda said. She reached out and her fingers wrapped around his skinny, pale wrist like a set of handcuffs. "Do you really want to get out of here?"

"Yes," he said.

"Getting out," Eda said, "*really* getting out means taking care of Baldilocks once and for all. This is his doing – all of this is his doing."

He nodded.

Eda took a step back. She flipped the katana around, offering the elegantly wrapped hilt to Number 64.

"Take it," she said. "I'm your prisoner. You're going to walk me down there to him and you're going to have the blade pointing at my neck. Alright?"

Number 64's pink face looked like it had been freshly slapped.

"What?" he said. "I mean, yeah okay."

"Listen out for my signal," Eda said. "You'll know it when it comes and when you hear it, release me. I'll take care of the rest, I promise."

She lowered her voice.

"No tricks," Eda said. "Frankie Boy's coming down there with us. As far as the rest of the Children are concerned, the dog isn't loyal to anyone. But we know different, right?"

"Right."

"I trust you Number 64," Eda said, "but if you betray that trust, if you try to hand me over to them for real, I'll give the word and Frankie Boy will rip your face off. And when that's done, I'll dress you up in this suit and throw you down to Uncle Sam. You can be President of the United States today."

"No tricks," Number 64 said, taking the sword. "But what if it doesn't work? Baldilocks is a lot of things but he isn't stupid you know."

"Then we're both dead," Eda said. "Alright?"

"Oh Jesus." Number 64 wiped the sweat off his forehead. Eda thought it was a miracle the kid had any fluid left to perspire. If he kept going like that, he'd shrivel up and turn into a pink raisin.

"C'mon let's go," Eda said.

They approached the winding road with the metal barriers. Peering towards the crater in the distance, Eda saw what was left of the Children. Thirty people at most, maybe less.

Baldilocks, with the Uncle Sam mask pulled up over his head, was deep in conversation with Number 10. They stood apart from the others, about twenty feet from the crater rim. Number 10, like the rest of the Children, was still dressed in a long gray robe. She held the dog skull mask in her hands, jostling it anxiously back and forth. Some of the others, like Baldilocks, had their mask sitting atop their heads. It looked very much like a half-time interval and that these people were waiting for the second part of the show to begin.

They had no idea most of their people were dead. Baldilocks had been too confident in the ability of the Children he'd sent after the warriors. He'd been too confident in numerical superiority. As a result, he'd left the coast clear for the one person in Great Piece Meadows who wanted him dead to return.

Number 64 was blowing hard.

"It's okay," Eda said. "Breathe slowly, in and out." She pointed to the sword in his hand and then gently pulled the tip of the blade towards her throat.

"Stand up," she whispered. "We're doing this."

They straightened up slowly together, like to hurry was a sin.

With Frankie Boy at their side, Eda and Number 64 began to walk towards the crater.

"Make it convincing," Eda whispered.

Number 64 didn't say a word.

The Children saw them when they reached the top of the hill. From afar, Eda heard a cluster of excited voices. These individual fragments came together to form a loud murmur of approval that drifted high above Uncle Sam's crater.

"They're going to love you for this," Eda said.

Most of the Children rushed forward to greet the boy and his prisoner. Eda walked downhill into a pack of eager, rejoicing faces. Praise was heaped upon Number 64. They would treat him like a hero, Eda knew that. She only hoped the acclaim wouldn't go to his head.

Number 64 kept the blade tight against Eda's throat. Eda tilted her head back as far as she could, knowing that Lex kept her katana razor sharp at all times. It didn't help that the boy's hands were shaking.

"I've got her," Number 64 said, as the crowd gathered around him. "I've got the President of the United States."

Eda's heart was pounding. She didn't know if the newfound confidence in Number 64's voice was sincere or not. Had he been playing her for a fool all this time, pretending to be a nervous kid?

Sweat trickled down her brow.

"Where's the other one?" Baldilocks said, marching through the crowd. He glanced at Eda for a second and then his eyes lingered on the road, as if he was expecting more to come. "Where's the Bank Manager?"

"She's dead," Number 64 said, leading Eda over to Baldilocks. "They ran onto the hunting grounds and the Bank Manager got caught in one of our circle traps. By the time we found her it was too late."

Baldilocks cursed quietly. Then his attention fell upon Eda and he scowled, as if Becky's death had been her fault.

"Uncle Sam won't be happy about that," he said. "He won't be happy at all and here we were today, hoping yet again that this was going to the last sacrifice. Not likely. And what about those fierce bitches? Have they been taken care of?"

Number 64 grimaced, his youthful face aging by ten years.

"There was a battle," he said. "We caught up with them on the hunting grounds and...I've never seen anything like it. They're dead, all of them, but we took heavy losses on the way. Most are dead, if not dying."

Number 64 looked at Baldilocks. Eda caught the fire in his eyes, even if no one else did.

"My dad's dead. They're all dead. This right here – all of us – is all that's left of the Children."

There were a few gasps from within the crowd. A barrage of frantic voices whispered back and forth, enquiring after the numbers they knew who were absent.

Baldilocks stood silent while the crowd panicked. But Eda saw the restrained horror spilling down the edges of the man. All the color had drained out of him upon hearing news of his people. She also noticed how he couldn't look at Number 64. Not since the boy told him about his dad.

And yet he didn't let the emotion spill out. His face remained cold, like a block of stone.

He pointed towards Eda.

"Bring her over here," he said. "And keep that dog back."

"The dog's with me now," Number 64 said.

Baldilocks didn't dispute the matter. After what had happened to Number 64's dad, he wasn't in a position to deny the boy anything.

"Uncle Sam is waiting for you," Baldilocks said, glaring at Eda.

He turned around and led them back towards the crater's lip. The other Children followed in a daze, still reeling in shock about the fate of their friends and family.

"We must finish it," Baldilocks said. "Uncle Sam will make it right, but only if we finish this. We must apologize and offer the President to him immediately. Quickly, quickly...c'mon!"

Number 64 walked behind Baldilocks, the sword jabbing at Eda's throat. They stopped at the edge and Eda realized she was back where she'd started that day with Becky, Mike and Murphy. It was hard to believe she was the only one left.

The small crowd formed a line about twenty feet back. At Baldilocks' command, they pulled the dog masks over their faces again. When it was done, Eda could still hear some of them muttering frantically to one another about what had happened. The doubt was tangible; it spilled out of the crowd like steam from boiling water.

"Bring her to the edge," Baldilocks said to Number 64. "Closer, c'mon!"

The last Sinner, aka The President of the United States, stood as far as it was possible to go without falling over the edge. As there was no rope left to bind her wrists, Baldilocks commanded Number 64 to keep a tight hold of her.

One of the boy's arms was locked tight around Eda's waist. The other held the sword at her throat.

"How unfortunate," Baldilocks said, addressing the spectators, "that we've been forced to keep Uncle Sam waiting today. Perhaps the tragic loss of our brothers and sisters, something that we will have time to mourn properly later, is a fitting punishment. We got complacent. Lazy. All of us. Just like people did before the war. I'm afraid to say it my friends, but with everything that's happened, I doubt very much that this year will be the last. Such a pity. Such a tragedy that we have to send the Seekers out again. We can only hope that the Great One won't ask for any more than four souls next year."

Baldilocks turned to face Eda. He lowered the Uncle Sam mask over his face and held a wrinkled hand out.

"Where's the dagger?" he asked. "The one you stole from our late friend, Number 47. Where is it girl?"

Because of the sword at her throat, Eda's head was tilted at a tight angle. Blood poured to one side of her skull. She had to resist the sensation of the world spinning and hold it together for a little longer.

"I must have dropped it when I ran off," she said.

Baldilocks clicked his fingers and one of the dog masks stepped out of the crowd. They came over and handed Baldilocks a short sword.

"This will have to do," Baldilocks said. The weapon was spotless, like it had never been used before.

Eda stared at Baldilocks, not daring to blink. She took slow, deep breaths to keep control of her temper. It wouldn't help anyone if she blew her top too early.

Baldilocks adjusted the red, white and blue mask. His hands, covered in dirt, dusted down the lapels of his matching jacket.

"The Seeker who brought this Sinner to us is dead," he called out. "Number 64, since you returned her to us, will you take this weapon from me and deliver the Sinner to Uncle Sam?"

"I will," Number 64 said.

Eda swallowed hard.

Baldilocks walked towards her, his mad, dazzling eyes peering out from behind the eyeholes of the mask.

He offered the short sword to Number 64.

"Put that foreign blade away," he said, gesturing towards the katana. His voice dripped with contempt. "The offering must be pure and so we use our own weapons. Besides, those women have offended the Great One by spilling the blood of the Children on this holy site. And they did it with that sword. It belongs to Uncle Sam now."

Baldilocks came closer. His arm was fully extended as he offered the short sword, hilt first, to Number 64.

"Take it."

Number 64 didn't move.

With a grunt, Baldilocks stabbed the sword in Number 64's direction, hurrying the boy along. Eda couldn't see the old man's face but she imagined that his bulbous, insect eyes were frowning.

"Take it for God's sake," he said. His voice was muffled. The tension in the air however, that was as clear as crystal.

"Are you going to keep Uncle Sam waiting?" Baldilocks said. His nasal voice cracked with emotion.

Eda inhaled slowly, picking up the toxic fumes off her suit. She still smelled of the ungodly river but that was the least of her worries.

"What's wrong with you boy? TAKE the sword!"

A burst of energy shot up and down Eda's body. It was a primitive response, a signal deep inside, readying her for action.

"Now," she cried out.

To Eda's relief, the sharp blade was pulled away from her neck. She heard Number 64 stagger backwards, as well as a chorus of loud gasping noises from the crowd.

"What...?" Baldilocks yelled. The mask stared at her, frozen in a devilish grin.

Eda charged towards Baldilocks and when she closed the distance, she threw a murderous right hand at his jaw. The blow connected flush and Eda's hand exploded with a sharp pain. There was a muffled grunt as Baldilocks reeled backwards under the force of the shot. Eda hit him again, this time in the ribs. The sword fell out of Baldilocks' hand as he doubled over in pain. One more punch to the face and he dropped onto his backside.

"Monster!" Eda yelled.

She reached into the inside pocket of her suit and pulled out the sacrificial dagger. It felt like it was made of paper after carrying the short sword for so long. Eda rushed over and yanked Baldilocks up to his feet. There was no weight to the man as she took a hold of his shoulders, trying to keep him upright as he staggered on jelly legs.

Some of the Children came forward, their swords drawn. Confusion on their faces.

Eda thrust the edge of the dagger against Baldilocks' throat. Then she backed away towards the crater. The advancing Children stopped in unison.

Number 10 pulled off her dog mask and stepped ahead of the crowd. Her jaw dropped in disbelief. It looked like she was saying something but Eda couldn't make out the words.

Since lowering the sword, Number 64 meanwhile, had put considerable distance between himself and the crater's edge. He'd already dropped the katana and now he stood alone on the outskirts, watching events unfold with a fearful expression. His face screamed, *what have I done?*

"One more death," Eda called out to the Children. She pressed the dagger tighter against Baldilocks' neck, not caring if she'd torn the skin or not already. "Uncle Sam needs one more death."

"Help me!" Baldilocks roared. He eyeballed the crowd through his mask.

"Shut up," Eda said. "Listen to me everyone. Uncle Sam is real, I know that now. But here's something you don't know – he doesn't just speak to Baldilocks. I heard his voice today. I heard it in this godforsaken swamp. Why else would I come back here if not for divine intervention? Huh? Want to know what he said to me? He said a name – one name. He told me who had to die to atone for what happened today. It's the person who's responsible for all this – Frank Church. And what Uncle Sam wants, Uncle Sam gets. Isn't that right Frank?"

She shook Baldilocks like he was a ragdoll. Keeping the knife to his throat, she used her other hand to tear the Uncle Sam mask off his face. Without thinking twice, Eda tossed the mask into the hole behind her.

Baldilocks' eyes were ablaze with terror. She could smell stale meat on his breath as he gasped for air.

"Help me!"

Eda twisted Baldilocks' head back, forcing him to look down into the jaws of Uncle Sam. There were specks of fresh debris barely visible at the bottom – Mike and Murphy perhaps? David was down there too somewhere, alongside the bones of all the other victims over the past thirty years.

"Are you ready?" Eda said.

Baldilocks screamed. "NO!"

"Uncle Sam says yes you are."

Eda turned to the crowd – a galley of stunned faces, some of them on the brink of insanity judging by their horrified expressions. Number 10 appeared to be the calmest of all. She was watching events unfold with an intense, thoughtful expression. Almost detached.

"Uncle Sam commands this of us," Eda said. "That's what he told me today. This man here failed to do what he was supposed to do. The sacrifice was a failure – the Bank Manager was taken by others. The President got away. And here's the worst thing – Uncle Sam told me he warned Baldilocks about the ambush weeks ago but your great leader here didn't believe that anyone would dare do such a thing in the Meadows. You hear that? He was too arrogant to protect you. That's why your friends and family are dead today."

Eda dug her boots into the ground, spreading her legs out to retain balance. The smallest misstep and she was a goner.

"The Great One is angry," Eda said. "He's so fucking angry right now. Can't you feel it? Can't you see it all around you?"

"Liar!" Baldilocks said. "Don't listen to a word she says."

"Uncle Sam!" Eda cried out, shouting as loud as she'd ever done. She no longer sounded like herself – she sounded like Baldilocks. "Uncle Sam! I have the last Sinner right here."

"She's a fraud!" Baldilocks said, fixing the crowd with a petrified stare. "Uncle Sam talks to me. Only me! You know it's true – help me for God's sake. I took you with me all those years ago – I forgave you, I saved you..."

Eda laughed – a deep, hearty rumbling noise that cut Baldilocks off in mid-speech. She looked over her shoulder. There was nothing between them and the long fall to the graveyard below.

"Frank Church!" she said. "It's time."

"God, no! Please no!"

"You are the President of the United States. You are the fourth Sinner. Go down into the..."

"No!"

"Why not?" Eda yelled. She pulled him so close that her lips grazed against his rubbery skin. "Why shouldn't I throw you in?"

Baldilocks shook his head. "Uncle Sam..."

"The Great One speaks only to me now," Eda said, running the tip of the blade over Baldilocks' exposed jugular vein. It was so fat that it looked like the man had a piece of taut rope trapped in his throat. "Please accept our apologies for today. We, the Children, sacrifice this man and beg..."

"Stop!" Baldilocks screamed like a frightened animal.

"Why?" Eda said. Rage spilled out of her like hot lava. "Why? Why? Why?"

"Because..."

"Speak up."

Silence.

Eda squeezed the handle of the dagger. "Fuck it," she said. "You're going in there you piece of shit."

"No!"

"Why not Frank? He called your name today. Uncle Sam called your name."

"He didn't."

"Why not?"

"No..."

"Why not?"

"BECAUSE HE'S NOT REAL!"

Eda had never heard anyone scream so loud. Instantly, she let the old man go and threw him down on the dirt. Baldilocks landed on his knees and without looking up, buried his face deep in his hands. "I made it up," he said. "I made it up dammit! Are you happy now? Is that what you wanted?"

He began to sob into the back of his hands.

Eda just stood there, listening to him cry. Gradually, the weeping burned out into a faint whimper.

Eda walked over and crouched down beside Baldilocks. She looked into the crowd of Children who hadn't moved. Their faces were eerily calm, as if the shock had passed. Nobody had moved since Baldilocks' confession. They were all just watching from afar.

"Say that again," Eda said, tearing the man's hands away from his face. "Just to make sure everyone understands."

When he didn't speak, Eda stood up and kicked him in the ribs. Hard. Baldilocks collapsed onto the dirt again, coughing his lungs up.

"Say it again," Eda said. "I'll throw you into that hole anyway, but not for Uncle Sam. For Becky, Mike, Murphy and all the other people who died here because of your bullshit."

"He's not real," Baldilocks croaked.

"There is no Uncle Sam?" Eda said. "He never spoke to you. Is that right?"

"Yes."

Eda looked at the crowd again, expecting to see at least a little shock register on their faces. There were only sad, almost empty expressions. They stood there in their robes, looking back at the broken man with an impersonal fascination.

She began to wonder – had they *really* known all along? Eda had suspected it but she hadn't dared to believe it was true. Had these people known from the start? Had they chosen to believe in Uncle Sam because it was easier to live with a demon under the ground than it was to live in the real world?

Number 10 turned around and whispered into the ears of several of the others. Muted exchanges took place. Heads nodded. Eda wondered if they might come over and throw Baldilocks into the hole themselves. That would have been something. But they didn't – the surviving Children simply began to walk away from the crater.

After about a hundred yards, Number 10 stopped and turned around. She beckoned Number 64 to go with them. To Eda's surprise, the boy ran over to them, smiling with relief at not being shut out. He walked away with the crowd, their arms locked around one another in solidarity.

Number 10 held back, staring over at Eda.

"Why don't you come with us?" she called out. There was no emotion in her voice. "It'll be easier out there in a large group of people."

"Go with you?" Eda asked. "Didn't you guys just try to kill me?"

Her words hit the mark.

"Understood," Number 10 said.

"A lot of people died here," Eda said. "Nothing's ever going to change that."

"I know."

"So where will you go?" Eda said. "Where will you take them?"

"Far away from here," Number 10 said.

The white-haired woman turned around and caught up with the rest of her people. Together they trudged back towards the road, exhausted and grieving. Some of them glanced over their shoulder, taking a final look at Baldilocks. Or at the giant crater. Most of them didn't look back.

Eda turned around.

Baldilocks was sitting in the dirt. His head was still buried in his hands, although he wasn't crying anymore. Frankie Boy was nearby watching him closely. The dog's head tilted with curiosity when Baldilocks let out the occasional, high-pitched groan.

Eda went over and sat down beside him, a few feet apart. She placed the katana at her side, out of Baldilocks' reach.

He rubbed his bloodshot eyes and looked at her.

"Judge me all you like," he said, in a tired, beaten voice. "But you don't know what it was like for me before the war. You can't ever know. The way people treated me, Jesus. I tell you, the End War was the best thing that ever happened to me. It turned this street bum into a prophet overnight. Suddenly, I was somebody."

"Yeah," Eda said.

"Purpose," Baldilocks said, nodding. "A sense of purpose, that's all I ever sought out of this poxy life. Without it, we're empty inside. Driftwood, going nowhere on a big cruel ocean. But in here after the war, I was complete. For the first time in my life people looked at me the way I've always wanted them to look at me. They thought I was a prophet. I took them out of the towns and cities and built this community because that's what they wanted me to do. They *wanted* this. We lived the End War, believing what we believed."

"But it was all a lie," Eda said. "Thing is, I think they knew that from the start. I guess worshipping a hole in the ground and sacrificing four people a year seemed tame compared to life outside the swamp. That's the world we live in I guess."

Eda watched Baldilocks rocking backwards and forwards. His

eyes were blank. He clenched his teeth like he was experiencing physical pain. It was as if all the ghosts he'd buried in the crater over the years were creeping out, their faces appearing between the cracks of his mind, clambering for revenge.

"Did David, I mean Number 47, tell you anything about New York?" Eda said. "About what's going on there?"

Baldilocks shook his head. "I don't care about New York."

Eda looked at him. "But you said you wanted purpose right?" she said. "Did you mean that?"

Baldilocks shrugged.

"You've still got time to make amends for this colossal fuck up," Eda said. "For all the innocent people you threw down that hole."

"How?"

Eda hesitated.

"There's a community in New York that I think might interest you," she said. "A small group of women known as the Complex. They're trying to rebuild."

"Rebuild?" Baldilocks said, glancing at Eda. "What does that mean?"

"They're trying to kick start the human species in America," Eda said. "It's a noble cause, I guess, but they're mostly women and they need men to help out with the fundamentals. The birds and the bees, you know?"

She looked at him.

"Purpose," Eda said. "It's there if you want it. If you can impregnate Helen of Troy you'll be the father of the new world. How's that for purpose?"

"Helen of Troy?"

"She's the most beautiful woman in the world," Eda said. "I've seen her with my own eyes. But so far, no man has been able to give her a baby. There's supposed to be this curse you see, and that's why the women in New York think Helen can't get pregnant. It's just superstition. There isn't any curse. She just hasn't found the right man that's all. They need a strong, virile man to show up and fix the problem. You've been looking for something all your life, haven't you Frank? Maybe, just maybe, this is it."

Baldilocks' eyes lit up. A few minutes earlier, he'd shriveled as his world had collapsed. Now the lights were back on and Eda felt a flicker of sympathy for the man. She hated herself for it.

"Why would you tell me this?" he said. "Why would you help me after everything that's happened?"

"I'm not helping you," Eda said. "Truth is, I wouldn't piss on you if you were on fire. You can go fuck yourself for all I care Frank. But I like what those women are doing in New York and the fact is they need men to get the job done. I guess you'll do. Everything works downstairs, doesn't it?"

He nodded. "Where will I find them?"

"Grand Central Terminal," Eda said. "Will you go?"

"I will," Baldilocks said. And then he laughed, which made Eda's blood boil.

He moved as if to get up.

"One more thing," Eda said. "The leader of the Complex is a woman called Shay. She's the brains of the operation. When you get there, tell her that Eda sent you. Tell her that and she'll treat you like a king."

Baldilocks rose to his feet, almost in slow motion. His old bones snapped. He rubbed his jaw where Eda had punched him and then he looked towards the road with anticipation, as if searching for the rest of the Children.

They'd been there a few minutes ago. They were all gone now.

"It's a long walk to New York," Baldilocks said with a sigh.

"Better get going then."

"What about you Eda?" he asked. "Where will you go?"

Eda shrugged. "Maybe I'll go back east. See what's happening in Boston."

Baldilocks, aka Frank Church, walked away from Uncle Sam's crater. He set off towards the road, laboring like an old man. He turned around only once.

"Goodbye," he called over.

Eda watched him go, excited at the thought of his fate in New York. She kept watching as he climbed up the steep incline and trudged across the road. Now that he was away from Eda, he walked differently. His step was light, like a young man.

Like a man who'd just walked out of his own execution.

THE END

THE END WAR (AFTER THE END 3)

Dedicated to the memory of Joan Barstad.

1

Eda Becker lowered the hood of her rain cloak. This tentative gesture was rewarded by a gust of damp, rancid air that smacked her hard on the face.

"Fuck," she whispered, putting a hand over her nose and mouth.

Even the breeze smelled like death.

She blinked hard and stared at what was coming her way. For the first time in several days, she wasn't the only human being on the road. There was a large caravan of people in the distance, walking towards her at a steady pace. They took up most of the road with three large carts taking up the rear of the procession.

Eda stopped dead in the center of the highway.

She strained her eyes, making sure it wasn't an urban mirage. People saw things in the emptiness, it happened. It was hard to digest anything that broke up the monotony of rotting cars, broken glass and emptiness that littered the highways of America.

The caravan consisted of around forty people. They were close now, moving steadily forward at a conservative speed that was surely deliberate and designed for the long haul. The people at the front had noticed Eda and although they seemed wary of the lone figure on the horizon, not to mention the large dog sitting beside her, they kept coming anyway. Two women stood at the head of the caravan and they began to walk ahead of their companions, seemingly taking on the role of scouts. One of the women had an ancient, leathery face. Deeply tanned and beautiful in its own way. She looked a hundred years old and yet her bright blue eyes could have belonged to a child. Dazzling eyes, like two sky-colored jewels.

Her long white hair was damp and tied into a ponytail.

The woman exchanged a few hushed words with her female companion. Then she came forward alone, wrapping her long gray coat tight around her tiny, shriveled body.

Frankie Boy's eyes were locked onto the strangers but at least he wasn't growling.

"We're not looking for trouble," the woman said, stopping a short distance from Eda. She held both hands in the air, palms facing outwards. "We're a peaceful people and we only wish to pass and continue our journey."

Eda's eyes scoured the barren surroundings. It could easily be a trap. She was relying on Frankie Boy to pick up on any potential nasty surprises that might come from behind. She didn't have much in the way of valuables in her bag, but Eda knew that people could make use of a woman's body in a number of sickening ways.

"Are you hungry child?" the old woman said.

At this, the other woman came forward and stood beside the older one. She was a lot younger, in her middle years. Blood red dreadlocks fell down to her shoulders while a pair of crisp blue eyes hinted at a family connection between herself and the old woman.

Behind these two scouts, the small caravan of men, women and children stood observing events in silence. Their supplies, which consisted mostly of bags, sacks and an old storage chest, had been loaded onto three massive wooden carts. These were quaint looking things, the type of cart that had once been attached to the backs of vehicles or animals but nowadays acted as supply carriers for large caravans such as this one. Each cart had four massive wheels with thick black spokes in the middle. Two wooden beams extended from the cart's body with a metal handlebar running across the top to connect them. Three large men stood behind these handlebars. They were the pushers or draggers – at least that's what Eda remembered calling them years ago.

As they stood there, looking at Eda and her dog, the pushers' fat fingers still gripped the handlebar. They were apparently eager to get back to hauling their load.

"I asked if you were hungry?" the old woman said. There was a look of concern on her face. "Can you talk? You look hungry, if you don't mind my saying."

Frankie Boy began to edge ahead of Eda. Eda caught it quick and tapped the dog's back, halting his advance.

"I'm hungry," Eda said.

The old woman's face broke into a smile. At the same time, a steady downpour began to fall from the gray, gloomy heavens. It had been coming for a while and Eda tilted her head back to the sky, letting the first drops of water land on her face. She licked her lips, devouring the moisture. Only when she'd drank a little did she realize how thirsty she was. She couldn't remember the last time she'd stopped for a drink even though there was still plenty of water in her bag.

"We ain't got much," the old woman said, pointing a thumb back at the stationary caravan. "But what we got, you're welcome to it."

She took a step closer to Eda and Frankie Boy.

Eda kept one hand on Frankie Boy's back. The other touched the hilt of her sword.

"My name is Louise," the old woman said, "and this here's my daughter Florence. As for the rest of our people here, we go by the name of Nomads. I'd introduce you to them all personally but well, it's raining and I guess you want to keep moving like we do. Right? Are you a peaceful traveler?"

Eda smiled. Her hand retreated from the handle of the katana hanging off her waist. She hoped the gesture would answer the old woman's question.

"I'm Eda," she said. "And this is Frankie Boy."

"Eda," Louise said, repeating the name slowly. "*E-da*. And where are you coming from Eda?"

"New Jersey."

"New Jersey? See much there?"

Eda shook her head quickly. "Nothing much."

Louise and Florence exchanged a brief glance. Eda observed that their side profiles, hooked nose, sharp chins, were identical. There could be little doubt now that they were blood relatives.

"How about the road?" Florence asked. "You see anything on the road in between here and Jersey? We'd appreciate you sharing what you know."

Eda shrugged. "A few animal encounters from a distance," she said. "Deer, horses, possums and other things. No people, until you that is."

Louise turned back to the caravan. With a thumb in the air, she signaled to someone in the group to come forward. A middle-aged man with murky salt and pepper stubble on his face signaled back. Then he took something out of the rear cart and approached the three women and the dog. In his hands, he carried a plastic box with a lid sealed tight on top. Like the rest of the travelers, this man was wearing weatherworn rags underneath a long waterproof cloak that trailed down to his knees.

The man greeted Eda with a blank-faced nod. Then he dropped onto one knee, opened the box and pulled out something wrapped in several layers of silver foil. Unwrapping the foil, a blackish-red object was partially revealed. It looked like the well-preserved organ of a large animal. The man cut a few slices and wrapped them up in a fresh piece of foil. Then he replaced the lid on the plastic box and stood up with a sigh. He handed the freshly cut slices over to Eda and his rugged face broke into a smile.

"You can eat it raw," he said in a gruff voice, "but it tastes a hell of a lot better if you cook it first."

Eda took the package and thanked the man.

"It's food," Louise said, laughing softly. "Even if it looks like crap and smells worse it'll keep you alive. It's fuel. It'll help you get to where you're going."

"Thank you," Eda said. She slid her backpack off her shoulder, pulled the zip and carefully put the foil package inside. There was plenty of room.

Louise squinted at the young woman and her dog. "How long have you been on the road Eda?"

Eda shook her head. "About a week I think. Maybe more."

The journey back east was a blur. In truth, Eda had been walking on autopilot since leaving the swamps of New Jersey, grateful just to be able to put some distance between herself and that place. The Nomads didn't need to know about what she'd encountered there – that particular danger had been removed and Eda sure as hell didn't want to revisit it. Now she was traveling northeast, having at first followed the road signs back to New York. Fortunately she didn't have to go through Manhattan or anywhere near the Complex to get where she was going. Thank God for all the books she'd read over the years, especially the history books containing maps of America. It was thanks to those books and to all the hours she'd spent looking at them that she possessed enough geographical knowledge to find her way back east.

"You're alone?" Louise asked.

Eda pointed to Frankie Boy. "Nope."

Louise smiled, showing off a set of pristine white teeth. Eda was impressed – it was rare to see anyone that old with so many teeth left. Good teeth too. Either Louise had taken care of her teeth all her life or she was hanging onto a great set of dentures, a souvenir from the old world.

"Sorry hon," the old woman said. "Jeez, I ain't seen one of them big, powerful dogs in a very, very long time. Look at him would you? He's a fierce-looking son of a bitch. Good protection I reckon. Loyal too so they say."

Louise looked like she wanted to get closer to Frankie Boy but something held her back. She blew him a kiss from a distance. Frankie's ears twitched in response.

"Yeah," Eda said. "He's sort of my guardian angel."

"And you're his," Louise said.

Florence cleared her throat.

"You two came all the way from Jersey?" she said. "That's a long trek. What are you heading east for?"

Eda didn't blink. "Got my reasons."

She glanced behind the two scouts, her attention drifting towards the rest of the Nomads. Eda saw the fear in their eyes, even though by now they must have sensed that this encounter was unlikely to escalate into a violent confrontation. She didn't blame them for being cautious. Strangers weren't to be trusted and it was smart to be scared sometimes. Those women in the group who were mothers clutched young children tight to their breast. Older children who tried to get too close to Eda and especially to Frankie Boy, were restrained with a strong hand and a stern expression.

"You're the first caravan I've seen in a long time," Eda said. "Where are *you* coming from?"

"A place called Brockton," Florence said. "You know it?"

"Never heard of it," Eda said.

"Massachusetts?" Florence said. "You've heard of that right? Northeast state."

"I know it," Eda asked.

"Right you are. Well we're bailing out of Massachusetts. Seeking fresh pastures."

Eda felt a shudder of relief inside. She was on the right road and thank God for a little confirmation. If these people were coming out of Massachusetts then she couldn't be too far away from the city of Boston now. America was big, so damn big that it was easy to get lost and stay lost. This was the boost she needed to carry her over the finish line.

Nearly there.

Louise called over to a young black-skinned girl standing by the lead cart. "Bring me a few of those apples darling will you?"

The girl, a statue just a moment ago, exploded into a flurry of activity. She rummaged around inside the nearest cart and after about a minute, pulled out three reddish-brown apples. She walked over and handed them to Eda. The girl was too shy or too frightened to look Eda in the eye.

"Thank you," Eda said, taking the apples and dropping them into her bag. "I wish I had something to give you in return."

"Forget it," Louise said.

Florence nodded. "We've got more than enough."

"You'll find orchards back that way," Louise said, pointing east along the highway. She raised her voice, her aging pipes battling to be heard over the rain. "People might have gone but the fruit's still growing like it always did. Might be radioactive but what the hell right? Just go off road, explore some of those little towns you'll see marked on the signposts. Nature still provides if you know where to look for her treasures. Stock up if you're going east because it's a concrete desert out there. That's where you're going right? East?"

"Boston," Eda said.

Louise exhaled, a whistling noise that sounded like disapproval.

"A ghost town," she said. "Right Florence?"

"Sure is," the dreadlocked woman said. She spoke gently, as if breaking bad news to Eda. "I think it was one of the first cities to go, not surprising seeing as how the harbor was used during the war. Boston was a big target for those fighting against us."

"Guess so," Eda said. "I'll see for myself soon enough."

"That where you're from?" Louise asked. The old woman stood motionless in the rain, seemingly impervious to the escalating downpour.

"I've never been there before."

"So why the hell are you going?" Florence said.

"I'm looking for someone," Eda said. "A woman by the name of Pam Burton."

Louise fanned her face, like she was brushing a swarm of insects away. "You won't find her, whoever she is."

"I have to try," Eda said. "Finding her, that's a bonus."

Louise and Florence glanced at one another. There was a brief, instant nod exchanged between them that Eda would have missed had she blinked at that moment.

"Say why don't you come with us?" Louise said, turning back to Eda. "We ain't got much but we've got each other and we've got food and water and sleeping bags. Huh? Safety in numbers honey, that's no lie in this world we're living in."

Louise pointed to the empty highway over Eda's shoulder.

"We're going west and then south," she said. "If you believe the rumors, there's some big tribes based down in New Mexico. It's a long walk for sure, especially for my old bones, but what the hell? Northeast is dead."

"What do you say Eda?" Florence asked. "Will you join us?"

Eda was tempted to say yes outright. The voice of instinct told her to accept the offer and to travel southwest with the Nomads to New Mexico. They seemed like good, genuine people. That was rare enough and it was a solid reason to turn back and go with them. Eda liked their faces too, honest and with kind eyes that didn't probe too deeply. These weren't the kind of people who'd squeeze her dry before leaving her for dead on the highway.

Say yes, damn it.

Eda smiled and slowly lifted her hood, pulling it tight over her head.

"No thanks," she said, looking at the two women standing in the rain. Louise's electric blue eyes had dimmed a little. "It's...it's hard to explain. But I have to go to Boston. I have to."

"Well the offer stands," Louise said, through gritted teeth. "Should you change your mind that is."

"I'll remember that," Eda said.

They said a brief goodbye and went their separate ways under the pouring rain. Eda and Frankie Boy continued east towards the coast while the Nomads took the road west and inland. It was a long time before Eda had the nerve to look back. With a gnawing regret, she stood rooted to the spot, watching the caravan as it disappeared around a curve in the highway.

2

Eda and Frankie Boy arrived in Boston two days later.

When she lived in New York, Eda always had a sense that something was there inside the emptiness – a presence, the possibility of running into some living thing on a street corner somewhere. The Big Apple was a shadow of its former self alright, but it wasn't all the way gone. The Complex was proof of that. Boston on the other hand, was all the way gone. Eda was crawling around inside the stomach of a giant corpse in Boston. The skyscrapers were tombstones. The city was eerily silent apart from the steady pitter-patter of the rain.

The scenery was familiar by now to anyone who'd traveled through various towns and cities of postwar America. Mounds of assorted debris were piled up on the street, abandoned cars sat on the road, reeking of rot and death. Shards of broken glass snapped underfoot with every step. Some of the buildings had come down, most likely in the war years, but some of them had probably only been damaged in the fighting, only to collapse later on.

In the distance, giant piles of rubble blotted out the horizon.

Eda slid the backpack off her shoulders and dropped it onto the wet road, dodging the puddles at her feet. Her joints were stiff and made a loud clicking noise as she moved. Everything felt tight.

She pulled the zip open and peered inside.

Her supplies were almost gone. She'd already eaten what the Nomads had given her and the truth was that Eda was no hunter. Even if animals showed up, Eda had no way to catch them except with the sword strapped to her waist. And that wasn't going to work. That meant she'd have to stick to what she knew. She'd been a scavenger since leaving the Complex. She'd have to scavenge some more in Boston while looking for a woman called Pam Burton.

She checked her boots, stamping them off the cracked asphalt several times. There were so many cracks on the road that it looked like a giant spider's web was hovering over the surface. The muddy soles of Eda's boots were intact, thank God. Her waterproof socks were still dry.

"We're going to South Boston," she said to Frankie Boy. The dog was sniffing at the door of an Italian restaurant, *Pizza Fritta*. The restaurant's front windows had been caved in at some point, revealing an empty shell inside. There wasn't even a piece of furniture left.

Frankie Boy turned around at the sound of Eda's voice. Taut muscles protruded from his thick legs as he trotted back over to her.

"That's where Pam Burton lived," Eda said. "Guess that's where we should start looking huh?"

She picked her backpack up off the road, strapped it on and shook her head.

"What the hell are we doing here boy?"

Eda walked along the middle of the road, eventually finding a sign that pointed the way towards South Boston. It was all she had to go on in the impossible search for Pam Burton. Not much, she knew that. But it was Becky's last wish that Pam be found. Becky wanted her sister-in-law to know what happened to the rest of her family and Eda was the only one left who was capable of delivering that message.

God, if only that wasn't true.

If Pam Burton wasn't already dead she was long gone from this big pile of nothing. And even if Eda found Pam alive, it still wouldn't be enough to erase the memory of Becky's grisly fate in the swamp.

Eda was thinking about the Nomads as she walked. Wondering how far they'd traveled since their meeting.

Frankie Boy strolled a hundred yards ahead of her. Now and then he'd stop and turn around, waiting for Eda to catch up with him. Eda thought she detected an impatient look in the dog's eyes. Or was it frustration?

She threw her hands in the air, signaling for him to keep going.

"I know!" she yelled. In the silence of the city she could hear the blood pumping to her head. She could hear her breath, her heartbeat. "You don't have to say it for God's sake."

The German Shepherd tilted his large, wolfish head. The tip of his snout glistened in the pale glow of mid-afternoon.

"We had to come here," Eda said. "We left her there to die in the swamp, you and me, trapped in those metal jaws. Alone. Do you know how scared she must have been, sitting there and waiting for the end? I told her I'd try to find her sister-in-law and that's what I'm damn well going to do. So just fuck off with your dirty dog looks Frankie and keep your nose in the air. Alright?"

Eda kept walking, her anger not yet fully exorcised. It wasn't Frankie Boy she was pissed off with. Truthfully, she didn't know what it was. A lot of the time there was no reason and so the brain tried to find one. To make sense of the madness of modern life.

As Eda followed the road, her eyes combed the empty streets, looking for something meaningful. Something to grab onto. Before getting here she'd hoped at least to run into some people – to find a small community grouped together in the likes of a train station or in a hospital or somewhere like that. There was nothing. Even the birds had fled the city of Boston, or so it seemed such was the absolute silence overhead.

Eda found a large road marked '90'. This led her southeast towards the region of the city where Pam Burton had once allegedly lived. She kept to the road following the signs marked 'S. Boston'.

Even when she reached South Boston, Eda found herself thinking about the Nomads traveling along the western road. They couldn't have gone far, not hauling that trio of large carts and all the supplies.

New Mexico, she thought. I've never been to New Mexico.

The abandoned neighborhoods of South Boston offered no clues to the whereabouts of Pam Burton. Eda walked up and down the streets for about two hours, reading nameplates on front doors, checking mailboxes, and looking at the intercoms on apartment buildings.

Nothing.

Soon she was back to where she started, not far from the highway marked '90'. And definitely no further forward in her search for Becky's sister-in-law.

Eda decided to take a break. She'd sit down, regroup and organize her thoughts. As things stood she was walking around in circles, chasing ghosts and getting nowhere. Not to mention wasting time.

She found a small park sealed off by a metal fence.

"C'mon Frankie," Eda said, walking through a large gap in the fence where a gate might once have been.

Eda flopped down onto a damp wooden bench. Now that she'd stopped moving, a sudden coldness stabbed at her skin. She sighed loudly. The park wasn't much to look at – the grass was badly overgrown, spilling over onto a zigzag maze of concrete paths that ran through the park like a series of ancient symbols.

So it was true – Bostonians were officially an extinct species. And that had to include Pam Burton. But where did that leave Eda? She felt caught between the promise she'd made to Becky and the grim reality of her situation. Without help there was no way she could ever hope to find Pam or even her remains. This was a big, empty city. It was all questions and no answers.

Frankie Boy leaned up tight against Eda's legs. He felt warm and heavy.

"You win boy," she said, scratching the back of his neck with all five fingers. "Looks like we're going southwest with the Nomads. New Mexico it is."

She sat with her back pressed up against the bench. Eda tilted her head towards the sky and felt drowsy.

The tree limbs, wild and unencumbered, reached for her. There was an air of menace in those fairy-tale arms – arms with crooked, wooden fingers that wanted to throttle her. Beyond the branches there was a gray swirling pattern in the sky, a rhythmic churning that threatened a fierce downpour.

"We'll go in a minute Frankie," Eda said, her voice thick and sluggish.

The cool breeze was soothing and gentle. Her head flopped forward and the drowsiness began to overwhelm her.

Just before she drifted off, Eda heard a rustling noise behind her.

Her head shot up. The first thing she saw was Frankie Boy standing on all fours in front of her. He was staring at something over Eda's shoulder, his ears up, the black tail erect. A low-pitched growl spilled out of him.

"Easy Frankie," Eda whispered, slowly getting up. She held her hands flat out, hoping he'd take the hint and stay put. Then she raised them higher, surrendering to the unseen threat behind her.

Slowly she turned around, hands over her head.

There was a man in the park with them. He walked towards Eda, each step full of caution, as if the park was rigged with landmines or some other hidden danger. There was a rifle in his hands.

It was pointing at Eda.

"Just stay right where you are young lady," the man said. "I'll shoot the dog and I'll shoot you too if I have to."

He was an old man. She recognized the familiar gray-blue uniform of the United States army that he was wearing. She'd seen many photographs of American soldiers over the years in her history books, mostly taken at the start of the war with China. Eda could also vaguely recall seeing that same uniform as child, wrapped around many a bedraggled and drunken soul during the wild years. Those were the soldiers that hadn't died during the war. At least in terms of physical death.

The famous bald eagle patch was visible on the old man's upper left arm, a little faded but the red, white and blue colors were hanging in there. A wrinkled army cap sat on his head.

"What are you doing here?" he asked. The majority of his mouth was hidden under a bushy but well-groomed white mustache. "Are you spying on me? Start talking or I swear to God young lady I'm going to put you and the dog to sleep right here, right now. Just to be on the safe side you know? Don't think 'cos you're a woman I won't pull the trigger."

Eda kept her hands up.

"I'm not a spy," she said. "I'm just passing through with my dog."

The man pointed the rifle at the sky. His mouth twitched as he squeezed the trigger and a loud cracking noise whistled through the air. Eda leapt backwards, almost tripping over her feet. At the same time, Frankie Boy bolted. He ran all the way to the gate before stopping to turn around again. His tail was tucked in between his legs.

At the sound of gunfire, a pack of birds fled a nearby rooftop.

Eda hadn't heard a gunshot in years. She continued to back away towards the exit.

The old man lowered the gun and grunted.

"Stop right where you are," he said. "I want to talk to you."

But Eda didn't stop. To stop was to defy nature. Some deep-rooted survival instinct had taken over, urging her in simple, easy to follow commands to get far away from this man and his killing machine.

Turn around. Run. Get the hell out of here.

Eda dropped her hands and ran for the gate. Frankie Boy was barking at her as she charged over the long grass, pumping her arms and legs as fast as she could. The sweat fell off her. Her eyes were glued to the gate, on the barking, overexcited shape of Frankie Boy.

She could feel the gun pointing at her back. Like there was a red-hot heat coming off it.

"Stop!" the soldier screamed. "I said STOP! I swear to God young lady. I'll shoot you dead right now. RIGHT NOW!"

Eda heard him chasing after her, his heavy army boots crushing the long grass as he ran towards the gate.

"STOP!"

He fired at her.

3

Eda charged towards the gate, somehow managing to stay upright as the second shot rang in her ear. Her heart was pounding. Her mind was scrambled with unfiltered spurts of information, a massive pileup of survival instinct that all came down to the same thing.

Run.

Frankie Boy was still waiting for Eda at the gate. He'd jumped at the second shot but he hadn't run off, not without her. Now he was barking wildly, screaming at her to catch up with him so that they could leave this park and the crazy old man behind.

"Go!" Eda yelled, waving her hands frantically in the air. "Run Frankie!"

There was another spurt of gunfire behind her. Eda ducked and ran at the same time, her insides contracting into tightly coiled knots. Either the old man was a lousy shot or he was just trying to frighten her. She wasn't going to hang around and ask him.

Eda closed in on the gate, running in a zigzag pattern. It was an incredible feat of instinctive memory – this was how she'd been taught to run as a girl back in the days when guns were common in America and bullets hit the streets like confetti.

"Stop!" the old soldier's voice yelled at her back.

Another explosive blast from the rifle made Eda flinch. A fresh flock of birds flew higher, seeking solace in the sky.

About a hundred yards from the exit, Eda's legs finally gave out under her. Her body was out of juice. Even as she fell, survival commands swirled around her brain – *get up, run, zigzag, run!* But the communication lines between mind and body had been severed. Eda toppled onto her hands. As she fell she twisted over onto her side, rolling onto her back with the backpack wedged in between her upper body and the wet grass.

Eda saw something move out of the corner of her eye. It was Frankie Boy. He was running back into the park.

"No," she groaned.

Up ahead, the soldier was galloping towards her now. Eda felt a sharp stab of fear in her guts. Behind her, Frankie Boy was racing over to intercept this strange, terrifying threat to his companion.

The soldier saw Frankie Boy coming. He stopped dead. Quickly he pulled the butt of the rifle tight to his shoulder and took aim at the charging beast.

"Stop!" Eda called out. With the last of her strength she scrambled back to her feet. Frankie Boy was on the brink of going past her. He was a dark blur, moving with purpose. Eda dropped into a wide crouch, her arms stretched out to make herself look big.

The timing had to be perfect.

When she leapt on top of Frankie Boy, she pushed him to the ground with all the strength she could muster. It felt like she was jumping into a fast moving brick wall but she managed to wrap her arms around his bulk quickly.

"No!" she said, her voice dripping with panic. "Frankie."

She pinned all of her weight on top of the dog. It wasn't easy to restrain him – he was a big block of solid muscle and he was putting up a damn good fight. As he tried to wriggle free, Eda could see the confusion in his brown eyes as she continued to force him down.

"Frankie! No. No!"

He stopped moving. It happened so suddenly that the stillness was jarring. Eda glanced over her shoulder at the gunman. He was peering over the rifle now, a confused expression on his wrinkled face.

"What the hell?" he said. "Is this some kind of mad circus or what?"

"Don't shoot him," Eda said, in between labored breaths. "Please."

The soldier's eyes zipped back and forth between Eda and the dog underneath her. Frankie Boy's head was flat on the grass, his brown eyes fixed on Eda, trusting yet confused.

She stroked his head.

"Easy," she whispered, easing up on the pressure she used to keep him down.

The soldier approached through the long grass. By now the rifle was slightly lowered to his waist but it was far from being in a relaxed position. Eda had to make sure that Frankie Boy didn't suddenly break free and lunge at the old man. It would be the last thing he did.

"Are you a moron or something?" the soldier said to Eda.

"No," Eda said, still breathing hard.

"I said stop and then you ran away. What's that if it's not a moron?"

Eda didn't answer.

The old man took a close look at her, his eyes peering across the park as if to check for others. "Are you American?"

"Yeah," Eda said.

She felt the ground trembling underneath. It took her a moment to realize what was going on – it was Frankie Boy's low-pitched warning growl going straight through her. The man was getting too close.

"Look mister," Eda said. "Is it okay if I sit up now? I'll keep a hold of the dog I swear. He's just frightened that's all."

The soldier didn't blink. He stood there, a flesh and blood statue rooted in the middle of the park. Eda could almost hear the wheels turning in his head as he tried to process.

"Alright," the man said. "Nice and slow."

Eda loosened her grip on the dog's torso. Frankie Boy's muscles felt like coiled springs, waiting to explode. He jerked upward. At the same time, Eda wrapped her arms underneath his thick neck, firmly but not too tight. With great difficulty she slid to the right, shifting onto her backside and into a reasonably comfortable sitting position.

"Stay," she whispered in Frankie Boy's ear.

Frankie Boy was a powerhouse of tension in her arms. His thick body was taut and primed for violence. The ears were up and the dark chocolate brown, so loving at other times, were now fixed upon the soldier with frightening intensity.

Eda nodded at the soldier, letting him know she had it under control. He began to approach and Frankie Boy was growling all over again.

"Maybe it's best if you stay there for now," Eda said. "Keep your distance and we'll talk that way."

"Just keep a hold of him," the soldier said in a raspy voice. He was looking down the barrel of the rifle again, his finger resting on the trigger. "Won't take me but a second to put him away for good."

Eda dug her fingers into Frankie Boy's coat. He felt as wet and slippery as the grass underneath.

"What do you want with us?" she said. "I told you we weren't spies. We're travelers and all we want to do is get out of here."

There was a strange, blank look on the soldier's face. Like he'd been reading from a script and now he'd forgotten the next line. "Uhhh, you can't be sitting out here in the open without your wits about you. Not like you were just there. You were damn near asleep."

The words staggered out, hoarse and tripping over his tongue.

Eda frowned. "Why not?"

"It's dangerous, that's why not."

"Here?" Eda said, unable to conceal the surprise in her voice. "You're telling me this city's dangerous?"

The old man looked at her like she was a crazed lunatic. "Damn right it is," he said. His voice trembled with anger, like she'd insulted him somehow.

"Sorry," Eda said. "I just don't see it, apart from you shooting that gun at strangers I mean. Since I got here I haven't seen anyone else.

Not a hint. Boston's as near to a full on mega-sized ghost city that I've ever seen."

The soldier lowered the sleek-looking weapon in his arms. This time it went all the way down to his side and Eda praised the gods in silence.

"Sheeesh...what's your name young lady?"

"Eda Becker."

"The mutt has a name does it?"

"Frankie Boy," Eda said.

The old man's furry white eyebrows stood up. Then he laughed out loud, opening his mouth wide and giving Eda a momentary glimpse of what was left of his teeth. One of the incisors was missing, along with a couple of molars. The fleshy gums, pale and a dark shade of pink, had almost completely receded.

"I knew a Frankie Boy once," he said. "Long time ago. Frank Marshall – he served alongside me in the 101st Regiment based right here in Boston. Boy, he was a real uptight asshole. We never liked each other. All because of a girl we fought over, a girl that I ended up marrying. Jeez, I haven't thought about old Frankie Boy Marshall in a long time. A bit of asshole reminiscing, why not?"

The old man stared into the distance for a second.

"Well now," he said, "it's been a long, long time since I saw a dog shuffling around these parts. I don't think you like me either do you Frankie Boy?"

Eda pointed a finger at the rifle in his hands.

"Can you blame him?"

The soldier began to laugh again. This time however, it lapsed into a mild coughing seizure. He doubled over, one hand covering his mouth. It was such a violent, unpleasant fit that Eda thought the old man was about to spit one of his internal organs out.

"Are you alright?" Eda said.

Frankie Boy twitched underneath her.

It was a while before he could answer. The man kept coughing for another couple of seconds. Eventually he held a hand out, registering to her that he was going to make it. He straightened back up, wobbling on rubbery legs.

"I'm old," he said. "That's everything that's wrong with me."

"What's your name?" Eda asked.

"Talbot Goldman," he said, wiping the spit off his mouth. "And if you're a loyal American citizen then you're alright with me young lady. I'm sorry about scaring you and all. Just so you know, I was shooting to miss back there. I wasn't actually trying to kill ya."

"I figured that," Eda said.

"Now let me tell you something," he said, "You're in grave danger. Just being here puts you in grave danger."

"Why?" Eda said.

"This city has eyes," Goldman said, lowering his voice. "Eyes that don't like the sight of Americans you know what I mean? You thought it was empty around ol' Beantown right? That was your first mistake and that's how you didn't hear me sneaking up on you when you were sitting half-asleep on that bench back there."

Eda looked at the rifle in Goldman's hands and shuddered. There was also a small handgun strapped into a black holster on his weapons belt, as well as a bone-handled dagger tucked into in a chunky hilt. A bald eagle logo was stamped onto the belt buckle, the same one that appeared on Goldman's uniform.

America the Brave.

Goldman noticed her checking out his arsenal of weapons.

"It's not even the tip of the iceberg," he said. "I've got a small armory back at my base I'll have you know. Guns, grenades, knives – you name it. I've got just about everything back there except a tank of my own. Never managed to find me one of those mothers, not one that still worked anyway."

"That's a lot of weapons," Eda said.

"Well yeah," Goldman said. "How else are we going to win this war? This isn't chess we're playing, you understand?"

Eda tilted her head.

"Win the war?"

"Yeah?"

"War?" Eda said, emphasizing the word with a verbal punch. "What war are you talking about exactly?"

Goldman laughed.

"Go downtown and take a good look around," he said. "Look at what happened to the once great city of Boston. That wasn't just a big fart that knocked down all those buildings you know."

"I know all about the End War," Eda said. "Who doesn't for God's sake? But it's over, it's been over for years."

The old man cackled. It triggered Frankie Boy who lunged forward. Fortunately Eda still had her hands wrapped around the dog and she held him back despite the growing numbness in her limbs.

"You better keep a hold of that dog," Goldman said, his rifle coming up again. "I'm starting to get nervous again and no one likes a shaky trigger finger."

Eda stroked the back of Frankie's head. His body trembled, accompanying the growl.

"Stay," she whispered into his ear. "It's okay."

She looked at Goldman.

"Please stop pointing that thing at us," she said. "Nothing's going to happen. I've got him."

Goldman's jaw was fidgety. Slowly he lowered the rifle again, sighing as his arms were relieved of the weight.

"I apologize for laughing like that," he said, looking at Eda with a sincere expression. "I must appear quite strange to you, right? I think I'm out of practice when it comes to the whole socializing thing, you know what I mean? Been a long time since anyone new showed up in Boston. And when it comes to dogs, well as you can see I'm all out of practice."

Eda let slip a half-smile.

"Can I ask you something?" she said.

"Shoot."

"Why do you talk about the war as if it's still going on?"

"Because it *is* still going on," Goldman said. "Don't you doubt it for a second."

"Well I don't see it," Eda said, with a cool shrug of the shoulders. "Have you been out there lately? Outside of Boston I mean? There's no war left, only a few survivors – men, women and children – doing their best to stay alive. The only war I've seen is the one between living and dying."

Goldman smiled, like a man with a secret to tell.

"I'm not alone here," he said. "There's someone else in Boston. And I'm not talking about you or Frankie Boy."

"Who are you talking about then?" Eda said.

"There's one more soldier at loose."

"One more soldier?"

Goldman's eyes scanned the neighborhood, roaming outside the metal fence and taking it all in.

"He ain't one of ours," he said, whispering. "He's one of *them*…"

Eda felt an icy jolt shoot up her spine. The old man's mind was gone, trapped in the past. It was horrible to see. In Eda's experience, the confrontation with madness was uglier than the one with death. Death couldn't hurt you. It couldn't hurt itself either. Those who were caught in the grip of madness however, were like animals suffering up close.

"One of them?" she asked.

Goldman tapped a finger off his skull. "Chink," he said. "There's still one chink running around here."

"*Chink*?"

"A Chinaman for God's sake!" Goldman roared. "You know? The slanty-eyed bastards who caused all this mess in the first place. I'm trying to tell you that there's one of them running around loose in the city. One soldier left out of an army of millions."

Goldman's eyes were bright and alert. He looked sane, at least on the outside. How long since the old soldier had tipped over the edge?

"I haven't seen him for a while though," Goldman said, looking around once again to check the coast was clear. "It happens sometimes and I start to think that maybe the old son of a bitch is lying dead somewhere. Natural causes, illness – something horrible like that. But if he has checked out, I've got to see it. Jeez, I've got to see that body."

The soldier squeezed down on the rifle barrel and his pink, jagged knuckles turned white.

"What if you don't see it?" Eda asked.

Goldman looked at her like she was crazy. Not for the first time either.

"I *have* to," he said. "He dies first, we win. God bless America and all those who perished inside her. But I gotta know for sure he's checked out or I'm always going to be guessing and looking over my shoulder for the man sneaking up on me."

Eda sat in silence, not knowing what else to say to this strange, broken man. She didn't feel like she was in any danger being close to him. Not anymore. The overwhelming emotion inside her was in fact one of great pity. She could only imagine what it must have been like for Goldman living like that for years, if not decades. Chasing his tail.

"I've got one thing left to do," Goldman said to Eda. "Just one. To make sure Mr. China dies before I do."

"Mr. China?"

Goldman smiled. "I call him lots of things. That's one of my nicer names. Seeing as how there's a lady present and all..."

"How long you been fighting him?" Eda asked.

Goldman shrugged. "Who the hell knows?" he said. "Right? Time doesn't stop just because the clocks aren't working anymore."

He let out a loud sigh.

"I was living right here in South Boston when the war broke out. Jeez Louise. This place was wall-to-wall Micks. Little Ireland, that's what we called it. And there were a few Jews like me of course. This is *still* my home. I never left Boston during or after the war – I fought for her, spilled blood for her, like so many others. And then it was over. Everything I ever knew or loved was gone. A long time passed and the America I grew up in began to shrivel and shrink into something else. And then one day, he showed up. Mister goddamn China. I don't know where he came from or what he was thinking about coming here. Probably came in from another state, trying to get back to the ocean. Trying to get to his boats, thinking they were still docked in the harbor. You can understand it I suppose."

Goldman covered his mouth with the back of his hand. It looked like he was about to cough again but he held off.

"Tell me something," Goldman said to Eda. "What the hell are you doing here? What are you *really* doing in Boston?"

"Long story," Eda said. "To cut it short, I came looking for someone."

Goldman shook his head. "Most Bostonians died at the start of the war. This place was a big chink target because of the harbor you understand? If anyone around here didn't die in the war they took off inland as fast as their burning, bloody legs could take them. Boston has a permanent population of two souls now. Mr. China and me. You wasted your time coming here Eda. That person you want, they're dead or gone. Long time."

"Wasted my time?" Eda said. "Oh really? You're one to talk mister."

Goldman flattened a stray hair on his mustache. "Now what in the hell are you talking about?"

Eda bit her lip. Goldman was a madman with a gun and she was about to lash out at him for telling the truth. She *had* wasted her time coming here. If she wanted someone to be angry at someone all she had to do was look in the mirror.

"You think I'm a loon?" Goldman asked. "Oh I see now. You think I'm a senile old dipshit chasing chink ghosts around this city for funsies? Or wait a minute...maybe it's worse than that. Maybe you think I'm a liar?"

"I don't think you're a liar," Eda said.

Goldman came a little closer. Thank God, Frankie Body didn't growl.

"It's not safe for you here," Goldman said. "You've been lucky so far because I found you first. But if you keep walking around this city long enough without your wits you'll get a bullet in your back cour-tesy of the Chinaman. That's a fact young lady. That son of a bitch is still out there fighting for the motherland. He wants to kill Americans. It's been a long time and his guns are hungry."

Goldman coughed and clamped a wrinkled hand over his mouth.

Eda saw a dark red stain on the man's hand as he lowered it to his side. Goldman noticed it a second later and he cursed quietly before pulling out a dirty-looking handkerchief from his pocket and wiping his hands clean with it.

She almost said something but stopped herself. Best not to agitate him.

"I think Frankie Boy's settled down," Eda said, patting the dog gently. "Okay if I let him go? You promise you won't shoot him?"

Goldman put the handkerchief back in his pocket.

"I like dogs," he said in a quiet voice.

Eda nodded her thanks. Then slowly, she let go of Frankie's thick coat, bracing herself in case he made a dash at Goldman. But the big German Shepherd stayed exactly where he was, sitting on the grass.

Eda straightened up and felt a sudden stab of pain in her left side around the hip. Without thinking about it she pulled up her rain cloak, peeled back the sweater back and saw a large scrape running down her side. Probably from the fall.

"Damn it," she said. The aches and pains were piling up fast.

"My god you're skin and bones," Goldman said, looking at her. He looked genuinely shocked.

Eda quickly pulled her top down. "I'm fine," she said in a flat voice. "Nothing that won't right itself in time."

"Hell you're not fine," Goldman said. "You're hungry, right?"

She said nothing.

"That's what I thought," Goldman said. "Listen. I got lots of food back at my place. Too much food for one old buzzard like me. I can't just leave you out here alone like this, all skin and bones and soaking wet."

Eda held a hand out. "I'm fine. Just let us go and we'll…"

"Don't be worrying now," Goldman said, slinging the rifle over his shoulder. He began to walk towards the gate, keeping a wide berth between himself and Frankie Boy. A wise move.

"I'm not a pervert or anything like that," he said. "Even if I was I don't have the energy for that kind of nonsense. Look here's what we'll do. You'll come back to my place and get some food inside you. The dog, he can eat too. And after that? We gotta get you out of this city. It's dangerous here."

"You said that already," Eda said.

"Well now I'm saying it again."

4

After about an hour's walk, Goldman brought his two companions to a small block of redbrick apartments located on a long, winding coastal road that stretched on forever like a giant asphalt snake. The apartment building was sandwiched neatly in between a public park, which looked more like a jungle now, and a stretch of golden sand beach.

The sight of the ocean captivated Eda. She'd seen it before somewhere – maybe it was inside a dream but perhaps not. Vast swathes of creamy sand. A blanket of dark blue water with tall, frothy waves charging recklessly at the land. And the delicious sound of it. It evoked a sense of familiarity in Eda, pointing her thoughts towards a nameless city she'd spent time in as a youth. Was she thinking about home? After all, there had to be somewhere out there that she could rightfully think of in that sense.

"What stretch of water is that?" Eda asked, turning to Goldman.

The old man had set a surprisingly swift pace since leaving the park. He walked with his head held high, stiff-backed, and with the assuredness of someone who had undertaken this journey many times.

"That's the old harbor out there," Goldman said. "You'll find more than a few islands if you keep going that way – Thompson Island, Long Island, Spectacle Island, to name a few. Some of the others escape me now. Beyond that you've got Massachusetts Bay and then it's the Atlantic Ocean. After that, Europe and Africa."

"It looks cold," Eda said. "The water I mean."

"I swim out there every day if I can," Goldman said. "Helps keep these old bones nice and limber. Even it's freezing cold, and I'm talking about ball-shrinking weather, you'll find me in the water."

"Impressive," Eda said, with a half-smile.

They walked up six flights of stairs to Goldman's apartment. Eda's legs throbbed as she tackled the concrete steps. She couldn't understand why the old man hadn't taken an apartment on the first floor.

Finally they reached his front door on the sixth floor.

Number 29.

Goldman aggressively jiggled a key in the lock, barged his shoulder into the door and then walked inside. Eda followed, with Frankie Boy trotting close behind.

There were photographs everywhere. It was the first thing Eda noticed as she walked into the otherwise modest and plain little apartment. So many photographs. They were on the wall, on the coffee table, the floor, and crammed side by side on the window ledges. There were a few others parked on the edge of the silvery blue cotton couch. They were family shots mostly but Eda caught a glimpse of a few others lying around with a serious looking young man standing front and center. This was a much younger Talbot Goldman, sporting a variety of bizarre hairstyles and clothes. He'd been a handsome, clean-shaven man back then. Pre-mustache. His hair was bluish-black and when it had been at its longest, a hint of thick curls could be seen forming around the edges. In most photos, solo and with his family gathered around him, Goldman wore a combat uniform featuring the old colors of the American army – a khaki, black and gold combo.

"Do you sleep with that uniform on?" Eda asked.

"As a matter of fact I do," Goldman said, laughing.

Eda looked closer at the family photos. Goldman was surrounded by a pack of adoring women. Three cute and smiling girls bunched up tight against their dad like monkeys hanging off a tree. A pretty red-haired woman stood beside Goldman, offering a knowing smile towards the camera. In the earliest photographs the girls were babies. The latest ones however, didn't go past their teenage years.

Goldman dropped his rifle on the couch.

"Back in a few minutes," he said. "Going to fix you two something to eat. Big plates all round right?"

"Sure," Eda said. "Thanks."

"You haven't tasted it yet," Goldman said, disappearing into the hallway.

While the old man was in the kitchen, Eda spent a little more time exploring the Goldman family museum. After that she crossed the living room and looked out of the small window. There was a decent view of the beach and harbor from up on the sixth floor. And she could still hear the dreamlike sound of waves in the distance.

"You alright in there?" Goldman called out from the kitchen.

"Fine," Eda said.

"Just make yourself at home. Food won't be long now."

"How long have you lived here?" Eda asked.

Silence.

A moment later, Goldman appeared at the door carrying a bright red plastic tray in his hands. Two plates and a large metallic bowl sat atop the tray, all of them spilling over with food.

"Can't remember how long it's been," Goldman said. "Damn long. Before I got married anyway. My uncle owned this apartment and because he didn't have any kids of his own he left it to me in his will. That was a big help back in the days when I worried about money and all that other material shit that doesn't mean anything anymore."

Frankie Boy tilted his nose up at the tray.

"Got some striped bass and vegetables," Goldman said, making a loud announcement. "Jumbo-sized portions too. Skinny thing like you, you gotta put the meat back on. Plus, it's a special occasion. God knows how long it's been since there was anyone besides me in this apartment."

"You grow vegetables around here?" Eda asked, lifting one of the plates off the tray and smiling in gratitude. Her stomach was growling with anticipation.

"I've got a garden of sorts not far from here," Goldman said. He gazed towards the window that overlooked the harbor. "There's a big old house down the road, they had lots of stuff growing out back. Well I found it abandoned and kept it going as best I could. It's given me a hell of a lot more than just a sack of fresh vegetables now and then I can tell ya. Gardening and fishing, my two pastimes. That's all I've got to wind down after a hard day's soldiering in the city of Boston."

"You fish out there?" Eda asked.

"Well that striped bass didn't just show up at the door asking me to eat it," Goldman said. "Yeah I do a little nearshore fishing. I like to go out every other day or so, preferably early in the morning if I can. It's nice at dusk too."

Eda got the feeling the old man was enjoying talking to someone else for a change.

"Catch much?" she said.

Goldman nodded. "You bet. With all the industrial scale fishing gone you won't believe the amount of fish swimming out there. It's funny because a long time ago they closed that beach down because the water was so damn dirty. Water's never been cleaner than it is now. You get all kinds of fish in there –striped bass, mackerel, cod, sea bass, and so on. The ocean is paradise again. I only take what I need to keep breathing."

Ed glanced through the window just as a huge, towering wave was churning its way towards the beach. "Must keep you fit," she said. "Steering a little boat in that."

"I'm not dead yet," Goldman said, walking further into the living room. "Besides I don't go out too far. Don't have to. The fish practically jump into the boat nowadays."

Goldman invited Eda to sit down on the armchair and eat. Then he crouched to a half squat and put the bowl on the floor for an excited Frankie Boy. The dog's tail wagged furiously. He shoved his snout into the bowl, slurping wildly as he ate.

"Are we friends now huh?" Goldman said, smiling at the German Shepard. The old soldier looked like he wanted to pat the dog but after he put the food on the floor he kept a distance, watching Frankie Boy tear into a large chunk of fish.

"Good appetite," he said, walking over to the couch. "I had a dog once. He always liked my June better than he liked me."

Eda nodded, shoveling a forkful of food into her mouth. Her appetite had been jolted into life by the taste of food. As she threw it down it felt like she was sinking into the armchair. Drowning in a beautiful dream.

"It's good?" Goldman said.

"Uh-huh," Eda said, her mouth full.

Goldman leaned back on the couch and closed his eyes. He kept silent for a while apart from a wheezy breathing noise that spilled out in a gentle rhythm. He made no effort to touch his own plate. Eda thought he might have fallen asleep. Either way she was grateful he didn't talk because it allowed her time to get stuck into the food without interruption.

It didn't take her long to finish. When she was done she wiped her mouth dry with her sleeve and at that moment the old soldier opened his eyes. He leaned forward on the couch, his wrinkled uniform making a dull creaking noise.

"Better?"

"Much better," Eda said. "Thanks.

"Alright," Goldman said. "So go ahead and tell me your story why don't you? And tell me why in God's name you're walking about Boston on your own like this. No offense to the big mutt there, I'm sure he's as tough as old nails, but I thought everyone moved around in packs and tribes these days. For safety. At least that's what I've seen passing through Boston on occasion. But solo travelers? That's just asking for trouble."

Eda pushed herself upright on the armchair. Her eyelids felt heavy after devouring the big meal and all she wanted to do now was fall asleep. The room was just the right temperature too, neither hot nor cold. Everything was quiet, apart from the waves in the distance. It was perfect.

But she was a guest in Goldman's apartment. He'd just fed her and he was at least entitled to ask a few questions about the stranger he'd brought home.

She fought back the sluggishness and told the old man about New York and the Complex. Then she told him about the swamp in New Jersey and what she'd found in there. Those were the things she could remember clearly.

The old man sat listening, wide-eyed and captivated throughout the telling. He didn't interrupt Eda once.

"I always wondered what it was like out there," he said. "I heard a lot of stories in the early days before this city emptied itself out. Seen those who passed through Boston over the years. A lot of sad faces. It didn't paint a pretty picture of the outside world."

Eda offered a tired shrug of the shoulders.

"It's a mess," she said. "I don't know how else to describe it."

Goldman sat forward, his straw-like eyebrows standing on end.

"You must have known there was no chance of finding this person you came here looking for," he said. "Surely you knew it was a waste of time. So why do it? Why did you walk all the way from New Jersey to Massachusetts for a losing bet?"

"I don't know," Eda said. "Because somebody asked me to do it. Somebody who deserves to have their dying wish fulfilled."

Goldman scratched his chin thoughtfully. Then he fell back into the couch, drowning in photographs.

"So there's still a little honor left in the world huh?" he said, glancing at a large silver-framed photograph of his wife. "I'm happy to hear that. It's good to hold onto some things. Right Junie?"

"Most people are holding onto revenge," Eda said. "They think it's going to fill the hole."

Goldman patted the butt of his rifle, which was sprawled out on the couch beside him like a favorite toy. He was smiling.

"Why do I get the feeling you're talking about me?"

"Don't know," Eda said. "Am I?"

Goldman sat forward in his seat again. He moved quickly for an old timer.

"Sure you are," he said. "You're...you're..."

He stopped. There was a blank, puzzled look on the old man's face. His eyes went dark, scanning the contents of the living room like he was seeing everything for the first time.

"Are you okay?" Eda asked.

"What?" Goldman said. He looked at Eda like she'd just appeared out of thin air all of a sudden. With a soft, low-pitched groan, he removed his cap and scratched the top of his head.

"Oh yeah, sure," he said. "I just..."

A pause.

"...sometimes I forget. I forget what I'm saying. Forget where I am, what I'm thinking. Uhh, what were we talking about?"

"Revenge," Eda said quietly.

Goldman nodded. "We were talking about revenge." He said the words as if reading them off a script.

"Your Chinaman?" Eda said. "Is that enough revenge for you?"

Goldman was staring at the family photographs in silence. Reestablishing the connection, temporarily severed by whatever had just happened.

"Right now," he said, looking up at Eda. "He's walking around the city and he's looking for me like I'm the cure to the fatal disease that's killing him. But that's good. Means we'll find each other again soon enough. As long as I get him before he gets me."

He wrapped his arms around the picture of his wife.

"It's victory for God's sake," he said, not to Eda but to the red-haired woman. "Victory."

Goldman put down the photograph. Then he looked at his plate of food, still sitting on the tray beside him. He picked it up and then put it back down again like he'd lost all trace of appetite.

He shifted nervously on the couch.

"I can almost feel him out there," Goldman said, staring at the window. "He's real close now. He's a patient son of a bitch mind you, not the mindless bastard our superiors tried to tell us the chinks were. Those people made good soldiers, I'll say that much for them. They were reading the Art of War when they were still in diapers. Meanwhile our kids were reading Spot the Dog books."

Eda put her empty plate down on the coffee table.

"I saw a caravan of people on the way to Boston," she said. "Nomads, that's what they called themselves. They asked me to go south with them."

Goldman was still staring out the window.

"You should have gone with them," he said in a quiet voice. "Something big's coming in and now more than ever, people need to join forces and stick together. Strength in numbers. Form groups, packs, tribes and learn how to work together all over again. Practice guerilla warfare. It's your only hope of survival because the trouble that's coming...it's big goddamn trouble."

The old soldier seemed to be talking to himself now. He shook his head, his lips pursed tightly together.

"Trouble?" Eda said. "What sort of trouble?"

With a groan, Goldman pushed himself back up to his feet.

"Forget about it," Goldman said, standing over Eda. "I'm an old man rambling on, don't listen to me. Now here's what we're going to do. I'll escort you out of Boston personally. If our friend Mr. China sees you on the street he'll shoot you stone dead. I'm telling you, he won't ask questions like I did."

"Alright," Eda said. "You want me to go now?"

"Hell no," Goldman said, shaking his head. "You need to get some sleep young lady. Look at you. You're beat."

Eda stood up and glanced out towards the coastline. The light was growing dim and the ocean sounded peaceful now. The world was winding down to a slow vibration and Eda was ready to climb aboard, to welcome oblivion.

"Thanks," she said. "I appreciate the food and the bed."

"Sure thing," Goldman said, smiling. "You can sleep in my Emily's room, alright? You and Frankie Boy. Sleep as long as you like. Tomorrow you guys are going to hit the road and by God I'll say it again, you're going to catch up with those Nomads and get the hell out of Boston. You hear?"

5

Eda slept in Emily Goldman's bedroom that night.

The room was neat and tidy. It was a small space with a single bed and Goldman had obviously kept it in good condition over the years. It smelled of scented candles – vanilla and fresh spices. And of course, like every other room in the house, it was filled with family photographs. Every last memory of Emily had been crammed into something tangible, locked inside a metal frame.

This was a sacred room in the Goldman shrine. After she'd said goodnight to the old man, Eda had sat on the bed with Frankie Boy for a while, not sure if she could sleep there or not. She felt like an intruder.

Pretty soon however, exhaustion overwhelmed all trace of discomfort.

As she lay in bed waiting for sleep, Eda's attention lingered on Emily Goldman's face on the other side of the room. It was only early evening outside and Eda hadn't bothered to pull the thick drapes over. A dull streak of light touched the surface of one of the metal frames sitting on the ledge. Emily was a black-haired girl with blue eyes and a strong jawline. She was the eldest of the three girls and if

Eda were to guess, she'd say that Emily hadn't made it past seventeen at the most.

The rest of the bedroom – the bookshelves, a closet, a small TV standing on a chest of drawers, paled in comparison to the photographs of the young girl.

At last, the room began to swim. Eda sank deeper into the soft sheets while Frankie Boy slept beside her, curled up on the end of the bed. He was snoring. His body felt warm against her legs.

Eda slept through the night without interruption. In the morning, she was bursting to pee. She slipped out of the sheets, her legs whipped by a blast of cold air. With Frankie Boy behind her, Eda crept out of the apartment, went downstairs, opened the front door and slipped around to the back of the building. She relieved herself, trying to shake off the fog of sleep at the same time.

It was a mild, dry morning in South Boston. Eda lifted her head to the sky and inhaled. Rain was coming.

Maybe even a storm.

After she was done, Eda stood up and stretched her legs. They weren't as stiff as she'd thought they were going to be after all the miles she'd covered over the past week. That was something at least. If she could set a good pace, she had every chance of catching up with the slow-moving Nomads.

She walked the length of the apartment building out back, following a narrow concrete path down to a small dirt strip. A faint rectangular outline on the dirt suggested that some sort of structure, a small building or a hut perhaps, had once stood there. Eda encircled the outline, almost in a trance and found herself looking at Goldman's apartment building from a distance. She noticed a row of six plastic trash bins lined up against the exterior. Something else was there, poking out behind the bins. It was barely visible. Eda walked over that way and saw that it was a large wooden chest, about the size of a coffin and of a similar width. The wood was damp and worn down.

Eda pinched forefinger and thumb over her nostrils. Something reeked badly. A small cloud of files buzzed furiously around the trash bins.

Resisting the urge to run, Eda took a closer look at the box. The lid didn't appear sealed or locked. She stepped closer, despite a voice in her head running through the worst possible outcomes of this investigation.

Frankie Boy rummaged ahead of her, nose to the ground. The rotting garbage cans were driving him crazy. Or was it something else? Was there something inside the chest? Someone? Eda's insides tightened up at the thought of finding the remains of one or more of the Goldman girls in there. The thought repulsed her but she couldn't shake it. What if the old man had killed his family in a violent, frenzied bout of postwar madness?

His mind was going, that much was obvious.

Eda's fingers trembled as they yanked the lid upwards. It flipped over easily and spilled to the side with a thud.

She took a step backwards, one hand clamped over her mouth. The box was full of weapons. A *lot* of weapons. Eda saw rifles, handguns, knives with serrated edges, and little ball shaped objects with turtle shell exteriors that she suspected were hand grenades.

She scoured the surrounding area, checking to see if anyone was watching. As far as she could tell, the coast was clear.

There was a sudden noise that almost made Eda's heart explode. It sounded like the front door to the apartment building opening and then being slammed shut.

Light, hurried footsteps. Coming towards her.

"Oh shit," Eda said, swatting a gang of marauding flies away from her face.

"Hello!" Goldman's voice called out from the other side of the building. "Are you there?"

Eda cursed again. The she picked up the lid and covered the weapons box, keeping as quiet as she could under the circumstances. She continued to brush the flies off as she straightened up, then walked back to the front of the apartments.

She met Goldman halfway. He was dressed in his military

uniform of course. Stray tufts of silvery white hair poked out from both sides of his wrinkled cap. The hair that Eda could see looked freshly combed, as was Goldman's thick, luxuriant mustache.

"Oh hi!" Eda said, trying to sound cheerful. "I was just…"

"Using the bathroom?"

Eda nodded, her gaze drifting off into the distance. "Yeah."

"I like going around the back too," Goldman said, whispering as if revealing some wonderful secret to Eda. "It's nice to have a regular place to relieve oneself you know? I just go around the back and bury it – I'm kind of like a cat in that way."

Goldman laughed and clicked his fingers at Frankie Boy. "You're okay with cats. Right partner?"

Eda laughed with him, nervously.

Goldman raised a hand in the air. "Sorry if I woke you last night," he said. "Truth is I don't sleep much nowadays, at least not during the night when I'm supposed to. And I can't stand lying in bed staring at the ceiling so I tend to get up and go into the living room and then into the kitchen and back again. Wandering around aimlessly, waiting for sunrise so I can get back out there and look for Mr. China."

"I didn't hear anything," Eda said.

"That's something at least."

The smile dissolved from the old man's face. He pointed a finger over Eda's shoulder towards the back of the building. "See anything else around there?"

Eda felt a chill in the breeze and shivered.

"What do you mean?"

Goldman let out another hearty laugh, his shoulders heaving up and down like someone was pumping him full of air.

"You should see your face," he said. "Awww, it's quite alright. I heard the lid of that box slamming shut from a mile away. Sounded like a clap of thunder, even to a deaf old coot like me."

Eda groaned and that only made Goldman laugh harder.

"You discovered my little stash right?" he said. "Curiosity got the better of you."

"I'm sorry," Eda said, feeling her face turn bright red. "I just saw the box and I was..."

"Interested," Goldman said, walking past Eda and heading towards the back of the building. There was a slow and carefree quality in his stride. "Of course you were. That's quite alright – as long as you're not Mr. China, I don't care if you see all that stuff or not."

Eda followed him back to the garbage and flies.

"You hoarded all those weapons over the years?" she asked.

"Sure did," Goldman said. He walked over to the chest, ignoring the flies as he pulled the lid open. He exhaled loudly, either from exertion or from the stench of the congealed garbage shooting up his nostrils.

"That's a lot of hardware," Eda said, taking another look at the layers of weapons stacked on top of one another. "How come you only carry the rifle and the handgun when you're walking the streets?"

"Dagger too," Goldman said, pointing to the small hilt on his weapons belt. "I've got another one of those taped just above my ankle."

All of a sudden he began to giggle like a child.

Eda frowned. "What's so funny?"

Goldman stole a glance over his shoulder, as if he thought someone might be listening in on their conversation.

"I've even got a grenade strapped next to my...you know?"

"No," Eda said.

Goldman grinned. "Down there," he said, nodding towards his crotch. "It's my *extremely* secret weapon. I call it my third ball."

"You put a grenade down there?" Eda said, taking a step back. "You put a *hand grenade* down your pants?"

"It's still got the pin in it for God's sake," Goldman said, looking a little embarrassed. The grin was gone now. "Relax. This is war and you've gotta be the slyest beast in the jungle if you want to make it through in one piece. You understand? Doesn't matter if the enemy's a better shot, a better fighter, stronger, has more weapons or whatever. The smartest fighter wins."

The way Goldman said 'smartest' it sounded like *smaaaaaartest*. Eda had never heard an accent quite like it before.

"Ain't nobody going to ever find it down there," Goldman said. "And that's the point."

Eda stared at the contents of the box again. There were dozens of turtle shell grenades scattered about inside.

"Do all those grenades work?" she asked. "They look like antiques."

"They work," Goldman said. "Everything works. Those grenades right there, that's a standard issue. All the troopers used to carry at least one of those back in the day. I prefer these to the old standard issue – there's a longer delay between pulling the pin and the blast. The old grenades used to go off after four seconds precisely. Jeez. That didn't work for some of the clandestine maneuvers we were pulling against the chinks. We lost a lot of good people who just weren't fast enough. These ones right here, they've got a longer fuse to burn. Twelve seconds. Means you can get right up close, drop one and haul your ass to safety."

Eda listened, nodding as Goldman spoke.

"I didn't think people used weapons like these anymore," she said.

"That's only because they don't have access to them," Goldman said. "I clung onto these babies like bankers hoarding up piles of money. Weapons meant survival. Still do. I don't know if you're old enough to remember what it was like back then Eda. There was no law. Nothing. The authorities, the old infrastructure had collapsed entirely. There was nothing to stop the man in the street plugging you full of lead and taking whatever he wanted to take from you. Whoever he wanted. Can you imagine how frightening that was for a man with a wife and three daughters to protect? There were murderers and rapists everywhere. Back then hate flowed like the rain does now. Fear too. So I started scavenging weapons. I searched dead bodies in the street, looking for treasure, and whatever I found I brought back here. The garbage here was fresh and a lot worse than it is now. On top of that the local junkies used to leave needles lying around. People kept away from the trash. Perfect hiding place, right?"

"But why don't you keep your guns in the house?" Eda said.

"June," Goldman said in a quiet voice. "She never felt comfortable with guns inside..."

"I understand," Eda said. "But now...?"

Goldman quickly shook his head.

"There ain't nobody to steal them now anyway," he said. "Apart from the chink I guess. I don't know. Truth be told, most of this lying here is useless now. I only need my old M4 rifle to win the war. Although if I get close enough to the chink I wouldn't mind dropping my third ball down the back of his shirt."

"That's messed up," Eda said.

"Didn't you say everything was a mess last night?"

Eda smiled. She looked into the chest again, scouring the pile of weapons that almost spilled over the edge. Despite the infestation of flies, she moved closer to the stash.

"I've never shot a gun before," she said.

Goldman pushed the visor of his cap up. "You wanna try?"

Eda was still staring at the gun. She replied in a quiet voice.

"I don't know," she said.

"Sure you do," Goldman said.

He squatted down, both hands reaching into the old box. After rattling around for a second, he picked up one of the black rifles and gave it the once over. It was identical to the M4 that he'd carried around with him the day before.

"These look heavy," he said. "But in fact they're made of light-weight materials and very easy to hold. I reckon it'd be a good fit for you."

Goldman put the rifle back in the box and closed the lid.

"We'll try mine for starters," he said, standing back up. "It's fully loaded and waiting up there in the apartment. What do you say we go pick it up, stroll down to the beach and do a little shooting practice?"

Eda smiled. "Thanks," she said. "But I should really get going. It's a long walk to..."

"C'mon young lady," Goldman said. "You never know when it might come in handy. Right?"

The old soldier was already walking back into the apartment to fetch his M4.

"Won't be a minute," he said.

Eda and Frankie Boy waited outside the front of the building, putting a little distance between themselves and the trash.

"Let's keep this short," Eda said, giving Frankie Boy a pat on the back. "The Nomads aren't standing around waiting for us."

When Goldman came back with the gun they crossed the quiet road and walked down to the beach. The old man did most of the talking as they approached the water, reveling in the opportunity to talk about the local attractions. He told Eda that the area they were in was called Carson Beach, although Eda thought he didn't sound too confident in the recollection. It had once been a popular spot, Goldman informed her. People everywhere used to flock to Carson Beach.

When they reached the sand, Goldman escorted Eda about a hundred meters along to where he'd set up a private shooting range. This consisted of three medium-sized wooden crates, lined up about ten feet apart. A small wire fence encircled the shooting range. Eda only understood why the fence was there when she spotted countless shards of broken glass lying on the sand close to the crates. The shards glistened, like thousands of tiny eggs waiting to hatch.

"Are the soles of your boots intact?" Goldman asked, pointing at Eda's feet.

"Yeah," Eda said, after she'd checked.

"Good. You don't want to be in here with naked tootsies. Not if you like walking."

The old man stepped over the fence, treading carefully across the small enclosure of sand and glass. He walked over to a black plastic bag flapping in the breeze, one that had been weighed down with a couple of large rocks. Reaching inside the bag he pulled out a trio of empty copper-colored bottles and lined them up, one on top of each crate.

"Alright," he said, walking over to Eda with a *let's get down to business* face. "Your targets are all set." He slid the M4 strap off his shoulder and let the weapon drop onto the sand. He looked at her. "You ready?"

"Yeah," Eda said, climbing over the fence and walking tentatively into the shooting range. She made a point of avoiding the larger chunks of broken glass. "Sure."

She stood facing him.

"Now show me a fighting stance," Goldman said.

"What do you mean?"

Goldman adopted a boxer's stance. "Just give me something like this," he said in a gruff voice. "Like you're about to square off with someone. Think about somebody you've encountered in the past, somebody whose head you wanted to punch off more than anything. Know anyone like that?"

"One or two," Eda said.

"Go ahead then."

"I thought I was going to shoot," Eda said.

"You are. You will. C'mon now, show me that fighting stance."

Eda stared at the old man like he was crazy. She clenched her fists and extended her left arm forward. The right arm stayed back, elbow tight to the body, her hand tucked in close to the chin the way a boxer would hold it. Likewise her left leg stretched out and her right stayed back, the foot pointing slightly to the side.

"Like this?" she said.

"Good," Goldman said. "That's really good."

"What's this for anyway?" Eda asked.

"I want your body to square off towards a target," Goldman said. "Now don't you move okay? I'm going to pick up the rifle and slide it into your fighting platform. Now remember this okay? Remember how you're standing because stance is super important. *Super* important."

"Alright."

Goldman squatted down and picked up the M4. Then he tucked the rifle into the pocket of Eda's shoulder. Still holding onto the gun he took a half step back and studied their progress, like a painter admiring the dawn of his creation.

"Close your hands around the rifle," Goldman said, coming forward again. "Stretch your arm far out on the forend – under the barrel, that's it. No, no – don't use the magazine as a grip. Grip the grip, that's what it's for."

Eda sighed and readjusted. She locked her hands around the weapon as instructed. It felt alien and inelegant compared to the samurai sword that she carried around with her.

"Like this?" she said.

Goldman made a slight humming noise.

"Trigger arm down, tight to the body. "Keep it tight now. You don't want that recoil bouncing the rifle around. That's especially important because you're a first-time shooter."

Goldman twisted Eda's shoulder forward as he kept spitting out instructions. She felt like a doll being bent into shape by its sadistic owner.

"Use that shoulder as a shock absorber," the old man said. "Listen to me Eda, you gotta have control of your weapon. Control means faster and better shots, and that's going to be the difference between you and the other bozo with a gun. Okay? Don't grip too hard now. Not too much pressure."

"Can I shoot yet?" Eda said.

Goldman walked around, studying her with a peculiar intensity. The old man's eyes were ablaze with concentration. Anyone would think he was sending Eda into battle instead of giving her a simple shooting lesson.

"It's nice and light right?" he said. "Keep a proper stance at all times and you won't get fatigued. All these little details will help you when the time is right. Make it work under speed and stress because that's how you're going to be shooting when they come for you. It feels alright?"

"It's fine," Eda said. "Can't I just shoot the damn thing?"

Goldman began to lighten up a little. He laughed and backed off a couple of paces. "Sorry," he said. "Old habits die hard I guess. I just want you to know what you're doing when you pick up a gun. Makes all the difference when it come time to shoot, I promise."

Eda waited impatiently while Goldman gave her more tips, including how to look down the top of the barrel and get the best aim.

"Ready to shoot?" he said.

"Uh-huh."

"Alright then," Goldman said, moving behind her. "Slowly take aim and squeeze that trigger when you think you've got the target locked in."

Eda's first shot missed by a mile. Her legs wobbled as the gun went off. She shot again quickly, trying to get used to the kick. When the rifle fired it felt like someone throwing a heavy weight into her arms and she struggled to control it.

Gradually the gun began to settle into her shoulder.

She fired, missing again.

"That's not good is it?" she said, looking at the three glass bottles, still intact on the crates.

"Well the aim's off a little," Goldman said. "But your stance and poise are actually pretty good for a first-timer. You say you've never shot a gun before?"

"Never," Eda said.

"But you've been in combat right?"

"Yeah."

"Try again," Goldman said, pointing to the crates. "Smash one of those damn bottles into smithereens."

"Smithereens?"

Goldman smirked and jerked a thumb at the three targets.

"Just shoot."

They spent a long time shooting on the beach together. While Frankie Boy went off exploring the sights, Eda absorbed as much as she could from Goldman about how to use the gun. She found herself enjoying this impromptu lesson.

Soon the Nomads slipped to the back of her mind.

When she finally hit the first bottle, Eda was ecstatic and wanted to shoot the second one to prove it wasn't a fluke. She did it. She cleaned them out and Goldman replaced the bottles and let her start over again.

Goldman didn't mention 'the chink' once. He showed a great deal of patience, showing Eda how to reload and how to do it fast while under pressure.

When it was done, he bowed in a show of appreciation.

"Now that's what you call a crash course in shooting," Goldman said, leading Eda back out of the enclosure. "You're a good learner. Damn good. You got the basics down real fast there – excellent work soldier."

The old man stepped over the fence. Eda followed and she noticed him tugging restlessly on the end of his mustache, as if overcome by a sudden rush of nerves.

"Are you okay?" Eda asked.

He nodded.

"Listen," Goldman said. "You've seen that box of weapons up at the apartment now right? And so you know I've got several spare M4s doing nothing better than collecting dust and stinking of garbage."

"Yeah," Eda said. "I know."

Goldman finally stopped fidgeting with his mustache.

"I know you've only had one lesson," he said. "But look...if you wanted to keep practicing, on your own that is, I could give you one of those M4s and a truckload of ammo to take on the road with you."

Eda flinched. "You'd give me a gun?"

"Damn right," he said. "I'd feel a lot better about sending you off on your own, knowing you were armed."

Goldman pointed to the katana hanging off Eda's waist.

"That samurai sword you're carrying – it's pretty and it's dangerous for sure if you get close. But it's not enough."

"Enough for what?" Eda said.

Goldman stood facing the water, looking out to sea.

"I've been lucky," he said. "Living on the coast like this, I've seen many things come and go over the years but this...this is something else we've gotta face up to. You've got to keep your eyes open Eda, no matter how empty the world might feel it's always got another surprise waiting around the corner."

He looked at her.

"I've seen them."

Eda hesitated. "Them?"

Goldman nodded. "Their scouts have already landed," he said. "They come ashore, look around and when they're done they go back out to sea again."

He pointed to the water.

"They're out there you see, biding their time for the main event. And one day they'll come ashore and they won't go back."

Eda didn't know what to say to him. It was painful to listen to Goldman's paranoid jibber-jabber about a Chinaman running loose in Boston, and God knows what other delusions that had infested his mind. Hard to see him like that. The old man, even though he seemed sharp at times, was further gone than Eda had first thought. A nice man, slowly losing his mind. She thought about hospitals in the Boston region and wondered if there were any still standing. If by some miracle one or two of those buildings had survived, she might be able to go there and find some sort of medication. They had every-thing back then and surely there was a pill that would stop someone from losing their mind.

Goldman began walking back to the road. He gestured for Eda to follow him.

6

Before hitting the road, Goldman and Eda went back to the apartment. They shared a quick breakfast and when it was over the old man crammed a pile of Tupperware boxes filled with foil-wrapped food into Eda's backpack. The seams on her bag were close to breaking point by the time she wrestled the zipper shut. Goldman had also managed to squeeze an extra water bottle in there, along with a winter beanie and gloves.

"Let's see now," he said.

He studied the contents of the bag. Nodding his approval, he checked out the M4 that he'd picked out for Eda from the chest out back. He'd already stuffed the bag full of spare magazines.

Even with all the food, water and extra clothing, Goldman still had a look on his face like something was missing.

"What is it I'm forgetting here?" he said, tugging on the ends of his mustache.

Eda looked at him, trying not to laugh.

"Nothing," she said. "Listen, I'll be lucky if I'm able to walk with that thing. She looked at the bag again – it looked pregnant, like there was a fat baby bag growing inside it. "I think we're good to go."

"You'll be glad of that weight," Goldman said, tapping a finger off the table. "Trust me. In fact you might want to think about picking up a bigger bag somewhere on the road."

"Sure thing," Eda said. She heaved the backpack off the wooden surface and wobbled a little as she threaded the straps through her arms. It was heavier than it looked. At this rate it was going to be hard work catching up with the Nomads. Maybe she'd have to eat into all those food supplies quicker than she'd thought.

She picked up the M4, gripped the sling and let the weapon slide over her shoulder. It felt strange, like something that she wanted to push away from her body. With the sword still hanging at her waist, Eda was fully loaded.

"Thanks for your help," she said, turning to Goldman.

"Sure thing," the soldier said. "It was great meeting you."

"Is there anything I can pick up for you before I leave?" Eda said. "Do you need anything? Anything from the hospitals or whatever? You know, to make you more comfortable."

Goldman shook his head. He'd already crossed the living room and now he was standing at the door.

"Forget it," he said. "Even if I did need something you won't find a hospital around here anymore. At least not one that's intact."

Eda ran a hand through her dark hair. It felt dry and knotty.

"Will you be alright?" she asked.

Goldman paused. His wrinkled hand fidgeted with the metal handle, pulling it up and down.

"Yeah," he said. The way he said it, it sounded more like a sigh than a word. "I'll be alright if I know you're going to catch up with those Nomads at some point. They sound like good people. That's what you need right now. Go south with them Eda. Go as far south as your legs will carry you. Find somewhere remote, somewhere that's not easy to access for the average traveler, and try to have yourself a life of sorts."

"And you'll stay here?" Eda asked.

"Yeah," he said.

He smiled sheepishly.

"I shouldn't have said some of the things I did," he said. "Back down there on the beach I mean. Jeez, you didn't have to hear that. You probably think I'm crazy or at the very least a delusional paranoid wreck."

"At least you're not boring," Eda said.

"C'mon," Goldman said, laughing as he pulled the front door open. Eda felt a cold draught seep into the apartment and rush across the room to greet her. She could almost taste the salt of the sea in the air.

They set off towards the road marked 93. That was the highway that would lead Eda and Frankie Boy back to the 90, which traveled west and inland out of Boston. With any luck the Nomads' caravan hadn't turned south yet. The only way to find out for sure was for Eda and Frankie Boy to cover the miles and to do it fast. They couldn't afford to stroll.

More walking. It wasn't exactly a pleasant thought but if there was something great at the end of it, it'd be worth it.

As they traveled west on the empty highway, Goldman exhibited occasional signs of distress. Eda was forced to slow down to keep an eye on him. At first, the old man just mumbled to himself. He sounded like he was berating someone under his breath. Eda touched him on the arm and he flinched. She asked him to repeat what he'd said but Goldman just shook his head and looked the other way.

Soon he wandered ahead of Eda, his head bowed like a repentant sinner walking to the gallows.

"Goldman," Eda called out in a shocked voice. "What are you doing?"

The old man stopped dead. After a long silence, he looked back at Eda, took off his cap and she saw the sweat gushing off his brow.

"Where am I?" he said.

Goldman's affable old features had degenerated into a mask of terror. His eyes were big and childlike. The world was a strange and terrifying place for this version of Talbot Goldman. He was a man falling with no safety net.

Eda walked over to him, staring into those vacant eyes.

"Emily?" he said when he saw her coming.

Eda stopped and shook her head.

"It's Eda," she said. "Remember? You're having one of your black-outs Goldman. You're escorting me and Frankie Boy out of the city. Okay?"

After a moment, Goldman's distraught expression began to fade. Thank God, the eyes cleared and he was nodding his head. Slowly he sat down on the road, cross-legged like an ancient yogi.

"It just comes all of a sudden," he said a minute later. "I don't understand it. It's like my whole identity falls into a black hole. Everything familiar is gone and I'm sinking. These lapses, they're happening more frequently."

He looked up at Eda. His pale, heavily wrinkled face was almost transparent.

"For a second there, I thought...I thought you were my Emily."

"I'm sorry," Eda said, walking closer.

She took the backpack off and her body shuddered with relief. Then she sat down on the road opposite Goldman. A warm breeze fluttered around her neck.

"I can't leave you alone like this," she said to Goldman. "You're sick."

As she spoke, she slid the rifle strap down her shoulder and lowered the weapon onto the surface of the road. Frankie Boy stood at a distance, eager to keep moving. When he realized it wasn't happening, the German Shepherd came back over and sat down, pressing his weight against Eda's back.

"I'm not sick," Goldman said. "When you're sick there's a chance of recovery. I'm dying."

"You don't know that," Eda said. "But just in case, I'm going to stay with you."

Goldman waved a hand in the air, like he was brushing the suggestion aside. He was about to say something when Eda cut him off.

"It's your mind," she said. "You're seeing things Goldman for God's sake. Things that aren't there. People that aren't there. Hallucinations, you know? And you're having these blackouts too. It's the war – it has to be. It did something to your head."

Goldman sat in silence, staring down at the road.

Eda felt something land on her head. She looked up and felt the muggy air pressing against her skin. Rain was coming.

She lifted up the hood of her rain cloak. Goldman sat opposite, now staring over Eda's shoulder into nothingness. Apart from the cap on his head the old man had no protection from the rain.

"Let's get you back home," Eda said. "You want my advice? You need to start taking it easy Goldman – all this running around chasing ghosts all day, it's not good for you."

The rain crashed down all of a sudden. It was as if the universe had flicked the switch to full power. Eda closed her eyes for a second, listening to the rat-a-tat rhythm of water exploding off the top of her hood. The rain felt like home, but today she couldn't sit there and enjoy it like she wanted to. Like she used to do back in New York when she'd sit down in the middle of the street and let it drench her.

The old man didn't need a cold or some other preventable illness on top of everything else.

"Let's go," Eda said, tugging on his arm.

But Goldman shook his head and stayed in a sitting position on the road. His uniform was peppered with dark raindrops.

"I don't have long to go in this world," he called out over the rain. As he spoke, he looked Eda dead in the eye. "You're not going to waste your time here in Boston with a dying old man for God's sake."

He smiled.

"Thank you though..."

The blankness in his eyes came back, flickering on and off like a light.

"Find the others," he said. "Run for your lives while you still can."

Goldman's eyes drifted towards the downtown skyscrapers. From a distance they looked like miniature tower blocks rooted to the skyline. Black shapes, at the mercy of time.

The old man's gaze drifted over Eda's shoulder.

"Jesus Christ," he said.

Frankie Boy began to growl. He was still pressed up tight against Eda's back and it felt like there was an electric drill going off inside her. The dog was staring in the same direction as Goldman.

East. The direction they'd just come from.

Goldman jumped to his feet. At the same time, Eda turned around, her heart thumping.

There was a man on the highway. He was standing about a hundred meters away, watching them.

"I knew it," Goldman said, stepping in front of Eda. He was wide-eyed as he pointed his M4 at the ghostly figure in the distance. "Son of a bitch. He's probably been tailing me for days. Tailing *us*. He coulda taken me out anytime. Taken *you* out."

The stranger began walking towards them.

Slowly.

Eda strained her eyes, peering through the gray haze at the man. He was wearing a faded, dark red military uniform with a matching cap on his head. There was a yellow logo splattered on the left arm of the uniform – it might have been a flag or some other kind of foreign symbol. Eda saw a white tuft of hair sticking out of his chin – a long goatee that added a devilish flavor to his exotic appearance.

The man shouted at them in an incomprehensible tongue. He had a deep, booming voice, angry and outraged. In his hand he carried what looked like a semi-automatic rifle, similar to the M4 that Goldman favored.

"Long time no see you bastard," Goldman yelled back.

He glanced over his shoulder at Eda.

"Time for you to go," Goldman said. "You and the dog. Get away from the east coast. Go. Go now! This is between me and the chink."

"No," Eda said, grabbing Goldman by the arm. "I can't..."

"GO!"

Goldman's eyes spilled over with rage. He was so far removed from the broken shell of a man he'd been just moments earlier that Eda found herself dragging Frankie Boy away like he told her to. The dog was barking at the mystery man further down the road.

Eda tugged on his coat.

"C'mon Frankie," she said. It felt like she was hauling a lump of dog-shaped iron across the highway. "C'mon!"

Goldman began walking towards the stranger. As he walked he yelled:

"So you waited till I was on open ground huh? Nowhere to run. Nowhere to hide. Well that sounds like a damn fine plan to me."

Goldman's rifle was tucked in tight to his body. He stopped walking and looked down the barrel. Mr. China was doing the same thing further down the highway. Taking aim.

"He's real," Eda said, backing off slowly. The highway felt like quicksand under her feet. And she was sinking fast.

7

Goldman and Mr. China fired off a couple of rounds each.

There was an explosion of noise and as the bullets whizzed back and forth across the highway, Eda jumped on Frankie Boy and pinned him to the road, trying to shield him from any stray bullets. The dog whined and fought hard. He thrashed around like he'd been shot already, desperate to flee the gunfire. Eda wrapped her arms around him and weathered the storm. She wasn't sure if she was making things better or worse.

Eda watched the action unfold from a distance.

Both men were on their feet, making little or no effort to dodge the shower of bullets flying their way. The grudge should have been settled quickly. When no one went down, Eda began to wonder if the two men were missing on purpose. Maybe they both wanted the manner of death to be more intimate than the sort of death offered by a gun.

By now, a pack of thick clouds had gathered in the sky; a giant gray mist hung low while the rain continued to fall.

The soldiers stood about fifty feet apart.

Eda couldn't keep Frankie Boy down. He was too big, too strong. With a grunt, Eda let go and the dog scrambled back to his feet in an instant. Eda went with him, her fingers grasping at Frankie Boy's coat and trying to reestablish a grip.

But then the shooting stopped.

The highway fell silent for a few moments.

Then Goldman and Mr. China started talking to one another again. Eda couldn't hear anything except the faint rumble of male voices further down the road.

She glanced over her shoulder.

The long, empty highway that led west was behind her. There it was, an open door, calling her back home. At the very least it was freedom. It was no longer Boston and all its dead skyscrapers filled with sad stories and ghosts. This was her chance to make a run for it and with any luck, to get the hell out of that two-man warzone in one piece.

Why wasn't she running already?

Frankie Boy had the right idea. He'd already put a significant amount of distance between himself and the shootout. Now he'd stopped and turned back, his face pointing at Eda. Surely he must have wondered why she wasn't doing the smart thing and getting the hell out of there.

"Damn it," Eda hissed.

She couldn't leave the old man like that. The shock of seeing Mr. China, of realizing that he wasn't a mere figment of Goldman's aging mind – that had been like a slap in the face. It had knocked Eda's thinking off balance. After that she'd been pushed into self-survival mode. But no, she couldn't desert him. Goldman *was* a sick man, even if he wasn't imagining everything that he'd spoken about during Eda's time in Boston. He sure as hell wasn't up to a gunfight, especially not in murky, wet conditions. Or any kind of fight for that matter.

Eda's hand went to the hilt of her katana. She held it there, her fingers wrapped around the narrow handle.

What good was a sword in a gunfight?

"Fuck."

She let go of the sword. Instead she reached for the rifle, its sling barely hanging off her shoulder. She held the M4 as she'd been instructed earlier, trying to convince herself that it wasn't a foreign object. That it felt as natural in her hands as a sword.

"Nothing to it," she said, moving onto one knee. Large puddles began to surround her on the asphalt. Eda realized that her hands were shaking, struggling to find the right things to grip onto on the body of the M4.

Mr. China looked like he was ready to end the war. With a murderous gleam in his eye, he raised his rifle and peered down the barrel. Eda guessed the foreign soldier was a little younger than Goldman. His movement was sharper. He was faster. If it came down to reflexes, the odds were against the fading Goldman ever seeing another sunrise.

Eda couldn't get a lock on the target. She placed her belly flat against the soaking wet blacktop. Mr. China didn't seem too concerned about the girl and the dog who'd been with Goldman moments earlier. Maybe he couldn't see her. Maybe he was too fixated on Goldman to see anything.

She looked down the barrel and immediately lifted her head up again.

"Damn it," she said.

From this far back she was more likely to hit Goldman than Mr. China.

Eda leapt back to her feet. A sudden disturbance in the sky caught her attention. A distant rumbling that sliced through the steady sound of the pouring rain.

She scoured the blanket of gray up above. Searching for the source of the rhythmic, guttural machine-like noise.

Then she saw it. The giant bird in the distance, leaving a long smoke trail in its wake. Now it no longer sounded like it was choking – there was a loud whooshing noise, like a scream. It came in fast from the east, from the ocean.

"GOLDMAN!" Eda yelled.

Both soldiers were well aware of the thing in the sky. Even in the midst of their hate-fueled battle to the death, it couldn't be ignored. Goldman and Mr. China were retreating away from one another, seemingly in slow motion. Their rifles lowered in unison. Both sets of eyes looked upwards, searching for the source of the interruption.

The dark dot with two arms extending outwards flew closer.

"Airplane," Eda whispered. "That's an airplane..."

She walked forward, hypnotized and forgetful of the danger. She'd seen airplanes before, large and small, but not for a very, very long time. They'd once been a common sight in the skies above all the big American cities, no more unusual than the cloud formations or birds.

But they were gone. Weren't they?

Mr. China spun around and shouted out a single word at the top of his voice. He looked back at Goldman, red-faced and snarling like a wild dog. He was infuriated that their shootout had been interrupted.

The Chinaman charged across the median strip towards the edge of the road. He was fast. When he reached a ten-foot wire fence he threw his rifle over to the other side. Mr. China leapt at the fence like it was the only thing preventing him from plummeting into the bowels of Earth. His arms and legs scrambled wildly at the wire strands, trying to secure a solid grip. He went up and over, jumping down onto the grass. As he picked up his gun, he took one last look at the plane overhead. Then, with another shriek of hatred towards the skies, he disappeared around the back of a yellow and brown building.

Goldman was already running back towards Eda. Fear had turned him into a talented sprinter. There was a manic glint in his eyes and he was waving his arms in the air, holding onto the M4 like it was a spear.

"Run!" he screamed. "Run!"

The small airplane shot overhead at a frightening speed. It was a low-flyer, probably no higher than five thousand feet up in the air. Eda watched closely, her hands covering her ears, as the jet traveled past them and made its way towards the skyscrapers of Boston.

"Scouts!" Goldman said, running up alongside Eda. He was

breathing hard, fighting to push the words out. "We need to get off the road, now!"

Goldman grabbed Eda by the arm. She felt a surprising strength in the old man's grip as she was pulled off the road. There was barely enough time to pick up her bag and rifle.

Frankie Boy was barking furiously at the plane.

"Shut up Frankie!" Eda said, glancing towards the sky. "And move it!"

They cut over the median strip, running to the edge of the 93. By now the airplane was a dot on the horizon but that wasn't enough to persuade Goldman to slow down. He led Eda over to a pair of corrugated iron huts at the side of the road in what looked like an old construction site. Goldman ran past the first hut to the one located furthest away from the highway. He trotted up a short set of metal stairs and tried the door. It opened and Goldman stepped aside, allowing Eda and Frankie Boy to run inside first.

"Ugh," Eda said, wafting a hand in the air as she walked into the small space.

The inside of the hut smelled like stale smoke. That and other foul, unidentifiable stenches permeated the room. There was a long table in the center of the room, rectangular with eight plastic chairs scattered around it. Four glass ashtrays sat atop the table, countless cigarette butts still lying inside, bathing in a shallow pool of ash.

Goldman closed the door and the room dulled to a blackish-gray. The remaining light trickled in through a solitary window at the side of the hut facing out towards the highway.

Outside the rain was easing off.

Goldman pulled back a seat and fell into it. He was sweating profusely, breathing hard. His body was calling in the debt it was owed after all that running. Looking at him, it was doubtful whether the old man could handle that debt.

"Are you alright?" Eda asked.

Goldman held up a hand as he continued to take deep wheezy breaths. *In, out, in out.* There was a good chance he'd topple off the chair at any second. Or puke on the floor.

"I just need a minute."

He took off his cap and wiped his glistening forehead dry with the sleeve of his uniform.

"I'll be damned," he said.

"That was an airplane," Eda said, taking a seat opposite Goldman. Her heart was thumping. Part of her mind was still out there on the highway, staring up at the big machine bird that might as well have jumped out of a history book.

"It was an observation aircraft," Goldman said. His voice was surprisingly calm now. "Right now it's undertaking a spying mission on the mainland. Going downtown by the looks of it. Probably seeing if there any survivors."

"Is it friendly?" Eda said.

"Nope," Goldman said without hesitation.

"Let's back up a minute," Eda said. "Mr. China is real, I can accept that and I'm sorry as hell for doubting you Goldman. But *that*...that wasn't supposed to happen. I haven't seen an airplane in the sky for twenty years or more. Who the hell flies an airplane in this country anymore?"

"Somebody who isn't from this country," Goldman said.

"What?"

"You weren't supposed to see that," Goldman said, fanning his beetroot red face with the army cap. "It's my fault for keeping you on the beach too long this morning. Truth be told, I was enjoying myself and time ran away. You should have been gone by now. Long gone."

"What exactly wasn't I supposed to see?" Eda said.

"The scouts."

"Scouts? You said that already. What does that mean Goldman? Where the hell did that airplane come from just now?"

"From the water," Goldman said. He had the look of a guilty man in the midst of a profound confession. "It came from the water because well, that's where the ships are."

"Ships?"

Goldman pushed one of the overflowing ashtrays away like it was radioactive. "Looks like I've got some explaining to do."

"Yeah you do."

The dry musty odor inside the hut forced its way up Eda's nostrils, an intrusion she paid little attention to.

"What's going on?" she asked.

Goldman put his cap back on despite the fact it was soaking wet. He lowered it so that his eyes were buried within the shade. Then he placed his large hands flat on the table and sighed.

"What do you know about the End War?" he said.

Eda thought it over for a second, wondering if it was a trick question. "The basic facts," she said. "What most people know I guess."

"Most people don't know jack shit," Goldman said. "How about this for starters? What if I told you that the thing people keep calling the End War wasn't really the End War?"

"Huh?" Eda said, leaning forward. "Are you having one of your blackouts right now?"

"No."

"So what are you talking about then?"

Goldman's eyes stared into emptiness, contemplating the past.

"Russia, the United Kingdom, Germany, Australia, Japan, just to name a few – all those powerful nations, they chose sides during the pre-conflict stage. They pledged their support, moral and military, to either America or China. Big mistake. They all became host battle-grounds in the end and all the people who lived there were chewed up. What a waste right? But..."

His voice trailed off into silence.

"But what?" Eda said.

Goldman coughed and wiped the spit off his lips. "Just because it was World War Three," he said, "that doesn't mean the whole world was involved."

"Quiet Frankie," Eda said. Behind her, Frankie Boy's shiny black nose was probing the corner of the hut. He was sniffing too loudly, distracting her.

"We called them the pauper nations," Goldman said. "None of the giants called on them to fight during the war because they didn't have much to offer in terms of military firepower. They were poor, third world countries. They were insignificant. Of no interest or value."

Eda jerked a thumb to the window. "Are you telling me that...?"

Goldman nodded.

"Who are they?" Eda asked.

"Don't know exactly what part of the globe they come from," Goldman said. "But wherever it is, they've spent decades in a world devoid of superpower bullies. And in the absence of superpowers, not to mention the absence of billions of people competing for resources, these backward nations began to grow strong."

Goldman stared out of the window.

"Look at them now," he said. "From beggars to conquering scavengers. They've come all this way to feast on the carcass of the dead giant."

The old man shivered and pulled the collar of his uniform in tight. He'd gone from sweating buckets to shaking like a leaf in a matter of minutes.

"Me and some of the boys in the unit," he said, "we used to speculate about it. Especially near the end when it was obvious the game was up. What would happen if the pauper nations survived? They'd bide their time, build up their armies and navies and come after us. It didn't feel too far-fetched at the time. Doesn't feel too far-fetched now."

Eda fell back in her seat. "So that's the End War out there?"

"Yes it is," Goldman said. "As far as you, me and all the other surviving Americans are concerned, this is the End War. Because it's *our* end. These invaders, they're strong. And smart too – the fact they've been using scouts for months tells you that they're patient about this conquering thing. And patience is a sign of wisdom in my book. But boy when they get out there...they're going to kill everyone and everything that moves. The rivers will run red with the blood of Americans. They'll kill all of us because that's how it works. A new nation is about to be born. And as far as *they're* concerned it's God's work. It's manifest destiny all over again."

8

"What do we do now?" Eda asked.

She was trying to digest the enormity of what Goldman had just told her, while at the same time realizing that they couldn't stay in the hut forever and bury their heads in the ashtrays.

"We stick to the plan," Goldman said without hesitation. "You go west. Nothing's changed except now you know the *why* of it."

"What does it matter if I run?" Eda said. "If this thing, this invasion, is as big as you say it is they'll catch up with me sooner or later. They'll catch up with everyone. Right?"

"There's more to you going west than just running," Goldman said.

"What do you mean?"

The old man's eyes lit up. The intensity poured out of him, flowing across the table to Eda.

"Now that you know," he said. "Are you willing to put that knowledge to good use?"

"How?" Eda asked.

"We need someone to take this to the survivors," Goldman said. His voice dropped to little more than a whisper. "I didn't want it to be you because it's a hell of a task and you've been through more than enough. But maybe it was destiny that brought you to Boston on the eve of the invasion. You probably didn't think of it like that of course."

Goldman paused all of a sudden, as if on the verge of another blackout. To Eda's relief, he kept talking.

"Men, women and children," he said. "At the very least they deserve a head start and the chance to organize some kind of armed resistance. Or if they can't fight, they need time to find somewhere remote where the invaders won't catch up with them. There has to be somewhere, it's a big world you know? We need a messenger. I'm too old and slow for the job and have been for a long time."

Eda felt like Goldman had just dropped a great weight on her shoulders.

"I'm beginning to think life was easier in New York," she said. "I had a nice room there and it was warm. I had my books."

Goldman didn't miss a beat. "New York won't escape this either."

There was a loud bellowing noise above their heads. Eda jumped to her feet and rushed over to the tiny window on the wall of the hut. Pressing her face against the glass, she caught a brief glimpse of two jet planes shooting across the sky. One of them was a fraction ahead of the other, but they were staggeringly close. They were flying at an incredible speed towards downtown Boston.

"How many?" Goldman asked. He was still sitting down, one hand slipping under the cap to wipe his forehead dry.

"Two," Eda said. "I think."

"Shit," Goldman said. "Never seen more than one myself."

Eda walked back over to the table and sat down. She didn't like the worried look on Goldman's face. "What does that mean?"

But Goldman didn't answer. He was lost in thought, so much so that he looked like the Thinker, a bronze sculpture Eda had seen photographs of in an art book a long time ago. When Goldman didn't answer, Eda decided not to push.

They sat in silence for a long time.

After a while, Goldman sat bolt upright. His wispy, snow-colored eyebrows stood to attention as the rest of his face creased up in concentration. Without a word, he slowly got to his feet, then moved towards the door like a man treading on razor thin ice.

"Hear that?" he whispered.

Eda heard it. It was a faint mechanical purring noise. Sort of like the airplanes but not as powerful or as loud.

"Cars," Goldman said.

"Cars?"

"Yep."

Eda hadn't seen or heard a working car in decades. The dead ones were everywhere, lying around like metal trash, clogging up every street in the country. But the constant chirping of human technology had long been silent. Now Eda had heard airplanes and cars all in the course of one morning. It was an unwelcome window back to the wild years.

The old man's face was chalk white.

"Oh God, they've made landing somewhere," he said. "This is it. It's happening."

Goldman leaned his head against the door. As he did, something small and black crawled away from the hinge and scurried towards the roof. Eda wasn't sure if Goldman was trying to listen to what was going on outside or if he was using the door to stay upright.

"You're right," Eda said. "We stick to the plan with one change – you're coming with me and Frankie Boy. I'm not leaving you here to face this thing alone. God knows what sort of people these are. We don't know anything about them, which means you have no idea what they'll do to you if they find you."

"I can't run," Goldman said, his eyes closed.

"You have to try," Eda said.

The old soldier shook his head. He opened his eyes and turned to face her.

"I don't want to run," he said. "When I die it'll be right here in Boston. If I'm lucky it'll happen in my apartment, surrounded by my family. And if I'm *really* lucky that chink son of a bitch will be dead before me."

"Forget about him for God's sake," Eda snapped. "There are bigger things to worry about."

Goldman shot her a furious look.

"*Forget about him*?" he said, his lip curling into a snarl. His voice was shaking and his neck turned reddish-purple. "Did you just say *forget about him*?"

Eda was shocked at how fast Goldman went from zero to raging basket case.

"Okay," she said, hands up in surrender. "I just meant…"

She was cut off by something outside.

Footsteps. Close to the hut.

Eda's body went stiff. She looked at the old man and without a word, pointed a finger to the window. Her face must have said the rest. Whatever outburst had been coming her way it would have to wait.

Finally Goldman caught on. He pressed a finger to his lips.

They listened as someone opened the door to the first hut. It was only a short distance from where they were standing. After that initial creak of the door swinging open, Eda heard the faint thud of feet walking back and forth in a slow, deliberate manner. Eda imagined someone inside the other hut, pacing around.

Looking for what?

Frankie Boy's ears had pricked up at the disturbance. Eda crept over beside him, dropped onto one knee and whispered.

"Quiet boy. Quiet now."

She stroked his back gently. Frankie Boy's low-pitched growl was building up to something momentous.

The door to the first hut clicked shut. Eda heard somebody walking down the metal stairs.

Clip-clop, clip-clop, clip-clop.

The footsteps got louder. Closer.

Eda and Goldman exchanged horrified expressions.

Goldman raised his rifle to shooting position. He took a couple of slow, quiet steps back, the barrel pointing at the doorway. There was no way he could miss if someone came in. It should have offered some hope and yet, the old man's hands were shaking.

There was a rattling noise outside.

Eda looked at the door handle. Waiting for it to move.

Another rattle, louder this time.

But it wasn't coming from the door.

Eda glanced towards the window, just in time to catch a flash of movement outside. Her back and shoulders were rigid with tension.

Outside, a pale-brown hand came into view. Long, crooked fingers gripped onto the edge of the metal frame and pulled softly. To Eda's horror, the catch on the inside was loose. It only took the slightest of effort to pull the window open.

It shifted about six inches.

The hand retreated, disappearing out of sight.

Eda gripped the handle of the katana. If whoever was out there dared to show their hand again they'd be going home without their fingers.

The hand did appear. But this time it was a blur – it was there and then it was gone again. The hand's sudden appearance was followed a series of light thuds. Eda looked to the floor. A tiny, ball-like object rolled ominously towards the corner of the hut.

Goldman's voice bellowed in Eda's ear.

"RUN!" he yelled.

Goldman yanked the hut door open, his aching bones drawing on the last reserves of energy.

"Move it!"

Eda hurled herself at the door, fueled by a primal fear of oblivion.

"Frankie!" she yelled. "C'MON!"

In a split second, Frankie Boy was galloping through the door ahead of her. Goldman waited as Eda charged outside. The old man's face was bright red, his eyes bulging with terror.

Eda grabbed Goldman by the arm, hoping that his paper legs wouldn't betray him. With little delicacy, she dragged him outside, down the stairs, and towards the road.

Everything was a blur after that.

The earth shook underneath Eda and it was like being catapulted into an altered state of consciousness. At the moment of the explosion, Eda felt as if she was experiencing the sensation of her body being torn apart. Her internal organs rattled violently. She remained on her feet for a matter of seconds after the blast, then she was knocked off balance, crashing hard onto a soaking dirt patch near the edge of the highway.

She'd never been so close to an explosion, not even during the height of the wild years. It was like pressing her face up against a supersonic wave of hot air. The energy was so intense that it felt like the world had flipped upside down. Had she and Goldman reacted a moment slower they surely would have been cut in half.

On the ground, Eda peered out from behind the shield of her forearm. Black smoke plumes gushed out of the wreckage. The deadly shock waves lingered, wafting an angry heat that raked her skin.

Eda rolled over onto her back, her body throbbing and yet strangely numb at the same time. As she looked up at the gray sky she saw more jets flying overhead in a procession. One, two, three, four – five of them!

Whoooooosh...

Eda heard movement to her left. She flipped back over and saw that Goldman was, miraculously, back on his feet already. He was staggering towards the road, his legs shaky and yet a determined expression on his face. There was a small cut at the side of his lips but apart from that he looked unharmed by the blast.

Eda glanced over at the road, trying to see what Goldman was running at.

The man in red.

He was standing on the highway. Waiting for Goldman.

"You slanty-eyed bastard!" Goldman yelled over and over again. His voice cracked with the hottest rage. "I'm going to cut off your head and when I'm done I'm going to spit and shit down your neck."

The planes kept flying overhead. Eda counted five, six, seven of them – small, silver and black jets of a similar size to the first one they'd seen. She wondered if they'd seen the explosion.

Of course they had. There was no way they could miss it.

The air was filled with an almighty roar.

Goldman opened fire on Mr. China. A tornado of bullets sprayed onto the highway and Mr. China, with slick reflexes, dove out of the way. As the gunfire chased him he rolled out of range with incredible agility for an older man. He came up on one knee, his rifle pointing at Goldman.

Mr. China squeezed the trigger and forced Goldman to take cover behind one of several metallic drums that lay scattered around the abandoned work site. It was just enough to shield Goldman's body from the volley of gunfire.

In between shots, Mr. China ducked behind an abandoned station wagon parked on the highway. He opened fire again and then took cover.

Goldman looked over at Eda. She was lying flat on the dirt, trying to stay invisible. Goldman made a pushing gesture with one hand, indicating that she was to stay put. Eda nodded her understanding and as quietly as she could, flipped onto her belly. She looked to her right, further down the work site to where a row of three white vans with faded purple logos on the side were parked. She'd seen Frankie Boy run off in that direction when the shooting started.

She hoped he wouldn't come back.

Goldman jumped out and peppered the station wagon with lead. Eda covered her ears, still reeling after the explosion. Goldman's M4 hit the frame of the car, smashing what little was left of the passenger side window.

Mr. China yelled something from behind the station wagon.

"Fuck you too!" Goldman said, cupping a hand over his mouth.

The tip of Mr. China's cap appeared over the top of the mangled station wagon. It was like a red shark fin breaking the surface of the water. The rifle came up too.

Rat-a-tat-a-tat.

Goldman winced as he took cover. Eda guessed the old man's

expression was one of frustration rather than pain. Watching the two soldiers square off it was apparent to Eda that Mr. China was faster and that so far at least, all his shots were closer to hitting the target.

If Eda could see that much, an old warhorse like Goldman wasn't going to miss it.

The old man looked over at Eda during a lull in the shooting. "When I cover you," he said, speaking as quietly as he could, "you get the hell out of here."

"No," she mouthed back at him.

"Please," Goldman said.

Mr. China sprang back to his feet. He ran around to the hood of the station wagon to get a better lock on Goldman.

Goldman fell backwards, his reflexes hanging on by a thread. He pushed his back up tight against the barrel while Mr. China unleashed a torrent of gunfire, giving the old man no chance to let off a round of counter-fire.

The sweat poured down Goldman's face.

Mr. China didn't retreat behind the car. Not this time. He came closer, edging off the highway and stepping onto the narrow incline that led down to the old work site. He let out a deep, terrifying roar that sent a shiver down Eda's spine. To Eda's surprise however, Mr. China slid his rifle strap over his shoulder. He marched towards Goldman, his face like stone. He looked like a man who believed he was invincible. Shooting wasn't enough for him. He wanted something more. Something slower, that he could enjoy.

Eda watched him from the dirt patch. Mr. China didn't seem to know she was there or if he did he didn't care. As quietly as she could, Eda grabbed a hold of the rifle lying beside her. She was still flat on her belly, slithering forward, trying to get closer to the man without being seen.

But it was too late.

Mr. China saw the movement on the dirt. There was a hint of confusion on his stern face. He tilted his head, like he was trying to solve a puzzle.

Eda froze, paralyzed by fear.

Mr. China's face softened a little. It was a sudden turn of mood that flipped a switch, making him appear like a different man.

He suddenly glanced over his shoulder as if he'd heard something at his back. Eda lifted her head up off the soggy dirt to take a look.

A procession of light and noise came speeding down the highway. Engines roared, forcing the earth to tremble.

Mr. China grunted in the direction of the disturbance. He turned and ran up the incline back towards the road. He was sprinting with all the intensity of a man half his age, no doubt trying to get back to the fence he'd climbed earlier. It was the only way out. Eda and Goldman watched him go, but it was obvious from the start it was too late.

Five dark green military jeeps took the final curve in the road. A chorus of excited male voices hollered and jeered over the deafening engines.

The jeeps screeched to a halt, forming a long barricade in front of Mr. China.

All hope of escape was gone.

9

About twelve men, all dressed in dark khaki green uniforms leapt out of the jeeps. They were well armed, wielding a combination of semi-automatic rifles, machine guns and handguns. Somebody yelled something at Mr. China, who was standing on the highway, a solitary figure trapped in the white headlights that cut through the gloomy day.

Some of the invaders ran over to the Chinaman and barked out a series of commands. Upon first impression, Eda found their language a harsh one that sounded more like hissing and spitting, than talking.

Mr. China placed his rifle down on the road and then very slowly, he unbuckled his weapons belt and threw it to the ground.

Two of the men, rake thin and robot-eyed, hurried over and patted Mr. China down, searching for any hidden weapons. When they didn't find anything they pushed the soldier towards one of the jeeps.

The other invaders turned their attention to Eda and Goldman. Since the arrival of the jeeps, the two Americans had been standing with their hands up about fifteen feet away from the road. The foreigners edged off the highway, stepping onto the old work site. Eda got a good look at them as they came closer. They looked young, most of them – late teens, early twenties at most. Skinny, wiry frames. Their skin was a light yellowish-brown color, their expressions uniformly fierce and impatient. And perhaps a little frightened too.

They were grunts. Foot soldiers of the invasion.

They talked to each other while the rain began to pick up again.

One of the grunts walked over to Goldman, muttering something under his breath. The old soldier was patted down and searched for weapons. After a brief examination, they took his belt and the dagger strapped to his lower leg. One of the grunts began pushing Goldman back towards the highway. To the old man's horror, he was thrown into the backseat of the first jeep next to Mr. China.

The two old enemies didn't even look at one another.

Several of the grunts approached Eda. She saw the hesitation in their eyes, spreading like a virus amongst them. Maybe they thought she was a foreign witch that would bedazzle them with magic spells if they got too close.

If only, she thought.

Eventually one of them, a tall skin and bones soldier with a pencil thin mustache, leapt forward and snatched Eda's sword out of the hilt with a loud gasp. He laughed wildly, then reached down and picked her gun up off the dirt. After he'd disarmed her, the grunt did a clumsy victory dance that went around in dizzying circles for about ten seconds. He held the gun and sword aloft throughout the celebration. When it was done he gave the weapons to another grunt, turned back to Eda and berated her in an outraged tone of voice, spitting out words in a machine gun, rat-a-tat rhythm. His breath was foul, like something was dead at the back of his throat.

Eda kept her hands up at all times.

The grunt came closer, examining her from head to toe. Slowly, he licked his lips. His skin was the color of jaundice. The lean, sinewy muscles on his forearm stood on end and Eda noticed a small faded tattoo on the right arm – the outline of a dark blue dagger with a single drop of blood falling from the tip.

When he was done, he pointed towards the huddle of military jeeps waiting at the side of the road, their engines still humming.

Goldman and Mr. China were ignoring one another in the backseat of the leading jeep. They were as stiff as two planks of wood.

"You want me to go over there?" Eda said.

The grunt pointed again.

"Okay," she said. "I'm going to walk over to the cars."

Another grunt jumped down from the road and escorted Eda towards the second jeep. As she walked past the first car, Goldman glanced at her briefly. His stoic expression folded, just for a second.

She nodded briefly.

Eda climbed into the backseat. The jeep reeked of piss and chemicals. One of the invaders jumped in the back with her – another underfed boy who couldn't have been more than nineteen or twenty. He laughed, a grating, obnoxious laugh like an unusual birdcall. For someone so young, he had surprisingly few teeth left.

The other grunts began to file back into the convoy of jeeps, shouting at one another in self-congratulatory tones. Seconds later, they set off, making a U-turn and traveling back on the 93 towards South Boston. Eda felt dizzy. She hadn't been in a moving car for at least twenty-five years and it didn't help that the soldiers were speed junkies. The engines screamed as they hurtled along the three-mile stretch of sandy beaches that lined the coast. Eda saw Goldman's apartment block go past in a split-second blur. Goldman didn't so much as glance in its direction.

Eda stared at the ocean, ignoring the crazy kid with the pistol sitting beside her. She saw past his toothless grin, her attention drawn to the water. Its shimmering surface was familiar. The water *had* been a part of her at some point. Still, home was a puzzle, one she might never solve. It was the same for a lot of people her age who'd been exposed as children to the traumatic aftermath of war. Faulty memories were not unusual.

The back of Goldman's head bobbed up and down as the lead jeep hit a bump on the road.

With each corner they turned, Eda expected to see the monster ships sitting on the horizon – the big ones, the kind of boats that were vast enough to transport airplanes and land vehicles thousands of miles across the ocean. If she saw them, Eda might understand what they were up against. But there was nothing except sea and sky out there. She wondered if the main fleet was elsewhere on the east coast. New York perhaps?

Eda didn't want to know.

At last the jeeps came off the winding coastal road, pulling into a large car park located a few miles northeast of Carson Beach. As the cars slowed, Eda's heart pumped faster. There were dozens of military vehicles in the car park – jeeps, vans, trucks – most of them drenched in a variety of badly faded camouflage tones.

Dozens of brown-skinned men and women dressed in khaki uniforms hurried back and forth across the car park. Quiet chatter filled the air like birdsong.

The gap-mouthed grunt sitting beside Eda said something. He spoke in a voice that sounded like it was in the midst of breaking. It was funny, almost. Eda guessed in his own charming way that the grunt was telling her to get out of the jeep. Eda pulled the handle, then pushed the door open. She stepped outside. With a soft groan, she stretched her legs on the concrete and felt the blood flowing reluctantly. Her body was still hurting from the fall she'd taken after the blast.

She stood in between the white lines of an empty parking spot. There was an ugly, dilapidated reddish-brown building up ahead. A faded sign hung over the building's sheltered entrance, the words once printed there now a mystery. Next to the building a paved pathway led uphill, cutting through a stretch of grass and trees – an oasis of overgrown forestland and a sight for sore eyes in the otherwise urban setting.

"What is this place?" Eda asked the scrawny youth who stood beside her now. Her personal guard, how lucky she was.

His answer was to start laughing again.

The three captives were led towards the large building. They were met by a man and woman standing outside the front door with clipboards in their hands. Some of the grunts started a conversation with the clipboard people, who were remarkably well groomed and clean in comparison to the scruffy, hungry-looking grunts. As she stood to the side, Eda felt wandering eyes all over her. The clipboard people would talk to the grunts, then write something down, then look at her like she was a cockroach on the dining room table.

After a brief discussion the grunts led the three prisoners towards the concrete path that continued uphill towards the greenery. The rain was starting to ease off and it was getting cooler. Goldman and Mr. China walked a few paces ahead, side-by-side. Eda thought it was weird that the enemies were walking together like that but then she thought it was probably because neither one of them wanted to go out front, to have their back facing the other.

Armed escorts surrounded the prisoners.

"Where are we?" Eda called out, hoping that Goldman would hear her.

Goldman twisted his head back and offered a brief smile of encouragement, which Eda appreciated.

"Fort Independence," he said. "On Castle Island."

"Castle Island?"

"Don't get too excited," Goldman said. "It's not really an island."

One of the guards growled in Goldman's ear. The conversation ended there. Eda watched the old man shuffle ahead of her in slow motion, breathing heavier as the incline got steeper. Meanwhile Mr. China walked in silence, chin thrust outwards. His short body was as stiff as a board.

Fort Independence was a five-bastioned enclosure built of granite. As they approached the structure, Eda saw the walls of the garrison first, at least thirty feet tall, towering over the three prisoners as they were escorted towards the entrance. Eda stole a glance up at the top of the fort walls. The dark outline of countless soldiers stood in scattered locations, watching everything unfold in silence.

The Boston skyline was a distant, shadowy backdrop to the fort. Eda could see a few dark specks flying over the city, the pilots inside those specks picking at the aftermath with a fine-tooth comb and almost certainly finding nothing in a once major American city that had at one point housed hundreds of thousands of people.

Eda noticed several silvery-black aluminum speedboats sitting out in the harbor, bobbing gently on the surface of the water.

The captives were led through a tall entrance cut into the fort wall. Going through this, they emerged onto a large grassy courtyard. There was no roof here and therefore no shelter from the rain.

Goldman coughed into the back of his hand, clearly struggling with the pace.

The small group approached a large white tent that had been erected in the center of the enclosure. It was the size of a small house with two stumpy turrets poking out of an otherwise flat roof. There were a lot of people inside the enclosure, rushing back and forth at a furious speed. Their voices were hushed, their eyes focused. Everybody was in a hurry, eager to stay busy. Eda couldn't help but think of the people here as machines, as robots that couldn't operate at anything other than full power.

The procession stopped outside the entrance of the white tent.

A handful of the grunts who'd escorted them from the highway to the garrison pushed back the tent flaps and disappeared inside. The others stayed out in the enclosure, their guns pointing at Eda, Goldman and Mr. China.

The toothless youngster was still at Eda's side, like a stray dog she couldn't shake off. But he wasn't laughing anymore. He kept shifting on his feet nervously as if he'd rather be anywhere but outside the tent.

After about five minutes, two of the grunts came back outside. There was an older man with them now, lean and bespectacled. He was tall and dressed in the same uniform as the others, although as with the clipboard people down the hill, he was well polished in comparison to the grunts. A red, white and green patch pinned to the breast of the man's shirt suggested that he was of a high rank.

"Welcome," he said in a soft, almost feminine voice. "My name is Walter Santos. I trust you have not been mistreated so far?"

Goldman cleared his throat.

"Yes we have sir," he said. "We've been brought here against our will for starters. Not to mention stripped of our arms. I'd call that a form of mistreatment wouldn't you? Now with that in mind, would you mind telling us why we're here? What do you want with us?"

Santos bowed his head.

"The Commander will explain everything to you," he said to Goldman. "I'm just here to personally escort you to her. If you're ready?"

With that, Santos turned back towards the tent. Before he opened the flaps however, Eda caught sight of a half-smile creeping onto the man's face. His sharp cheekbones poked out, knifelike. His was a sinister outline that sent a cold shiver down Eda's spine.

"This way," Santos said, walking inside.

10

They walked through a tall, arch-shaped entrance into the tent.

The air was warm inside. For a moment, Goldman abandoned the role of disgruntled prisoner and sighed, drinking in the comfort and shelter like a thirsty man who'd stumbled upon an oasis. Daylight trickled into the tent, sneaking past a set of white transparent curtains that swayed along to the breeze.

As Eda walked forward, raindrops fell off her cloak, dripping onto the groundsheet.

Commander Torres was waiting for the prisoners on a wooden platform, raised about twelve inches off the ground. Three narrow steps had been carved into the center of the platform, each one with a small and exotic mural depicting some kind of jungle scene with wild animals. Torres was sprawled on a bright orange and red couch, like a grand queen of ancient times. She was a fierce-looking young woman, somewhere in between twenty and thirty, with cropped black hair. Her military uniform, peppered with brightly colored badges, clung to her lean and muscular frame like an extra layer of skin. Underneath the medals, a metal dagger pin was fastened to her shirt.

There were four other people gathered around her on the platform – a tight-knit circle of high-ranked officers, two men and two women, standing on either side of the luxury couch. One of the men and both women were much older than Torres, in their fifties or sixties at least. The other male officer however, was younger and he bore a striking resemblance to Torres, so much so that Eda suspected they might even be twins.

All eyes were on the captives as Santos, the delivery boy, brought them closer.

They stopped short of the platform and stood in a neat line. Santos nodded to the platform, then quickly made his retreat.

Torres signaled to one of the guards standing by the platform. The guard executed a swift, flawless salute and hurried over to where a row of spare folding chairs was stacked up against the tent wall. The guard brought back three of the chairs, unfolded them and set them down behind the line of captives one at a time.

When it was done, Torres gestured for them to sit.

Goldman and Mr. China jumped on the outside seats, making sure there was a gap in between them. Eda frowned, then sat down in the middle.

"Welcome to Fort Independence," Torres said. "I'm so happy to see you all today." She spoke English effortlessly, like someone who'd been around the language her entire life.

"What do you want with us?" Goldman said.

Torres looked at Mr. China for a second, then turned back to Goldman.

"Both of these uniforms I know well," she said. "So you are both veterans of the old war yes? American and Chinese foot soldiers. Yes?"

Torres adjusted her position on the couch, sitting forward as if on the brink of getting up.

"You understand my words okay?"

"I understand your words," Goldman said. He suppressed a cough and then pointed at Mr. China. "And yes we're soldiers of the old war, which by the way we were trying to finish when your goons came along and interrupted us. What's the world coming to when two men can't settle a score in peace anymore?"

"My apologies gentleman," Torres said.

The commander turned her attention to Mr. China once again. She spoke to him in a foreign language, retaining the elegant, confident tone she'd used while speaking English to Eda and Goldman. Mr. China's eyes lit up at the sound of his native tongue being spoken aloud. His dour expression lifted like a slow moving fog.

"What are you saying to him?" Goldman said. "This is still America you know. At least have the decency to speak English."

Torres looked at Goldman with a puzzled expression.

"What am I saying?" she said. "The same thing I'm about to say to you and the woman. But why should you get to hear it first?"

"Like I said," Goldman snarled, "this is *still* America."

"Is it?" the commander said with a sneer.

Torres kept talking to Mr. China. The old soldier responded with a shake of the head, which seemed to displease the woman on the platform.

With a shake of the head, she turned back to the Americans.

"What I want from you today," Torres said, her eyes skipping back and forth between Eda and Goldman, "is information. Specifically, information about the city of Boston. The Chinaman here claims he doesn't know anything. What about you two? What can you tell me about Boston?"

"They used to call it Beantown," Goldman said. "That the sort of info you're after?"

Torres's didn't bat an eyelid.

"So far our scouts report very little in terms of activity," she said. "Personally, I doubt a city as vast as Boston is as quiet as it looks from the sky. So, if you can tell me about what's going on in this region – networks, tribes, survivors of any kind, I'm willing to spare your lives. What do you say?"

Goldman responded with a short burst of laughter.

"You haven't got a clue what happened here have you?" he said. "Networks? Take it from me Commander, I've lived in this city for more years than you've been alive. The chinks hit it hard during the war, real hard. Not a lot of people stuck around to watch you know?"

"And now?" Torres said.

Goldman shrugged. "It's a ghost town."

"I don't believe you," Torres said.

"You underestimate the effects of war on the civilian psyche," Goldman said. "And I'm talking about the type of war that shows up in your backyard, not on some television screen. One day you're living a normal, boring life – work, routine and taxes, maybe a little drinkie poo at the weekend with friends you know? The next minute you're drowning in hellfire and so is everything and everyone you ever loved. You don't have to believe me when I say that Boston is empty, that's your right commander. Waste your time, waste your jet fuel all you want. But don't expect to find any networks or tribes around here. And I sure as hell won't help you either."

Torres nodded in Goldman's direction. Then she stared long and hard at Eda.

"You're very quiet," she said. "What do you have to say?"

"I'm just passing through the city," Eda said, shaking her head. "I'm not from here and I've got no intention of staying here either."

"Where are you from?" Torres asked.

"Don't remember," Eda said. "I've been on the move a lot."

"You've seen America?"

"Some of it."

"And what about the people?"

Eda shrugged. "What about them?"

"How many?" Torres said. "Survivors. Roughly speaking of course. Is the population sparse or is it growing again? Are we talking hundreds, thousands, tens of thousands or more?"

"I have no idea," Eda said.

Torres smiled. She gestured towards the older male officer standing a few feet behind her. A short, weasel-faced man, he waddled to her side and leaned over the commander. They conversed briefly before she dismissed him.

Torres stood up. As she got to her feet, everyone in the room leapt to attention, their hands frozen in a rigid salute pressed against their heads. The commander walked to the edge of the platform.

"Your knowledge of this country is invaluable to us," she said to Eda. "We have maps, lots of maps, but there's a type of knowing that can't be found on a piece of paper. That's what we seek as we push inland. If you were to work for us in an advisory role you'd be well rewarded."

Eda glanced at Goldman sitting beside her. His face was like a piece of ancient rock, a solemn expression carved into its center.

"Well?" Torres said.

"No."

The commander didn't look surprised.

"What's your name?" she asked, her voice softening ever so slightly.

"Eda."

"Do you understand what's going on here Eda?" Torres said. "I'm offering you a *good* life. A better life than you've ever known I'd wager."

Eda heard the rain easing off on the roof outside. All eyes were on her, she could feel it.

"No," she repeated. "I know what you want. You want me to help you find and kill survivors. Just to get them out of your way. There are people out there, starving, frightened and desperate, who're trying to find someplace safe to live for their friends and families. That's a hard thing to do. I don't know how many there are but even if I did and even if I knew where they were all hiding out, I wouldn't tell you. They've earned better."

Torres appeared to be only half-listening. As Eda spoke, the commander dabbed at a small blemish on the oversized breast pocket of her uniform. From a distance, it looked like a bloodstain.

"Do you think America when she was at full strength was innocent of bloodshed?" asked Torres.

"No," Eda said. "I don't."

Torres paced back and forth on the platform with her hands locked behind her back.

"I was told you had a Japanese sword in your possession," she said. "Are you a fighter Eda?"

"Not really," Eda said. "Just another one of those survivors you want to kill so badly."

Torres ignored the quip.

"I have a wonderful collection of samurai swords," she said, "dating back several centuries. If you like, you could own any one of them. Ask anyone around here how I reward loyalty. I'm very generous to those who serve…"

"Some things commander," Eda said cutting in, "just aren't up for grabs."

Torres glared at Eda through narrow, burning eyes.

She turned around and spoke to her officers for a few minutes. When that was done Torres summoned a couple of grunts to the platform. The grunts scurried over, bowing their heads like they were approaching an angry god.

While this was going on, Goldman leaned closer to Eda.

"Proud of you," he said. "That took guts what you did there, telling that bitch to shove it."

"Thanks," Eda whispered. And yet some part of her was convinced she'd just made a terrible mistake.

Torres dismissed the grunts with a wave of the hand. They ran off with a look of excitement on their faces as if they had some great secret they couldn't wait to tell all their friends.

"Looks like we've found another use for you and your companions," she said, staring over at Eda with a chilling smile.

"Spit it out," Goldman said.

"We've decided to take you all to Dead Island," Torres said.

She repeated this in Chinese.

"Dead Island?" Goldman said with a bewildered shake of the head. "What the hell is Dead Island?"

Torres smirked.

"It's one of those islands in the harbor," she said. "We've renamed it. How best to describe Dead Island? It's very small with a rocky shoreline. When we first landed we found evidence of mass graves."

Goldman's eyes flickered with recognition.

"It's probably Rainsford Island," he said. "At the start of the war when people thought that civilization was still salvageable, bodies were taken out there by the boatload. When things got worse they started using the bigger islands. But it all started on Rainsford."

"Well it's not a graveyard anymore," Torres said. "It's become something of a playground since we got here. You see, recreation is important on long military campaigns. I don't want my people to become bored or frustrated, you understand? They're a long way from home and from their families."

"What are you getting at?" Goldman said.

"Why keep the prisoners locked up?" Torres said, pacing the stage again. "Why execute them when they can provide entertainment? Entertainment maintains good morale. Good morale is essential for final victory."

Torres stopped pacing and turned to the prisoners. Her lip curled into a snarl.

"If you won't join us," she said, looking at Eda, "then I have to make good use of you somehow. I'm sure you understand."

She pointed a finger at Goldman.

"So the America-China War isn't finished? Two old men have kept the flame burning all this time in Boston. Well how about we let you settle the score? And while you do that my troops will have the chance to do a little gambling. Running bets on a duel between an American and a Chinaman, this is big. The winner of the duel will be granted their freedom and given a head start on the mainland. The loser, we'll drop them off in the ocean. After all, fish have to eat too."

Torres turned back to Eda.

"And you?" she said. "There are many other forms of entertainment that we require to pass the time. A pretty girl like you can help with that."

11

That evening the three prisoners were transported to Rainsford Island.

They traveled in a small armada of speedboats, heading southeast past some of the other harbor islands en route. The rain had mellowed to a gentle spit. The temperature offshore however, was icy cold. Eda wrapped her rain cloak up tight, the hood pulled over her head to shield her from the fierce wind that cracked like a whip.

The boats were as reckless on the water as the jeeps had been on the highway. They hopped wildly over the waves in Quincy Bay, riling up the surface and generating a ferocious spray that machine-gunned into the faces of those onboard. The invaders cheered every time they conquered another wave, as if goading the ocean into trying harder to tip them over.

Goldman coughed a lot during the journey. Sometimes he doubled over with the force of his seizures and although Eda offered her cloak to him many times he always refused. His uniform offered little protection from the biting cold but Goldman was a stubborn old bastard who wouldn't accept help. Eda got the impression he'd rather die than take a woman's coat.

She put a hand on his back, reassuring him in silence.

When Goldman wasn't coughing he was pointing out the sights. He directed Eda's attention towards the likes of Spectacle Island and Long Island in the distance. Despite his worsening condition, Goldman seemed to enjoy the offshore landscape as it passed them by. He delivered a croaky and brief history lesson about the harbor islands, about how they'd been used by the Native Americans prior to the American colonial period. Eda listened intently, forgetting the dire reality of their situation for a few moments. The old man would have made a fine tour guide.

Eventually a small island appeared up ahead. Eda watched it emerge over the bow, an icy chill running through her veins. Somehow she knew this was the one.

Rainsford Island.

Dead Island.

Goldman's tour of the harbor continued as the speedboats closed in on the small dot of land on the horizon. According to the old man, the island was about eleven acres in total and composed of a large east head and smaller west head connected by a sand spit. The shore-line was predominantly rocky, which Eda saw for herself as they got closer. The rugged beach looked anything but inviting in the fading light.

The speedboats at last slowed down, cruising into the shallows. Anchors were soon dropped and gangs of overexcited young soldiers began to leap over the edge. They splashed through the knee-high water, laughing out loud, like it was the best thing in the world. Quickly they made their way onto land.

With an armed escort beside her, Eda waded through the freezing water towards the beach. Goldman and Mr. China weren't far behind. When the prisoners reached land, the invaders quickly surrounded the prisoners, stabbing their rifles and pistols in the direction of the unfortunate trio.

Many of the grunts were young boys, their trigger fingers twitching in a way that made Eda nervous.

She avoided eye contact with the mob around her. Instead she looked past them, down both sides of the beach. Two parallel rows of camping tents were pitched to the left, the outer walls flapping in the wind. Beyond that, Eda noticed a hint of stone ruins poking out of the rocks and dirt. She guessed it was one of of the old institutions that Goldman had told her about – a hospital or school or something like that.

Dead Island was a desolate place. It was fragile too. The constant pounding of the ocean, combined with the northeastern winter storms were slowly eroding the island from existence.

The three prisoners were lined up on the beach. They stood there shivering, waiting for Commander Torres and her officers who had traveled in on the last boat. When she arrived, Torres strode through the shallows with the swagger of someone who'd already conquered the North American continent. Her officers followed like shadows. The only one who looked out of place amongst the bravado of these high-ranking foreigners was the young officer who Eda had assumed was the commander's brother. He was a frail-looking youth, with a long neck and restless eyes that blinked too much.

Eda felt a hand on her shoulder. It was Goldman. He was swaying on unsteady legs and grasping at Eda for support. The old man, his skin pale and sweaty, looked at her as if to ask – *is this okay?*

"You need to lie down," Eda said. "And you need to get out of the cold."

Goldman whispered. "I'm fine."

Commander Torres approached the captives, her breath shooting out like a fog. She rubbed her hands together to generate heat.

"You'll spend the evening here," Torres said. "You won't be mistreated but I'm only going to say this once, don't think about trying to escape. You'll be shot in the leg and crucified here on Dead Island. Imagine the slowest, most painful death you can and multiply it by ten. Your fate has been decided my friends. You are my play-things now. Back at Fort Independence, the wagering has begun for tomorrow's duel and we are all very excited at the thought of some sport."

"*Sport?*" Eda said, pointing a finger at Goldman who was still hanging onto her shoulder. "He can barely stand up."

Torres glared at her.

"Tomorrow morning," she said. "After sunrise."

The commander turned her attention to Mr. China. She spoke to him and the Chinaman listened intently, his stoic expression never wavering. Torres might as well have been reading out a dinner menu. When the commander was done, Mr. China spoke back in a deep, reflective voice. Torres' response to whatever he said elicited a spark of excitement in the old soldier's eyes. Eda wondered if Mr. China had just realized he was getting another chance to kill the American.

Goldman doubled over again, coughing into the back of a clenched fist.

"He can't fight," Eda said, her eyes pleading with Torres. "For God's sake, look at him will you?"

"Bet your ass I can fight," Goldman said, wiping the spit off his chin. He let go of Eda's shoulder. "And I will."

Torres watched their exchange and smiled. The angry scar under her lip twitched like a living thing.

"Nothing is going to stop this duel from taking place tomorrow," she said. "But I'm not a monster Eda, no one is going to force you to watch. This sort of entertainment isn't for everyone."

"And what about me?" Eda said.

"You already know what's in store for you," Torres said. With that, she turned around and spoke to the soldiers at her back. This announcement in the foreign tongue was met with a blistering cheer of approval from the invaders.

"And they know too," Torres said, turning back to Eda. "Unlike the duelists, you're a plaything that can be used more than once."

Eda shook her head and took a step back. At this, one of the grunts leapt out of the crowd, rushing past Torres and charging straight at Eda. He made some kind of animal, snorting noise as he caught up with her and grabbed Eda's raincloak at the waist. He pulled Eda off balance and reeled her towards him with the cloak. She staggered forward. When she was close enough, the grunt reached at her with a claw-like hand and grabbed Eda's breast.

He twisted hard, hissing with satisfaction.

Eda shrieked at the sudden jolt of pain. She reached for her belt but the katana was gone.

The puffy-faced grunt watched her grasp at thin air. With a mindless laugh, he crept forward again.

There was a blur of movement at the grunt's back. Torres drew the dagger on her belt and rushed at the man. Her attack was lightning fast – a dizzying swirl of arms and steel. A loud slicing sound was followed by a shrill, sudden gasp.

Eda backed off, retreating further up the rocky beach. Her head was spinning, her heart racing. When she regained her focus she saw Torres' dagger embedded deep in the grunt's throat. A stream of dark blood gushed out of his mouth. It flowed down his chin, splashing onto his collar and upper torso. Eyes bulging, the man reached for the blade while staggering backwards on rubbery legs. The other soldiers got out of his way fast as he moved past them, edging closer to the water. There was neither sympathy nor excitement on the faces of the spectators as they watched him go.

The dying man tipped over, landing on the rocks. His face was by now a yellowy shade of pale. With a gasp, his red hands clawed towards the sky and then his body convulsed as he spewed out a series of violent choking noises.

It felt a long time before he stopped moving.

Torres walked over and with a single sharp thrust, pulled the dagger out of the grunt's neck. There was a wet squelching noise as the blade came free.

The commander wiped the bloody dagger dry on the deceased's uniform. She then examined the blade with a bored expression before walking back over to the prisoners.

The crowd parted quickly as she went past. There was a collective look of bug-eyed fear on their faces, like they were in the presence of something more than just a woman.

"You *will* be a plaything," she said looking at Eda. "But when I say so, not them."

She jerked a thumb towards the grunt pack.

"The older ones grew up during the occupation of my country,"

Torres said. "Back then the American soldiers thought they could do anything to the local girls and get away with it. And they could. But that's not how I run things, they know that now."

"I guess so," Eda said.

"I'm going to give you one more chance," Torres said, taking a step closer to Eda. "Do you want to be a toy? Or would you rather be our advisor? That offer stands for another ten seconds."

Eda looked down at the rocks that littered the beach. She could still hear the wet gurgling noise the grunt had made as he'd choked on his own blood.

"I can't help you," she said.

Eda heard the air coming out of Torres.

"I won't ask you again," the commander said. "No matter how much you beg for it in the days, weeks, months and years to come. Okay? I'll see you tomorrow for the sport Eda."

Torres turned around and walked back to the boats. On her way she exchanged a brief conversation with the young officer who Eda had taken for her twin brother. He nodded his head as Torres spoke to him.

The majority of grunts returned to the boats in silence. This was in stark contrast to the boisterous entrance they'd made not long ago. Two of the grunts went over to the dead man and grabbing him by the arms and legs, began to haul him towards the boats.

The young officer stayed behind along with ten grunts. He stood on the shoreline watching as the speedboat engines fired up. Moments later, Torres and her unit were on their way back to the mainland.

By now the sky was dark grey, fading to black. With a heavy step, the officer walked back towards the prisoners, his cap pulled low over his forehead. On his way he muttered a few words to two of the grunts walking alongside him. The grunts set off, hurrying over to a small tent about a hundred meters further down the beach. Eda watched as they went inside and then a minute later, came out carrying a large block of firewood each. The wood was dumped into a rickety old, wheelbarrow parked beside the tent. The men repeated the maneuver, going in and out of the tent for the next five minutes, filling up the barrow with wood.

"Feeling the cold?" Goldman said, as the officer came within earshot.

The young man pushed his cap up and smiled.

"Yes," the officer said in his strange accent. "A little."

As the soldiers prepared a fire on the beach, the officer showed Eda, Goldman and Mr. China to their quarters in one of the larger tents that had been set up elsewhere on the island. The tent, which was shaped like a tunnel, was located uphill on a stretch of dirt and grass, far from the water.

"It's not much," the officer said, holding the entrance flap open for the captives. "But it's better than sleeping outside."

Eda walked in, followed by Goldman. Mr. China lagged a few paces behind. There were a large number of worn down, filthy sleeping bags scattered across the groundsheet. At a push, about twenty people could have slept inside the tent.

"So we're stuck in here all night?" Goldman said. He was looking at Mr. China with a quiet loathing as he asked the question.

The officer stood at the door, a tall shadow, close and yet somehow distant. Eda couldn't equate all those brightly colored war medals on his uniform with the soft-spoken young man standing in front of her.

"You're all most welcome to come and sit by the fire tonight," he said. "There's plenty of food and water and tea. It's my job tonight to take care of you."

He repeated all this in Chinese. Mr. China responded in a calm, muted voice, bowing his head once.

"Our friend here is hungry," the officer said, looking at Goldman and Eda.

"Friend?" Goldman said, spitting out a chesty cough. "How about you put my *friend* in a different tent tonight? Or us for that matter. Chink son of a bitch is going to strangle me in my sleep. Who knows? Maybe I'll do it to him first. And then where will your commander's precious duel be? Huh?"

The officer shook his head. "The situation has been made clear," he said. "If he tries something like that he'll be crucified. So will you. The commander is quite fond of that particular method of execution so I urge you to take note. Now on the other hand if you're both willing to wait about twelve hours before trying to kill each other there will be a reward involved. Win a fair fight tomorrow morning and you'll be set free."

"Torres is really going to let the winner go?" Eda said. "Just like that?

"She will," the officer said. "And then she'll try to hunt him down afterwards. The victor gets a head start on the mainland and that's all he gets. I'm sorry. Now, will you be joining us at the fire tonight?"

Eda looked at Goldman.

"You have to eat something," she said.

Goldman glared at the man in red.

"I don't want to break bread with that bastard," Goldman said. He turned back to the officer at the tent door. "Tell me this son, why can't we just duel now and get it over with?"

"Money," the officer said. "Back at Fort Independence there's a lot of excitement being generated about tomorrow. For most soldiers, good quality entertainment is few and far between and the commander needs this event to keep up the morale. Conquering is a strangely dull affair most of the time."

"You're eating something," Eda said, nudging Goldman with her elbow. "You don't have to look at him okay? Just eat, drink and rest before tomorrow. Think about it this way if you have to – you'll kill him better on a full stomach."

Goldman said nothing.

"We'll go with you," Eda said to the officer. "Thank you."

The four of them went to the fire and sat down. It was a tiny oasis of light burning in the vicinity of the harbor islands. From the sky it would have been no more than a dot of bright orange shimmering on the beach. The flames crackled and spat, kissing thick beams of maple and oak. The ocean was so close that at any minute Eda expected to feel the water rushing over her legs.

The heat drifting off the fire was divine. Eda put her hands out to soak up the flames and she sighed. At last, some comfort.

A couple of grunts came over and passed four plates of food around the fire. After that, the officer dismissed them and Eda watched as the two men walked down the beach with plates in hand, eating and talking in hushed voices. She wondered if they were debating on who would survive tomorrow's duel. Or were they discussing what they'd like to do to the American plaything when it was their turn to play?

"Some rice," the young officer said, poking a fork around his plate. "Beans. Vegetables. Let me pour you some hot tea too."

He put his plate down, got up and went around the small group, pouring a steaming hot liquid out of a metal pot into the cups the captives held out. Eda drank the tea and it was glorious. It felt like another fire, this one being lit inside her.

"What's your name?" she said, once the officer was sitting down again. "You're related to Torres right? Are you guys twins or something?"

He smiled.

"The commander is my cousin," the officer said. "My name is Manny Torres and I'm a colonel in the Third East Coast Unit. That's this unit, the one based out of Fort Independence."

"How many units are there?" Eda said.

Manny stared into the fire. "A lot."

"They're all over the east coast," Goldman said, chewing slowly on his food. "Aren't they?"

"Yes," Manny said. "And the west coast."

Goldman nodded.

They sat in silence while they ate. Eda devoured the food, thinking about Frankie Boy and wondering where he was. Although she missed him terribly, she was glad he wasn't with her. The grunts on the highway would have shot him if he'd stuck around. Running was the smart move.

Goldman was having a tough time getting his dinner to stay down. Every second mouthful was spat back out in a violent coughing seizure that lasted for about ten seconds. When the coughing was over, the old man would groan and apologize for putting people off their food.

Manny put his plate down and turned to Goldman. "Have some water," he said, pouring out a cup and handing it to the American. Goldman took the water with a grateful nod and forced it down the hatch in one go.

"Damn this getting old shit," he said, putting the cup down.

The redness in his face was less angry.

"He can't fight," Eda said, looking at Manny. "You can see that right?"

"Don't you start," Goldman said, patting his chest down. He was watching Mr. China on the opposite side of the fire. The two enemies eyeballed each other through the flames. "If it's the last thing I do on this earth – and it probably will be – I'm going to shoot that bastard and watch him die."

"Bullshit," Eda said. She took a sip of tea and listened to the fire. "You can barely stand up without help."

Goldman grunted, but said nothing.

"So your country didn't fight in the war?" Eda asked, turning back to Manny.

Manny shook his head.

"We stayed neutral," he said. "That was always our official position. The government didn't listen to the international threats or to all the talk that there was no neutral – not in *this* war. Still, we wanted no part of it. Let America and China and all their warmongering allies fight to the death. A poor nation like ours – we sent no soldiers and offered no allegiance to either side. That didn't stop the Americans from invading though. The occupation lasted for...well, more years than I can remember."

"What was it like?" Eda said.

"The American soldiers tried their best to build a little America on our homeland," Manny said. "And they did a good job of it for a while. My people were second-class citizens, pushed off their most fertile land in great numbers. My parents lost their home. The commander's parents too. But our new masters, they didn't realize how organized the common people were. Early on they'd established a sophisticated chain of secret networks. The rebels stole weapons from the Americans with surprising ease and began a large-scale guerilla war against them. In the end the rebels won because they had the support of the people. But victory came at a great cost. No family that I know of escaped the suffering and certainly not mine or the commander's. However, unlike so many other nations in the great global war, we hadn't been bombed. We were intact. And so we could rebuild. Grow strong."

Manny sipped at his tea and the fire reflected in his eyes, giving him a supernatural appearance.

"And it was always the plan to come here?" Eda said.

"Like most of the people back home," Manny said, "my cousin wants to take this country. Even though China is much closer to home, this is what we want. *America.* All we have to do is clean it out, claim it as one of our territories, and rebuild."

"Pauper nations," Goldman said, staring into his teacup. "We always knew you'd come."

"Yes," Manny said. "So did we."

Eda looked at Manny. "You don't seem like the soldiering type to me," she said. "If you don't mind my saying."

Manny laughed softly.

"I wanted to stay home," he said.

"Won't be hard for you lot to conquer this country," Goldman said gruffly. "There's no one left to fight. In fact, I'm surprised it took you so long to get here."

Manny smiled. "We are a cautious people. It took a lot of effort and planning just to ship everything here."

"You got fuel?" Goldman said. "Right son? Got enough food and ammo?"

"Those were the priorities, yes."

"And you've got the numbers," Goldman said. "By God you've got the numbers..."

Goldman's body jolted forward. He lapsed into a ferocious

coughing fit and dropped his plate, spilling the contents all over the place.

Eda hurried over and put an arm around him. "Goldman," she said. "Are you alright?"

He couldn't answer.

Manny jumped to his feet and called the grunts over from the other side of the beach. They arrived in less than a minute, their guns pointing at the jerky figure of Goldman. Manny pushed the guns away and then gave the order. The grunts nodded, then pulled the still coughing Goldman up off the ground. Taking an arm each they led the old man away from the fire and back towards the tent.

"It's alright," Manny said, gesturing for Eda to sit down. "They'll make him some tea and put him to bed. He won't be harmed, I swear. The guards will take it in turns to stand outside your tent all night should he need anything."

Eda flopped down in Goldman's space. She looked at the scattered food items – a mix of rice, beans and chopped green vegetables – and realized that Goldman hadn't eaten much, if anything at all.

Across the fire Mr. China sat in silence.

"He can't fight for God's sake," Eda said, turning towards Manny. She could hear the desperation in her voice. "Can't you see that?"

"I'm very sorry," Manny said, gazing into empty space. "But there's nothing I can do about that now."

"Yes there is."

He looked at her with a puzzled expression. "What?"

Eda took a deep breath.

"Well," she said, lowering her voice to a whisper. She leaned closer to Manny. "It's America versus China isn't it? If Goldman can't fight then it's no big deal. All you need is another American to take his place."

She tapped a finger off her chest.

"See anyone like that around here?"

Manny sighed but he didn't look surprised.

"Why would you do that?" he said. "Let the old men finish their war Eda. Let it end, for God's sake."

"No," Eda said. "Your cousin used the word sport. Sport means a fair contest, or at least that's what it should mean. You know? Let me take Goldman's place in the duel tomorrow morning. It's still America versus China and that's what they're betting on back there at the fort. Isn't it? Who's to say that Goldman will even make it through the night? What happens to the duel then? Isn't it better to have a sure thing when tomorrow comes?"

Manny kept her waiting a long time.

"You realize if this was to happen," he said, "that I'd have to go back to the fort now – right now – and report this to my cousin. The soldiers are making bets on a shootout between two old men. Money is being wagered as we speak. There's a big difference between betting on the reflexes of an old soldier and those of a young woman. And nobody knows if you're any good with a gun or not."

"Go then," Eda said. She glanced across the fire at Mr. China. She could feel him concentrating on the sound of her voice. "Please Manny. Even if I lose the duel it's better than being a plaything. Right?"

Manny's face was grim. It looked like he'd aged ten years in five minutes.

With a sigh he got to his feet.

"I'll go back to the fort," he said to Eda. "But I don't like this. It feels wrong."

"Thank you Manny," Eda said, her mind racing in multiple directions. If the commander approved the switch she'd probably just signed her own death warrant. And yet she felt strangely elated.

"I appreciate it."

Manny bowed his head.

After informing the grunts that he was taking a trip back to the mainland, Manny waded through the cold water towards the sole remaining speedboat. The boat bobbed up and down restlessly on the black, shimmering surface. Once he was onboard, Manny waved at Eda. She waved back and then watched the boat as it disappeared into the night. It felt like forever before the sound of the engine faded away.

Eda thrust her hands towards the fire, soaking up the heat. How long before he came back? Before she knew for sure.

She looked at the shadowy figure sitting across from her.

"Guess it's just you and me," Eda said.

She flinched as Mr. China slowly got to his feet. For a second, Eda thought about jumping up and running back to the tent. That's what her instinct told her to do. Who cared if she came off as a coward? She should be with Goldman anyway, not this foreigner. Not somebody that she might have to face off with in a matter of hours in a fight to the death.

He was just standing there, staring at her over the fire.

"What?" Eda said.

With a sigh, Mr. China walked around the tall flames and sat down where Manny had been sitting. Right beside Eda, just inches apart.

An excruciating silence lingered. They both listened to the fire for a long time without saying a word. Then to Eda's surprise, Mr. China's tight face relaxed into a smile.

"You want to fight me?" he said.

Up close, his voice was deep and powerful. It was like being shoved backwards by a gust of wind.

Eda gasped.

"You speak English?"

"Of course," Mr. China said. "You think I don't know language of my enemy? All Chinese soldiers were taught English. No speak English, no fight."

"So you've understood everything so far?" Eda said. "And there you were, making that nice commander woman translate everything for you."

Mr. China's skin was a brilliant shade of red in the firelight. He was like an ancient eastern god who'd materialized onto the mortal plain to share wisdom with lesser beings.

"Don't fight me," he said. "I saw you with gun...back there on the highway, I saw you. You don't know gun."

Eda felt the evening chill on her skin. She budged a little closer to the fire.

"I don't have a choice," she said.

"Have choice," Mr. China said. He pointed back towards the tent they were all sleeping in that night. "Let old American man die."

"I can't do that," Eda said.

"I'll kill you," Mr. China said without hesitation. "Stand in front of me, you leave me no choice."

"I know," Eda said. "But I *will* be standing in front of you."

Mr. China groaned and it sounded like an earthquake. He reached into his back pocket and pulled out the tattered remains of a black wallet. He opened it up and Eda saw that it was empty, apart from one thing. There was a photograph inside one of the inner pockets.

"They give wallet back after searching me," he said. "Because I ask. Because of this. More important than all the guns in the world."

He handed Eda the photograph. The image hadn't aged well over the years – it was scratched and faded and Eda had to tilt it towards the fire before she could make sense of it. She was looking at a young Chinese girl, about three years old. The girl was impossibly cute with long black bunches and a gap-toothed smile that beamed back at the camera.

She glanced at Mr. China. He was staring at the photo, not blinking.

"Your daughter?" Eda asked.

He nodded.

"Daughter."

"This was taken before the war?"

"Yes. Same dark hair as you. Same age, if she had lived."

Eda handed the photo back and stared out towards the crashing surf that pounded towards the Dead Island shoreline. White foam sprayed everywhere. The horizon that had swallowed up Manny's boat was now pitch black.

"Why are you showing me this?" Eda said.

"Don't want to kill you," Mr. China said.

Eda smiled. "Didn't you try to blow me up in a hut today?"

"Not you. Him. Enemy."

"That makes me feel so much better."

They sat in silence, watching the fire together. It was a long time before anyone felt the need to talk again.

"Don't fight me tomorrow," Mr. China said, staring at the photograph in his hand.

12

That night, Eda lay inside her sleeping bag listening to Goldman toss and turn beside her. He coughed on and off throughout the night like a man trapped underground, gasping for air. Occasionally he'd drift off into a light sleep, snoring softly.

His old hand, speckled with lines and sunspots, resembled a giant bird claw. While half asleep, Goldman would mutter names that Eda didn't recognize, and the hand would hover several inches off the mat, grasping at thin air.

Eda watched the old man, frightened that he might slip away at any moment. She'd once read a book about people who died and came back with stories about the afterlife. Eda recalled that many of these 'returners' reported seeing the spirit of one or more of their loved ones waiting for them. It was a nice idea and Eda hoped it was true. But this kind of scenario raised one problem.

Who'd be waiting for her?

She closed her eyes, knowing that sleep wouldn't come. Outside, the guard at the door was breathing every bit as as loudly as Goldman snored. Was he asleep standing up? When another guard showed up to take watch later on, the two men spoke at full blast for at least ten minutes, disregarding the fact that there were people inside the tent trying to sleep.

Eventually the night fell silent. Eda could see the shadowy outline of the second guard standing at the door. It was bright outside, considering the late hour and a full moon had broken through the clouds, bathing the Dead Island shoreline in a crystal white light.

Eda's thoughts turned to the duel.

Manny had returned to the island about an hour ago. He'd stopped by the tent to let Eda know that Commander Torres had approved her offer to take Goldman's place in the morning.

Of course she had.

Torres couldn't call off the duel, not now. The troops were ecstatic at the prospect of some light relief, at the notion of America and China dueling it out for nothing more than their viewing pleasure. Cancelling the shootout would be a sickening blow to morale.

Eda had never doubted that she'd be fighting Mr. China. Not once she'd made the offer.

She tossed and turned inside the thick sleeping bag, which at the very least was keeping her warm. She wanted so badly to drift off, to sleep and to forget about the duel for a few hours. But although it came in spurts, proper rest evaded her.

The sound of crashing waves was a constant companion throughout the sleepless night.

Eventually the first rays of sunlight crept into the tent. More and more birds began to squawk and sing somewhere over the island, announcing the new day.

It wasn't long afterwards that Eda heard the first load of boats in the distance. The engines gradually got louder, going from a faint hum to a loud, piercing growl as they closed in on Dead Island. Even from afar, she could hear the grunts singing and shouting and laughing.

Eda lay in a daze, staring at the worn fabric on the roof of the tent. A scattering of threads hung loose up there, some several inches long and reaching down for her like strands of rope.

She stared at these threads, listening to the arrival of the Third East Coast Unit.

They sounded drunk already. In all likelihood they hadn't gone to bed the night before. How could they? The excitement of the America-China duel had been too much for them. All that was left of the two hated superpowers and their great armies had now become sport for the pauper nations. Dead Island was the final battle of the old war. Not surprising then, that the grunts had kept the party going all night. This was an early victory in the conquest and victories were to be celebrated.

Hurried footsteps approached the tent. A moment later one of the invaders – a fifty or sixty something man with gaunt, sunburned features poked his head through the entrance flap. He grinned at Eda first, showing off a set of yellowy-brown, tobacco stained teeth. Entering the tent, he walked over to Mr. China's sleeping bag in the corner and shook the old soldier on the shoulder.

Mr. China rolled over in slow motion. Dark shadows surrounded his eyes and Eda wondered if he'd spent most of the night lying awake too, just a few feet away from her.

Mr. China climbed out of his sleeping bag, fully dressed. He picked his cap up off the groundsheet, dusted it down and put it on his head. He wiped down the front of his red uniform and sighed.

He followed the grunt out of the tent. Eda watched him go but Mr. China didn't look at her.

Eda had to block out their unexpected exchange on the beach last night. Seeing Mr. China as anything other than Goldman's boogeyman would get in her way when she was looking down the rifle barrel. She had to forget about the gap-toothed girl with the cute bunches. The girl was dead anyway, what did it matter if her old man joined her?

Goldman was sound asleep at last. Eda took a closer look just to make sure he was still breathing. She saw his chest going up and down slowly. The stubborn old man was hanging in.

Not long after Mr. China was taken away, a pair of young soldiers marched into the tent to collect Eda. They seemed sober enough.

Between them they carried a basin of water and some breakfast, which was no more than a bowl of oaty mush. Eda grimaced as the plate was set in front of her, but she picked out a spoonful and brought it to her mouth. It was hot and sugary. She gulped it down quickly.

The food revived her a little. It also revived the butterflies in her stomach, which began to flutter again.

She knelt before the basin and splashed cold water on her face. At the same time Eda replayed the shooting lesson with Goldman over and over again in her head. In her mind she was back on Carson Beach, back in the shooting range, standing amidst a thousand shards of broken glass and firing at the bottles on the wooden crates. She hit the target every time. It was all coming back to her – technique, stance, everything she needed to remember was slipping through an open door in her head.

But was it enough? Could she kill faster than an aging, but experienced veteran?

The answer leapt out at her.

She shoved it away.

The invaders stood at the door, waiting and watching. One of them shuffled about nervously, hopping from one foot to another like he was standing on hot coals. Eda remembered that it was a big day for the spectators too. There was a lot of money riding on this duel.

How many of them had backed her?

Eda signaled that she was ready to go. She turned back to look at the sleeping Goldman. Walking away without saying goodbye felt wrong but if she woke him Eda would have to tell the old man that she'd hijacked his place in the duel.

And that wouldn't go down too well with Goldman.

She followed the guards, stepping outside. It was a cold morning on Dead Island, a mild wind blowing in from the water. Eda walked over the dirt and grass, down towards the rocky beach where a large crowd had gathered. Before she got far however, Manny appeared in the distance. He walked over quickly, dismissing the two soldiers who nodded and kept walking towards the crowd further down the beach.

"Good morning," Manny said. Purple-blue shadows under the officer's eyes hinted at a rough night. His shirt was crumpled, suggesting he'd slept in his clothes.

"Morning."

"How are you feeling?" Manny asked. He made a face as if to scold himself. "Stupid question I know."

Eda nodded. "Stupid question."

Manny scratched at a dark shadow of fluff that had sprouted on the base of his chin.

"It's not too late," he said. "You do know that right?"

"I don't think your cousin would agree with you," Eda said. A gust of wind crept past the collar of her rain cloak, clawing its way down her neck. She pulled the collar tight to her skin.

"But it's not your fight," Manny said. "This is *not* your fight."

"Of course it is."

Manny looked down at his boots. "Why don't you accept my cousin's offer?" he said. "Become an advisor and just tell her what she wants to hear? All you'd have to do is point at a map and travel with us – you wouldn't have to take part in any of the...details. You'd just be an advisor. I could go and talk to her right now, work it out. Surely that's better than being shot dead on the beach?"

"You think I'm going to lose Manny?" Eda said.

Manny let slip a quiet gasp. "Aren't you scared?"

Eda glanced over at the large fleet of speedboats floating in the shallows off the coast of Dead Island. Further down the beach it sounded like a carnival was building up steam.

"I'm scared," Eda said. "But I'm not sure I'm quite as scared as you are. You don't look too hot Manny."

Manny nodded. "I hate this," he said. "All of it. I hate it more than you'll ever know Eda. I hate the fact that I'm looking at someone who might be dead in an hour..."

He bit his lip.

Eda listened to the boisterous crowd in the distance. "Aren't you supposed to be a soldier Manny?" she asked. "Shouldn't you be with them?"

Manny laughed softly. "You want to know what I did back home?"

"Sure."

"I wrote poetry," the young man said. His brown eyes drifted towards the waters off Dead Island. "And not one person in my family ever knew about it, back then or now. Nobody knows, except you."

There was a roar from the crowd. Loud whoops and cheers drowned the island in noise.

Eda cast her eyes towards the action but she couldn't see much except the swaying of a large, drunken crowd. They were like one giant organism, moving in time with one another. She wondered if this latest bout of raucousness signaled the arrival of Mr. China on the dueling ground.

The butterflies kicked hard.

"You were a poet?" Eda said, trying to ignore the background noise.

"I used to disguise myself in rags," Manny said. "About three or four days a week I'd go into town, far away from our nice home in the suburbs. I'd sit down on the sidewalk and lay out sheets of poetry that I'd written. Just for pennies. I never thought I'd sell any but I did. I was quite the hit for a while – people seemed eager to consume what I'd written. Why not? Many of the people back home had lived through the hardships of the occupation. They valued love, nature and beauty – these were the things I wrote about most. I'd sit side by side with all the other traders and artists and while there I'd write some more poetry."

"So what are you doing here?" Eda asked.

"I love my cousin," Manny said. "And she loves me. We've always been close you see; we both inherited our family's hatred for tyrants. Our destiny is here in America, both of us."

"And what does that look like?" Eda said.

"We're going to build something new," Manny said, "something better than the Yankees ever built."

"Why don't you let your cousin build it without you?"

Manny shook his head. "My cousin needs me to help her run the unit. Where I come from, military leaders don't tend to last long and the Third is a notoriously fickle regiment. She's under constant pressure to project strength and you've seen it already. That's why she killed that man on the beach yesterday."

"I didn't think she was sticking up for the sisterhood," Eda said.

"It was nothing more than a show of strength," Manny said. "If you're a woman it's even harder to lead a regiment so you've got to be twice as impressive as a man. It's tough. I'm here to guide her decision-making as best I can. Family is everything and as her next of kin, I'm the official second-in-command of this unit. So you see Eda, we're in it together, all the way to the end. Blood is blood."

"Sounds like a good title for a poem," Eda said.

"I'm sorry Eda," Manny said. "You're about to fight a duel and I'm rambling on. Forgive me, it's just that there's no one else I can talk to around here without pretending."

"It's been good talking to you Manny," Eda said, offering her hand. "And don't worry, if I lose, the dead don't tell secrets."

Manny took it and squeezed. His grip was surprisingly strong.

"Are you ready?"

Eda nodded. "Yeah."

"Good luck," he said, letting go of her hand.

"You bet."

Manny called the two grunts back over and they escorted Eda down the slope and back onto the rugged terrain of Dead Island's beach. At least two hundred people in military uniform swarmed the dueling ground. There was a lively, jubilant atmosphere and most of the grunts carried transparent cups with an amber-colored, frothy liquid swirling around inside.

Eda could smell the alcohol, a toxic wind shooting up her nostrils. Her head was pounding. The rank chemical odor that filled the air made her feel dizzy and that was the last thing she needed right now.

The crowd let out a feverish roar upon her arrival. They parted reluctantly as the guards delivered her onto the dueling ground where Mr. China was waiting. He didn't look at her as Eda was taken to her mark, about fifteen paces directly across from her opponent.

A small wooden platform had been erected for the occasion. Commander Torres sat upon a high-backed metallic chair, dead center on the platform. Eda's attention was drawn to a bright red and yellow oriental style-pattern running down the armrests of the chair. The pattern appeared to be in the shape of a long dagger or a sword.

Torres picked at a bowl of fruit as she watched Eda arrive. The commander's high-ranking advisors, including Manny, stood behind her in a neat line.

"Our brave substitute is here," Torres yelled.

This was met by a deafening howl of approval from the grunt horde. Eda wondered if they understood what their commander said or if they were just cheering at the sound of her voice.

Torres put the fruit bowl down and stood up slowly. She said something in her native tongue and the crowd went wild again.

Mr. China's face was a void on the other end of the dueling ground. He wasn't blinking and Eda got the impression he saw nothing of the outside world.

Two grunts carrying M4s approached the duelists. One of them went over to Mr. China and the other walked towards Eda. They dropped the rifles on the ground simultaneously, a few feet from the duelists' feet.

"Your weapons," Torres said. "It's what you were carrying when we found you."

She clapped her hands together and stared into the crowd.

"Music."

A man stepped out of the swarm of drunken bodies and walked to the edge of the dueling ground. He was carrying something in his hands – it was a plaid bag with five black pipes poking out like tentacles. The man waited for a signal from Torres. When he got it he began to blow into the end of one of the pipes, emitting a low, unpleasant droning noise. His face puffed up with the effort. Eda winced at first when she heard the ugly sound coming out of the bag. A moment later however, the droning transformed into a cheerful high-pitched melody. The music whistled through the air and the invaders went crazy, dancing arm in arm with one another and singing at the top of their voices.

"Bagpipes," Torres screamed over the music.

She was dancing alone on the stage, clapping her hands, and surveying the happy crowd in front of her. Eda got the impression of a delighted parent watching her children play.

After a few minutes, Torres hollered into the crowd again. The piper ceased to play and when the music suddenly dropped out the island fell eerily silent.

"The rules are simple," Torres said, addressing the duelists. "What we have here is the final battle of the End War, also known as the Great Global War or the America-China war. Eda represents the United States of America and the man who won't tell me his name is fighting for the People's Republic of China."

Eda looked at the crowd. By now they'd lined up on either side of the two duelists. Excited, sweaty faces leered back at her. As they listened to Torres introduce the duelists the grunts guzzled cups of beer like it was a race to see who could pass out first.

"Guards," Torres called out.

Ten grunts spilled out of the crowd, all of them carrying rifles. They split into two groups, standing on either side of Torres, and slightly ahead of the four officers. Five of the gunmen pointed their weapons at Mr. China. The other five aimed at Eda.

"Pick up your weapons," Torres said.

Mr. China reached for the M4. Eda, moving a little slower, picked up the gun at her feet, ignoring her frantic heartbeat. Her throat was dry and scratchy. She had to block out all physical discomfort now.

There was the man in front of her and nothing else.

Torres' metallic voice cut through the blurry edges.

"Rifles begin at the combatant's side. When I give the word you fire and you keep firing until the opponent is dead or until you are dead. Once again, the victor will be granted a head start on the mainland."

Eda's rifle arm was shaking. Doubt had flooded her mind at the last minute, an unwelcome visitor that reminded her of her inadequacies. She wasn't a gunfighter.

What had she done?

She looked over at Mr. China. He was in position, rifle lowered at the side. That blank, stoic expression was still on his face.

"Ready," Torres yelled.

Eda froze. At that moment she was as good as dead. Her thoughts had congealed into mind mush. Everything she'd learned about shooting a rifle was gone. She could only hope now that Mr. China would kill her quick – a bullet to the head or to the heart. No pain. She didn't want to die slowly, listening to the sound of grunts slurping beer.

"FIRE!"

Mr. China was like a ghost. He was already looking down the barrel of the M4 before Eda's rifle arm had even twitched.

Nothing flashed before her eyes.

But then she saw the old soldier twist his body to the left, swinging the weapon along with him. In the blink of an eye he took aim at Commander Torres, who was still nibbling grapes on the platform.

An explosion of gunfire lit up the beach. One of the marksmen went down while the other four shot back at Mr. China. The other five gunmen on the platform whose weapons were trained on Eda didn't flinch. She was still their target.

Mr. China took out another guard that had jumped in front of Torres. The Chinaman edged closer to the platform, miraculously dodging the first round of bullets that came his way. Seconds later however, he fell backwards, bellowing out one last word in Chinese as he collapsed onto the beach.

He landed on his back, arms and legs spread out in a star shape.

Eda dropped her rifle and put her hands up. Her ears were ringing after all the snap gunfire.

Torres stepped out from behind her guards. She looked unruffled, if a little annoyed.

The sudden silence that followed the shootout didn't last long.

The crowd immediately began to jeer the disappointing outcome. Drunken, angry voices yelled out words that Eda didn't understand. But she understood they were pissed off. She looked around, sensing their dissatisfaction and seeing the beginnings of an opportunity. It was a heat of the moment thing, not to be ignored. It was crazy and yet she had no choice but to listen to the madness.

She yelled at the top of her voice.

"WAIT!"

All the guns on the island pointed at her.

She turned towards the platform and looked at a nervous Manny. "I have something to say," Eda said. "Will you translate for me? I want everyone here to understand."

Her voice was trembling but she had to keep going.

"Will you translate for me?"

Manny's skin was a yellowy-pale color as he glanced at his cousin. Torres said nothing, so he turned back to Eda and managed a slight nod of the head.

"I'll translate," he said.

Eda cleared her throat.

"I was promised a duel this morning," she said, conjuring up a tone of outrage. "I was promised a fight with the Chinaman in exchange for my freedom. This was my chance to win the war for America, my chance to get the hell out of here, and it was taken away from me."

Manny translated quickly.

Eda pointed a finger along both sides of the crowd.

"YOU were also promised a fight," she said. "But what did you get instead? A half-assed assassination attempt. Now I'm sure you're all delighted that your commander is still alive but I can only imagine how unsatisfying this outcome must be for you all. All that money you gambled. You were promised entertainment and instead you got tricked."

She nodded at Manny. He translated and the crowd mumbled their discontentment.

"Who wants to see a real fight?" Eda said.

She waited for Manny. After his translation, the crowd responded and the mood began to lighten again. At that moment, Eda knew she had them where she wanted them. And she had Torres where she wanted her too.

She turned to the commander who was sitting down on the metal chair, dipping her fingers into the fruit bowl.

"Commander Torres," Eda said. "I challenge you to a duel this morning on Dead Island. This time, we fight with swords."

After Manny's translation, there were a few gasps in the crowd. Muted conversations were cut short when Eda kept talking.

"We're swordswomen," Eda said, glaring towards the platform. "So let's have a real fight. If I win I get a head start on the mainland as promised. But something else too – the old man in the tent comes with me. And if I lose, well it's one less American in the world. If you kill me Commander Torres, you'll have shown yourself to be a worthy leader of the Third Unit."

Eda held her arms out wide, allowing the island breeze to wash over her.

"What do you say?"

13

Torres must have known that everyone was looking at her.

The sheer audacity of the challenge. It was nothing short of crazy. After Mr. China's death Eda had every reason to believe that she would have been considered the winner of the America-China duel. And as the winner of that fight, she would be sent back to the mainland as promised.

Why then had she challenged Torres?

Was it for Goldman's sake? Eda wasn't so sure. Was there some other reason, something more primitive and selfish?

Did she want to see Torres dead?

Eda saw the confusion reflected in the faces of those standing around her. Confusion mingled with nervous excitement. After the disappointment of the first duel would there now be another one?

They turned towards their leader. The grunts were still clutching onto their beers but for now the festivities were on hold.

The commander still hadn't responded to the challenge.

It didn't matter. Eda already knew how Torres would react. She'd spun a spider's web and trapped the commander like a helpless fly, leaving her with no choice but to accept the challenge. The alternative? Back down in front of her regiment and become something less than a warrior goddess.

The weasel-faced officer behind Torres leaned in and whispered something in her ear. As he spoke, his thick jugular stood up, exposed.

Torres batted the officer away like he was a mosquito.

She glanced at Manny, then turned to the crowd.

"I accept your challenge," Torres said. "You're a smart girl Eda but not as smart as you'd like to think. You'll find out what a mistake you've made soon enough. So be it. All bets remain as they were – as far as today's sport is concerned it's still America versus China on the battlefield. I'll fight the American on behalf of the troops who voted for a Chinese victory. Nothing changes except this time we duel with swords. Apart from that, there are no rules. Anything goes."

Torres repeated this to the grunts in their language. Just like that, the crowd switched back into carnival mode. They jumped up and down on their feet as the piper struck up another tune. They also seemed to remember that they were drunk and that they were supposed to be having a good time on their play day.

As the music played Mr. China's body was dragged away from the dueling ground. Two grunts pulled him towards the boats, his head clattering over the rocks on the shoreline. His arms and legs were limp like a ragdoll.

Eda watched from afar as they threw him onto one of the boats. She was grateful at least that the grunts hadn't looted the corpse. The old soldier deserved to go down into the deep with his wallet in his back pocket, not to mention the beloved photograph inside it.

She turned back to the front and saw Manny, stiff as a board on the platform like an exotic mannequin. Beside him, Torres was dishing out orders to her officers and troops. Now and then she stopped to scowl at Eda who was still standing in the dueling area, a lone figure amongst the rowdy revelers.

Torres called for quiet and the crowd obeyed. The piper cut off the cheerful ditty he was playing and retreated back into the horde.

"I've just ordered a boat to go back and get our swords," she said. "Until they return you'll wait under guard in the tent."

Torres gestured for one of the men to take Eda away. Before she left, Eda exchanged a grim look with the commander. For the first time since she'd walked into Fort Independence, Eda saw a flicker of discomfort in the woman's eyes.

Goldman was still asleep on the floor when Eda arrived back at the tent. Snoring loudly. Apart from the one guard standing outside, the two Americans were left alone. As Eda walked over to the sleeping bag she'd barely slept in last night, she glanced over at Mr. China's spot in the corner. Then she dropped onto her bag, flat on her back, both arms on her chest. Now that everything was quiet she could feel her headache again.

"What have I done?" she said, rubbing a hand over her throbbing temple.

There was a loud groan beside her. Goldman's eyes were half-open and he was trying to sit up.

"Jeez Louise and then some," he said, glancing at Eda. All things considered, the old man didn't look too bad. His eyes were bright and his skin had a nice touch of pink about the cheeks. "How long have I been out? Feels like I've been asleep for a month goddamn it."

"Hey," Eda said, lying on her side and facing him. "How you feeling?"

"Head's a bit foggy."

"I'll bet."

Goldman lowered himself back onto the bed with a long wail of a sigh. "Is today the day?"

Eda flipped onto her back. "What's that?"

"The duel for God's sake," he said. "What else? Me and the chink. We need to do it soon by the way, while I can still summon the strength to stand on two feet. You know what I mean?"

"Are you serious?" Eda said.

Goldman shot up to a sitting position. "You bet your ass I'm serious. I've still got enough juice left in the tank to take that son of a bitch out, don't you doubt it. And when it's done, maybe then I'll start thinking about dying. But not a second before."

He leaned forward, trying to look past Eda towards the corner of the tent where Mr. China had spent the night.

"Where'd the chink go anyway?" Goldman said.

He tried to get up but Eda placed a hand on Goldman's chest and gently lowered him back onto the bed. Goldman went down, coughing, covering his mouth with the crinkled sleeve of his uniform.

The truth would break Goldman's heart. Killing Mr. China had been his sole reason to live, along with winning the war for America and getting revenge on those he believed were responsible for everything he'd lost. That's how he'd survived all those years in Boston in such grim circumstances – with purpose. It was a testament to the power of having a dream.

She waited until Goldman had stopped coughing. Checking that his eyes were clear she leaned closer.

"Mr. China's dead."

Goldman looked at her in horror but he didn't speak. As he digested the news his face gradually creased up into an angry, frightened and confused mask. Eda got the impression the old man wanted nothing more than to sink into the groundsheet and burrow deep into the darkest bowels of the island.

"Dead?" he croaked.

"Yeah."

"How? When?"

Eda paused. "He tried to run last night and they shot him," she said.

Goldman's body jerked backwards in a short, sudden fit of outrage.

"I knew it," he roared at the top of his voice. "Cowardly son of a yellow bitch! He'd rather run than stand toe to toe with me. A-haaa, great war hero he turned out to be right?"

"Right," Eda said quietly.

She tried to shut off the gnawing guilt inside. Goldman deserved better. Mr. China deserved better. She was also worried that somebody else on the island would tell the old man what really happened to his sworn enemy. If that happened the shit would really hit the fan.

"I'm getting us off this island," Eda said.

"Doesn't matter anymore," Goldman said. He was staring up at the roof of the tent. He clapped his hands together, like he was signaling to the gods that he was ready. "It's over. The war's over but I'll be damned, I don't feel like much of a winner."

"Of course it matters," Eda said.

"Doesn't matter," Goldman said. "I'm dying here for God's sake. They can do whatever they want to me now."

Eda felt like slapping the old man across the face to rouse him out of his self-pity. "Wouldn't you rather be at home right now? Surrounded by your family?"

Goldman pursed his lips. He nodded.

Eda took a deep breath. "Right," she said. "I challenged Torres to a duel this morning. With swords. If I win we get a pass back to the mainland – you and me. That's enough time to get you home to your apartment and get me back on the road."

Goldman sat bolt upright, rigid with terror. "You challenged Torres to a fight?"

"Yeah," Eda said.

"What the hell did you do that for?" Goldman said. "She's a killer for God's sake. Listen to me Eda, I've been in war. I've seen people – men and women – with the same bloodthirsty look in their eyes as Torres. It's the mark of a monster. They've been around too much violence in their life, too much death, too much pain. Something snaps in their brain and that's it – they become numb to suffering. There's no filter to control the violence that spills out of their soul."

Goldman started to unzip the sleeping bag.

"I'll do it," he said. "She wants to kill an American right? Well, let it be this one. I'll fight her on condition she takes you back to the mainland whether I win or lose."

He looked around the tent.

"Where's my gun?"

"It's too late for that," Eda said. "You don't understand. I chal-

436

lenged her in front of everyone. She *has* to fight me and that's exactly the way I want it. With a sword, I have a chance of winning and getting us both out of here. Apart from that it's a no rules fight. Anything goes."

"To the death?"

"To the death."

Goldman's bird-like hands wrestled with the bag's zipper.

"God damn it!" he yelled, his neck turning purple with frustration. "I watched all of my children die. All three of them, one at a time – beautiful, innocent young lives snuffed out for no good reason. Do you think I'm just going to sit here while you face off against that bitch? You can't trust any of those people out there. Think about it. Even if you win they'll rip you to shreds for killing their leader. What else are they going to do?"

Eda shook her head. "I won't lose," she said. "And we'll get back to Boston afterwards, I know we will."

With his other hand, Goldman finally got a handle on the zipper and with a grunt he pulled his legs out the sleeping bag. He tried to stand up and shrieked with pain.

"Ugh," he said, dropping back onto the floor with a thud. "My legs feel like they're in a coma."

"Will you relax?" Eda said.

"Relax?" Goldman said. "Bullshit. I'm coming out there with you."

Somebody tapped on the tent door. Seconds later, the dark outline of a grunt slipped his head through the entrance flap. He muttered something and while Eda didn't understand the words, she understood the meaning.

"The swords are here," she said. "It's time to go."

Goldman tried to get up again but he wobbled before he was even halfway upright. "What the hell..."

"Listen," Eda said in a reassuring voice. "You need to stay here for me. I can't concentrate on fighting her if I'm thinking about you and what you're doing. Please, for me. I need you here."

Goldman's tired old face was beaten. He sat there in limbo,

neither fully in or out of the sleeping bag. Eda walked over and helped lower him back into a horizontal position.

"Anything goes," Goldman said. There was still a faint spark in his eyes. "Eda listen to me. I..."

"Gotta go," Eda said, cutting in.

She squeezed his hand and straightened back up again. Without a word, she walked to the entrance where the grunt was waiting for her.

"Anything goes," Goldman called out.

Eda stopped. She could hear movement at her back. When she turned around, Goldman was once more clumsily trying to get out of bed, cursing his body as it betrayed him.

"There's something I need to tell you," he said.

The grunt stabbed the butt of his rifle in the direction of the beach. Then he hit it off the groundsheet. He shouted something in an urgent, impatient tone of voice.

"I'm coming," Eda said, looking at the man.

"Eda!" Goldman called out.

Eda glanced over her shoulder. Goldman was sitting up, eyes alert, his arms stretched out wide and beckoning her over.

"Don't worry about me Goldman," she said.

"Let me say goodbye properly," Goldman said. "For God's sake young lady, you come back here and say goodbye to this old man."

Eda felt a knot tighten in her guts. She looked at the guard, then turned around and walked back to Goldman. Behind her, the grunt unleashed a torrent of verbal abuse.

"Give me a hug will you?" Goldman said. His arms were still wide open.

Eda threw her arms around the frail body of Talbot Goldman. He felt light, absent. Like a paper man.

She could hear the grunt's feet slapping off the groundsheet behind her. He was coming in fast.

"Better go," Eda said. She kissed the old man on the cheek and looked at him.

Goldman's eyes were burning with excitement. With a smile he slipped something into Eda's hand. He quickly wrapped both her fingers around the offering, concealing it from the view of the grunt coming up fast behind her.

"A gift," he whispered. "Hide it. Fast."

It took Eda just a second to register what Goldman had given her. With a quiet gasp, she dropped it into the inside pocket of her rain cloak.

"Anything goes," she said.

"Anything goes."

The angry grunt caught up with Eda and yanked on her arm like he was trying to break it clean off at the shoulder. She got up and let him drag her away from Goldman. He was cursing and berating her in his native tongue but Eda didn't care. As she was roughly pulled towards the entrance flaps, Eda turned around one last time to see Goldman sitting on the floor, saluting her with a clenched fist raised aloft.

He was grinning.

"Good luck," he said.

14

The crowd was on the beach waiting for the second duel to begin. This time they'd formed a tight circle around the dueling ground, their bodies becoming a sweaty, drunken amphitheater that was alive, constantly edging closer to where the blood would soon be spilled.

Eda's long walk to the lion's den was accompanied by a howl of derision from the spectators. The grunts weren't just betting on two strangers this time around. This was something more than entertainment. It was personal and the hatred was palpable. Some of the grunts jumped in Eda's path, booed and after a swig of beer, spat the cold, disgusting liquid in her face. Then they'd disappear back into the crowd only to be replaced by another drunken heckler.

She had to keep going.

Finally Eda reached the dueling ground. As she stepped into the clearing, escorted by two guards, she wiped the foul smelling spit off her face. Even the spit reeked of alcohol, or so it seemed. The guards' faces and clothes were covered in it too although they didn't seem to care.

Torres was on the opposite end of the dueling ground, waiting for Eda.

The commander's right hand was wrapped around the handle of

a lavish samurai sword. She held it aloft and the curved blade glistened in the morning light as if the gods of war were blessing the weapon. Torres' sleeves were rolled up for battle, showing off her sinewy light brown forearms. Her large breast pocket was unbuttoned, the top flapping around in the breeze. She'd taken off her badges and medals for the duel, and the top two buttons of her shirt were loose, exposing the hint of a crooked scar above her breasts.

Lex's katana lay at Eda's starting point. Eda bent down and picked it up, slashing at the air a few times to loosen her wrists.

"Why don't you take your cloak off?" Torres said. "C'mon now Eda, let's at least try to make this fight entertaining while it lasts. That thing is only going to slow you down."

The commander grinned, hatefully so.

"I'm an ambassador for the Complex of New York City," Eda said in a voice that defied her nerves. "This is my uniform. If I'm going to die here, I'll die wearing this."

Torres lowered her sword.

"Are you trying to make it easy for me?" she said. "Did you challenge me because you're too much of a coward to kill yourself?"

Eda turned her head away from the commander. She glanced to her right and saw Manny and the other three senior officers standing at the edge of the wooden platform. The officers stood like dead-eyed robots. Manny tried to copy their detached air of superiority but his fast-blinking eyes gave his true feelings away.

"All bets are in," Torres said, silencing the crowd with a wave of the hand. "In this fight there are no rules. We start with swords and anything goes from there. Death is the only judge today. You understand?"

"I understand," Eda said, staring back at her opponent. She then pointed a thumb towards Manny and the other officers to her right. "Just one thing first. Tell your second-in-command what happens if I win the duel. I want to hear you say it out loud and I want it confirmed on your honor that both Goldman and me get a head start on the mainland. Chase us all you want, but we get that head start first. Swear it."

Torres' gleeful smile faded. With a look of disdain on her face, she spoke in the foreign tongue, directing her words at Manny. When she was done, it was Manny who nodded.

"Happy?" Torres asked Eda.

"In English," Eda said. "Say it in English and then I'll be happy."

"If you win, you get a head start on the mainland across the water. On my honor as a soldier. As commander of the Third Unit."

Torres smirked as she said it.

"And the old man too," Eda said.

"The old man too."

Eda turned to Manny. "I want to hear you say it."

"You have my word," Manny said in a voice that Eda could barely hear. "You'll be released, of course."

Torres lashed out, striking the air with the katana. There was a loud whooshing noise as she sliced through the breeze with frightening speed. She bounced up and down, testing her feet on the rocky surface. The way she moved, Eda recognized a graceful warrior at work.

A dark shadow swept across the commander's face. Her sword arm twitched hungrily.

"You won't be the first American that I've killed," she said in that cold voice of hers. "But I'm going to enjoy it like it's the first."

Eda's heart was like a drum.

"Ready?" Torres asked.

"Ready."

Torres marched down the dueling ground towards Eda, black-eyed and with both hands gripping the handle of the sword.

Eda held her ground. Her katana was outstretched, waiting to greet the invader chief.

Torres fired off a couple of probing thrusts, gauging the distance between herself and Eda. The crowd backed away as the action began, giving the fighters more room to move. The drunken grunts were at least sober enough to be wary of any wayward blows that might cut them open by accident.

The rowdy atmosphere began to cool down, although it was far from silent on the beach.

Eda circled the ring, using her feet to stay out of range of these early attacks. She fought back but Torres' lighting fast reflexes were extraordinary. Every time Eda thought she was within striking range the commander was already somewhere else. Fast, so damn fast. And her arms were long for such a small woman. Eda had the impression that she was facing off against someone who'd been born to fight with a sword.

Eda strained her eyes, scrutinizing every feint from the opponent's sword. She knew that Torres was capable of springing into life like a cobra.

After feeling Eda out a little, Torres sprang forward with a savage yell. Eda was pushed back onto the defensive, parrying each of Torres' blows with instinct rather than skill.

Sweat gushed from her forehead. Some of it was already running into her eyes and forcing her to blink furiously in order to protect her vision. As for the rain cloak, Torres had called it – it was weighing her down worse than she'd thought it would.

Steel clashed against steel.

The crowd was silent, a flock of shadowy faces in the background.

Torres backed off from her attack and now it was Eda's turn to charge forward. But her arms felt like they were moving underwater. She was always two steps behind her opponent, no matter what she did. As the fight progressed it became clear that skill and not stamina were going to be the deciding factor. And Eda's skills were no match for the commander, that was painfully obvious. Eda's swordsmanship was good, but not elite.

Torres was on another level.

Still Eda came forward, remembering something that Lex had told her back in New York. That fights were won and lost in the mind. Recalling those words, Eda hacked at the slippery shape of Torres, missing every time. Despite these failures, she continued being the aggressor, well aware that she was emptying the gas tank at an alarmingly fast rate. But if she gave Torres a moment to breathe it was much more likely that the commander of the Third would strike her down.

The crowd was pushed back further as the dueling ground opened up. The fighters moved onto rockier stretches of the Dead Island beach where the footing was unstable.

They were close to the water's edge now.

Torres blocked all of Eda's attacks. Eda, out of sheer stubbornness, kept it up but the missed blows were becoming more exaggerated and she was leaving herself open for longer.

Sure enough, a moment later Eda overstepped and Torres brought her katana down in a slicing, vertical motion. The edge of the blade scraped against Eda's left arm, shredding up the bulky sleeve of the rain cloak like it was made of paper.

Eda hissed at the sudden, searing pain. Her arm was exposed and a long cut emerged on the length of her pale skin. Streams of blood spilled downwards, running onto the wrist and hand.

At least it wasn't her sword arm.

Torres smiled, like she could smell the blood. She'd glimpsed victory waiting around the corner.

Lex's voice screamed in Eda's mind like a drill sergeant.

You have to be first. First, first, first – don't wait for her!

Eda roared like a wounded animal. She charged forward, swinging at the shadowy figure of Torres.

Torres dodged Eda's sluggish attack, flipped her around and pushed her towards the water. Now the commander began to mix it up, throwing punches and kicks to body and head. Her blows were crisp – the cat-like limbs moving in and out like a well-oiled piece of fighting machinery.

Heavy punches landed. There was no pain – that would come later if she was still alive to feel it. Eda went backwards, staggering into the shallows and hearing the waves behind her as they crashed towards the island. Torres was thinking now – she was laying traps by using her sword to lure Eda into a position where the punches could land.

Eda continued to retreat, not looking at anything except the blurry shape of the woman in front of her. She almost tripped over the rocks several times but somehow managed to stay on two feet.

Back into the water, back into the water.

Her sword arm was numb. Useless. It was still a shock however, when Torres attacked her with a slashing blow that knocked Eda's katana clean out of her hands. The sword flew through the air and landed in the shallows with a splash.

The cold froth lapped at Eda's feet. Torres marched towards her with the swagger of a conqueror. *Chasing, chasing, chasing.* Eda went back on unsteady legs, not even thinking about the fact that there was nothing but miles of ocean waiting behind her. Finally her legs gave out and she toppled over into the icy water.

It felt oddly refreshing.

Eda flipped herself over and her fingers clawed at the gravelly seabed. Behind her, the sound of someone charging through the knee-high water.

She pushed herself onto her knees and began to crawl out to the deep.

Before she could get very far, a hand grabbed Eda by the shoulder. The hand, which felt like it was made of steel, pulled her backwards, tipping her over so that she fell face first into the shallow water. A great weight landed on top of her and when she looked up, a leering Torres was on her knees, pinning Eda down with one hand against the chest. With the other hand, the commander threw a devastating blow to the head. Eda's neck snapped backwards as it landed.

Torres had apparently tossed the sword somewhere. Like Goldman and Mr. China, she wanted her enemy's death to be as slow as possible.

Anything goes.

The commander's hands gripped Eda's collar. Her serpent eyes were emotionless as she gazed down at the bloody, beaten shape underneath her.

Torres said something in her native language. With a gloating smile, she then pushed Eda's head under the water and held it there.

Eda's body shook violently as it begged for air. A whirlwind of pressure built up inside her and it felt like it was building to a terrifying crescendo. This wasn't going to be a peaceful death. Before Eda blacked out however, Torres pulled her up again and Eda's lungs grasped for oxygen. She heard Torres laughing and it was a terrible, mocking sound. In the distance, the grunts were singing. The piper was playing and the music sounded like someone being strangled.

Eda was pushed under again. Gurgled sounding laughter filled her ears, while saltwater poured into her lungs.

The world was dimming at the edges.

Eda closed her eyes.

It was now or never.

She took her hands off Torres' arms and stopped struggling. Almost immediately, she felt the commander's grip loosen on her shoulders. Torres must have thought that Eda had accepted her fate or that she was already slipping away.

Eda's right hand reached for the inner pocket of her rain cloak.

It took her a moment to find the pocket. The cloak swayed underwater as Torres throttled her opponent a little more for good measure. Eda's back was slammed hard against the gravel but she did all she could to resist the dreamy pull of the darkness that was calling her in.

Her fingers slipped into the pocket. They wrapped themselves around the turtle shell texture of Goldman's gift. At that same moment, a strange, euphoric calm began to wash over Eda's mind.

No.

Don't give into it.

She yanked the grenade out of her pocket.

Eda screamed and felt a rush of saltwater pouring into her mouth. Her body was instantly engorged with the ocean. This maddening sensation gave her a sudden burst of seizure-like energy that allowed her to grab Torres by the arm and sink her teeth into the exposed, wiry flesh. She bit down hard. A reddish-brown liquid sprang out of the brown skin, dispersing quickly across the water like an underwater fog.

446

Eda heard something above the surface that sounded like a choir of angels in her head.

It was Commander Torres screaming in pain.

Eda jolted upwards, breaking her battered body through the surface. Somehow she climbed back to her feet and found her balance was good. The dizziness faded, giving way to cold clarity. Torres was standing a few feet away, staring at her profusely bleeding arm. There was a look of shocked outrage on her face. Eda didn't waste a second. She crashed through the shallows and threw a murderous right hand at Torres' exposed chin. The blow knocked Torres back but she managed to stay upright. Eda chased after her again. She grabbed a hold of the dazed commander's throat and hit her again. Then Eda shoved her off-balance, forcing the invader down into the water.

Eda looked at the grenade in her hands, her heart pounding. With a gasp she pulled the pin, hoping that this was indeed one of those long delay grenades that Goldman had told her about. When the pin finally came out she felt a stab of terror.

How long?

Ten? Twelve seconds?

Eda raced over to where Torres was floundering in the shallows. She jumped on the commander and threw a hard elbow to the temple. It landed flush. Torres was out of it, her eyes rolling around in her head. With her hands shaking, Eda quickly opened up the flap in Torres' breast pocket. Then she slipped the grenade inside.

Eda ran back to shore, pumping her arms and legs with every-thing she had left. As she left Torres in the water, she saw the soldiers standing on the beach laughing at her. They were pointing, doubling over at the hilarity of the situation.

The American was a coward. She was a coward because she was running away from the fight.

The piper played the first few notes of a victory song...

And then the blast came.

It felt like a deep, thunderous avalanche inside Eda's head. She dropped onto the rocky beach in a split second, her hands pressed tight over her ears. Dead Island rattled underneath her like it was trying to get rid of the infestation of human fleas on its back.

When Eda finally looked up hundreds of gleeful faces had been silenced. Eyes bulged in the direction of the ocean. Mouths hung open.

In the aftermath, a chilling silence emerged on the island.

Eda lay perfectly still on the rocky shore, breathing hard, trying to recover her senses. Soon there was a flurry of movement on the beach. Eda heard it and she lifted her head, the bright morning light hurting her eyes. When her focus cleared she saw countless machine guns, automatic rifles and pistols pointing at her head.

The entire Third Unit had her surrounded.

Eda could taste the salt in her mouth, along with the metallic flavor of blood trickling down from her nose. She didn't even have the strength left to surrender.

Face down, she gritted her teeth and braced herself for the end. Let it be quick, she thought. A part of her yearned for it and she found herself thinking about the afterlife again – who would be waiting to greet her on the other side? Would the white light be empty? Or was death nothing but a black void where all pain, thought and sensation ended?

Eda heard a solitary voice yelling out in a foreign tongue. The voice, which was familiar, cut through the tense silence. There was a noise up ahead – the rough sound of boots scraping off the rocks. Getting closer.

The tall, skinny figure of Manny barged through the sea of grunts who stood around with murder in their eyes. Then he stopped dead. His glistening eyes zipped back and forth between the bloody figure of Eda and towards the ocean where the remains of his cousin were now fish food.

His mouth hung open.

Behind Manny, the invaders edged forward like a menacing pack of tribal vigilantes. Angry words were muttered. Their guns were still trained on Eda, the Yankee plaything who'd killed their god.

"Where is your honor?" a man's voice called out in the distance.

"Where is your honor?"

Eda could just about turn her head to the right.

Talbot Goldman was staggering down the beach. His legs were unsteady. His skin was pale and gaunt, but although he looked like a freshly resurrected corpse the fire in his eyes still burned bright.

"Where is your honor?" he said for the third time. The old man battled against the rugged terrain as it tried to tip him off-balance. As he walked, the waves lapped ashore and chased after him. A fierce gust of wind made the hairs on his mustache dance at the tips.

"Her death was fair." Goldman said. He finally caught up with the crowd gathered in the center of the beach. He pointed at the water, then addressed Manny as well as the other three haunted-looking officers on the platform. "It was a duel. Anything goes, isn't that right?"

Manny was still staring out to sea. Very slowly, he tore his eyes off the water and his body turned towards Goldman. Some of the invaders had by now turned their guns on the old American soldier who'd appeared out of nowhere. There was a look of uncertainty in their eyes.

They were waiting for the order to shoot.

One of the female officers, a poker-faced woman with dark brown skin, yelled something from the platform. Manny spun around and quickly raised a hand. He responded to the officer with an impassioned outburst, one that was directed towards all the officers and the grunts too. His voice was fierce, at odds with the gentle soul that Eda had come to know.

The grunts lowered their guns and backed off a few paces.

Eda felt like she could breath again.

"A deal's a deal," Goldman said. He went over and stood in front of the downed Eda, his outraged expression daring anyone to point their gun at her again.

Goldman looked at Manny. "Right? A deal's a deal?"

Manny's eyes had drifted out to sea again.

"You kill this girl and your word means nothing," Goldman said.

He coughed into the back of his hand. "If your word means nothing, then nobody will ever take you seriously again."

"Help me up," Eda said.

With Goldman's help, Eda climbed back to her feet. She got up slowly, leaning on Goldman's shoulder for support once she was back on two legs. Dead Island was still spinning like a bad dream. As well as that, she could hear the bagpipes playing in her head.

"Stop the music," she said groggily.

"You alright?" Goldman said, peering at her. "You look like shit young lady."

Eda shrugged, then turned to the front. She pawed at thin air, at all the faces looking back at her.

"I want my head start," she said, trying to focus on the blurry shape of Manny. "You promised me…"

"A head start," Goldman echoed. "Nothing more, nothing less."

15

The bow of the speedboat pointed towards the mainland. It cut through the choppy blue waters of Quincy Bay, traveling northwest and conjuring up a long white frothy tail in its wake that stretched all the way back to Dead Island.

Manny stood in the bow cockpit, staring hypnotically at the Massachusetts coastline up ahead. Nearby one of the grunts was driving the boat while two others were pointing their rifles at Eda and Goldman, who'd been told to sit in the stern cockpit during the short crossing back to Castle Island. It was a tense journey; nobody spoke and Eda still harbored fears about being shot and dropped overboard halfway through the trip. Or dropped overboard without being shot first. Back on Dead Island, she'd breathed a sigh of relief when Manny had climbed aboard the speedboat along with the three grunts, announcing that he'd also escort Eda and Goldman back to the mainland.

Any plans the grunts might have had about getting rid of the Americans would have to wait.

The new commander didn't look at the two passengers throughout the journey. Eda watched him standing there like a carved figurehead, staring out to sea. She tried to imagine the turmoil going around in his head. That morning he'd woken up as Manny the shy, secret poet and now, just a few hours later, his cousin was dead and he was the Commander of the Third East Coast Unit.

The Castle Island pier approached on the horizon with the shadow of Fort Independence sprawled out behind it.

The boat pulled up next to the pier and rocked back and forth on the surface of the water. Manny turned around at last, looking like a much older version of the young man who Eda had spoken to before her first duel with Mr. China. His skin was grayish-white. At the very least he looked seasick. Walking over to the cockpit, he said something to the grunt at the controls. Then he signaled for Eda and Goldman to approach. When they did, he informed them to climb the small ladder on the pier that would take them up onto the Castle Island walkway.

"You first," Eda said, looking at Goldman.

Goldman grumbled, then put his hands on the bottom rung and began climbing. Eda followed behind, sticking close to the old man who battled his way to the top slowly and with great difficulty.

Manny went up with them. When they reached the top, he stood on the pier, looking back south along the water. With a sigh he leaned over the metal railing, signaling to the three grunts in the boat that he'd be back onboard in a minute.

Goldman was halfway towards the car park. He turned around when he noticed that Eda wasn't alongside him.

She was still at the edge of the walkway, standing beside Manny.

"I'll be right there," Eda said, calling over to Goldman when she noticed his confused expression. "Keep walking and I'll catch up."

The old man nodded. But he stayed exactly where he was.

Eda lowered the hood of the rain cloak and a stinging pain went up and down her arm. The long, jagged wound she'd acquired in the duel had been whipped by the harsh wind on the crossing, sometimes to the point of it becoming unbearable. She'd done her best not to poke at it. Not to look at it.

"You're free to go," Manny said. His voice was strangely hollow. "Congratulations."

"I don't know what to say to you Manny," Eda said, her long brown hair flapping in the wind. "About your cousin...about what happened..."

"It's not your fault Eda," Manny said. "She would have killed you. We both know she would have killed you and wouldn't have lost a wink of sleep over it."

Eda nodded. "So I guess you're commander now?"

"Yes," he said.

Eda stole a glance down at the boat. The grunts were standing on deck talking amongst themselves and paying no attention to what was going on up on the walkway. Like most of the other grunts back on Dead Island, they were stone cold sober now. Fun day was over.

Eda took a step closer to Manny.

"Come with us," she said, lowering her voice. "You told me yourself Manny, this isn't who you are. This war bullshit, it's not meant for you. Now your cousin's gone and there's no need for you to pretend anymore. If you want, you can leave it all behind and never look back."

A gang of seagulls flew overhead, pondering the possibility of food scraps appearing on the walkway.

"I belong with my people," Manny said. "As commander, I'll pretend I didn't hear that Eda."

Eda frowned. "Bullshit," she said. "A few hours ago you were telling me about a boy who used to sit on the street and write poetry. Where is he now? You've just changed into a war god all of a sudden?"

"Sometimes reluctant leaders are the best leaders."

"They'll kill you for God's sake," she said, pushing a clump of hair off her face. "Are you going to keep proving yourself to them like your cousin did? Are you going to slit a grunt's throat now and then to make a point? What was it you told me? They challenge their leaders all the time. Right? Are you up for that?"

Manny said nothing.

"Come with us," Eda said. "You won't have much on the road but at the very least you can write. We'll pick up pencils and paper. You only have to know where to look to find them and I know where to look."

"No."

Manny was backing off towards the ladder.

"Manny," Eda said. "Don't..."

"Goodbye Eda."

He put a hand on the top rung and signaled to the men below that he was on his way down. Before he began the descent however, he gave Eda a look that chilled her blood. In that moment Eda saw Manny's cousin alive and well, as if her evil ghost was staring through his eyes.

"We'll be coming after you," Manny said. "It doesn't matter if it's me at the helm of this unit or someone else. As we speak, there are over a hundred units stationed on both the east and west coasts. Soon they'll be making moves. Going further inland to stake a permanent claim on this land. What I'm trying to say is, this isn't your country anymore."

He climbed down the ladder towards the speedboat. Eda watched his head disappear under the pier and then listened for a moment to the loud metallic clunking noise of his boots on the metal rungs.

"Eda," Goldman yelled from behind. There wasn't much pop in his voice anymore, having burned it out back on the beach with his last-minute entrance after the explosion.

She turned around and saw the old man shivering in the cold. He beckoned her over.

"Let's get out of here," he said.

"Sorry," Eda called out, running over to catch up with him.

She locked her hand around Goldman's arm. They walked back towards Fort Independence, keeping at a slow pace because it was all Goldman could manage now. Every couple of minutes he'd have to stop, double over and cough his lungs out. When he straightened up, Eda noticed a bluish tinge to Goldman's lips that she didn't like.

"You look like shit," Eda said, trying to make light of something so dreadful. "How are you feeling?"

Goldman laughed weakly. But he didn't answer.

454

"How the hell am I going to get you back to your apartment?" Eda said. "You can't walk that far."

"We're not walking," Goldman said.

"What do you mean?"

"You'll see in a minute."

When they reached the crowded car park, which was full of pauper vehicles, Goldman marched over to the nearest jeep. Upon closer inspection he realized the keys were missing. He shook his head and immediately moved onto the next vehicle. The second and third cars were no good either. The fourth one however, had a long silver keychain dangling beside the wheel.

"Bingo," Goldman said. He patted the jeep like it was a faithful old sheepdog lying at his feet.

"Get in," he said, looking at Eda who was standing on the other side of the car.

"You're kidding right?" Eda said. "You're going to drive a car when you're half-dead?"

Goldman shrugged. "That's how most people drove cars back in the day."

Eda looked at the jeep. Its lower half was plastered in several shades of dried mud but more importantly, all four of the tires were dangerously bald. Even Eda, with what little she knew about cars, knew that the tires weren't supposed to be smooth like that. Even if the damn thing went, it was death on wheels.

"Are you saying that you want to drive?" Goldman said, stepping back from the driver's side.

"I've never driven a car in my life," Eda said.

Goldman smiled. His eyes were bright again. Young.

"God damn it," he said. "It's been a long, long time since I've driven anything."

"Maybe you can show me how to do it?" Eda said. She wiped a patch of dry blood off the skin around her nostrils. Another souvenir from the battle with Torres. "How hard can it be anyway?"

"We don't have time for another crash course," Goldman said impatiently. He was about to open the door when he noticed the worried look on Eda's face. "Listen Eda. It's only a five-minute drive from here back to Carson Beach. And there's no other traffic to worry about. Five minutes. I reckon I've still got that much left in me. Don't you?"

Eda leaned on the car. With a sigh she took off her belt and sword and threw them down onto the back seat.

"What the hell?" she said. "I've escaped death once today. I can do it again."

Goldman whooped like an overexcited teenager. It was strange how he kept jumping back and forth between the top of the world and death's door. For the moment at least, he was as fresh as a puppy but Eda knew it wouldn't last long. Hopefully it would be long enough to get them back to Goldman's apartment in one piece.

The old man opened the door and climbed behind the wheel. With a silly, boyish grin on his face, he turned the key very slowly. The engine spluttered into life and Goldman fell back in his seat, closing his eyes and listening.

"That's what I'm talking about," he said. "Oh sweet God in heaven, are you ready for this?"

"Sounds like it's about to break down," Eda said.

"No way," Goldman said. "In God I trust."

Eda dragged herself into the passenger seat, trying to ignore a chorus of aches and pains all over her body. She knew it was only going to get worse before it got better.

Goldman backed the jeep out of the parking spot, then cruised through the lot and onto the road. From the start he drove like a maniac. The jeep rocketed south on William J Day Boulevard and halfway through the journey Goldman threw his US army cap onto the road. His wispy hair flew back and he laughed like it was the best day of his life. Eda, despite her concerns, couldn't help but laugh with him.

A short while later, Goldman pulled up outside the front door of the apartment building overlooking Carson Beach. He turned the engine off and glanced up at the sixth floor window.

"Home," he said in a quiet voice. "Thank God Almighty."

With a sigh he stepped out of the jeep. Before going inside however, Goldman stared across the road at the deep blue ocean.

"Wish I had time for one more swim," he said. "But I reckon if I went in there now I wouldn't make it back to the apartment."

Eda stood next to him, listening to the waves. Thinking how peaceful it all looked from afar.

Goldman refused any help from Eda as they made their way upstairs to the sixth floor. Stubborn pride fueled his limbs, carrying him all the way to the top.

"Goddamn it," he cried out, when the climb was over. "Getting old is no fun. And dying isn't much better."

Inside the apartment, Eda helped Goldman onto the couch. That's where he wanted to stay, so he said, surrounded by his photographs. Eda put a fresh blanket over the old man and slipped a soft pillow behind his head. Goldman gathered as many family photos around him as he could, scooping them up off the floor and asking Eda to get some others that were scattered around the apartment.

After she'd made Goldman comfortable, Eda went into the bathroom to clean her wounds with soap and water. She found a case of medical supplies and patted her cuts dry with a towel. After that she self-bandaged as best she could, wrapping foam padding around her hand and then layering it across the length of the arm. It wasn't much, but it was better than nothing.

"Make sure you take as much food and water as you need," Goldman said, when Eda returned to the living room.

"You got a bag?" she asked. "Mine's still somewhere out there on the highway."

"Take one of Emily's," Goldman said. "Look in the closet in her bedroom."

"Are you sure?"

"I'm sure," Goldman said, sinking deeper into the couch.

Eda took an old Nike backpack out of Emily's room and filled it with food and fresh ammo. She then went downstairs and helped herself to one of the many spare M4s in the weapons chest. Its removal didn't even make a dent in Goldman's pile of killing machines. Eda brought the rifle back up to Goldman who looked it over for her.

"It's good," he said, after examining it as best he could. "I showed you how to reload didn't I?"

"Yep."

"And you've got plenty of ammo."

"More than I can carry."

Eda dropped the rifle at the front door beside her bag and sword. She then went back inside the living room and sat on the floor beside Goldman who was flat out on the couch.

She took his hand. It was like touching thin air.

"Maybe I should stay," she said. "I don't feel good leaving you alone like this. You know?"

Goldman shook his head. It was clear the old man still had a chunk of stubbornness left in him should it be required. "No you won't," he said. His voice was a whisper now. "There's no time for any of that watching me die crap."

Eda nodded. "Sure there is."

"No," Goldman said, looking at her. His breathing was fast, erratic. "Young lady, I hate to say this but it's up to you now. It's up to you to warn the people. A thankless task I'm sure – no one will want to hear what you have to say. Fewer still will believe you. Thing is, they all think the worst is behind them, the poor bastards, but you gotta tell it like it is. You're the messenger now. Okay?"

"Okay," Eda said.

"I'm sorry it has to be you," Goldman said, squeezing her hand as best he could. "The last thing you deserve is another End War. And here's the thing Eda, don't forget that there's never going to be an End War. No matter how many fights they call the End War another one will always show up after it. Sooner or later. That's the shitty truth of it."

Goldman let go of her hand. Wheezing softly, he pulled one of the family photos towards him and pressed it tight against his chest. Eda stole a quick look. It was a nice portrait of them all – the young

Goldman, his wife and three girls, sitting around a picnic table with a shimmering blue lake in the background.

"I enjoyed that drive," he whispered. "You're crazy for letting me behind the wheel."

"I know," Eda said.

The old man chuckled. His eyes stared up at the damp-infested ceiling.

"Go now," he whispered. "Before it gets worse."

Eda nodded. "Okay."

She pushed herself back up to her feet. An explosion of white-hot pain shot up and down her limbs.

"See you," she said, limping towards the front door.

"Hell of a day," Goldman said.

"Hell of a day," Eda said.

She left the apartment, closing the door gently behind her. She had Emily Goldman's bag strapped onto her back. Lex's katana hung from the scabbard on her belt and Talbot Goldman's M4 was draped over her shoulder. Her rain cloak was shredded at the left arm but it would do until she found something better.

She made good time despite her injuries. She was back on the 93 and traveling north, chasing after the Nomads and anyone else out there who would listen to her warning. It was still early morning in Boston and the rain hadn't come yet. Being on the road felt familiar to Eda. It felt good.

Movement is life.

Close to the old South Boston bypass, Eda heard a light tip-tapping noise at her back. At first she thought it was the rain. Then she stopped dead on the highway and a smile emerged on her battered face.

"Where the hell have you been?" she said.

Frankie Boy strolled up casually, like nothing was amiss. Like he'd been gone for five minutes chasing rabbits. He sat down beside her on the road and Eda crouched down, letting him lick her face and inspect her wounds.

"Missed me huh?" she said.

She let her hands rummage around his thick coat. Then she patted him on the back three times and rose stiffly to a standing position. She looked down the 93 again. A long, spiraling road stretched out in front of the two travelers. Eda had found the Nomads somewhere on this same road a few days ago. It felt like a lifetime ago.

Manifest destiny.

Is that what she was up against? Was it the divine right of the pauper nations to conquer the continent of North America and to turn it into something new?

Time would tell.

Eda and Frankie Boy exchanged a knowing look, one that would commit them to each other for the war ahead.

They walked together down the highway, side by side.

It began to rain.

THE END

OTHER BOOKS BY MARK GILLESPIE

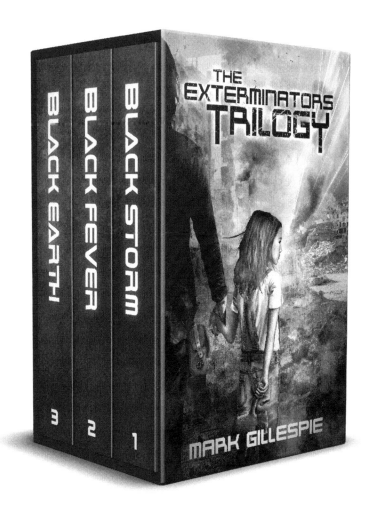

'A pulse-pounding post-apocalyptic horror series.'

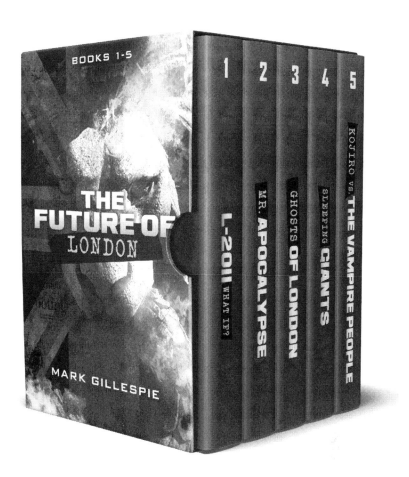

'Civic terror, apocalypse, gangs, horror, complete decline of civilization... read it and weep!' - Mallory A. Haws

The Future of London (Books 1-5)

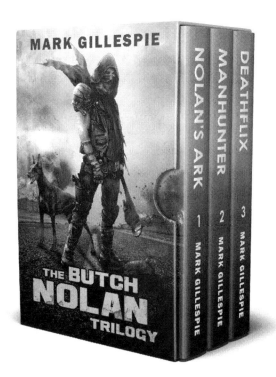

Butch Nolan wants revenge. And not even the end of the world will get in his way.

The Complete Butch Nolan Trilogy

'Stories you won't want to put down!'
  Five first in series post-apocalyptic and dystopian books...
  Apocalypse No.1

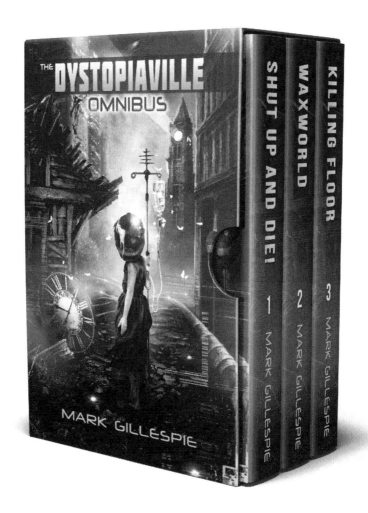

The Dystopiaville Omnibus: 'Think Twilight Zone or Black Mirror, but with books...'

If you love taut, fast-paced, claustrophobic horror, you'll love The Hatching

THE BUTCH NOLAN SERIES

Nolan's Ark (Butch Nolan #1)

ManHunter (Butch Nolan #2)

Deathflix (Butch Nolan #3)

Mad Max meets John Wick meets Clint Eastwood's spaghetti westerns in this rollercoaster ride of a post-apocalyptic action thriller...

THE FUTURE OF LONDON

L-2011 (Future of London #1)

Mr Apocalypse (Future of London #2)

Ghosts of London (Future of London #3)

Sleeping Giants (Future of London #4)

Kojiro vs. The Vampire People (Future of London #5)

The Future of London Box Set (Books 1-3)

The Future of London Box Set (Books 1-5)

"Modern dystopian at its very best." - Kirsten McKenzie, author of Painted.

THE EXTERMINATORS TRILOGY

Black Storm

(The Exterminators #1)

Black Fever

(The Exterminators #2)

Black Earth

(The Exterminators #3)

"Part-horror, part post-apocalypse...all brilliant."

DYSTOPIAVILLE

Is this fiction? Or is it the future?

Shut Up and Die!

WaxWorld

Killing Floor

All Dystopiaville books are stand-alone novels/novellas that can be read in any order.

GRIMLOG (TALES OF TERROR)

Apex Predators

Air Nosferatu

Rock Devil

"What's not to like about zombies and sharks, or zombie sharks?" - CJ (5 stars)

"Brilliantly fast-paced horror that was unputdownable." - Chantelle Atkins (5 stars)

JOIN THE READER LIST

If you enjoy what you read here and want to be notified whenever there's a new book out, join the reader list. Just click the link below. It'll only take a minute.

www.markgillespieauthor.com

(The sign up box is on the Home Page)

You can also follow Mark on Bookbub.

WEBSITE/SOCIAL MEDIA

Mark Gillespie's author website
www.markgillespieauthor.com

Mark Gillespie on Facebook
www.facebook.com/markgillespieswritingstuff

Mark Gillespie on Twitter
www.twitter.com/MarkG_Author